HELGA'S WEB

Also by
JON CLEARY

★

HELGA'S WEB

*

JON CLEARY

THE
COMPANION BOOK CLUB
LONDON AND SYDNEY

This edition, published in 1971 by
The Hamlyn Publishing Group Ltd.,
is issued by arrangement with
William Collins, Sons & Co. Ltd.

To
Renée and Fred Zinnemann
with affection

*Made and printed in Great Britain
for the Companion Book Club
by Odhams (Watford) Ltd.*
SBN/S. 600771350
SBN/D. 600871355
7.71

CHAPTER ONE

I

Monday, December 9

'SHE'S NOT A CATHOLIC,' Brigid Malone had said. 'She's not even an Australian!'

'At least she's white,' Scobie Malone had said. 'I could be marrying a black Zambian Methodist.'

'I wouldn't put it past you,' said Mrs Malone, conceding nothing. 'What's a Zambian?'

'Someone from Zambia. In Africa.'

'Oh, one of them new places—' Dismissing three and a half million Zambians of all denominations, even the Catholics, Mrs Malone turned back to her ironing. She never read the cable pages in her daily newspaper. The rest of the world was turning upside-down day by day, but she neither knew nor cared about it; what mattered was only what turned up on Sydney's doorstep and when it did she would read about it in the home news pages. She had given up reading the *Catholic Weekly* because lately it seemed to be full of nothing but what was going on in Rome.

'Well, is it still on tonight?' Malone said. 'I mean, can I bring her home to meet you?'

'Bring her home for tea,' said Mrs Malone, slamming the iron on to one of Scobie's shirts as if he were in it. 'But don't expect me to whip up any of that foreign muck for her. It'll be chops. And I'll make a trifle.' Which was something, Malone thought: it could have been rhubarb tart.

'I'll bring a bottle of wine.'

'Please yourself. Don't expect me to drink any of it.'

Malone grinned at his mother behind her back. At least she was consistent: her prejudices extended to everything. She had lived all her life here in this same terrace house in a narrow street in Erskineville; she had borne him in the

5

same bed where she herself had come into the world. No, not *the* world: *her* world. Long ago, long before she had married, she had drawn her boundaries and he would never know why. There had never been any desire to escape from this tenement district, to come to know what was outside and to understand it. And when the Italians and the Greeks, *foreigners*, had moved into Erskineville in the immigration years since the war, she had shut the front door of her house, which in Scobie's childhood had always stood wide open, and retreated still farther into the iron lung of her bigotry. Malone had learned that the only way to tolerate her narrow, myopic outlook was to smile at it. Sometimes the smile had to be forced, but it was better than getting angry with her. He did not want her to shut the door against him.

'I'll see you tonight, then.' He looked at the shrivelled back of her neck bent over the ironing table and wondered what she would do if he kissed it. He was an only child, but he couldn't remember when he and his mother had last gone through the usual gestures of affection. Her prejudices ran even to a hatred of demonstrative sentiment. She kissed her rosary three times a day without embarrassment, but he had never seen her kiss his father.

'Six o'clock. Your father likes his tea on the table when he comes in.'

Malone wondered how Lisa would like that: dinner at six o'clock. In the month she had been back in Sydney she still lived to the pattern that had been established for her when she had been private secretary to the Australian High Commissioner in London: dinner at eight, wine on the table, conversation over the coffee cups. She was in for a shock tonight when his mother grabbed the plates as soon as the last mouthful of trifle had been eaten. Any after-dinner conversation in the Malone house was held at the kitchen sink above the rattle of dishes and the clink of cutlery.

'You can pick up your ironing tonight.' Every week he took his washing to a laundromat, then brought it home to be ironed. He had once objected that he was imposing on her, but his mother had only got angry and grabbed the washing from him as if it were hers and not his. Since then he had

6

come to recognize that it was some sort of bond between them, just as was the weekly visit to clean out his flat at King's Cross. It was the only way she knew of showing love.

He went out of the house, got into his car and drove away from the memories that still clung so stubbornly to him. When he had been growing up in this street there had been only one or two cars parked outside the terrace houses and those had been third- or fourth-hand, bought cheaply and made to go only by the ingenuity of their new owners. Now the street was lined with cars, none of them older than his own 1964 Holden and some of them looking brand-new. Not everyone in Australia was affluent, but hire purchase at least allowed some appearance of it; most of the population was infatuated with prosperity, even if it could not afford it. Con and Brigid Malone, both of whom had been brought up to believe that the hire purchase man was a relative of the Devil, were the only couple in the street without a car. When Malone came occasionally on a Sunday to take them for a drive, Brigid Malone boarded his car as if she were heading for a wedding or a funeral: it was an occasion. Con Malone, more exposed to the world than his wife, would get into the car with no show of expression at all; but the impassivity of his face was intended for the neighbours and not for Scobie. It was bad enough having a policeman for a son; it would not do to show that he was even on good terms with such a wayward bastard.

As he drove down the street this morning Malone was aware of women and one or two men standing at their front doors staring silently at him as if he were a plague-carrier. Maybe I should turn in my badge, he thought, and start carrying a leper's clapper. Even the Italians and Greeks living in the street, not knowing him, never having spoken to him, had learned to suspect him. Cop-hating was a good starting point for assimilation in Australia. We have our uses, Malone thought; and clashed his gears as he slowed to round the corner of the street. The people at their front doors only smiled and shook their heads: the bloody coppers didn't even know how to drive properly.

Now, an hour later, Malone sat in the detectives' room at

Y Division and once again caustically wondered why he had become a policeman. His mother had prayed that he might become a priest, but God in his wisdom had recognized a religious no-hoper when he saw one: the Church had enough to worry about without recruiting a fellow who had trouble staying on his knees longer than two minutes. When Malone had come home and announced he had joined the police force, his mother had retired to her room and her rosary and his father had gone up to the local pub and got blind weeping drunk. In those circumstances it was difficult to believe that he had been driven to his decision by any sense of vocation or spiritual message visited upon him by the Police Commissioner. It had been a job and nothing else.

'Why did you join the force, Russ?'

Russ Clements looked up from his betting calculations. 'I won another hundred and forty dollars Saturday. I'm beginning to wish I'd never become a cop. I've won fifteen hundred bloody dollars on the horses this past three months. Who's gunna believe I'm not taking something under the counter?' He shook his big crew-cropped head, anguished at the thought of being a wealthy cop. Twenty-six years old and six feet two, he wasn't yet old enough or strong enough to carry the weight of public opinion; Malone had noticed that it was the old and the atrophied who best stood up to public abuse. They had learned the uses of indifference. 'Why'd I join? Christ, I dunno. The bird I was going out with at the time, she didn't talk to me for a month after.'

'You still going out with her?'

'After six years? You're kidding.' Clements shook his head again, staring at the blackmail note in his hand: three winners, all at good odds. 'It buggered up my social life completely. That was why I took to betting on the nags and dogs, just for something to do. I'd rather be in bed any day with a bird. People will take that, it's natural. But a cop with a bank account with money in it, they won't go for that.'

Malone slumped farther down in his chair, staring through the grimed window at the blank wall of the building next door. This police building had been erected in 1870, a year when the local public thought even less of its police than it did now. It sometimes seemed to Malone that every year since then had laid its cold, dusty dead hand on this room where he sat. Police circulars hung from the walls like peeling wallpaper; a fly-speckled picture of the Queen hung above four equally-speckled photographs of four Wanted men. Clements stood up and opened one of the lockers in the corner: it groaned like an ancient sarcophagus and Malone would not have been surprised if a convict from the First Fleet had fallen out. On Malone's desk stood a typewriter in which he was expected to take some pride, as if he were some sort of antique dealer: it had been used to type out the first report on a famous murder case of the early Twenties. The only bright, new note in the room came from the early Christmas cards that Clements had now begun to arrange on the mantelpiece over the old blackened fireplace. It's a job, Malone thought, but has it made me into a dull, stupid clot? Does Lisa really know what she's marrying?

Then Smiler Sparks, the duty sergeant, came into the room. 'Better get down to the Opera House.'

'Why?' said Malone. 'They finished it at last?'

Sergeant Sparks didn't laugh; he had never been known to be amused by anything. 'They found the body of a girl. Looks like murder. You owe me thirty cents, Scobie, for those meat pies I got you on Friday.'

Malone shelled out thirty cents. 'They were cold.'

'Don't blame me, mate. Anyone deserves cold pies if he spends an hour trying to give advice to a pro.'

'She was only a kid. Sixteen.'

'I checked on her card. She was nineteen and she'd had twenty-two convictions. She was laughing at you, mate.'

'That's more than I've ever seen you do,' said Malone, and went out of the room and out of the building, followed by Clements, his partner. He felt his mood improving as he went, glad as he always was to escape the sour, drab atmosphere that successive governments had considered the right environment for its law officers of Y Division.

The early summer humidity swamped them at once; even by the time they had crossed the road to the parked police car, Malone was damp under the armpits. People struggled up the

9

small hill from the Quay, faces shining as if they had come straight out of the waters of the harbour, the older ones inwardly cursing the climate that, on cooler days, they claimed was the best in the world. Another police car drew up and Inspector Fulmer got out. The cold-blooded bastard, Malone thought, he looks as if he's come straight from the ice-works. Malone told him where they were heading.

'The Opera House's first dramatic performance,' said Fulmer, and Malone and Clements smiled dutifully at his flat heavy humour. Fulmer did not go in very often for jokes and when he did they fell on the ear with a dull thump. 'Well, I hope it's a straightforward case, one that won't spoil your Christmas.'

He left them, walking in his stiff-backed way that suggested he was leading a review past the Commissioner.

Clements looked after him. 'I wonder what he was like as a kid?'

'I don't think he ever was a kid,' said Malone. 'He was born thirty years old and in uniform..

Clements nodded and got into the car. 'Well, let's go and have a look at this girl, see if she's gunna give us an easy Christmas or not.'

2

Malone pulled the Falcon out from the kerb, wondering if the force would ever run to air-conditioned cars for its officers. He went round the block and drove down Macquarie Street, the glittering window-eyes of new office blocks on one side of the road glaring down on the green oasis of the Botanical Gardens on the other. They drove into the work compound surrounding the Opera House. Clements showed his badge to the gate-keeper just as a uniformed policeman came down the road from the main building site.

'Nobody in or out, Ted,' Malone told him. 'And no outside phone calls, especially to the newspapers.'

The policeman looked at the gatekeeper, who looked hurt, as if he had been accused of high treason. 'You heard that.

You've just been made a deputy marshal. Sergeant Malone will send you a badge for Christmas.'

'You know what you can do with it,' said the gatekeeper. 'I hope it has points on it.'

The policeman gave him an official smile, then turned back to Malone. 'I'll keep an eye out, Scobie. Jack Radcliff is still down with the body.'

Malone drove on. The Opera House loomed before them, the huge towering shells that were the roofs of the various concert halls seeming to Malone to be like giant ears turned to the sounds of the harbour and to the suspect whisperings of the local citizens. The building, over the years of its long chequered history, had become variously a joke, an object of anger at waste of public money, a source of tremendous excitement that at last Sydney was going to have a centre for the performing arts: no one, except perhaps visitors from other States, remained indifferent to it. So far work on it had been in progress ten years and there was said to be at least another two years before it would be completed.

'When opening night finally arrives,' said Malone, who blew hot and cold in his reactions to the project, 'I wonder if God will be free to cut the ribbon? They won't be able to get anyone less than him, not after waiting this long.'

'Not if Labour's back in power,' said Clements, ignoring the police rule to be apolitical. 'Whoever heard of a Labour politician letting an outsider steal the limelight?'

They drew up before the vast expanse of steps that led up to the open podiums below the shells. A short wiry man in shirt and tie, dark shorts, long socks and desert boots was waiting for them. He handed them each a construction worker's helmet and slipped one on his own head. His hat was too big for him and with his thin legs tapering away beneath him he reminded Malone of a tight-headed toadstool.

'Kerslake's the name. One of the engineers. Bit of a shock.' He sounded as if he would have a continual mouthful of words, any one of which could be spilled out like a lottery marble. He led them up the steps, into a wide opening, then across what he told them was going to be the main concert hall. The concrete shell soared above them like a vast ribbed tent. A scaffolding staircase reached up to the fluted roof, like a tall metal reredos beneath the vaulted ceiling of a cathedral. Workmen moved like bats among the high scaffolding catwalks, their voices and the clash of their tools on metal magnified in the huge chamber. It was the first time Malone had been so close to the project and for the moment he felt a sense of awe.

Then Kerslake said, 'The body's down here,' and led them down a long flight of rough steps, talking all the way, sketching an angular embroidery of words: 'Might never have found her. Just sheer chance. Old plans changed when Utzon, the original architect, left. Spaces down below, closed up, now being utilized. For new rooms. Watch your step.'

He had switched on a workman's lamp and Malone and Clements followed him carefully as he led them through a labyrinth of passages that were only occasionally lit by electric globes hanging like fungi from the concrete walls. Malone sniffed, conscious of the smell of sea water.

'Below high tide level,' said Kerslake, and brought them to a small group of men standing like a queue of unemployed outside an opening in a wall. Timber had been torn out of the opening and lay scattered about. Somewhere far above them a pneumatic drill thumped away like an aural nerve. Malone sniffed again, but there wasn't the sickly sweet smell he had expected.

'She hardly smells at all.' A uniformed policeman, Jack Radcliff, stepped out of the dark opening, balancing like an overweight ballet dancer on the pile of timber. 'The air in there's pretty dry, Scobie. And no light got to her.'

'Who found her?'

Everyone looked around, then the familiar lumpy figure leaning up against the wall said, 'I did.'

'G'day, Dad,' said Malone, and hoped he didn't sound as surprised as he felt: policemen were supposed to be never surprised by anything. 'When did you start work here?'

'Your father?' Kerslake fired a couple of lottery marbles, bonus prizes. 'What d'you know! Small world!'

'Come in this morning,' said Con Malone, still leaning against the wall, his helmet tipped like a challenge over one

12

eye. 'I'm labouring for one of the sub-contractors. Just my bloody luck.'

Malone didn't ask what his father considered bloody luck: whether it was the fact of discovering the dead girl or having his own son as the investigating officer. Malone knew what the answer would be.

He stepped gingerly over the heaped timber and, guided by several lamps, went into the large chamber.

'Pretty appropriate,' said Clements. 'This could be a tomb. What were they gunna do—bury politicians down here like those Egyptian kings?'

'Break it down, Russ,' Malone said, and Clements blushed, abruptly aware that these men around him were not as used to murder as he and Malone.

'It was going to be a dressing-room,' said Kerslake. 'But don't know now. Know what theatrical types are like. Will reckon the place is haunted.'

There'll be other ghosts before this place falls down, Malone thought, this is just the first. The girl lay in the spotlight of two lamps, her nude body half-exposed beneath a green silk dressing-gown, old newspapers and the fossilized remainders of workers' sandwiches scattered about her like the debris of funeral tributes. Her blonde hair hung like straw beneath her curiously twisted head; her mouth was open for a scream that she might never have made. There were dark bruises on her throat and her wide open eyes were veined with haemorrhaging. She had that peculiarly ugly look that only beautiful women get when they have met a violent death. Malone had noticed it before: the living ugly seem to get no uglier in death.

'Anything on her to say who she was?'

Radcliff shook his head. 'Nothing. I didn't move her, Scobie. That's your job.'

'Thanks,' said Malone dryly: the police force had its own lines of demarcation. He looked around at the other six or seven men in the high narrow room. Shadows hung in the corners and in the angles of the ceiling like dark cobwebs; a couple of the men glanced furtively about and one of them blessed himself. Malone noticed now that they were all

Italians; most Australian construction would come to a standstill without the unskilled labour that the newly-arrived immigrants offered. Only one man had remained outside in the passage, the Old Australian with his helmet still cocked derisively over his eye and the cigarette hanging from the corner of his mouth like an old fang.

'Nobody leaves the work site,' Malone said to Kerslake. 'We'll want to interview everybody. Everybody,' he repeated, and looked out at his father. The fang came up, glowed red, then dropped again. 'Where's a phone?'

Kerslake, letting fly with today's quota of unused words, spitting them out to the rhythm of the faraway pneumatic drill, led Malone back through the passages, up several flights of steps and into an office that looked directly out on the harbour. Gulls hung in the shining air like small crucifixes and a man sat in a rowing boat, his head bent as if he were praying for fish to bite at the rosary of his line. A ship went by, its decks crowded with passengers waving frantically at the wharf and the relatives they had left behind; streamers trailed the sides of the ship, giving it an air of tattered gaiety that must have pained its captain. The Manly hydroplane scooted by, hell-bent for the city with its load of housewives desperate to spend their money. No one has any time any more, Malone thought, remembering his days as a kid when a ride on the ferry to Manly was an overseas experience.

He gratefully took off the helmet, which was already giving him a headache, picked up the phone and dialled Police Headquarters.

'Thought you'd have cars with radio,' said Kerslake.

'We do. But the newspaper blokes listen in on the wave-length. We try to keep them off the scene as long as we can.'

'That good public relations?'

'We're old-fashioned,' said Malone. 'We don't think murder calls for any public relations.'

And left Kerslake with a mouthful of words that were useless.

Malone asked for a police photographer, a doctor and someone to take fingerprints. He hung up, looked wistfully

14

out at the water preening itself under its nor'-easter breeze, then turned to Kerslake and said, 'Send up Mr. Malone.'

'Your father?'

'Mr. Malone,' Malone said emphatically, aware of the two mini-skirted secretaries poised like carrier pigeons on the edges of their desks: they'd be away as soon as he'd let them go, carrying gossip between their ring-of-confidence teeth.

Kerslake went away, helmet bobbing on his head like a loose cranium, and Malone looked at the two girls. 'Do you know why those rooms 'way down below were boarded up?'

The two girls looked doubtfully at each other, then the older of them, twenty-year-old face half-hidden between two scraggly scarves of dark hair, said, 'It all happened while Mr Utzon was here. You know, he was the original architect——' Malone nodded, trying not to look wearied by a story that even the metho drinkers in the Domain now knew by heart. 'In Mr Utzon's conception——' There was no mistaking her tone: she was one of Utzon's army. When the battle between the Danish architect and the State government had reached its peak, sides had been drawn on lines as distinct as those in the Wars of the Roses or the American Civil War; only the demonstrations over the war in Vietnam had produced as much heat. Malone himself had once been called out to separate two architects who, fired by drink and opposite aesthetics, had tried to demolish each other as a slum. The girl went on: 'In Mr Utzon's conception all that space down below was not needed, it was just part of the basement structure. When he *resigned*——' She underlined the word to emphasize that her hero had not been sacked. 'When he resigned and the *new* people came in——' Malone waited for her to spit, but she had been to a good private school where spitting had not been permitted. 'The new people said they needed that space down below.'

'When were these changes known?'

The two girls looked at each other and now the younger one, face as blank as a clock's without hands, took her cue: 'Oh, *we've* known about them for some time. In this office, I mean. I don't know about the, you know, workers outside.'

There were lines of demarcation here, too: the office workers and the, you know, workers outside. 'Why, Inspector?'

'Sergeant,' said Malone, unflattered. He looked them up and down, wondering what they'd be like in bed; maybe he should have brought Clements up here with him, got his mind off his winning bets. The blonde sat higher on the edge of her desk, mini-skirt tucked into her lap so that it was almost invisible. I don't know why rape is a crime, Malone thought. Being eye to eye with a girl's crotch all day and half the night should give a man certain privileges. A man, unwittingly leaving his fly unzipped, could be arrested for indecent exposure; a girl, exposing her crotch or her behind, was just considered to be fashionable. Women were subtly providing their own answer to the double standard for men. The blonde girl was aware of Malone's look, but evidently she trusted policemen.

Then Con Malone, who wouldn't have trusted the Police Commissioner, came in with Kerslake. Malone excused the engineer and the two girls and closed the door after them, then turned to his father. 'Take off the helmet, Dad. You look like something out of *All Quiet on the Western Front.*'

Con Malone took off his helmet, held it tucked against one hip and tapped the ash of his cigarette into it. He was not as tall as his son and he looked much shorter because of his broad figure. His thick grey hair was close-cropped above the wide face with its door-knocker nose, its long Irish upper lip and the years marked like notches in the cheeks and around the eyes. It seemed to Malone that his father had looked this old for as long as he could remember, yet Con still kept going, working as hard as he had ever done, never mentioning the word retirement. He was sixty-three or four and he still had another good ten years in him. Only the worry and disgrace of having a copper for a son might wear him out.

'I'm not gunna be mixed up in any of this,' he began, taking over the interview, showing who was senior and who was junior. 'It could've been any one of us, me or the Dagoes, who found her——'

Dagoes: the Old Man was like the Old Lady, still carried

16

his prejudices like football club ribbons. 'Dad, you *are* mixed up in it. Nothing serious, you'll probably just be called as a witness at the inquest——'

'No bloody fear!' Con Malone shook his head emphatically, as if he had been asked to denounce the Pope. He never went near a church except on Christmas Eve when, as his Christmas present to Brigid, he went to midnight mass with her. But he believed in the institution of the Church and considered the Pope worth a dozen kings or presidents. He had got drunk when Pope John died, but didn't think he'd go that far for this new bloke Paul. He'd get drunk all right, cause a, whatyoucallit, disturbance before he'd go into bloody court as a police witness.

Malone sighed and looked out the window again. Another liner was going down the harbour, another means of escape. Since his one and only trip abroad two years ago, a short and not very happy trip, when he had gone to arrest the Australian High Commissioner in London for murder, he had been dreaming of another journey to Europe. He had been saving every cent he could, even investing in some of Clements's surefire tips, and now he had enough for a three months' economy tour of Europe. But a week ago he had asked Lisa to marry him and now the money was earmarked as down payment on a house. He was trapped, tied down to the routine of investigations like this one and the irritation of witnesses who did not want to get mixed up in anything. Angry at himself as much as at his father, feeling he was being disloyal to Lisa, he spun back and said sharply, 'You'll be called when they want you, Dad.'

Con Malone sucked on his cigarette, then, without taking it from his mouth, asked with massive sarcasm, 'You want me name and address, then?'

Malone grinned: it was hard to take the Old Man's antagonism seriously. 'I'll get it from the wage sheet. When you got down there this morning, did the timber in front of the opening look as if it had been disturbed? Or had it been put neatly back in place?'

Con Malone scowled, then said grudgingly, 'I didn't notice nothing. I mean, whoever done it, he done a neat job of

17

putting all the timber back. It wasn't nailed or nothing, but he'd put it all back the way it'd been.'

'You were pretty observant.'

'Not at the time. I been thinking about it since, like.'

'You see where I get my detective instincts from?'

'Christ!' said Con Malone, and almost spat into his helmet. 'Whoever dumped that girl there must have worked here at some time.'

'He could work here now.' Despite himself, Con Malone could not resist hazarding an opinion.

Malone shook his head. 'No, he must have been a bloke who worked here in Utzon's time. You've worked here before, Dad. How long ago was it?'

'You accusing me of dumping her down there?'

'If I were, I'd just turn the case over to Mum. She'd have you up against the wall in no time.'

Con Malone looked out the window and remained silent for a while as if he were not going to give any more answers. But Malone knew how to handle his father and he waited patiently.

At last, doing the Police Force a great favour, Con Malone said, 'About six years ago. I used to work down in that particular bit.'

'If you had worked here, knew your way around, and you wanted to dump a body, how would you go about it?'

'You're making it pretty bloody crook, ain't you? Asking me to think like a crim!'

'I thought you'd rather think like that than like a cop.'

Con Malone eyed his son warily. 'You're too bloody smart.'

Malone waited patiently, knowing the Old Man better than he knew himself. Con Malone's life had been so empty of any importance he could not resist any temptation to pontificate, even if it meant helping a mug copper. 'It'd be easy as falling off a log. Plenty places around the harbour where you could dump the body in a boat, then bring it around here. There's only a coupla security men on guard here at night and the Water Police patrols only get around here a coupla times a night. They'd never cotton on to a small rowing boat, not if you kept close to the shore all the way around. Then it's dead easy to slide in under this place, in between the pylons.'

'How would you get into the actual basement, though?'

'There's air ducts all around the bottom, just faced over with some steel netting. Good pair of pliers'd snip 'em in no time. What the hell am I telling you all this for, but?'

'I don't know,' said Malone innocently. 'But you'd have made a good cop.'

Con Malone reeled and looked out the window, seeking his own escape. Malone himself looked down at the week-old newspaper spread out on the desk. A story was ringed with red pencil: Minister Would Welcome Ideas, said the headline. Malone read on: 'Mr W. P. Helidon, Minister for Cultural Development, said yesterday that he would welcome any serious suggestions for the first year's programme of the Opera House. He would study further the Returned Soldiers League's suggestion of an Anti-Communism Pageant. He did not take seriously the Students' Union's suggestion of a nude version of *White Horse Inn* or *The Sound of Music* . . .' Malone shook his head in amusement. Everyone had his problems, especially Ministers saddled with the responsibility for cultural development.

Then Kerslake came back with Clements. 'Get anything more?' Malone asked.

Clements just nodded, disappointing both Con Malone and Kerslake who had set their ears forward in the hope of catching up on something they had missed. Kerslake chewed on a mouthful of questions, but thought better of asking them and finally shrugged and said, 'We'd been hoping to stay out of the news. Had far too much publicity. Just our luck. Sorry for the girl, of course.'

'Who isn't?' said Malone, and managed to make the remark toneless.

Twenty minutes later the doctor, the fingerprint expert and the photographer arrived and Malone and Clements went down to the basement with them. Kerslake wanted to lead the way again, but Malone, doubly perverse, insisted that Con Malone was enough as a guide. Con, grumbling in his throat like a bronchial dog, switched on his lamp and led the way.

Kerslake, disgruntled, took off his helmet, sat down and invited the mini-skirted girls to join him in sniping at the arrogance and rudeness of the Police Force. The girls, as practised as all Sydney citizens in such abuse, willingly joined in.

The photographer took a dozen photos, his flash sparkling with indecent brightness, like a carnival cracker, in the gloomy room. The doctor examined the girl, going over her body with that casual detachment that Malone, even after years on the force, still found hard to accept. He knew that a dead body was no more than a piece of evidence, that the soul, if you believed in such a thing, had gone and left only a clay vessel, that no amount of sympathy or grief could ever bring the body back to life. But it had once been a person and somehow he thought it deserved more than the cold unconcern that a butcher might have shown towards a side of beef. In some odd way Malone felt a sense of guilt that the girl should be handled in such a way. But then, he told himself, it wasn't his job to protect the dead.

The doctor, a young man who wore a strip of plaster across his nose from last night's squash match, stood up. 'Strangulation. Pretty vicious, too.'

'Done by a man?'

'Probably. But it'd be hard to tell. Could've been done by a woman with strong hands. There are some scratches on the throat, but that doesn't mean anything. Even blokes are wearing their nails long these days.'

'Any sign of rape?'

The doctor swung back one of the girl's legs as if he were opening a gate. 'There are some bruises on the inside of the thigh there, but that doesn't prove anything, either. There's no sign of bruising around the vagina.' He looked down at the girl, for the first time showed a spark of interest. 'She would have been quite a looker. Why do they kill the good-looking ones? There are plenty of crows around.'

Then he stepped back, already impatient to be gone. 'You'll be able to get some fingerprints, Herb. This room must have been pretty airtight. Her hands have mummified a bit.'

The fingerprint man knelt down beside the body and Malone jerked his head and led Clements out into the passage. They walked round the curve of it and came to an opening that looked out through a pattern of concrete pylons to the waters of the harbour. Steel netting covered the opening, but when Malone pushed against it a section fell out, leaving a hole about three feet square.

'That's how they got in.'

'They?' said Clements.

'You want to lose some of that money of yours? I'll bet it needed more than one bloke to get that girl in here. What did you find on her?'

'There's half a dry-cleaning tab on her dressing-gown. And —you're not gunna believe this—there are two nipples tattooed on her arse. One on each cheek.'

'There's your filthy imagination at work again. They were probably rat bites. The doc didn't say anything.'

'He probably didn't see them. You know what a perfunctory bastard he is. But they'll see them right enough when they get her into the morgue.'

Malone stared out at the water lapping against the pylons. A fruit box floated by, a stick of celery sticking up out of it like a bedraggled flag on a child's home-made boat. 'If she went in for that sort of caper, she must have been in the game one way or another.'

'Oh, I dunno. You never know with kids these days, even the so-called nice ones. Anything for a giggle.'

'She's around twenty-seven or eight. When she was a kid, the nice ones weren't doing that sort of thing for a giggle. I think we'll start assuming she's *not* a nice kid. Anyone in my day had tattoos on her bum, she wasn't captain of the school.'

My day: I'm thirty-five and I'm talking like my dad. The generation gap was opening quicker every year. 'Maybe we'll have her prints in the records. But I thought I knew most of the recognized performers.'

'I've never seen her before,' said Clements. 'And I've been

to all the most exclusive places.' He, too, looked out at the
dirty, heaving water under the pylons. He sniffed the air,
cold and damp here despite the heat farther out, and his big
basset-hound face suddenly drooped. 'Makes you wonder,
though. Why would a good-looking bird like her finish up
down here?'

CHAPTER TWO

I

Tuesday, November 26

THE FISHING TRAWLER bumped against the jetty, rocking gently on the backwash from a speedboat that had pulled out from the other side. Jack Savanna, still feeling queasy from the long hours out at sea, clambered awkwardly up from the trawler's deck on to the jetty. The cameraman and his assistant were already ashore, festooning themselves with their equipment before they moved along to the truck that was waiting for them out on the roadway. Savanna could see the sign on the side of the truck: Olympus Film Productions; and he shut his eyes against the bitter joke of it. When he opened them the skipper of the trawler, Bixby, was standing beside him.

'Feeling all right?' The look on the man's weather-carved face was as sardonic as the sign on the truck.

'I'll survive.' Savanna's voice croaked, the words sticking like splinters in his throat. Twenty years as a radio announcer, ten years doing voice-over on television commercials, and he sounded like W. C. Fields with a cold. He cleared his throat, as a matter of professional pride as much as anything else, but then decided against saying anything further. The less he said to this chap, the sooner he got away from him, the better.

He was conscious of Bixby watching him as he walked along the jetty after the cameraman and his assistant. He had the feeling that Hopkins, the cameraman, should be walking backwards before him, camera raised for a tracking shot: this was the sort of scene one saw night after night in the cheap melodramas that filled in the time between the commercials. The hero, debonair and indistinguishable from any of the heroes in the commercials, walking away from the villain who

23

might at any moment decide to take a shot at him. Then the ridiculousness of his imagination tickled him and he laughed, a cough of embarrassment. Hopkins looked over his shoulder. 'Something funny, Jack?'

Savanna shook his head, looking past Hopkins at the biggest joke of all: Olympus Film Productions. No bigger now than when he had started it ten years ago, eighteen thousand dollars in the red this year alone, still making the shoe-string budget documentaries that were to have been the first step to feature production, still chasing agencies for the odd commercial that would pay the wages of his small staff. Everyone else in the game was coining money, but he might just as well be turning out Rupert Bunny and Flora Finch silents for all the money he was making. Something funny, all right. But Hopkins, a good cameraman, had never had a sense of humour. He would certainly not understand the humour of Grafter Gibson's trawlers being used to pick up drug parcels out at sea.

Savanna had known he and his crew were unwelcome when they had reported to Bixby yesterday afternoon. 'You weren't supposed to be coming on my boat,' Bixby had said.

'I know that. But the other trawler has broken down or something. They just rang and said we were to come to you.'

'Pity they don't give a bloke a bit more warning. I don't like the idea of it.' Bixby looked like a man whose ideas would be as simple and hard as the knuckles on his rock-like fists. There appeared to be no fat on his big square frame and he gave the impression of being all bone and muscle, the content extending even to his head. 'I don't think much of advertising, commercials, things like that. Okay, just don't get in the way, that's all. Stay off deck while we're working.'

'But that's the whole point,' Savanna protested. 'We're supposed to be shooting fishermen at work, then you all stop for a smoke.'

'What sorta smoke?'

Savanna named the brand.

'Never use 'em,' said Bixby. 'We all smoke Benson and Hedges. Only the best,' he smirked, 'when only the best will do.'

'I know,' said Savanna wearily. 'I did the voice on that one myself for a couple of years. Well, we shan't shoot too close to you.'

'Just don't get in our way, that's all. I dunno how you got permission to use our boats, anyway. Old Grafter Gibson ain't one for public relations or anything like that.'

'Mr Gibson is my brother-in-law,' said Savanna, and thought, Put that in your Benson and Hedges and smoke it, pal.

Bixby's face became as hard and bony as his fists, then he turned abruptly and went up into the wheelhouse of the trawler. Savanna looked at Hopkins and young Colegate, the assistant. 'Welcome aboard. But you heard what the admiral said. No getting in his way.'

It had not been easy. They had shot several hundred feet of film late yesterday afternoon as the trawler's crew had set their nets, but Hopkins had had to get his close shots with his zoom lens; as soon as he had moved in close, one or another of the crew had snarled at him to get out of the bloody way. When Savanna and his two men had gone below to eat their supper, Bixby and *his* men had remained up on deck talking quietly amongst themselves. Savanna, Hopkins and Colegate reluctant to wear out their welcome any further, had not looked at any of the bunks, not knowing if any of them were spare, and had gone to sleep propped in corners of the tiny mess-room. At two o'clock in the morning, cramped, his head aching from the stale air, Savanna had woken and, moving cautiously so as not to disturb Hopkins or anyone else who might be sleeping down here, had gone up on deck for a breath of air and a smoke.

The breath of air he had taken in one short quick gasp and he had never had the smoke at all. Bixby and the trawler crew were working at the stern of the boat. There was no light hung there, but a broken lantern of moon silhouetted them.

A net had been hauled in and Bixby was taking half a dozen oilskin-wrapped parcels from it, each of them attached to a small buoy no bigger than a toy balloon. He passed one of the packages to a crewman who opened it and said, 'It's okay.

25

Pound packets as usual.' He bounced the package in his hand. 'It's hard to believe, ain't it? That's worth more than gold.'

'Don't get any ideas,' said Bixby sharply. 'You work for your cut and that's all. Our job finishes when we get it ashore.'

'Christ,' said the crewman in a hurt tone. 'I'd never peddle the stuff. I've seen what it does to some of 'em. I could never look a junkie in the face, you know what I mean?'

The other crewmen laughed softly. Savanna backed cautiously down the stairs, slid back into his corner and sat staring into the darkness, his sudden information pressing down on him as unwanted and uncomfortable as a load of wet fish. He was still staring into the darkness when Bixby, coming noiselessly down the stairs in sandshoes, flashed a torch on him.

'Hullo, you still awake?'

Savanna shut his eyes against the brutal punch of the torch. 'You just woke me,' he said, and hoped that the nervous rasp in his throat sounded like the voice of a man just disturbed from sleep.

Bixby held him pinned by the torch beam for a moment, then he grunted and switched it off. He went through into the bunk area and Savanna sank farther down into his corner.

He fell asleep, but he tossed restlessly all night, disturbed by his knowledge and by a queasiness brought on by the rolling of the trawler and the stale air of the mess-room. He was glad of daylight when it finally crawled weakly down the steps and gave some shape to the ugly clutter of his surroundings. He got painfully to his feet, went up on deck and a moment later was followed by Bixby.

'We're finished,' said Bixby. 'We'll be heading back. You want any more shots, you better get 'em in a hurry.'

Savanna nodded weakly. 'Can't get back soon enough for me.'

Bixby grinned sadistically. 'Takes all sorts, don't it?'

'What?'

'To make a world.' Then he looked more carefully at Savanna. 'You got something on your mind, mate?'

Savanna shook his head, managing a smile that rested on

26

his face like a momentary scar. 'It's my stomach that's worrying me, not my mind.'

Bixby stared at him a moment longer, then shrugged and went up into the wheelhouse. He continued to look down at Savanna as the latter moved to the bow of the boat, and when Savanna glanced back he saw that both Bixby and the man at the wheel were staring at him. He turned his face into the morning breeze and thought: twenty-five or thirty years ago I'd have shrugged this off as none of my business. It's still none of my business, but why am I—scared? (He said the word doubtfully in his mind, as if he were scared of *it*.) Does the backbone go in middle age, along with the hair, the muscles and the jawline? Is atrophy of the spirit, of guts, part of the process of ageing? Twenty-six years ago he had proved to himself and the army that he had courage and the army had decorated and promoted him for it. But his courage now seemed as faded as the long-forgotten ribbon they had given him to mark it.

Now as he walked along the jetty in the early sunlight, the same thoughts still cluttered his mind, like rocks in a bed that, though lumpy and sagging, had up till now at least been bearable. Nothing was perfect, he had been telling himself for the past six months, throwing himself straws to save from drowning, and the negative optimism had been enough: something was bound to turn up sooner or later. But not this morning: last night's discovery, the fear (fear? Was that too strong a word?) of Bixby's knowing what he had learned, the queasiness of his stomach, the bitter joke of the sign on the side of the truck: it all added up to a despair that he had suspected for a long time was eventually going to hit him. Some men lived in the resigned expectation of cancer or heart disease. His expectation had been despair and now it had come this morning, finally triggered off by something whose connection with him was so tenuous as to be ignored. Except that he had always found it impossible to ignore Grafter Gibson . . .

He heard the toot of a car horn and looked along to see Helga sitting in her car twenty or thirty yards along the road.

'I'll see you at the studio,' he said to Hopkins and Colegate, and walked along to Helga. Her car was a low Datsun sports model and he had to lean down, feeling his spine crack, as she put her face up for him to kiss her. Out of the corner of his eye he saw Hopkins and Colegate watching him, but there was nothing he could do about it. If your mistress expected you to kiss her in public, you couldn't blame the public for taking a free seat. Except that Helga, in the past, had always been more discreet than this.

Tired, sick and nervous, he turned his irritation on her. 'What the hell are you doing down here at this hour?'

'Darling.' Thank God she wasn't coy; that was always one of Josie's worst sins. There were some women who would never learn that coyness was as unattractive on them as a bad complexion. 'I shouldn't be here if I didn't think it was necessary. I'm usually asleep at this hour.'

'Then I didn't make the mistake of being flattered, thinking you had come down here just to see me.'

'But that's why I did come, darling. To see you. I want some money.'

He swore, jerking his head up as the truck went past. In it Hopkins and Colegate sat with their heads turned aside in exaggerated discretion; some men could act coyly, too, blast them. 'What makes you think I carry a walletful of cash on me at this hour, getting off a fishing trawler after being all night at sea?'

'I only want forty dollars, darling. I have to go to my dentist and I'm afraid he won't do anything unless I've paid my bill for the last time.'

'What time's your appointment?'

'Ten-thirty.'

'The banks open at ten.'

'Not for me. I'm overdrawn far too much.' She smiled, unworried as only the habitual extravagant can be. He looked along the promenade, saw the truck disappear; he was so far in debt he couldn't remember if the truck was paid for. He looked down at her, at the broad beautiful face, the golden hair that looked so unreal and the voluptuous body that was her snare. Sex and overdrafts, he thought, our mutual interests.

She continued to smile up at him, reading his thoughts. 'There's time, darling, if you feel up to it.'

He reached for his wallet, took out forty dollars as he slid into the seat beside her, bending his long legs beneath the dashboard. 'I'll feel I'm paying for it.'

'It doesn't worry me if it doesn't worry you.' She was cool and unoffended; she reached across and kissed him on the cheek. '*Ich liebe dich.*'

'You don't,' he said, but it didn't worry him.

Then Bixby was standing over him, towering above the tiny car. 'Be seeing you again, Mr. Savanna?'

Again there was the tightness in his throat. 'I don't think so. We got all we needed.'

'Well, that was all you come for, wasn't it?' Bixby took a match out of his pocket, began to chew on it. 'Hooroo, Mr Savanna. Put in a good word for us with old Grafter when you see him.'

Helga started up the car and pulled it away from the kerb. 'What's the matter, darling? You sounded afraid of him. Funny, I never thought you would be afraid of anyone.'

'You don't know me.'

How can you, he thought, when I'm just starting to find out things about myself?

'No, except on Tuesdays and Fridays. I really don't know what you are like the rest of the week.'

'We're quits, then. I don't know you.'

'No,' she said, smiling to herself. 'It's better that way.'

Later in her flat he lay in bed and watched her as she came out from the bathroom drying herself. Whether by instinct or by practice, she had a talent for making even the most everyday action look sensual; she towelled her body with the slow lazy grace of a strip-tease artist unaware of her audience. He liked that: she ran the towel lazily over her full breasts, conscious that he was watching her but making no attempt to put on a cheap titillating act. Josie would have done that; or retreated coyly to the bathroom. He felt a twinge of conscience and, much worse, a sharper stab of pity for Josie. There was not much hope for a marriage when the deepest pain you could feel for your wife was pity.

29

Helga turned away from him and he saw the ridiculous tattoo marks on her buttocks, the crude sniggery joke that fitted so ill with her personality.

'I still wonder what you *did* in Germany.'

She turned back, knowing what had prompted his remark. Then she wrapped the towel round her hips, the one modest thing she had done since they had entered the flat almost an hour ago. But she did not blush nor lose her poise; along with everything else she had learned, she had acquired the art of cool self-possession. He knew he was not the first man who had queried her about the nipples on her plump behind.

'I've *told* you—I was a secretary. And I did some modelling. But not *that* sort. Those marks, they were a stupid joke. I was only fifteen. Didn't you do things as a dare when you were a teenager?'

'That's a cruel question. I can't remember back that far.'

She came across, sat on the side of the bed and kissed him on the cheek. 'I wouldn't be cruel to you, darling. I never think of you as—whatever you are. I don't even know how old you are.'

'Fifty-four.' That was how low he felt this morning, that even vanity was no longer worth the effort.

Her surprise was genuine. '*Really?* Darling, you're marvellous!'

'Louis the Fourteenth was doing it twice a day when he was seventy.'

'I don't mean *that*. I mean your *looks*. Nobody would take you for more than forty-three or four, even with your grey hair.'

He looked at himself in the big mirror on her dressing-table across the room. It was not easy to see himself clearly even at such a short distance; myopia made the man across the room a stranger. He looked back at her, put a hand on her breast, on one of the real nipples. In a moment or two he saw the dark myopic look come into *her* eyes as the nipple rose under his fingers.

'*Nein.*' Her voice became guttural as it always did when her passion was aroused; it was almost as if she changed nationalities when she was in bed, became a natural German again; no one, she had once said, ever took their citizenship papers to bed with them. '*Nein, Liebling.*'

He hesitated, then he took his hand away. 'Better get dressed or I'll start to try proving I'm a better man than Louis.'

'You are, darling.' The guttural note was still in her voice as she sat back.

He shook his head, suddenly depressed again. 'No. Louis was always wise enough to take the long view. I've never had that talent.'

She continued to look at him, the dark look now gone from her eyes. 'Darling, what's the matter? There's something worrying you. Was it that man this morning?'

Him, and a thousand other things. But for the first time he took her into his confidence; he had reached a depth where he had to talk to *someone*. And who better than a mistress? Louis, secretive though he was, must have confided a few of his troubles occasionally to his mistresses. 'I don't know, maybe I'm taking it too seriously.' He told her what he had seen last night out at sea. 'What do I do? Forget all about it? Or go and tell my brother-in-law?'

'That could be embarrassing, couldn't it? What if he already knows what is going on? If he is the organizer of it?'

'Grafter has made his money. He wouldn't need to get into something like this.'

'Darling, you don't know how greedy people can get. People make fortunes out of smuggling drugs. Why shouldn't Mr Gibson want to make another one?' She stood up, letting the towel drop from round her hips, and moved across to the wall-closet to pick out a dress. 'Why don't you go and see him?'

'What do I say when I get there?'

She looked over her shoulder, smiling at him. 'Blackmail him. Maybe then you could retire and we could see each other *every* day in the week.'

He returned her smile, thinking: she has been no help to me at all, she has the same frivolous outlook as Josie. He got out of bed and stood in front of the mirror.

'No,' he said when he saw her look at his reflection and nod approvingly. 'You're flattering me, just like a good mistress should.' He looked in the mirror again; even the myopia didn't help at this distance. He might be what you would call handsome, he decided, if you overlooked the tired eyes and the slackness round what had once been a very strong jawline. He still carried his tall body straight, but there was no disguising the thickening round the waist and the wrinkling skin over the muscles under his arms. An honest man always accepted the truth of his own mirror: he might look better than most men of his age, but: 'The decay has started, love. There's only one muscle in all that body that's still any good and it's never been praised for its looks.'

She smiled more widely and he saw the faint glint of metal in the corner of her mouth. 'Australians are like Americans. They think the only thing worth having is youth. All those men jog-trotting round the streets on Saturday mornings, just so they can get into condition for beer-drinking on Saturday night. At least, darling, you know how to treat a woman as a woman.'

I don't know that Josie would back you on that. But all he said was, 'When you're at the dentist this morning, get him to replace that tin cap on your tooth.'

She shook her head, looking in the mirror and pulling back the corner of her mouth to look at the cheap cap on one of her canine teeth. 'No, it's my lucky charm.'

'How's your luck been lately?'

She made a face. 'That was why I had to ask you for the money this morning. It's that youth fetish again—photographers don't want twenty-six-year-old models these days. All they want are what they call *birds*, eighteen-year-olds with blank faces and minds to match. Do I sound like a middle-aged bitch who is just jealous?'

He kissed her bare shoulder, went past her and into the bathroom. 'We'll go out Thursday night, show these kids what a couple of middle-aged squares can really look like.'

'Not Thursday night.'

He put his head round the bathroom door. 'Why not? I know it's not Tuesday or Friday. Let's have a bonus night. For the both of us.'

'Not Thursday, darling,' she repeated. 'No questions,

remember? I never ask you why or why not, you never ask me.'

He looked at her, then he shrugged and went back into the bathroom, feeling curiously relieved rather than disappointed. A wife and a mistress, he thought, neither of whom ever asked questions. In a way, he guessed, he was lucky.

2

He left the flat before Helga went to her dental appointment. He went downstairs and out into the silverplate atmosphere of Double Bay. Even at this early hour of the morning women were coming and going through the expensive boutiques, shopping at nine-thirty for a seventy-dollar pair of silk slacks with the same casualness as they might shop for a pound of sausages in Woolworth's supermarket across the street. The women of this well-to-do harbour suburb always reminded him of well-groomed dogs: between the entrance to Helga's block of flats and the taxi rank he passed two poodles, a borzoi and a pekinese: the pekinese woman confounded the image by having a real pekinese on a pink lead. He beat a toy bulldog in lime green slacks to a cab, ignored her broken-accented comment on Australian men, gave the cab-driver the address of Olympus and sank back on the stained and fraying vinyl upholstery.

'Bloody reffo women,' said the cab-driver, a naturalized Australian from Calabria. 'You get 'em all da time down thisa way, you know? They treat you like dirt.'

Savanna just nodded, not wanting to get involved in a xenophobic discussion with a cab-driver who, among his mates out at Fairfield or one of the other Italian communities, might say exactly the same thing about Australians. Reffo was a term that had been out of date for years; he wondered where the Italian had picked it up. There had been refugees arriving in Australia since the war: Balts, Yugoslavs, Hungarians and, just recently, Czechs; but they were never referred to as reffos. That was a term that belonged to the Jewish refugees of the Thirties, the fugitives from Hitler, the people thirty years resident now in Australia but still saddled with an epithet that Savanna found even more insulting than the official *New Australian*. He wondered if the cab-driver, noticing any trace of Helga's German accent, would have classed her as a reffo. Probably not: it seemed a name reserved strictly for Jews. It suddenly struck him that he had never asked Helga what she, as a German, thought of Jews. It was one question that, perhaps, he never should ask her. Come to think of it, he had never asked her what she thought of Australians, though occasionally she dropped hints that had a stiletto-sharpness to them.

The cab dropped him at Olympus and he went into the narrow, three-storey building squashed between the brewery and the meat-pie bakery. Olympus's single sound stage was on the top floor, heavily soundproofed to keep out the noise from both sides; but they had been able to do nothing about the smells, and the technicians, actors and agency people reeled between the overpowering whiffs, depending on which way the wind was blowing, of yeast and hot meat pies. Savanna's office was on the middle floor and, like the workers in the brewery and the bakery, he had learned to close his nose against the odours that surrounded him. But the agency people had not and gradually they were dropping him as a maker of their commercials. But with the soaring rents in Sydney, he could not afford to move elsewhere. Perhaps he should try for beer and meat pie commercials, to be shot on alternate days.

The phone rang as soon as he sat down at his desk. He waited for Betty, his secretary, to take the call outside; but she was not at her desk, was in the Ladies' or upstairs dodging Hopkins's hands as he zoomed in on her. There were plenty of people he wanted to avoid talking to these days, but he could not complain if she was not around to take the calls. She was worth far more than the fifty dollars a week he was paying her, but he could not afford more; and he was forever afraid of losing her. Reluctantly he picked up the phone, and knew at once that it was not a creditor. Well, not a *business* creditor.

'Sweet——'

34

He had known it would be Josie even before she spoke; he had an instinct for recognizing her presence even on the end of five miles of telephone cable; her very humility had its own nagging quality. 'You didn't call. I was worried——'

He looked around his office, not really seeing it, not having to see it: this was one print that would never fade or crack. The grey walls that hadn't had a coat of paint since he had moved in here; the desk, very mod*erne*, as the salesman had called it, that now looked like a plywood antique from the Twenties; the clients' two leather chairs that had finally revealed their plastic cow's origin; the carpet, worn so thin that the floorboards beneath created their own pattern in it. The row of bookshelves beneath the one grimy window: books on film by Rotha, Grierson, Manvell, books that hadn't been opened in God knew how long; the books on advertising, by Mayer, Ogilvy, that also hadn't been opened in the same time; the stacks of trade papers. Not a thing in the room that identifies me, he thought. Unless you could salvage enough out of the dust and debris of dreams to identify him.

'I stayed with one of the fishermen to dig up some background.' Lies slid off his tongue these days as easily as saliva.

'I rang the wharf. They said you left over two hours ago.' But there was no accusation in her voice, no protest or question: if there was an abstraction of voice, she had achieved it. Then she went on: 'You haven't forgotten Glenda and Les are coming for drinks? And Father Wrigley.'

He *had* forgotten. 'No, I hadn't forgotten. I'll be home early.'

'Sweet, could you bring home a cheque? There's no money in my account.' No whine, no rebuke, nothing: she had refined humility to a point where it was a deadly weapon. Yet he couldn't bring himself to believe that she was intelligent or cunning enough to have done it wittingly.

'I'll do that. I'm busy——'

'I'm sorry, sweet. It was just that I was worried.'

The phone went click in his ear. The timing was too exact: she had cut him off as if she had heard him draw in his breath to reply. He looked at the instrument in his hand, then slowly put it back in its cradle. He had felt for some time that Josie suspected there was another woman, but it had not perturbed him. Not because he was callously conscienceless about his infidelity; he had had a conscience once and there were still some dregs of it left in him somewhere. He had not worried about Josie's suspicions because he had convinced himself she would do nothing about them; it was as if, falling far short of other people's targets, she had achieved her own complacency of self-fulfilment. But now he wondered: had she done something about her suspicions, found out about Helga? And then quite suddenly he didn't care. Life was becoming so bloody complicated that any untangling of it, even if it meant argument and heartache, would be welcome. He suddenly longed for everything to come to a head: the bank to foreclose, Josie to divorce him, Helga to tell him that their affair was over. He would be bankrupt and alone, but it would give him the detachment that he now found he craved.

3

He did not manage to get away from the office as early as he had hoped and when he arrived home, Grafter Gibson, Glenda and Father Wrigley were already there. As he pulled his seven-year-old Jaguar into the drive he saw the black Rolls-Royce, so new that he imagined he could smell its leather upholstery from here, parked at the kerb, the chauffeur slumped in his seat with his cap pulled down over his eyes. He wondered if Wrigley had come in the Rolls with the Gibsons: it would be just what the smug little bastard would revel in.

The smug little bastard was pouring the drinks as Savanna came into the living-room. 'Ah, Mr Savanna! Your good wife asked me to act as barman. However, your brother-in-law thinks I'm a trifle light-handed with the liquor. He thinks whisky should not be dispensed in the same small measure as altar wine.' He giggled, his plump face, smooth as a cake of expensive soap, showing not a wrinkle as he smiled. Unctuous, a product of one of the worst elocution schools, an ambitious man who had decided that doubters never got on in the Church, he was a priest who at the early age of thirty had managed to take on the image of a spinster aunt, a career aunt. He had spent all his priesthood in well-to-do parishes and you knew he would never find himself in a poor district: he was too good a politician for that. 'What can I get you, mine host?'

'How'd the trip go?' Leslie Gibson lolled in Savanna's favourite chair, one short thin leg crossed over the other, half a dozen inches of bare white skin showing above the black silk socks. He was a small, wizened man, his thick grey hair cut short back-and-sides, his skin mottled with sun cancers, his blue eyes still as bright and shrewd as the day he had first played another man for a sucker. His silk-and-mohair suit hung on him like a Chinese peasant's pyjamas and the ten-dollar tie he wore could have been a piece of string for all it did for him sartorially. Glenda tried hard to make her husband look like the millionaire that he was but he remained looking like the New Guinea gold fossicker he had once been. He was fond of quoting that fashion was for fools who had no confidence in their own taste, and did his best to advertise that he had no taste at all. Savanna hated him with that comfortable sort of contempt that is often as good for a man's well-being as a feeling of charity.

Savanna took the drink Wrigley brought him and sank down on the couch beside Josie. He pressed her knee with his free hand and was surprised when she gently lifted his hand and dropped it on the couch between them. Savanna saw Glenda's eyes narrow and at once he thought: hullo, you two have been having a little chat about me. On a sudden impulse he winked at Glenda and almost laughed with delight when she straightened her neck in surprise. Then he looked across at Gibson. 'It went all right. Except'—he wondered how far he dared go—'except I don't think your skipper welcomed the idea of having us aboard.'

'Who was it? Bixby? Wouldn't take any notice of him. He's always got shit on the liver.'

'Les——' Glenda glanced warningly in the direction of Father Wrigley.

'Oh, don't mind me,' said the priest, raising his glass. Savanna noticed the level of whisky in it; it hadn't taken

37

Wrigley long to switch from his altar wine measure. 'Obscenity, not brevity, is now the soul of wit.'

Gibson screwed Wrigley to the wall with a gimlet glance, but the priest seemed unaware of his gaffe. Savanna smiled into his glass and said, 'Do you ever go out on the boats, Les?'

'I won't let him,' said Glenda. 'He's too old for that sort of thing any more.'

She said it with affection and in her fluttery, high voice, but Savanna knew that what she dictated, Gibson did without argument. The vulgar old bastard had more enemies than the Minister for Defence, treated everyone he met as someone to be exploited; but Glenda had defeated him years ago, he had succumbed to something that he recognized in no one else: love.

She sat there on the edge of her chair, corseted upright at great expense, her pale pink face bright with that impregnable blankness that Savanna found in women of no imagination. He looked across at Josie: she was even worse, but at least she didn't try to run his life. He felt a sudden warmth of feeling for her. Not love: he could never remember feeling *that* for her. And, hard on the heels of the warmth of affection for Josie, was the cold stab of conscience that he didn't feel, had never felt, anything more for her. He had never loved any woman but his first wife Silver, and she had left him twenty-two years ago and was now the wife of another man. He looked back at Gibson, wondering what the bastards of the world did to merit happiness in their marriages.

'You should go out some time,' he said, feeling malicious in his knowledge of what went on on at least one of Gibson's trawlers. 'Just to keep up with things.'

'He's too old,' Glenda repeated, hurting her husband as only a woman with too much love can; Gibson shook his head, trying to struggle out of the grave she was digging for him. 'Anyhow, we're going abroad again soon. We're going to Rome again,' she said, and turned her face to Father Wrigley as if looking for a benediction.

'Wonderful!' exclaimed Wrigley, chalking up indulgences for himself. He had been pressing this trip on Mrs Gibson

.or months, hoping that she might suggest taking him with them as their personal chaplain; he had read, with an envy that had required an Act of Contrition, of those priests fortunate enough to be chaplain to the aristocrats of Europe. It would be difficult to see as an aristocrat the sinful old reprobate who would be paying for the trip, but perhaps a miracle would be worth praying for.

'Dunno why we're going there again,' Gibson grumbled. 'Last time we were there I got sick as a dog. Had some sea-food stuff in a restaurant down the arse-end of the Colosseum.'

The arse-end of the Colosseum: so much for the antiquities of Europe with Grafter Gibson. Savanna smiled, holding out his glass to Wrigley for a refill; the priest leapt to it as if he were an altar boy. 'Stick to steak, Les, wherever you go. Steak and beer, you can't go wrong.'

'He's poking fun at you, Les,' said Glenda. 'Trying to make out you're nothing but an Australian.'

But Gibson wasn't offended. He winked at Savanna, realizing he had an ally against the priest. 'I don't find that such an insult. I been called a bloody lot worse. I bet Father Wrigley here's called me a thing or two.'

'I pray for you all the time,' said the priest, pouring himself another drink. 'Mrs Gibson asked me to.'

'Father is going with us,' said Glenda, her smile expanding as she saw the priest's face swell with delight. 'It's time we told you, Father. Les agreed to it this morning.'

'Our own bloody personal chaplain,' Gibson growled. 'How's that for buying your way into heaven?'

Savanna had felt Josie tense beside him and when he looked at her he could see the slight quivering round her mouth, as if she were about to burst into tears. You poor old cow, he thought. I can't afford to take you to Surfers' Paradise for even a week, and here's this smarmy bastard being shouted a three months' trip to Europe. Grafter doesn't deserve to keep his money if he's going to waste it like that.

He stared across the room at the photographs on the book-shelves, one of Josie taken fifteen years ago when she had had no weight problem and when she had still believed that happiness was one of nature's gifts and didn't have to be worked at, and one of their daughter Margaret taken the day she had graduated, the day she had told him she no longer believed anything he would ever tell her. I had every opportunity for happiness, he thought, and I've buggered it. And started to feel sorry for himself, something he would have despised in himself on any other day.

The conversation of the others spun on about the coming trip, meaningless words clouding the room, while Savanna sat back beside Josie, his eyes half-shut, and began to half-dream, a dream that after a while took on some of the chill of a nightmare as he realized what was taking shape, like a sudden tumour, in his mind. And all because a tight-fisted old scoundrel, instead of using some of his money where it would come in handy, was going to give a free trip abroad to an unctuous fat little priest whom probably the Vatican couldn't stand. He stared glazedly across at Gibson and wondered how the old man would respond to the suggestion that Helga had frivolously made this morning. Twenty thousand dollars, Les. That's all I want, and I shan't say a word about the drugs your men are bringing in. Twenty thousand dollars, Les, and I might even join Wrigley in saying a prayer for you.

'We must be going,' said Glenda. 'We're putting Jack to sleep.'

She stood up, giving him no time to make a polite protest. Gibson also stood up, glad of the opportunity to be gone; he had never acquired a taste for the bon-bons of small talk. Father Wrigley rose more reluctantly, knowing he was soon going to be dismissed, dropped off at the presbytery to return to the company of the two older priests whose only talk was of cards, football and the Holy Father's problems with the upstarts of the Church. Oh, wait till he told them tonight he was going off on leave to Rome!

He shook hands with his host, aware that Savanna hated him as much as if he were some fire-eating Redemptorist who had forced his way into the house on some evangelical mission. Why, and all he wanted was a little social ecumenism! 'It's been a pleasure, Mr Savanna.'

'You should come up here some time before we go, Father,'

said Glenda, acting like a Mother Superior. 'Have a talk with Jack.'

'What about?' asked Savanna; and even Father Wrigley looked blank.

'The Church, of course,' said Glenda, and looked at Josie for support.

But Josie shook her head, and Father Wrigley looked relieved: he was not built for the role of evangelist. 'Jack's all right as he is.'

'Well——' said Glenda, making it apparent she thought otherwise. She put on her coat and gloves, straightened her hat, picked up her small elegant parasol. Christ, Savanna thought, she's become a typical Society matron, making every outing look like Ladies' Day at the races.

'You should get Les to church more often,' said Josie, and Savanna loved her for the sweet delicate way she placed the barb. 'Especially if he's going to have a personal chaplain.'

Gibson winked at Josie, an evil grimace. 'Your point, Josie. You two women can go off to Mass as much as you like. Me and Jack will say our prayers over a beer.'

'Would you care to have me join you?' said Wrigley brightly.

'You better stick to the women,' said Gibson, nodding at the Savannas and heading for the front door. 'They're the ones keep you fellers in business.'

Glenda straightened her hat again, as if it had been blown off centre by her husband's rudeness to the priest, salvaged a smile for the Church, kissed Josie affectionately, pecked at Savanna as if she would prefer to bite him, and followed her husband out to their car. Father Wrigley, hide as thick as the cover of a family Bible, shook hands again, complimented Savanna on his whisky and scuttled out to the Rolls before Gibson gave the order to the chauffeur to drive away.

The Savannas stood side by side in their front doorway watching the big black car glide away. It turned the corner at the end of the street, the late sun catching it for a moment: the golden reflections seemed to take on an extra carat or two from their source. 'I'd love a Rolls-Royce,' Josie sighed.

I couldn't bite him for that much, Savanna thought; not

41

that *and* the money we really need. He had looked up the
price of the Rolls when Grafter had bought the latest Silver
Shadow: twenty-four thousand dollars; that had been the day
the bank had sent him a particularly sharp note about
Olympus's overdraft, and he had almost turned Communist
on the spot. Yet, in a way, he didn't begrudge Grafter the car
nor the way the old bastard lived; he would live that way
himself if he could afford it. He put his arm about Josie's
plump shoulders and squeezed her. 'Would you settle for a
vintage Savanna?'

He could feel her body stiffen. She and Glenda have been
talking about me, he thought again; or she's been listening
and Glenda has been doing the talking. But he kept his arm
round her, his fingers working gently on her bare shoulder.
Across the street a woman hosing her garden watched them,
her eyes sore with the effort to be discreet; here in Rose Bay
there were still pretensions of gentility; you did not stare at
your neighbours unless you were wearing dark glasses.
Savanna *did* stare across at the woman, telling her silently:
I'm trying to seduce my wife and I'm a bastard. Then he felt
Josie relax and he felt even more of a bastard. But what else
can I offer her but some love-making? She knows I don't
love her, but she's willing to take the substitute. She looked
up at him, her eyes going blank, and said, 'Now?'

She turned quickly and went inside. He stood at the front
door looking out across the shining scab of red-tiled roofs on
the lower side of the street to the thin streak of water, a blue
mote in the eye, that the estate agents called a harbour view.
He and Josie had moved here to Rose Bay when they had
first married; she because, born and raised in Ashfield, a
respectable lower middle class suburb, she hungered to move
up to a higher scale of respectability; he because he had been
born and raised in Rose Bay, anyway, and it was close to the
city. They had paid five and a half thousand pounds for the
house and he had not been too proud to finance it on a War
Service loan. Today he could sell the house for fifty thousand
dollars, or twenty-five thousand pounds, and wipe out all
his debts with the sale. But they would be left with nothing
to start all over again and he had no confidence in his powers

of recovery. Unlike Grafter Gibson he had never really started at the bottom and at fifty-four he did not want to go looking for the experience of it. Beyond that there was another, more important, reason why he would not sell the house. It was the one solid, constant thing in their marriage, Josie's rock; she did not love it more than she did their daughter, but she depended on it more; it would always be there, but Margaret was already gone, was in England now and might never come back. If he took the house away from Josie, their marriage would be over. And he could not bring himself to do that to her.

He closed the front door, shutting out the scratched and dented Jaguar, the driveway that he couldn't afford to have resurfaced, the dusky sky whose serenity was a mockery. He would give Grafter a call in the next day or two, but first he would have to work out what to say. He had never spoken the commercial for blackmail.

'Hurry up, sweet——'

On his way to the bedroom, he stopped by the phone, took it off its cradle and dialled two digits to break the dial tone. It had a habit of ringing at the worst possible moment. The Postmaster-General had been responsible for more hernias than he knew of.

CHAPTER THREE

I

Monday, December 9

'I THINK you might've let your father off,' said Brigid
Malone, doling out trifle in Irish-sized helpings. 'Getting him
mixed up with the police and things like that. There, Lisa.
Is that too much?' She handed the plate to Lisa Pretorious,
daring her to knock it back.

'I'm Dutch,' said Lisa.

'I know,' said Mrs Malone, looking as if the knowledge
gave her indigestion.

'We love big helpings. They never served me enough when
I was in London.'

'Not even at them big fancy dinners and things at the
embassy houses and places like that?' Mrs Malone shook her
head in wonder at how the rich tried to economize.

'That wasn't a bad picture of me in tonight's *Sun*,' said
Con Malone.

'It was a good one of Scobie, too,' said Lisa.

'Yeah,' Con Malone said. 'Pity they had to take us together,
but.'

The visit had been awkward, but not quite as bad as Malone
had expected. His father's connection with the Opera House
murder, slight though it was, had been enough to take the
heat off Lisa, even if only occasionally. Brigid Malone, Irish
as a peat-bog as she was, had missed out on one of her fore-
bears' talents: she could not wage war on more than one
front. At last she had put aside her antagonism towards Lisa
for another night and had concentrated on her son's bad
taste and lack of filial feeling in getting his father involved
in police business.

But Malone knew how to handle that sort of situation and
it had not worried him. He poured some more claret into his

44

father's glass and said, 'I never talk business when I'm eating. Lisa says it's bad for the digestion.'

'What do ambassadors and people like that talk about when they're eating?' asked Mrs Malone.

'About each other,' said Lisa. 'Excepting the French. They only talk about themselves.'

In the house next door an argument suddenly started up, words booming and crackling beyond the thin kitchen wall like a distant barrage. Malone looked at Lisa and grinned. 'There's some diplomatic chit-chat for you.'

A woman's voice, strident as a cracked siren, yelled, 'You drunken bastard! I dunno what I ever seen in you——' Her voice cut off sharply as something thudded against the wall with a metallic clunk.

'Something's gunna come right through the wall one night,' said Con Malone, sipping his claret, thinking maybe there was something to this business of gracious living or whatever they called it.

'Two or three times a week it happens,' said Mrs Malone. 'Next thing you'll hear him clout her.'

On cue there was a scream from the woman. Lisa jumped and looked across at Malone. He shook his head. 'If I went in there and interfered, they'd both go for me. That's their own argument. They don't want any outsider butting in.'

'Least of all a copper,' said Con Malone, taking another sip of the Cawarra Red, wondering what the wife would do if one night he brought home a bottle of it. Probably throw him out of the house for being a pervert or something.

'But he might kill her!'

Mrs Malone shook her head, an armchair general wise in the ways of such battles. 'They never do. It's the cold-blooded ones do things like that. Like the one who killed your girl.' She nodded at Malone, giving him a proprietary interest in the dead girl of that morning.

Then she noticed her mistake and for the first time looked sympathetically at Lisa. 'I didn't mean you, dear. I meant the other one.'

'I suppose in a way she is his girl,' said Lisa. 'At least till he finds out who murdered her.'

45

'Dad tells me it ain't gunna be easy.' Mrs Malone attacked her trifle.

'We have to find out who she is, first,' said Malone.

'And if you don't, you'll just forget her.' Mrs Malone's teeth clicked as they slipped on a piece of loose custard. 'Pigeonhole her.'

'They never try very hard when it's a nobody,' said Con Malone.

'We don't know she's a nobody,' said Malone, used to this sort of criticism and still unoffended by it. 'She could be a *somebody*, for all we know.' Though in his mind he doubted it: *somebodies* didn't have tattoos on their behinds.

'If she is, you still hush it up,' said Brigid Malone, her Irish logic breaking out like a rash tonight. 'You hush up so many things. I don't mean *you*. The police. You've never told us yet why you went to London that time.'

Malone felt Lisa look at him: he had never told *her*, either. 'That was security business.'

'I don't believe in security,' said Con Malone, a revolutionary from the age of ten. 'In a real democracy there oughta be no secrecy.'

'In an Irish democracy there wouldn't be,' said Malone, just beginning to be irritated. 'Not with the Irish gabbiness. Look, we'll find out who this girl is. It may take us a while, but we'll find out. And when we do, she won't be pigeonholed. We'll find out who killed her.'

Then the phone rang. Malone had had the phone put on when he had first joined the police force and when he left to live on his own he had insisted that it would remain in the house and he would continue to pay for it; it was another link with his parents and religiously he called them every day, as if to compensate for the disappointment he knew he had caused them when he had walked out to live alone. He got up now and went out into the narrow hallway in which the phone clamoured with what seemed twice the noise of phones elsewhere. When he lifted the phone, stilling the ringing, he noticed that the row next door had abruptly ceased. He could imagine the battling couple taking time out to press their ears against the wall.

Clements was on the other end of the line. 'Scobie? We're making a bit of progress. She was clean as far as we are concerned, nothing on her in the records. But that dry-cleaning tab, it belongs to a company that operates in the eastern suburbs, from Bondi back to the harbour. That should place where she lived.'

'Good,' said Malone, unimpressed. He had never yet met a case where some progress was not made, but that didn't mean it would be solved. 'What else?'

'Looks like she's some sort of European, or she's lived over there. Germany, the dentist thinks. The doc down at the morgue had a good look at her, then called in the dentist. She's got what he called a jam-tin cap on one of her teeth. It's a pretty cheap sort of cap and evidently they used it a lot in Europe up till a while ago.'

'What about her fingerprints?' Malone kept his voice to a whisper; he could almost hear the heavy breathing on the other side of the wall. 'You get a good set?'

'Beaut,' said Clements. 'Soon's I heard the dentist say she might be a European, I bunged a set off to Melbourne. They are already on the way to Interpol. Pity we gotta waste time routeing the stuff through Melbourne, though.'

Malone clucked sympathetically, not being as parochial-minded as Clements. The Victorian Commissioner of Police was the Interpol representative in Australia and all other State forces had to work through him when requesting Interpol co-operation. It rankled with certain New South Wales men, who considered their own service far superior to that in any other State. Clements, in his own way, was as narrow-minded and bigoted as Con and Brigid Malone.

Malone said good night to Clements and hung up. He stared at the wall in front of him, then he knocked loudly on it. 'Righto! You can start fighting again!'

Then he thought, I'll never leave here. No matter where I go, even if I finish up as Commissioner, there'll still be a bit of Erskineville in me. And how will Lisa react to that? He stood a moment longer, regretting his shout of good-humoured abuse. He had felt no shame or embarrassment at bringing Lisa here to his old home; there had never been any snobbish awkwardness about his beginnings. Police work had taught him the impossibility of hiding your origins; the next few days would prove that, when they learned where this morning's dead girl had begun her life. But acknowledging one's start in a slum district did not mean he had to act as if he had not learned there were some social graces worth cultivating.

Lisa, the product of a middle-class Dutch family and the best schools in Holland, a girl who had spent three years living at embassy level in London, had shown her own social graciousness when she had walked into the tenement house as if she had known such surroundings all her life. Warned by him of the antagonism to be expected from his mother, she had greeted Mrs Malone with a smooth friendliness that he could only imagine must be diplomacy at its best. Her reaction to the fight next door had been a humane rather than a social one: she had been afraid for the safety of the woman with her drunken husband. Lisa had learned to adapt; he would have to learn to do the same. He walked back down the hall to the kitchen, determined to ignore the fight which had once more started up next door.

He stood in the hallway for a moment looking in at Lisa at the kitchen table. I don't know how I ever did it, he thought. How did I get a girl like that to agree to marry me? Her blonde hair gleaming like a helmet under the hard electric light, she sat leaning forward to listen to his father. Her face in repose looked flawless to Malone; then when she smiled the perfection was not broken but, if possible, improved. But it was not just her looks that fascinated him. She had something else, a poise that placed her at ease with the world and the individual. At first he had thought it was what was called sophistication, then he had come to recognize that it was something deeper than mere social imperturbability. There was a tranquillity about her; not a resignation but an acceptance that there were certain things, grief, duty, the demands of love, that would always have to be faced. Then he looked at the lined face of his mother and felt the pain: Brigid Malone would never achieve that serenity of spirit till she died. He loved them both, but he was glad he was not marrying a girl like his mother.

Later, as they were leaving, when Lisa had stepped outside into the tiny back yard to the outside toilet, he said to his mother, 'Well?'

'Well what?'

'Well, what do you think of her?'

'She's all right.' Mrs Malone was already tidying up, emptying the two old brass ashtrays that had been in the house as long as Malone could remember, straightening the two velvet cushions on the faded couch in the front room; it was as if she feared even the imprint left by visitors on her retreat. 'She's too good for you.'

'I thought you hinted this morning she wasn't good enough for me. Not being a Tyke or an Australian.'

'I don't mean religion and things like that. That way there'd be trouble, too. I mean, well, you know. Education, things like that. *Position*.'

'She's well spoken,' said Con Malone, trying to say something not too extravagant in favour of Lisa. He had liked the girl, but he wasn't going to get into any argument with the wife over her.

Malone shrugged in exasperation. He recognized what his mother and father were both trying to say. Without conceding that there was such a thing as class distinction in Australia, they were telling him Lisa was a class above him. His father had used the classic euphemism for breeding: Lisa was *well spoken*.

'For a couple who hate the Poms for having a Queen and an aristocracy, you don't sound very democratic. Dad, ever since I was a kid you've always been telling me everyone is born equal.'

'They are,' said Con Malone, Labour Party to the core. 'Only in the system like it is, some have advantages. She's had 'em.'

'It won't work,' said Mrs Malone. 'But it's your life. You do what you like with it.'

Then Lisa came in from the back yard, aware that they had been talking about her but unruffled by it. Outside the toilet gushed noisily like a young Niagara; everyone in the terrace of houses knew when everyone else heard the call of

49

nature. It gurgled, gave a final spasm that jangled the chain, then died away. Lisa, as composed as if she had come from the powder-room at the Savoy in London, said good night to Mr and Mrs Malone.

'That was the best dinner I've had since I left Holland,' she said.

'Just what we always have,' said Brigid Malone, not taken in by diplomacy.

2

'They didn't like me,' Lisa said as she and Malone drove away in the Holden. When he had come out he had seen the finger-scrawled message in the dust on the boot: *Get stuffed, copper*. He hadn't said anything, but had helped Lisa into the car, bade a quick good night to his mother and father and driven away before some public-spirited citizen yelled a vocal postscript to the message. He had to educate Lisa gradually into what it was going to be like to be a copper's wife.

He drove down Erskineville Road, a childhood trail, threading his way through the cars pulling away from the corner pub at closing time. He hoped there were no mugs out tonight to thumb their noses at the breathalyser test; he had too much on his mind to get caught up with a drunken driver. He swerved to avoid a car pulling out sharply from the kerb and was thanked with a yell of abuse for his caution.

'Mum's a little bit, well, conservative.' Then he made a confession that was also an excuse: 'Actually, I've never known her to take to anyone first time up.'

Lisa put her hand on his knee. 'Darling, I know it's not going to be easy. But I'm marrying *you*, not your parents.'

'How d'you reckon your parents will go for me? Do they hate coppers, too?' Her parents lived in Melbourne and he had met them only once, when he had gone down to Melbourne on holiday a year ago and introduced himself to them. At that time they had not seen him as a possible fiancé for their daughter, and they had been politely friendly but that was all. Hans Pretorious was the Australian general manager for a big Dutch textiles company, and though he and Mrs Pretorious had been in Australia almost ten years they had given Malone the impression that eventually they would retire back to Holland. They had written him a polite note when he and Lisa had become engaged and told him how much they were looking forward to seeing him again when he and Lisa went down to Melbourne for Christmas.

'That worries me, you know,' he said. 'You marrying a cop. Do you know what you're letting yourself in for?'

'I know that isn't going to be easy, either. I've had a long time to think about it. I was thinking about marrying you long before you asked me. But *someone* has to marry policemen.' She smiled and leaned across to kiss him on the ear.

'That takes a load off my mind,' he said with gentle sarcasm. 'You're marrying me as a public duty.'

'That's right. So we can have lots of little policemen and keep up the supply.' She moved her hand farther up his leg, squeezing it.

'Don't do that, or you'll have me running us up a pole.' He cast a quick glance at her and smiled, and she smiled back. She wore a moderate mini-skirt that, though several inches longer than the fashionable minis, had raised Brigid Malone's eyebrows a corresponding distance. The knees, to Brigid, were what ankles had been to her mother: no decent girl exposed them. As for the thighs that one saw walking the streets of Sydney these days, she kept her eyes averted and prayed that Sodom and Gomorrah would not burn down before she got back home to Erskineville. Lisa's skirt had now crept up as she sat back in the car seat and Malone was seeing enough thigh to make him wish that Sodom and Gomorrah, Lisa's flat, was only at the end of the street instead of another ten minutes' drive.

He looked back at the road, drove for a while in silence, then said, 'Is that the first time you've been to an outside toilet?'

'Yes. Do you want me to say I liked it?'

'No. But while you were out there, somehow it seemed to sum up the difference, the distance, if you like, between us. I don't know what your home was like in Rotterdam, but

51

I'll bet it didn't have an outside toilet. Your home in South Yarra certainly doesn't. Do you think we'll make a go of it?'

She said nothing for a few moments and when she finally spoke she chose her words carefully. 'Darling, we're both intelligent, that's the main thing. I'll admit I didn't think I'd ever marry a policeman. I thought I might finish up marrying a diplomat—I know that was what Mother would have liked.' Even in the dim light from the dashboard she saw the expression on his face, as if he had flinched. 'Sorry. I shouldn't have said that. But as I said—we're marrying each other, not our parents. I'm in love with *you*, and it doesn't matter a damn to me whether you're a policeman or a diplomat or a—a garbage man. You're intelligent. And we both have something else—curiosity. We both want to *know*. About everything. I've had the advantage of an expensive education and I've travelled more than you have, and, well, there was that sort of life I lived in London.'

'That's what I mean. You're bound to miss all that. A Sunday barbecue at one of my mates' place—that's not much of a substitute for an embassy dinner.'

She looked at him coolly. 'I hadn't finished. I was going to say that I have an education, but you have it, too. In another way. You know more about people than I might ever know if I live to be a hundred. You aren't as dumb as you try to make out, darling.'

'I've never been this way before. But you give me an inferiority complex.'

She said half-angrily, 'Then why did you ask me to marry you?'

He grinned, at himself as well as at her. 'Maybe I'm a masochist.'

'You make any more silly remarks about your inferiority complex and I'll give you something for your masochism.' When she got angry the Dutch accent of her girlhood came back.

'I love you, you know that?'

'I'm glad to hear it.' Then she smiled and moved closer to him. He was tempted to take a hand from the wheel and put his arm about her; but there had been a time, when he had been on traffic duty, when he had arrested drivers for doing just that. 'There's just one thing, darling.'

'What's that?'

'I don't know that I like being back in Sydney. I find it, I don't know, *dull*.'

Oh, that's great, he thought. I'll have to see the Commissioner, see if he will give me a beat in London or Paris. Maybe he could get them to swap me with Maigret or Gideon of the Yard. 'I was afraid of that.'

'Does that make me sound—unpatriotic?'

'Why should it? You weren't born here. What makes Sydney so dull for you?' He was ready to defend the city, but first he had to learn what was her attack. Not so long ago, before his visit to London, he would not have even listened to any criticism of Sydney.

She was aware of his hurt civic pride and she hung back now with her estimate of what made the city unattractive to her. 'I'll probably change my mind in six months or so. Sydney itself isn't so bad. I like the climate and the harbour. What I miss is—dignity, I suppose you'd call it. But perhaps a city has to be old to have that. How many young *people* have it?'

'You have it,' he said.

She kissed him for that. 'What troubles me is the people. They are, I don't know, so—so insular, I suppose. They seem to think this is Babylon itself, as if no other place could compare with it.'

'Even the people you work for?' As soon as she had arrived back she had stepped straight into a job with a public relations firm and she was making almost as much money as he did and would soon be earning more. That was going to be another bone that would stick in his throat; and in his mother's. It wouldn't please Brigid Malone to have a daughter-in-law who made as much money as her son: that wasn't the way the world was supposed to be run. 'Not the people you work *with*. Your clients, I mean. You think they're insular?'

'Some of them are the worst,' Lisa said. 'I have a date on Wednesday with one of them. Ostensibly I'm supposed to be helping her promote the Blue and Red Ball. What she really

53

wants me to do is make sure she'll be the Queen Bee of Sydney Society. That's Society with a capital S. She wouldn't be interested in the general sort.'

'Aren't there any Queen Bees of London Society?' he said, defending a type of Sydney woman he had never met and whom he privately sneered at on the rare occasions when he read the social pages of the newspapers.

She saw she had made a mistake in opening up the discussion. She kissed him again. 'Let's forget her. Instead, I'll promote you into being Police Commissioner.'

'My mother would never be able to take that. It would be worse than being promoted as the Anti-Pope.'

CHAPTER FOUR

I

Thursday, November 28

WALTER HELIDON came out of State Parliament House and stood in the sun on the veranda. Across the street were the buildings that housed the city's medical specialists; every doorway stood in the midst of its own discreet aureole of brass plates. Next door to Parliament House was Sydney Hospital, a Victorian massif designed to depress approaching patients. Whoever had planned Macquarie Street had been a man with a wry sense of humour: standing politics and medicine side by side, he had invited the citizens to choose their own palliatives.

Helidon mopped his brow, cursing that he sweated so easily; it destroyed the image he so meticulously tried to create. It was difficult to be urbane when your face was shining, your shirt was sticking to your back and your glasses were misting up. He took off his glasses, the thick horn-rims that he thought made him look business-like as well as urbane, wiped them and put them back on. Then he took out his pipe, another part of his image, and began to fill it. He sometimes regretted the pipe. It suggested a resemblance to Harold Wilson, a politician he would hardly have chosen as a model; but he had adopted the pipe long before Mr Wilson's image had been so universally projected and it was too late to change now. Passers-by in the street looked across the court-yard at him and he saw the sudden stiffening of the head on one or two of them that showed he had been recognized. That warmed him more than the afternoon sun, but didn't make him sweat: politicians only sweated when they were *not* recognized. He wondered if he should nod to them, then decided against it; nods and smiles got you no votes unless they were for someone in your own electorate. Better to look business-like, perhaps a little preoccupied with the affairs of government.

An Opposition member came out and went down the steps, hurrying back to Party headquarters and further instructions on how to think. 'Another wasted afternoon, Wally. Why don't your mob learn how to get some business done? You're supposed to be the businessmen's party.'

'Just keeping you fellows in a job.' He wished they would give up calling him Wally: that didn't have much suggestion of dignity about it for a Cabinet Minister, even a junior one.

A long crocodile of students went past on the opposite side of the road, their banners demanding an end to the war in Vietnam. As they passed they gave a perfunctory chorus of boos to Parliament House, but the off-handedness of their manner was more of an insult than their abuse; their main target was the Commonwealth offices some blocks away and they dismissed the home of the State parliamentarians as if it were no more than a suburban town hall. Helidon's resentment of them was double-edged: he did not believe students were entitled to the voice they were assuming, but, if they were going to demand a voice, they should have more respect for their *State* representatives.

Then he was aware of a woman standing beside him and he turned to her, the smile automatically on his face before he recognized her. 'You wanted to see me—oh, Mrs *Plummer*.'

'I'm sorry to keep troubling you, Mr Helidon. I know you're busy and all that——' She was a pretty woman whom worry had made plain; she carried scars that no beautician could ever erase. 'It's about my son——'

'Mrs Plummer, you know I am only in parliament to do what I can for you and people like you. I am never too busy to listen to your problems. A politician has no problems of his own, only those of his constituents.' He was fluent in banality, his clichés honed by constant use. 'In your case I am here to see that justice is done——'

'That's it, but, Mr Helidon, justice hasn't been done. Oh, I know you've tried. But couldn't you try again? Bud, that's my son, he never hit that policeman at all——'

Helidon stifled the sigh that welled up in him. He had

56

already made inquiries and been assured by the police that the woman's son had been particularly violent in a recent demonstration. But you couldn't tell a mother, especially one from your own electorate, that her son was a liar and a beater-up of policemen. Perhaps the police had told a lie or two, too, but you never queried the police too closely about things like that. You never knew when you might need them on *your* side. 'All right, I'll look into it again, Mrs Plummer, indeed I will. It's not for want of effort on my part, I assure you——'

The woman went away, half-convinced, not from any reassurance on his part but from the stubbornness of her own hope. Helidon looked after her, feeling sorry for her; thank God he and Norma didn't have any delinquent kids to worry about. That would shake up the old urbanity a bit, to be a Cabinet Minister and have a son up on a charge of belting a policeman.

He walked down to the Members' car park, acknowledging the nods of the Assembly staff as he passed them. It had been a dull day in Assembly and he knew he had done nothing to relieve the boredom. He had the reputation of being one of the dullest speakers in the State parliament and today he had been below his usual form. But it didn't worry him; no politician was ever elected on his performance in parliament. He had once bought a book of Churchill's speeches, studied them and then tried a new approach on his own speeches. It had got him nothing but laughter and suggestions to 'Cut out the bull, Wally, and give us some facts.' Oratory and rhetoric were no longer fashionable in Australian politics; speeches were made for today's newspapers, not for history; a populace attuned to the brassy bibble-babble of disc jockeys was not likely to be patient with a speaker who tried to show the values of a silver tongue and golden phrases. But Helidon sometimes bored himself with what he had to say and how he said it, and today he had been desperately bored. He needed a pick-me-up.

He got into his car and switched on the air-conditioning. He had sold their Pontiac and bought the Mercedes 300SE last year when Norma, an arbiter in such matters, had told him that American cars were no longer right for the Right People in Sydney. He sat for a while, cooling himself and drying off the sweat he had raised in his short walk. Then he headed the car towards Double Bay. Rather than use an official car he always drove himself on Mondays and Thursdays: those were Helga's days. When he reached Double Bay he pulled into the car park behind the main section of shops; from here he could slip out of the car park into a side street and walk the short distance to Helga's flat. Before he got out of the car he substituted dark glasses for his usual pair, wondering just how much of a disguise they were.

He had not gone ten yards from his car when a woman's voice shrilled, 'I *thought* it was you, Walter! What on earth are you doing out this way? Mending fences or whatever you politicians call it?'

'Hullo, Louise.' Louise County was a thin sword of a woman, every side of her a cutting edge. He knew there had been a time, long before he had moved up into her circle, when she had been one of Sydney's leading amateur whores; as a girl of eighteen she was rumoured to have ruined an entire school Rugby team on the eve of a Great Public Schools final and gone out the next day and cheered on the other side, whom she had accommodated that night. But now she was respectable and had once played hostess to Billy Graham. Helidon did not know her well, but he had met her several times at Norma's charity functions. He knew that she and Norma hated each other with all the smiling, cheek-kissing hatred of rival society queens; and for once he was now on Norma's side. 'No, this is private business.'

He backed off and escaped into the side street. God, that had been close! How would it have been if he had bumped into her right outside the entrance to Helga's block of flats? Private business, indeed. If Louise had guessed why he was there, it would not have been private for long. He knew her type: reformed whores always made the worst gossips. As he climbed the stairs to Helga's flat he found himself sweating again. He waited on the landing outside till he had cooled down.

Helga was waiting for him as he let himself in with his key.

No matter what time he came on Mondays and Thursdays she was always there waiting for him, with never a complaint that he might be late. He assumed that patience must be one of the major differences between a mistress and a wife; Norma looked upon punctuality as one of her conjugal rights. Helga kissed him, wrapping him in her arms and the musky smell of the perfume that was his favourite. He sometimes wondered if she wore it on the other days of the week, but he had never asked her about it. His life with her never went outside Monday or Thursday.

They went to bed at once, the pick-me-up he needed, and later she made him his favourite gin-and-tonic and brought it to him in bed. She sat naked on the side of the bed and looked at him with fond amusement.

'My own Cabinet Minister. Did you ever think, darling, when you first started coming to see me that you would one day be where you are?' Yes, he had, but he was not going to tell her that. He knew that his ambitious outlook was now being held against him in certain places, that it was starting to tarnish his image.

'You do sweat, don't you?'

She had brought a towel with her and was lazily wiping his face and chest.

'I'll sweat if ever anyone finds out I'm coming here.' Without his glasses he looked older than his forty-six years. He had a bland, sleek-cheeked face, but there was a tiredness about the eyes that aged him. There was no grey in his sandy-coloured hair, but it was thinning along the front temples and he had to comb it carefully these days. He had once been a keen surfer and still had broad, powerful shoulders, but the rest of him was running to plumpness. He would think twice about sitting around naked as Helga did. He drew the sheet a little higher on his chest, making the pretence of using it as a coaster for his ice-cold glass. He sipped his drink and bent his head forward as she straightened his mussed-up hair with her fingers. 'Maybe we should adopt some of the Japanese customs, now we're trying to be friends with Asia. No one there would take any notice if a politician had a geisha girl.'

59

'I'm not your geisha, darling,' she said, still smiling at him. 'They are much too—what's the word?—servile?'

He smiled back at her. He always felt so at ease with this girl; she really knew how to make a man feel at home. But then home had never been like this: sex at five o'clock in the afternoon, gin-and-tonic brought to him in bed, Norma sitting naked on the side of the bed. At five every afternoon Norma was halfway between her charity bridge parties and her cocktail parties, changing from one expensive dress to another, watching her social diary as carefully as she watched her diet chart. He groaned inwardly: when he left here he was due to meet Norma at a cocktail party. He took his mind off her and went back to looking at Helga.

'And you're not servile?'

'No, *liebling*.' She got up, moved across to her dressing-table and took a chocolate from the box there. She bit into it, smiling suggestively at him as she did so. God, he thought, why can't Norma be like this?

'Walter darling, I'm broke.'

At once he was wary, a reflex action, the politician coming out of him even in bed. 'Broke? You mean you're a trifle short?'

'More than that.' She picked up the box of chocolates, came back and sat down on the side of the bed again. She chose another chocolate and bit into it, this time without any suggestiveness. 'I've decided to go into business, open a boutique. But I'll need capital.'

'How much?' Still wary, he looked at her over the top of his glass.

She pushed the expensive-looking box towards him, but he shook his head. She picked out another chocolate and said, 'About twenty thousand dollars.'

He shook his head; even Norma had never asked him for that much. 'Try someone else, Helga.' He nodded at the box of chocolates. 'Try the chap who buys those for you.'

She gave him a mildly reproachful look. 'You sound like a schoolboy. How do you know I don't buy them myself?'

'Every time I come here, there's a new box. For a girl who's always complaining about being broke——'

'I do not complain, darling.'

'No,' he admitted reluctantly. 'No, indeed you don't. Not like——' He buried the comparison in his glass.

'Not like your wife? Are you afraid that if you give me twenty thousand dollars, she will complain?'

'I'd make damned sure she didn't know.'

'But I might tell her, darling. About us.' She picked over the chocolates carefully till she found a soft centre. 'Of course I shouldn't do that if you gave me the money. I might even pay you interest, just so it would look legal and business-like.'

'How much?'

She shrugged. 'Half per cent?'

He laughed, the glass on his chest jumping and spilling some of his drink. 'You think my accountant would consider that businesslike? Forget it, Helga. I don't have twenty thousand dollars to hand out like that.'

'You do, darling. I've been watching the shares of all your companies. For instance, New Sydney Development has risen thirty per cent in the last three months. You own two hundred thousand preferential shares in it.'

'How do you know that?'

'I bought some shares, darling, not many, then asked for a copy of the original prospectus. It was all there in black and white.'

He looked at her admiringly, even though he was now beginning to feel something approaching dislike of her. 'And I used to think you were a girl who only knew about one thing.' He gestured at the bed. 'What sort of business were you in when you got those tattoos on your behind?'

She stood up, holding the box of chocolates carefully in front of her. She looked at him steadily, then she hit him in the face with the box, scattering chocolates all over the bed, spilling his drink and making him yelp with pain as the corner of the box split his eyebrow. Cursing her, he fell out of bed, blood pouring from his cut eyebrow, his body marked with dark splotches where he had rolled on the chocolates. He caught a glimpse of himself in the dressing-table mirror; he looked ridiculous and the image only added to his anger.

He swiped at her, but she moved quickly backwards and he stumbled past her and into the bathroom.

When he came back into the bedroom ten minutes later she was sitting in a chair by the window doing her nails. She wore the green silk dressing-gown he had given her for her birthday and her hair was pulled back with a matching green ribbon. She had stripped the bed and the bloodstained and chocolate-daubed sheets were nowhere to be seen. Looking at her and the room one might have doubted that any scene had taken place. He knew how house-proud she could be, the whore in her ruled by the *hausfrau*, but this today seemed just a bit too cold-blooded to be called house-pride.

But he wasn't going to let her sweep him under the bed like that. 'I think I've paid my last visit here. You can find someone else to fill in your Mondays and Thursdays.'

'As you wish, Walter.' She didn't look up at him, just went on filing her nails. 'But I still want the twenty thousand dollars.'

It was difficult to be righteously angry when pulling on your underpants. He teetered on one leg, waited till his loins were clad, then said, 'You know what you can do, Helga. With your experience you should find several interesting ways of doing it.'

She looked up at him then, her face puckered just slightly with contempt. 'You're still what you were at the beginning, aren't you? A nasty little schoolboy trying to be a big man. Everything you've been since has not made a bit of difference to you.'

A mistress flattered you; a wife and a whore told you the truth. He recognized the difference now: she would never be his mistress again, not if every day in the week for the rest of his life was blank of sex. He finished dressing, doing his best to ignore her. He had regained control of his temper and was regretting the cheap abuse he had flung at her. He hadn't shown much urbanity up till now; at least he should try for a suave exit. He combed his hair, put on his dark glasses and patted the strip of plaster he had fixed above his eyebrow. Then he turned to her.

'I apologize for what I said. But it doesn't alter the fact

that you and I are finished. Very much finished, indeed. Goodbye, Helga. You just made the mistake of being greedy. Hitler was the same.'

He went out of the flat, wondering if the last barb had been a worthwhile one; there had been no change of expression on her face nor had the rhythm of the file on her nails faltered. Maybe she was right: he was only capable of school-boy's abuse.

She waited till the door closed, not even bothering to get up and follow him out of the bedroom to the front of the flat. Then she put down her nail file, opened a drawer in the dressing-table and took out a small leather-covered diary. Its pages were thick with her heavy Germanic hand, but the entries were in English; even in her private moments she had drilled herself to put her past life behind her. Only occasionally did the German words creep in and they were more numerous in the later entries; there was a point in the diary where one could almost read the beginning of the decision to return to Germany. If everything went as she hoped she would be back home in Germany for Christmas: well, not *home*, but in Germany. Home, the farm near Hanover, had been farewelled forever. The last pages in the diary would be written in German.

She ran her finger down the list of names and phone numbers in the front of the book. She had never called Walter before, either at his office or at his home; but it was part of her thoroughness that she had both numbers in her diary. She chose the home number, picked up the phone, dialled and waited. Then: 'Mrs Helidon? We haven't met——'

2

Norma Helidon floated through the cocktail crowd like a very elegant and not unattractive porpoise, catching balls of greeting and throwing them back to the guests. There had been a time long ago when she could not have exchanged a *bon mot* with the milkman, when it had been agony for her to meet anyone outside her immediate family. But ten years ago,

63

when Wally, as he then was, had told her bluntly that she would have to do something about herself, when he had come home and said he was moving up from local government as a councillor into State politics and that she would have to pull her weight as his wife, she had begun the reconstruction task that today was recognized as Mrs Walter Helidon, society hostess and woman about town. It had not been easy at first, but time, practice and hard study had finally brought success and enjoyment. She had taken voice lessons, a slimming course and instruction in some of the more obvious aspects of politics. When Walter had been made Minister for Cultural Development she had bought a twelve-foot shelf of Great Books and now she was only four feet six inches from graduation. Her confidence had increased to the point of arrogance as she had looked around her and realized that practically all her competitors had had to go through the same process of manufacture and not all the results had been as good as her own. An egalitarian society did not breed natural hostesses; and once the hostesses developed themselves, they did their best to eliminate the egalitarian society. Norma just wished that some of the egalitarians were not so necessary to her charity causes.

She floated up to one of the worst of them. 'Mr Gibson, your lovely wife just told me you'll give us a *thrilling* cheque!' She had not been to an expensive school, but her quick ear had soon told her that the product of an expensive school could always be told by its extravagant adjectives. 'You don't know how awfully humbled I am by your generosity——'

'Don't bust your girdle,' said Grafter Gibson, rich and rude enough never to need extravagant adjectives; he had the sour face of a man who would have paid to have had the whole cocktail crowd dumped in the harbour. 'Your Wally could match my cheque any day. You oughta get *him* to humble you some time.'

He does that more than you know, Norma thought. But the smile had not slipped: she wore it permanently in public, like the double strand of pearls that were her trade mark. She put her hand up to the pearls now, the only nervous gesture she had. 'Charity should begin at home, but not with

64

Walter. He thinks the voters would suspect a politician who contributed to a good cause.'

'He's probably right,' said Gibson grudgingly. 'I see he's just arrived. Who donged him—some suspicious voter?'

Norma moved towards the door to greet her husband. She kissed his cheek with her teeth, her lips still open in the smile. 'What happened to your eyebrow? Did Miss Brand give you that?'

Before Helidon could reply she had drifted away into the crowd, the smile turned back at him like a dagger being withdrawn. Feeling slightly sick he headed for the table at the end of the room where the drinks were being served. Carrying the crutch of a gin-and-tonic he then sidled through the crush towards where Grafter Gibson stood in the big bay window that looked out on to the harbour.

'Not a bad place, this,' said Gibson. 'You a member here, Wally? That how Norma got it for her shindig?'

Helidon had joined the Yacht Club a year ago, after three years' waiting and three applications: he had found it much easier to get into parliament. It had cost him only a hundred and five dollars to join and the annual subscription was eighty dollars; it was not an expensive club, but it was as exclusive as if its dues were twenty times what they were. He was a member of twenty-seven other clubs, ranging from football clubs through national clubs to returned servicemen's clubs; but they had been political joinings and he frequented none of them unless he had to. This yacht club and his golf club were the only two that ever saw Walter Helidon as a participating member.

'Norma and I do quite a bit of entertaining, here, Les. You and Glenda should come for dinner with us one night.'

'You think they'd have me as a member? Or don't trawler blokes qualify for a yacht club?' He grinned fiendishly and Helidon managed a smile in return. He knew that Gibson could have owned the world's largest yacht, have won the Sydney to Hobart race three years in a row, and he would still never have been accepted as a member. 'Don't worry, Wally. I won't embarrass you by asking you to nominate me. You gotta be a bit careful, now you're in the Cabinet, eh?

65

Minister for Cultural Development. My word, that was a turn-up. I nearly bust a gut when I read about it. What d'you know about culture, Wally? You wouldn't know the difference between Van Gogh and Van Johnson.'

Helidon knew that Gibson, vulgar and uncultured as he was, had one of the finest art collections in Sydney. He was saved from an honest answer by the arrival of Glenda Gibson. 'What did you do to your eye, Mr Helidon?'

'Bumped it on my car door,' said Helidon, looking across the room at Norma. She was standing with Louise County, both of them looking as if they were suffering from smiler's cramp, the society queen's occupational disease; a photographer appeared and they grasped each other with loving claws. Then Norma looked across at him and without her lips changing, the smile hardened. Again he got the sick feeling and he took a hurried gulp at his drink.

'Doesn't your wife look wonderful? But then she always does.' Poor old Glenda, he thought. She might have been pretty once and if old Grafter had given her money to spend in those days she might have kept her looks. But the purse strings had been opened up too late and Glenda would be forever several laps behind in the race to retain her looks and keep up with fashion.

He guessed she was about sixty now, too old to recover the years that had been lost. 'Every photo I see of your wife in the newspapers, she looks as if she's just stepped out of a bandbox.'

'And she's in the papers every day,' said Gibson, smiling into his drink. 'More than you are, Wally.'

'Now don't be nasty, Les. I'm sure Mr Helidon doesn't envy his wife all the publicity she gets. It must help you, too, doesn't it, Mr Helidon?'

'Oh, she's a great help, indeed,' said Helidon, struggling for enthusiasm: across the room Norma had left Louise County and was moving about among the guests, occasionally looking across at him with an expression that said she was going to be no help to him when they got home.

'Men in public life would get nowhere without their wives, I always say.'

66

'Hitler managed without one. And Mrs Stalin didn't get her picture in the papers much.' Gibson spent his time taming his wife's wild generalizations, but he always did it with fond good humour. He had little, if any time, for other women, but he would have killed anyone who harmed Glenda. 'Wally would have made it, with or without his missus. Ambition is more help than publicity, eh, Wally?'

'You insulting old bastard,' said Helidon, losing his urbanity, and walked away, leaving Gibson chuckling and Glenda Gibson remonstrating with him.

'You shouldn't have done that, Les——'

'Don't waste any sympathy on him,' said Gibson. 'His wife's got more intelligence than he has and he knows it. He must be getting a bit worried, too—you notice how he kept looking across at her all the time? Trouble for him is, she's got as much ambition as he has. Don't ever get ambitious, hon.'

'As if I would,' Glenda said, patting his arm.

Helidon went out to his car. Angry and confused as he was, he had some trouble at first in finding it: the car park seemed to be full of blue Mercedes. Christ, he thought, the more affluent we become the more conformist we become. Per head of population Australia was now supposed to buy more Mercedes than any other country; that was a fact Helga had mentioned to him with some pride. Helga! With what he recognized as juvenile spite, he wished now he was looking for the old Pontiac.

He found his car, got into it, wound down the windows and sat staring out at the small bay of the harbour where the yachts rode like sleeping gulls. A cool breeze came across the water and he turned his face towards it, towards the south and Coogee where everything had started. Only seven miles and twenty-five years, but it seemed like another country and another century.

He had come back from the war, after six months in New Guinea, a twenty-one-year-old determined to be rich by the time he was forty. He had started out in a real estate agent's office and within three years had his own office. He had married a girl from Coogee, but she had left him after two years, tired of sharing her bed with a man worn out by long hours and ambition. He had divorced her after three years, then married Norma; he had loved her, but he had also married her because he needed a woman to look after him. And she had looked after him, at least up till he had forced her to go into public life with him. Then she had become too busy for sex, for taking trouble cooking his meals, for running the house as a haven where he could come home to rest. Sex had become a Sunday morning ritual, like washing the car or mowing the lawn was for other men; they went out for most of their meals and when they did eat at home it was only to have a snack; and their home was no longer a haven but an aviary for chattering charity committees. He had never had much sense of humour, but he had been in politics long enough to appreciate irony. If it had not been for his ambition and his insistent spurring of Norma's own ambition, there would have been no need of Helga.

He and Norma no longer had any financial worries. He did not need his Minister's salary of nineteen thousand dollars, but Australians were too cynical about their politicians ever to accept a man who might model himself on some of the wealthy Americans who had worked in Washington for a dollar a year. He would be classed as either a fool or a crook. And he could not risk the latter epithet. Half-buried seven years back in his political past was the one piece of skulduggery he had ever indulged in. As a real estate man he had bought some land several years after the war, but had been thwarted when a State Commission had zoned the area as green belt. But when he had got into parliament, become tuned to the atmosphere there, he had seen his opportunity. He had sold the land to Norma's brother, a wheeler-dealer like himself whom he could trust. He had bided his time, then after two years had quietly worked to have the area re-zoned. He had been successful, his brother-in-law had sold the land for a three thousand per cent profit, had turned over the proceeds to Helidon, taken his commission and conveniently died six months later. There had been a few inquiries, even the police had been brought in, but they could prove nothing. On the face of it Helidon was clean and since then the matter had been forgotten. The profit from the deal had been the foundation of Helidon's current fortune. It was part of the irony of his whole life that with the current boom of the past three years, when money could be so easily made by anyone who could add two cents together, there might not have been need of that skulduggery of seven years ago.

Helga had come into his life two years ago. Again there had been the irony: she had been a mannequin at a charity function arranged by Norma. He was not unhandsome, he was well-groomed and, even if it was still an effort, he was urbane; it had not been difficult, once he understood Helga's arrangements, to get the key to her flat. She had cost him fifty dollars a week, an expense that his accountant accepted as a legitimate entertainment of constituents. The arrangement had been ideal, though he had known in the back of his mind that eventually it would bring its own complications and it would have to end. He had not expected it to end this way.

Guests began to drift out from the party, got into their cars and drove away. Scraps of conversation floated across to him, the metal filings of cocktail gossip:

'Did you see that interior decorator and the antique he had with him? She must be old enough to be his mother——'

'I thought Norma Helidon looked marvellous, didn't you? That hand-made face of hers never shows a crack.'

'I loved that little black Givenchy Louise County was wearing. It went so well with her dandruff accessories——'

'All right, you women! This was supposed to be a charity show. How about showing a bit of charity?'

'Oh, shut up! I heard you and Harry talking about that girl in the see-through blouse. What's the difference between a little bit of gossip and sex talk?'

'If you don't know by now, I dunno why you married me. Come on, get in.'

'Aren't you going to open the door for me?'

'Christ, what's the matter, you crippled or something all of a sudden?'

'Men!'

Despite his depression, Helidon smiled. Other married

69

couples had their problems and their frictions. He saw the Gibsons come out and walk across to their Rolls-Royce; there was one couple who did not seem to have any problems. He felt suddenly resentful of Grafter Gibson, the unscrupulous old bastard whom everyone hated but whom one woman loved with all the devotion that better men yearned for. Married bliss never made any sense; it happened to the most unlikely partners. He and Norma had once had it, but it was gone now.

At last Norma came out of the clubhouse, looked around, then came across and got into the car. A government car had brought her to the function and he knew how much she liked that: it gave her a small cachet above her rivals. 'I've been looking all over for you. I thought you might have gone back to Double Bay for another dressing on your eye.'

He grunted wearily. 'Sarcasm doesn't become you. How did you find out about her? Did she phone you?'

She was still wearing her smile, like jewellery she had forgotten to remove. 'She was lucky to catch me. I had to go back to answer the phone. It could have been something important.'

'Jesus!' He rarely swore, but her attitude had for the moment left him without any adequate words. He started up the car and they drove out of the car park and up towards the main road that led towards home. They rode a mile or more in silence, till at last he said, 'All right. What are you going to do about her?'

'It's not what *I'm* going to do. It's what *you're* going to do.' She had taken off her smile and now in the dim light from the passing street-lights she looked old, haggard and unhappy. He felt a stirring of the old love for her, a regret that he had hurt her. But they had grown apart: he, who was so voluble with his constituents, could not now talk to his own wife. She looked at him when he didn't answer and said, 'You're going to tell her to go to hell.'

'I've already told her that.' He brought the car to a halt under the bloodshot eye of a traffic light. 'When she asked me for some money this afternoon.'

'How much?'

'Twenty thousand dollars.'

She uttered a sound that was halfway between a gasp and a laugh, a whinny of disbelief. Then she leaned her head against the window of the car and said, 'I could kill her.'

The light turned green and he drove on. 'Don't say things like that.'

'I could!' she said fiercely through her teeth. 'If she breaks us up, I could kill her! I'd never let you go, Wally—never!'

It was years since she had called him Wally; not since the early happy years. He turned off Pacific Highway and swung down the long tree-lined street where they lived. They had lived for years south of the harbour because that was where his first electorate had been; three years ago he had been offered this much safer seat on the North Shore and both of them had leapt at the offer: he because he knew it guaranteed him a seat in the Assembly for as long as he wanted, she because at last it meant they would have a good address. It had been a cunning ploy on her part and he had admired her for it. Everyone these days was moving into the Eastern suburbs, but they were becoming much too fashionable: they were plagued with social climbers. Norma had chosen Pymble, one of the older, exclusive addresses, and some of the more bitchy social columnists, ready to score a point off some of her rivals, had remarked upon her taste and good sense. They had bought an old colonial style house, invited Sydney's most expensive interior decorator to swindle them, then moved in with that pleasurable pain that accompanies the realization that there is nothing more to be desired. Helidon drove down the street towards the house, suddenly looking forward to it as a haven again. Once there he knew that, though it might take time, he would be able to explain to Norma the why and wherefore of Helga.

He swung into the drive and the lights of the car lit up the other car parked before the front door. Even before he had braked sharply to a halt he had recognized Helga's Datsun.

'Your maid let me in. I said it was business. Which it is, of course.'

'Why did you come here?' Norma demanded.

'I thought I should come and see you both,' said Helga. 'I thought it would save time.'

'How's that?' said Helidon, unable at this moment to get any grasp at all on the situation.

'It would save you running back and forth to Mrs Helidon for instructions.' She looked at Norma. 'I'm sure you will make the decisions, anyway.'

They were in the Helidon living-room, surrounded by all the expensive comforts of home. There were bars on all the windows, each outside door had two locks and there was a burglar alarm system. The decorator, who had done six months for importuning sailors, had given the Helidons the benefit of his experience in gaol without telling them where he had acquired his knowledge. 'You *just* don't know what tricks these awful professional housebreakers get up to! Security, my dears—you can't have *enough* security. Especially with all the lovely treasures I'm going to give you——' But he had neglected to build in any security against blackmailers. Helga sat there in the red velvet empress chair that was Norma's pride as composed and secure as if she were a buyer come to make them an offer for their home that she knew they could not refuse. She was dressed in a dark linen suit, carried white gloves and wore a thin strand of pearls. She looked coolly elegant, as only some women can, and Norma, suddenly feeling over-dressed in her cocktail dress, choked by her double strand of pearls, hated her even more.

'We could turn you over to the police,' Norma said wildly.

Helga smiled and Helidon looked pained. 'Darl——' He hadn't called her that for several years: short for *darling*, there had been a time when he had called her nothing else. But somehow or other it had slipped out of his vocabulary over the past couple of years. Since he had met Helga, he realized with a sour taste in his mouth. 'Darl, that's the last thing we could do.'

Norma, recovering, nodded dumbly. She had been standing up ever since they had entered the house, but now she sat down opposite Helga, as if acknowledging at last that they were not going to be rid of her easily. She sat with her knees together, her hands folded primly on her lap, the way the nuns, years ago, had told her a lady should sit. 'Miss Brand, what made you come to me so soon? I gather you only asked my husband for the money this afternoon.'

Helga sat back at ease, crossed one beautiful leg over the other. She's lovely, Helidon thought, but why does she have to be such a bitch? And felt an ache in the pit of his stomach that was a sense of loss and not of fear. 'I thought about it, Mrs Helidon. Walter'—she used his name with a slightly proprietary note, a reminder to Norma that they had shared him—'would not have paid the money without a great deal of trouble on my part. It might have taken me weeks to get it out of him.'

'I told you,' said Helidon, 'you won't get a red cent.'

'I think I shall, Walter. That's why I came to see Mrs Helidon. You see, she is just as afraid of bad publicity as you are. I've followed your career, Mrs Helidon. If everything goes right for you, you should soon be the Number One hostess in Sydney. I think the *Sunday Telegraph* referred to you the other day as the queen-elect.'

Norma flushed, a habit she thought she had conquered. 'Go on.'

'It would not be difficult for me to make known my relationship with Walter. There are several political scandal sheets that are always ready to print stuff like that.'

'You'd get no money out of *them*,' said Helidon.

'I'm not looking for money from them,' Helga smiled. 'I'm looking to you for it.'

'You mean you'd give them a story like that just out of spite?' said Norma.

'Of course not. I'm not spiteful, Mrs Helidon. I'm just— *practical*? Or what's that new word they use about politicians —*pragmatic*? I know you'll give me the money before you'd let me go to those people.' She stood up, smoothing down her skirt. Norma looked at her with grudging admiration: the

skirt was just the right length, not too short but just short
enough to be fashionable: no one would ever take her for the
whore she was. 'Think about it. When Walter comes to see
me on Monday, he can bring the cheque. Made out to Helga
Brand Proprietary Limited.'

'Proprietary Limited?' Helidon echoed.

'I formed a private company a little while ago. It will be
much more discreet. It will just look like a business investment
for you.' She looked at Norma and smiled. 'You see, I'm not
really spiteful. I don't want to ruin Walter's career any more
than you do.' The smile widened a little. 'Nor do I want to
ruin yours. It must mean an awful lot to you, the money you
have spent on it. Good night. Monday as usual, Walter.
Well——' The smile was even wider, but even then was not
ugly. 'Well, not as usual. Just business.'

CHAPTER FIVE

I

Tuesday, December 10

MALONE AND CLEMENTS had to wait two days for the answer to their query to Interpol on the dead girl's fingerprints. In the meantime they worked with the only other clue they had.

'It's the wrong half of the tab,' said the manager of the dry-cleaning chain. 'If it was the other half it'd give us the number of the shop where the dressing-gown was cleaned. This'll mean going through every order book in every shop we have.'

'Then that's what we'll have to do,' said Malone. 'Constable Clements will start in right away.'

'Why me?' said Clements.

'Because I'm the senior bloke and because you're better at figures than I am. Just imagine you're reading the form sheets and looking for another winner.'

'What are you grinning at?' Clements said to the manager.

'Listening to one cop telling another one what to do,' said the manager. He was a cheerful stout man who looked as if he might be put through his own dry-cleaning process every morning; his shirt was immaculate, his trousers had a knife-edge crease, even his dark hair looked as if it had been cleaned and pressed.

'Do you want to start here? This is our head office. We have another twenty-seven branches.'

Clements looked at Malone, his big dark eyes as mournful as those of a dog that had just been told it was going to be locked up in the pound. Malone took pity on him. 'Okay, you take half, I'll take half.' He took the dressing-gown out of its brown paper bag again and showed it to the manager. 'When do you reckon that was last cleaned?'

The manager twisted his mouth in what Malone took to be

a facial shrug. 'I'd only be guessing. Say within the last three months.'

'Could we have all the order books from all your shops for the last three months? We'll go around and collect 'em this morning.'

'That's gunna be a bit of a bind, isn't it?' said the manager. 'Going through all that paper?'

'Most police work is a bit of a bind. It's only in movies that cops have all the fun.' As they were going out of the shop he stopped and sniffed. 'Doesn't that dry, clean smell ever get you down?'

The manager nodded, smiling broadly. 'Does it ever! Weekends, I don't even shave or shower. Sat'day to Monday, I'm the dirtiest coot in Sydney. Good luck with your paper chase. You want any dry-cleaning done, bring it here. I'll do it free.'

'Why?' asked Malone.

'I like a clean cop,' said the manager and creased his shirt as he bent over laughing.

'I love funny bastards,' said Clements as they got into their car. He looked down at the pile of order books the manager had given them from the head office. 'Twenty-seven more. Maybe we should've brought a trailer.'

It took them three hours to collect all the order books from shop assistants who ranged from the eagerly co-operative to the aggressively antagonistic. 'I'm too busy,' said the woman with henna'd hair, the pink-framed glasses and the mouth so heavy with lipstick she had difficulty in opening it. 'Come back t'morra and I'll see if I got 'em ready by then.'

'I'd like them now,' said Malone patiently. He stood aside as two women came in with armfuls of clothes and dumped them on the counter. He waited five minutes till they had gone, then he said, 'The order books, please.'

'I told you, come back t'morra——'

'If you don't give me those books,' said Malone, 'I'll be back in half an hour with a warrant. I'll close this shop up and you can explain *that* to your boss. Now get 'em and stop mucking about!'

The woman, muttering like a distant storm, went out to the rear of the shop, came back with some books and dumped

76

them in front of Malone. He thanked her sarcastically, picked them up and went out to the car. 'Some days I think there might be something to be said for a Police State. I'd have the time of my bloody life with some of these voters.'

'The day before I retire,' said Clements, weary, irritable and sweaty from sitting in the hot car, 'I'm gunna book every bugger who even *looks* at me.'

They spent the rest of that day going through the books. They knocked off when their eyes began to cross from deciphering the variety of scrawls on the pink slips. 'I've been seeing things here that I thought were extinct,' said Clements. 'Camisoles, antimacassars—there's something here that looks like a chastity belt. Who'd be wearing one of those these days?'

'The Vice boys picked up a feller in drag the other night who was wearing one. He said he didn't want to go all the way.' Malone threw down a book, rubbed his eyes. 'Everything but a green silk dressing-gown. You want to come back and finish these off tonight?'

'No,' said Clements. 'I'm going to the dogs tonight, see if I can lose some of the money I've been winning on the horses.'

2

Wednesday, December 11

Clements came into the detectives' room next morning shaking his head. 'I can't *lose*. I backed a mong last night that had only three legs and was three months pregnant and it finished up beating the bunny home. Twenty to one, it paid. At this rate I'm gunna have to retire pretty soon. Come up with anything yet?'

Malone held up a book. 'Double Bay. A green silk dressing-gown turned in by someone named Brand.'

Then Smiler Sparks, lugubrious as a camel, came in and dropped a sheet of paper on Malone's desk. 'Telex from Melbourne. Something to do with Interpol.'

Malone read the sheet, then looked across at the expectant

Clements. 'No doubt about these Germans, they're efficient. They've given us everything here except her brassiere size.'

'Who was she?'

'Her name was Helga Schmidt. Or anyway that's the one she was booked under—not very original. She came from Hamburg. She was a pro there. That probably explains the tattoos on her bum—the Germans like their sex a bit kinky. They first booked her in 1958 when she was supposed to have been sixteen. They haven't had a record of her for the last six years.' He laid the sheet beside the dry-cleaning book. 'She's our girl, all right.'

They drove out to Double Bay through another steaming morning. The bottom of the sky was smudged with haze; in the dazzling brilliance high overhead a plane melted and disappeared. It was not a day for good tempers. Malone walked into the dry-cleaner's and the henna'd-haired woman glared at him through her pink-framed glasses. 'I hope you haven't lost any of those order books——'

Malone dumped the books, neatly tied with string, on the counter. Then he produced the green silk dressing-gown. 'Recognize that?'

The woman inspected it, her face tightly concentrated behind the thin screw of her long nose. 'I've seen it—yes! A foreign girl—German, I think——'

'That's the one,' said Malone. 'Where does she live? It's not on the order slip for this.'

'We only take the address when someone first comes in.' The woman was a little more amenable; obviously something was wrong and she was *dying* to know what it was. She reached under the counter for a master order book. 'What's the matter, might I inquire?'

'She's dead,' said Malone.

Even the weight of lipstick couldn't keep her mouth closed this time. 'Oh, migod, isn't it terrible! Where did it happen? How?'

'The address, please,' said Malone, nodding at the book lying on the counter and now ignored by the woman. When he had first become a detective he had been impatient and frustrated by the scrub of obstructive people you had to beat

78

your way through to get to a certain point. But now he accepted that detection work was much like old time exploration: days and days of hard slogging till you reached a high ridge and looked out and saw something in the distance that kept you going. He had reached a ridge now, seen a name and an address. But it was really only the beginning of the journey and there would probably be more thorny obstructions like this woman before he reached the end of it.

He went out to the street and got back into the car. 'The address checks with one of those in the phone book,' he told Clements. There had been three H. Brands in the phone book, all of them with addresses within two miles of Double Bay. The greater majority of German-speaking migrants to Sydney tended to congregate in the area along the southern shores of the harbour: the map of Europe, with its national boundaries, was being re-drawn ten thousand miles from home. 'Now all I'd like is for the feller who did her in to be sitting there waiting for us. I don't want this bloody thing to drag on over Christmas.'

They drove round to the address they had been given and parked in a *No Standing* section of the kerb. Clements had to squeeze the Falcon in between two other cars and he got out cursing drivers who ignored police signs. 'I oughta give the bastards a ticket.'

They went up into the flats and met more scrub that had to be beaten through. They rang the buzzer of Helga Brand's flat, not expecting any answer and getting none. Then they rang the buzzer of the flat next door. The woman, garrulous as a disc jockey, took five minutes to tell them where they could find the managing agents. Clements went away to get the key and Malone went into the woman's flat to have a cup of tea.

'I've never seen her, you know. We moved in a week ago, but I've never seen her, definitely. Milk? Matter of fact, haven't seen anyone here except for the first day we come. There was two fellers here—matter of fact I thought one of 'em was the hubby, you know what I mean? He had a key. But you said her name was *Miss* Brand, isn't she? Down on her letterbox there's just Brand, no Mrs or Miss. Is she all right? I

79

mean, there's nothing wrong with her or anything, is there? Sugar?'

Malone was thinking: the gabby ones are often a help. The ones with the sharpest tongues are the ones with the sharpest eyes: Malone's Law of Physiology. 'You saw *two* men come here?'

'Oh, definitely. Separately, not together. She wasn't a——?' The woman gestured. 'I mean, I wouldn't wanna think the worst of anyone I hadn't met——'

'No,' said Malone, giving Helga Brand the benefit of the doubt. 'She wasn't in business, Mrs Woolton.'

'*Wasn't?* You mean, she isn't—I mean she isn't dead or something, is she?' Malone nodded, and the woman whacked her head hard enough to knock it back on her shoulders. 'Oh, migod, that's a shock! Definitely. We come here for peace and quiet, we useta live up in Darlinghurst, and only a week and there's a death right next door! She isn't dead in *there*, is she?' She jerked her head at the wall that divided the two flats.

'No, she's not there. Those two men—would you recognize either of them if you saw them again?'

'Oh, definitely. One was a tall feller, not bad-looking, with grey hair. But not *old*, if you know what I mean. Just gone grey early, I'd say. Dunno why we all don't, the things we have to put up with these days. Oh, he was very well spoken, too. Real nice voice.'

'What about the other chap?'

'Well, I didn't speak to him. Fact is, I'm not even sure he come to see her. But there's only her flat and ours on this floor and he certainly didn't come to see me, definitely. He looked sorta familiar, you know what I mean? Wore horn-rimmed glasses, very well dressed, sorta—*smooth*, you know what I mean? He could've been an estate agent or one of them fancy women's doctors, you know what I mean? Very smooth, definitely.'

Then Clements came back with a young man from the agent's; he didn't look *smooth*, Malone thought, but perhaps he hadn't been in the game long enough. Mrs Woolton wanted to follow them into Helga Brand's flat, but Malone assured her she wouldn't be needed for the moment and gently closed the door in her face. He took one quick look at the chaotic condition of the living-room, then opened the front door again and nodded to the young man.

'Thanks. We'll call you from here when we're leaving.'

'But they said I had to stay with you——'

Still protesting, he was gently pushed out of the flat and the door was closed behind him, too. Then Malone went into the living-room where Clements was already sniffing about like a bloodhound. I wish I could get the dog image of him out of my mind, Malone thought. One of these days I'm going to whistle him instead of calling him.

Malone put in a call for a police photographer and a fingerprint man, being careful to hold the phone only by its mouthpiece where he was unlikely to disturb any fingerprints left by a previous user of the phone. Then he and Clements set about searching the flat.

It was Clements who found the torn-up cheque in the waste basket and Malone who discovered the manilla folder under the heavy lounge chair. They found a lot else that might or might not be clues and they spread it all out on a sheet of newspaper on the small dining table.

'Five chocolate boxes—why do women save chocolate boxes? My mum does and so does my sister.' Clements shook his head at the inexplicable whims of women. 'These coupla chewed matches—I don't reckon they'd be hers. This blood-stained sheet—I found that in the laundry basket. There are some prints on those pieces of broken glass. And this key might have some on it.'

'We're doing all right so far,' said Malone. 'Keep the chocolate boxes. That's an expensive brand of chocolates and women don't buy themselves expensive chocolates. They always depend on men for that.'

'Not me,' said Clements. 'A box of Black Magic is as far as I go, or Cadbury's Milk Tray. What about these pearls and the broken bits? You reckon they belonged to her? She wasn't wearing any stuff when we found her, so maybe that could be the motive—robbery.'

Malone shook his head. 'I've looked in the bedroom. There's

81

a stack of stuff there that wasn't touched. Not much expensive stuff, but there's a good watch and another strand of pearls. It wasn't robbery. Why would he go to all the bother of carting her from here down to the Opera House?' He picked up the pieces of the cheque, laid them together till the pieces formed a ragged whole. Then he raised an eyebrow as he saw the name printed above the flourishing signature. 'This feller, for instance, wouldn't need to lift a few pieces of jewellery. Walter S. Helidon. The woman next door said she saw a man come down from this floor who looked vaguely familiar to her. That's about all Cabinet Ministers are to anyone—vaguely familiar.'

'If he's involved in this,' said Clements, 'I think I'll ask to go back on the beat. It's likely to get too complicated for me.'

Malone opened the manilla folder. The cuttings were all marked with the name and date of the newspaper or magazine from which they had been cut: none of them he noticed was more than six months old. The majority of the cuttings featured photos of Mr and Mrs Walter Helidon, together or alone; there were half a dozen of Mrs Leslie Gibson, one of Mr and Mrs Gibson together, and a scowling one of Mr Gibson alone; and a single photo of Mr and Mrs John Savanna, Mr Savanna's grey hair high-lighted by the photographer's flash bulb. Helga Brand's portrait gallery was limited but interesting.

Clements looked over Malone's shoulder, then made a clicking noise with his tongue. 'I don't like the looks of this, Scobie.' He put a finger on the torn cheque, then nodded at the cuttings. 'Blackmail?'

'It would be a good bet.' Malone went across and sat down in the heavy lounge chair. There was a smell of perfume to the chair, as if it had been the favourite chair of one woman for a long time. He got up, feeling he had been sitting in the lap of Helga Brand, and moved to another chair. He felt uneasy and he wished there were some way he and Clements could walk out of this flat and leave the case to someone else. He had already been engaged in one case involving politicians and he had sworn to do his best to avoid another. Years of experience had taught him that the criminal mind, though cunning, was fairly predictable; but the political mind, equally cunning, was something that, as with most voters, baffled him. In Australian politics it could be vicious; the stab in the back was an occupational hazard. He had seen politicians with independent minds who had bucked their party and finished up with independent heads, carried under their arms; he hated to think what might happen to a policeman with an independent mind, especially one who would link a Cabinet Minister with the murder of a call girl. It would not help if Helidon had a long memory: he might remember the constable named Malone from the Fraud Squad who had been to question him seven or eight years ago on some land dealings.

Malone looked up at Clements. 'What do you reckon would be a nice easy beat to be posted to?'

'I've got mine picked out,' said Clements. 'Place called Wilson's Tank, out the back of Tibooburra. It's got a population of two.'

'That'll do us,' said Malone. 'We'll double the population in one go.'

'Go ahead with it as if it were a routine case,' said Inspector Fulmer. 'Politicians, even Ministers, are liable to the law just like the rest of us.'

'I just thought I'd ask,' said Malone.

'You did the right thing,' said Fulmer, and Malone could almost feel himself being patted on the head. 'But I'll take the responsibility. You and Russ Clements do the donkey-work and I'll see you get the credit if you wrap up the case.'

'I'm not worried about the credit. I was thinking about the boot in the behind if Helidon really had nothing to do with this and decided to get nasty.' After the police photographer and the fingerprint man had arrived and done their job, Malone and Clements had put a seal on the front door of Helga Brand's flat and come back to Y Division headquarters.

Already feeling anxious and wanting someone else to make decisions for him, Malone had gone in to see Fulmer. 'He may not have had anything to do with the girl, except on business. The cheque was made out to Helga Brand Proprietary Limited. Call girls usually don't register themselves as companies. It would be a bit difficult listing their usable assets.'

'All right, Scobie. Enough of that.' Fulmer sat back, putting his hands together in the position that had earned him the nickname of Steeple-Fingers or The Bishop. He was a very tall, lean man who might have been handsome if he had allowed his expression to relax. He had thick black hair, deep-set eyes and thick black eyebrows that seemed to clamp the one severe expression on his face as a vice might. He had come into the police force thirty years before with rigid ideas about right and wrong and had never changed them; he had never been known to swear or tell or listen to a dirty story; and it was on his record that after six months on the Vice Squad he had asked to be transferred to something less sordid. Still, as Malone knew, he was a good detective and he had been promoted on his merits. But he would never make Commissioner and that was the one bitter disappointment of his life. He had learned too late that black and white were not the only rungs in the ladder that took you to the top. There were now too many men between him and the Commissionership and he would be too close to retirement before he reached the rank from which the chief executive was chosen.

'Report to me each day on how you're progressing. Don't wait till things get too sticky.' He allowed himself a moment of surmise, something he rarely did: 'It would be interesting to see the reaction in high places if you had to arrest a Minister for murder.'

Malone said nothing. Only the Police Commissioner and two senior Superintendents knew why he had been sent to London two years ago; politics had been behind that case and when the expected outcome had not eventuated, politics had seen that everything was conveniently buried. Malone knew that it was only the justness of the Commissioner that had prevented himself from being buried somewhere out in the bush, maybe even at Wilson's Tank. Though right now that looked a desirable posting.

'But be discreet,' Fulmer went on, every inch the bishop; Malone waited to be given absolution. 'No comment to the Press at all. It might be an idea not to let on to our public relations boys that you know anything. That will save them having to cover up if the reporters worry them.'

'Will you tell the Commissioner?'

'Naturally. I'll see the Superintendent and he and I will go and see the Commissioner together.' He demolished the steeple of his fingers. 'You have nothing to worry about, Scobie. Just approach it as a routine case.'

'But discreetly?' said Malone dryly.

'Naturally,' said Fulmer, who had a tin ear for nuances.

Malone left Fulmer's office, collected Clements and drove out to Pymble where Walter Helidon lived. It was a suburb he rarely visited, either officially or socially: it was off his beat on both accounts. It was a suburb as solid and respectable as a law court; judges and lawyers were liberally sprinkled among its population; at Christmas the garbage collectors were said to go their rounds chanting 'Fiat Justitia' instead of the usual season's greetings. The Helidon house looked a little more palatial than the others in its street, but it was still eminently respectable.

'I have a cousin lives up here on the North Shore,' said Clements as they got out of the car. The North Shore was a region that had no definition, only a cachet; it had nothing to do with any shore and, by rough estimate and depending on where one lived, began some five or six miles from the shores of the harbour. 'He always makes it sound as if he comes from another country.'

'Well, let's hope we don't have to extradite Helidon.'

Two cars stood parked in the red gravel driveway, a pale blue Mercedes and a small white Renault. Malone with a jolt suddenly recognized the smaller car, but it was too late to draw back now.

'Don't recognize anyone,' he said cryptically, and Clements looked at him blankly. They went up on to the wide veranda surrounding the house and rang the bell. A maid opened the door, a young pretty girl with an Italian accent and a look of instant fright at seeing two burly men standing on the doorstep.

'It's all right, love,' said Malone. 'We're harmless. We'd like to see Mr Helidon.'

'Mr Helidon, he not at home——'

'Who is it, Rosa?' Malone recognized Norma Helidon as soon as she came through into the large entrance hall behind the maid. The pictures in the cuttings, he thought, did her more than justice; in real life she looked strained and older, a good ten years older. But then maybe she had aged suddenly, since the photos were taken. She might even have aged in the last week.

Malone introduced himself and Clements. 'Just a routine inquiry, Mrs Helidon. We'd like to wait for your husband.'

Norma Helidon hesitated, then managed her hostess's smile and waved them into the hall. Only then did Malone notice Lisa standing in the living-room two steps down below the level of the hall.

'Hullo, Mrs Pretorious——'

'*Miss* Pretorious,' said Lisa. 'I'm not married—*yet.*'

'You've met?' said Norma Helidon.

'Miss Pretorious came to us once for some information. Still in public relations?' He looked at Lisa, wondering if he was doing a good job of appearing only casually interested in her. Behind him he could guess at the expressions chasing each other across Clements's face: the big fellow would never put Olivier, or even Lassie, out of a job.

Lisa nodded, her own face as cool and blank as that of a girl who did not think much of policemen. '*Constable*—Moloney, isn't it? We met some time ago,' she told Norma Helidon. 'He is the only policeman I've ever met with an inferiority complex. Remember that, Mrs Helidon, and you'll be safe. I'll call you tomorrow about those press releases.' She nodded coolly to Malone and Clements and went out the front door. The maid closed it behind her, then disappeared towards the back of the house, leaving Malone and Clements alone with Norma Helidon.

She knows why we are here, Malone thought. For a career

86

hostess she was much too ill at ease. But the reason for their visit had to be kept under wraps until Helidon himself came home; Malone was cautious enough to know that this was one case where protocol had to be observed. Norma Helidon waved them to seats and all three of them sat down, the policemen as stiffly and uncomfortably as their hostess.

'My husband has probably been delayed. Parliament rises tomorrow for the Christmas recess, you know.'

The three of them sat for an hour, tossing the conversational ball that bounced awkwardly every time it was missed, and it seemed to be missed on every second throw. They talked about the weather, gardens, the dullness of both police work and politics, and even about the Blue and Red Ball.

'I don't suppose you go to that sort of function much, Sergeant. Do the police have balls?'

Malone kept a straight face, while Clements suddenly found something of intense interest in the garden outside. Then mercifully there was the sound of a key in the lock of the front door. Walter Helidon came in, pulling up sharply when he saw the two strangers sitting in the living-room with his wife. All three rose as he came down the steps into the living-room and Norma Helidon went to her husband and took his arm, almost seeming to lean on him.

'We've come about a certain Miss Helga Brand,' said Malone after he had introduced himself and Clements. 'Did you know her, Mr Helidon?'

Helidon, in the few steps it had taken to come down from the hall into the room, had collected himself. Malone recognized the control: Helidon had been too long a politician to be caught by the question fired from the hip. He looked at Malone closely. 'Haven't we met before?'

'Yes,' said Malone reluctantly; he did not want the issue complicated *this* early. 'Several years ago. It was on something different to this.'

Helidon's face stiffened and beside him his wife blinked, as if she had just been reminded of a long-forgotten memory, one that had been deliberately locked away. Helidon said, 'About this girl. Yes, I knew her, but only in a business way. Has there been some trouble?'

'She is dead,' said Malone, and watched Mrs Helidon instead of Helidon: she went pale behind her expensive make-up, her hand dug into her husband's arm. 'You might have read about her. She was the girl found down at the Opera House.'

'Of course I read about it. Anything the newspapers have to say about the Opera House lands on my desk.' He gently freed his arm from his wife's grip, took off his glasses and polished them. Again Malone recognized the control: any small action or gesture to distract the attention while the mind got into the right gear. But the smooth-cheeked face gave nothing away; the eyes were as steady as those of a police marksman. He put the glasses back on and said, 'But why come to me?'

'We found a torn-up cheque of yours in her waste basket, Mr Helidon. Made out to Helga Brand Proprietary Limited.'

'That was part of a business deal.' Helidon moved across to a small table beside a big leather chair and took a pipe from a rackful of pipes; he methodically and unhurriedly began to fill it from a tobacco bowl beside the rack. 'She had come to me for some financial backing on a boutique she wanted to start.'

'Who recommended her to you, sir?'

'I did,' said Mrs Helidon. 'She had acted as a model for me at a charity function and had spoken to me casually about it. The boutique, I mean.' She, too, was in control of herself now. She had retreated to a red velvet chair, sat stiffly there like a woman on a throne. Even society queens go in for the regal touch, Malone thought. Then he chided himself: Come off it, Malone. Don't start acting like your Old Man, dragging the old class bit into this. Cops are supposed to be apolitical and asocial. But he could feel a resentment building up in him against the Helidons that so far lacked any real definition or cause.

'Did you know her well, Mrs Helidon?'

'No-o.' The denial was just a little too drawn out. 'I assumed my husband would look into her background if he wanted to put some money into her boutique. I just thought the idea had possibilities at the time. Women in Sydney now have more money to spend than they have ever had in their lives before.'

'I'm sure they have,' said Malone, trying to sound as if he were grateful for the information; he wondered how his old mum would respond to it. 'Did *you* look into her background, Mr Helidon?'

Helidon had his pipe filled now but made no attempt to light it. He stood in front of the large marble-faced fireplace; behind him the mantelpiece carried a chorus of very expensive Christmas greetings: Y Division never got cards such as these, not even from reformed crooks. 'I don't see the point of all this, Sergeant.'

'There's a point to it, sir,' said Malone with quiet emphasis. 'We're trying to find out who killed Miss Brand. Even the slightest bit of information you can give us may help.'

Helidon pressed the tobacco more firmly into the bowl of his pipe. He glanced at his wife, then said, '*Well* . . . I couldn't discover much. There didn't seem to be anything *against* her, if that's what you mean. She seemed to me to have a good business sense, a very good sense, indeed.' He glanced at his wife again, then looked back at Malone. 'My wife assured me she knew clothes and their quality.'

'But I'm afraid we don't know any more about her than that,' said Norma Helidon, and Malone waited for her to stand up, to tell him that the interview was over.

He got in first: '*We've* looked into her background. She had a police record in Germany. She was a prostitute in Hamburg for five or six years.' He had addressed himself to Norma Helidon. It had been a shot in the dark, but he got the reaction he had hoped for: the sudden look of distaste, the flash of contempt in her eyes as she looked at her husband. Then he looked back at Helidon. 'Could you think of some reason why she would have torn up your cheque? Did you have a disagreement with her?'

Helidon seemed to be taking a moment to recover, not from the revelation of Helga Brand's background but from the look his wife had given him. 'No-o. None at all. To me it looked as if it was going to be a very amicable partnership, indeed. I'm—I must confess I'm shocked at what you say she

89

was. There was no hint of it in her manner, none at all. She was most ladylike. Very ladylike, indeed.'

'All prostitutes aren't female larrikins,' said Malone. 'Some of them could pass for housewives. Ask Constable Clements. He was on the Vice Squad for three years.'

'That's right,' said Clements, glad to be able to say something. He usually let Malone do all the questioning while he took notes, but he liked to be recognized occasionally. He would be a sergeant himself one day and he wanted the practice of being able to handle people as well as Malone did. 'But as soon as we stripped this girl Brand we knew she was in the game. She had——' Then he looked at Norma Helidon, his face collapsing into a bag of embarrassment. 'Sorry, Mrs Helidon. I won't go into the details.'

'Thank you,' said Norma Helidon. She had recovered her poise, was once more the Queen of Pymble. 'But if Miss Brand was what you say, doesn't a girl like that——?'

'Deserve what she got?' said Malone.

Norma Helidon realized she had been about to say the wrong thing.

'No-o, I didn't mean that. I meant——'

'I think my wife meant that a girl like that stands the chance of being murdered,' said Helidon quickly. 'I mean, she might meet *anyone* in her—her profession.'

Malone nodded. 'That's true. But the law doesn't recognize whether people deserve to be murdered or not.'

Both Helidon and his wife recognized the rebuff. They both stiffened, then Helidon said sharply, 'I think we've told you all we can, Sergeant. You'll have to excuse us. My wife and I have a dinner engagement—a charity dinner——'

'Just one more question, sir,' said Malone, doggedly remaining seated. Clements had been about to rise, but he sank back into his chair as he saw Malone make no move. 'Did you ever visit Miss Brand in her flat at Double Bay?'

'Once,' said Helidon without hesitation. 'We looked at some possible sites for the boutique in Double Bay. Then I went back to her flat to discuss them with her.'

'Was that when you wrote out the cheque?'

'Yes. For a thousand dollars. It was what you might call

starting money—a deposit on a lease on a shop she had picked out.'

'The date of the cheque was the second of this month, Monday of last week. Was that the day you visited her?'

'I'm not sure.' Helidon pursed his lips. 'Yes. I think so. Yes, it was Monday.'

You know bloody well it was Monday, Malone thought. 'What time were you there?'

'I'm not sure. Between five and six, I'd think.' Then his voice became sharp again: he was the Cabinet Minister putting a public servant in his place: 'Sergeant, you're not implying I might have had something to do with her death?'

'No, sir,' said Malone, putting on his own political face. 'But we had to check——'

'I'm afraid I don't appreciate the honour,' said Helidon, but his wit had no more spark than his unlit pipe.

'It was better, wasn't it, that we found the cheque rather than someone else?' Malone's voice had its own sharpness now.

'Oh yes. Yes, indeed.' Helidon abruptly changed his face and his tone of voice; he could have been canvassing a wavering voter. 'I'll do all I can to help, Sergeant. But I'm afraid it won't be much.'

Malone stood up and Clements, snapping his notebook shut, rose, too. 'If we have to come back, Mr Helidon, it will only be to clear up some minor points. Good night. Enjoy your dinner. What charity is it for?'

'The Police Widows Fund,' said Norma Helidon, and Malone felt the sharp prick of her smile. 'Are you and Constable Clements married?'

'Not yet,' said Malone. 'We're still looking into our girls' backgrounds.'

Norma Helidon looked at her husband as if waiting for him to tick off the impertinent policeman. Malone waited too, realizing he had gone too far; but there was too much Irish in his tongue for him ever to be able to control it completely. But Helidon said nothing, just stood there waiting for the two detectives to go: he had learned the political value of saying nothing.

When they were at last outside in the car, Clements said, 'That was a bit rough, wasn't it? That bit about our girls' background?'

Malone nodded, still looking back at the big low house half-hidden in its garden. 'I shouldn't have said it. But somehow they got under my skin. Neither of them said a word of sympathy about our girl Helga. I could have been telling them some stray dog had been run over. She was a whore and she might have been a blackmailer, but ordinary decent people don't take someone's death as casually as all that. They even looked *relieved*.'

'I noticed that. Especially the wife. Do you think he did have something to do with the murder?'

'I don't know. Maybe not. But he had more to do with her than just thinking of going into business with her. The look on his wife's face told me that.'

'You didn't mention the folder of newspaper cuttings.'

'I wanted a reason for coming back to see him again. Do you lay all your bets at once or do you wait to see how the track is running?'

'Doesn't matter what system I use,' said Clements dolefully. 'I always bloody well win.'

4

'But wasn't it a coincidence?' said Lisa.

'In the police game you soon realize coincidences are more common than most people suppose.' Malone took off his shoes, lay back on the divan, sipped the beer Lisa had given him. 'You come to half-rely on them. Without 'em, a quarter of our cases would never be solved.'

'Are you going to discuss the case with me? Are detectives allowed to do that—discuss things with their wives and girl friends?'

'Officially, no. But if you and I were in bed together and I had a sudden idea about a case, would I get out of bed and call the inspector or would I discuss it with you?'

'Depends what we were doing in bed.' She sat down on

the divan beside him, stroked his forehead. 'You look worn out, darling. Do you want to talk about it or not?'

Lisa's flat was what was called a bachelor flat; even when occupied by a girl, bachelors were usually trying to gain entry. It had one largish bed-sitting-room, a bathroom designed for a skinny midget, and a minute kitchen that pre-supposed the tenant would never want to use it: the walls of the tiny alcove seemed to bulge outwards when even steam blew out of the kettle on the fairies' gas stove. Malone had once stepped in there to get a glass of water and had almost dislocated his hip trying to extricate himself from between the stove and the sink. But the flat had a large picture window that looked out on to the city skyline and Lisa was willing to pay the high rent for the view. It was better than Malone's own bachelor flat a mile or two away, which looked out on to a narrow street and the entrance to a strip joint.

He put his hand on her thigh and grinned. 'Till I've finished my beer, anyway. Then we'll see. . . .' He took another mouthful of beer. Lisa did not like beer, but she went to the trouble to get some in for him because she knew he preferred it to any other drink. This was a Dutch beer and he wondered if she was trying to prove to him that not all the best things in the world were Australian. 'When you were with Mrs Helidon this afternoon, did she seem to you to be a bit, well, distracted? As if she had something on her mind besides the Blue and Red Ball?'

'Take your hand away from there. Is that how you usually interrogate your witnesses?' He grinned and took his hand away. 'No, she was not what I should call a hundred per cent *with* me. It was almost as if she did not care whether the ball went on or not. I was a bit surprised, because this is her first year as president of the committee. Her sort of coronation, if you like. But then I thought perhaps she was having one of *those* days. Women of her age do. She's in the middle of her change of life, I'd think.'

'You see? That's the advantage of discussing a case with your girl friend. What man would have an antenna as sensitive as that? I have great difficulty in telling when a girl is a virgin.'

'From now on that's a question that's not going to concern you. I'd rather you stayed away from the menopause matrons, too.'

'I think I have to go back and visit Mrs Helidon again. She and her husband know more about Helga than they let on. Do you have to see her again?'

'At least once a week for the next few months. The ball isn't till Easter. Are you going to ask me to do some detective work?'

He put down his empty glass, shook his head. 'No. You're not going to get paid for my headaches. But if you found out I'd been seeing another girl and that she was trying to blackmail me, what would you do? Strangle her?'

'No, I'd strangle you.'

'You're a great bloody help,' he said, and pulled her down on to the divan beside him. 'Hullo. No underwear. How'd you know I'd be in the mood for it tonight?'

'I know you Australians.'

'What are Dutchmen like?'

'Ah, you don't catch me like that. Ask some other girl. Put your hand back where it was and interrogate me some more. But not about Mrs Helidon.'

'Do you love me?'

'That's the sort of question I like. Darling——'

94

CHAPTER SIX

I

Friday, November 29

'A HUNDRED THOUSAND DOLLARS!' Savanna said. 'You're out of your head, Helga. Eat up your lobster.'

He had brought Helga here for an early dinner at the Summit restaurant at the top of the Australia Tower. He occasionally took her out to lunch or dinner, reasoning that the risk was minimal: if he were seen by Josie or one of their friends he would just introduce Helga as a model he was planning to use in a commercial. So far he had never had to use such an invention and he had reached a stage of depression where he no longer cared what was discovered about him.

'I am not joking, darling.' Helga ate her lobster with relish; she was not a girl who picked at food as if it were the oddments table in a bargain sale. 'He could easily afford it. There was a profile on him in *The Bulletin* a few months ago. It said he was worth at least six million dollars, probably more.'

'You've worked pretty fast, haven't you? What have you been doing since I saw you last—digging up research on him?' He was careful not to mention Gibson's name. They were at a window table and the two tables on either side of them were still vacant; but waiters had ears like radar and he knew that his own voice, even as a whisper, could carry like another man's shout. This was no time for voice projection.

She wiped lobster sauce from the corner of her mouth. 'Darling, I've had a folder on him'—she, too, was discreet —'ever since I found out you were related to him.'

'Jesus Christ!'

Instantly a waiter was beside him. 'Something wrong, sir?'

Savanna waved him away, turned his head and looked out the window. Sydney stretched away to the west beneath them: the coffin-like dock sheds, swatches of water corduroyed by the wind, then finally the tiled roofs of the suburbs caught like red mackerel in a vast net of their own shadows. Though it was summer, the day had been cool and windy and the sun-streaked sky had all the cold resignation of a winter sunset. It fitted his own autumnal mood.

'I'd like to think you're pulling my leg. But the worst of it is, I don't think you are. You're in earnest.' He looked back at her, at the smooth, clean-lined face gently lit by the fading sun. There was no hint of evil or malice in that face, but neither was there any hint of love; yet she had made a profession of love and had been successful at it. Not, perhaps, to the extent of gouging a hundred thousand dollars out of one of her clients. 'Have you been planning something like this for—*months*?'

'No.' She pulled a claw off the lobster, squeezed out the flesh from it. 'I just thought he might come in useful some time. And now he has.' She looked up and smiled behind the red claw. 'For both of us, darling.'

He shook his head emphatically. 'Not me, Christ I—' He shook his head again. Her estimate of what she thought Grafter would pay had suddenly put his own half-formed idea of blackmail into some sort of perspective; he had been ridiculous even to think that he could get away with such a scheme. 'You don't know him. He'd, I don't know, *laugh* at me.'

'I don't think so. Haven't you had even the tiniest thought that you might ask him for some money, after you found out what they are doing with his boats?' She looked carefully at him, then nodded. 'I can see you have. You see, *liebling*, I know you too well. You don't have quite as many scruples as you like to think.'

'I used to,' he said defensively, bitterly.

'You mean till you met me?' It was her turn to shake her head. 'No, darling, you had started to lose them a long time before you met me.'

Perhaps she was right. You did not make your own character: it grew out of the influence of environment, cir-cumstances, other people: all you could do was polish up the distinctions you became aware of. And perhaps when erosion

96

set in other people became aware of it from the outside before you saw it from within.

'You can make a new start after he gives us the money.' She reached across, put a hand on his; from the other side of the room the waiter watched them, envying the grey-haired joker whose young bird so obviously loved him. Christ, what money could do for you these days! Because that must be all the grey-haired joker had. 'Fifty thousand for you, fifty thousand for me.'

'What'll you do if I tell you to go to hell?'

'Then I'll go and see him myself. And take the whole of the hundred thousand. Eat up your steak, darling. It's getting cold.'

Automatically he bit into a piece of steak, found it tasted like indiarubber, spat it out on to his fork and pushed the plate away from him. The waiter was beside him at once. 'Something wrong with the steak, sir?'

'No. No, I've just lost my appetite. It's the—the height, I guess. Vertigo.' He looked out the window, saw a freighter pulling out from a wharf. Where was she headed: London, Hong Kong, Tristan da Cunha? If only he had a passage on her, anywhere would do. 'I'm used to basement bistros.'

The waiter laughed politely, took the plate away and Savanna picked up his wine and gulped a mouthful.

Helga said, 'Wine isn't good for vertigo, darling. Please, you mustn't think I'm awful. Have I ever tried to blackmail you?'

He laughed, feeling giddier than ever he might have from vertigo. 'You'd have been wasting your time. They don't allow overdrafts for blackmail.'

'Darling, it wasn't just that you did not have enough money. I *like* you—no, really, I do. But *him*! You've told me yourself what an awful old villain he is. He's the really unscrupulous one—you have told me that a dozen times. What is the difference between blackmailing someone and swindling them? None, as far as I can see.'

'There is a difference, a slight moral one. But you're myopic when it comes to morals, aren't you?'

'Don't be nasty, *liebling*.' Her voice wasn't raised nor

quickened; but he was an expert in voices and he detected the hard note that was suddenly there. 'I don't think your wife would think much of *your* morals.'

'Are you thinking of going to her, too?'

'Why should I? I suppose she has less money than you have. And I would not go to see her just out of spite. Whatever else I am, darling, I am not spiteful.'

'No,' he admitted. 'At least not up till now. But you're greedy and that's what I'm afraid of as much as anything else. What if you aren't satisfied with what he gives you? Are you sure you won't go back to him in six months, twelve months, and ask for more?'

'I shan't be here in six months. I shall be back in Europe. I am not foolish, darling, nor brave. If he gives us the money, if he is as bad as you say he is, he would want to keep an eye on us all the time. He can do that with you and there is nothing you can do about it. Unless, of course, you come back to Europe with me?'

'There wasn't enough invitation in your voice when you said that.'

She put her hand on his again. 'No, *liebling*. I think it would be best, once we have the money, if we never saw each other again. I don't want to be anywhere near our friend after we have—er—negotiated with him. So I'll go back to Europe.'

'To Germany?'

'I think so. Germany is booming again—there are wonderful opportunities for investment there—people work hard—' Was he mistaken, was her voice becoming more guttural, more German? They never lose their pride in their Fatherland, he thought, never lose their German-ness; then wondered why he should think that was a fault. They had a remarkable talent for turning a blind eye to their faults, but then so did a great many other nationalities; the first nation to face the truth of itself would become the first country of saints and would at once be invaded by all its neighbours, afraid that the disease might spread. Helga had casually (and without spite, he had to admit) often pointed out to him faults with Australians that he had never bothered to examine. But now, unreasonably, he hated the German arrogance that he thought he saw rising in her.

'Where will you go, back to Hamburg?'

She shook her head. 'München. The people are gayer there, especially the men. I shall invest my money, find a nice rich husband and settle down.'

'How will you explain the nipples on your bum to him?'

Her mouth hardened, her eyes went pale. He had never seen such a coldly fierce look on her face before; she turned sallow with hatred and anger. 'Do not bother to go near your brother-*in*-law.' She did not name Gibson, but it was as if she did not care now who heard her identify their victim. Or rather *her* victim: Savanna had been wiped from the scheme: 'I shall go myself. You won't have to worry yourself about him. You can start cleaning up your dirty little scruples again.'

'Please yourself.' He felt relieved, as if she had just taken a loaded gun away from him. 'But do me a favour. Don't tell him where you got your information. I have to go on living with him.'

She was gathering up her gloves and handbag. 'Oh, I shall tell him, darling. You will have to pay *something* for your insults.'

'You *are* spiteful,' he said, feeling suddenly sick.

'Only when other people are.' She looked up as the waiter materialized beside them; the professional lover managed the bright easy smile: 'We must rush, darling. Otherwise we're going to miss the show.'

They were half-way across the restaurant when Savanna saw Silver step out of the lift. He half-halted, not knowing where to go but not wanting to meet Silver at exactly this moment; but Helga had already reached the lift, had turned back to wait for him. He stumbled up the few steps to the foyer, desperately trying to work his face into an expression of pleasure.

'Hul-*lo*, Silver!' Jesus, he thought, I sound like the Lone Ranger. He had thought it a beautiful name for her when he had first heard it, that it had suited her ideally; but now, dismayed and fumbling like a schoolboy, he had made it sound ridiculous. He was still in love with her and nothing,

nothing in the wide world, would ever change that. 'This is Miss Brand. Mrs——' He fumbled again, his mind blank. It was farcical that he could not remember his first wife's married name; but it was always the same. As if his mind refused to accept that she was now another man's wife. 'Mrs.—*Carson*.'

'Hullo, Jack.' She looked at Helga with a quick glance of appraisal that was not long enough to be offensive but that missed nothing. He felt an odd relief that her judgement of Helga seemed approving, that he had not come down to going around with tramps. 'You look a little peaked. Been working hard?'

'Never harder,' he said, thinking how hollow his bluff sounded. 'Are you down for long?'

'Just to pick up the children from school when they break up. And do some Christmas shopping.'

He heard himself say, 'Maybe we can have a Christmas drink before you go back?'

Silver glanced at Helga, who smiled. 'It is all right, Mrs Carson. Mr Savanna and I work together occasionally. I am not his girl friend or anything.'

Silver smiled in return, but the smile told Savanna nothing. She looked back at him and said, 'I'm at the Wentworth, Jack. Phone me.'

Then she went across to join two women who were waiting for her at a far table and Savanna followed Helga into the lift. It was an automatic lift and they were the only passengers. Conversation was safe here: about blackmail, about ex-wives.

'That was your first wife, wasn't it? She must have been beautiful when she was young.'

'She still is,' he said with angry emphasis. He sometimes saw Silver's photo in the newspapers: at country picnic races, at the polo, at the Carson beach house at Palm Beach; and each time she looked as beautiful to him as that first night they had met during the war. This time was the first for four or five years that he had seen her in the flesh and he was still feeling the sudden heartache it had given him.

'Don't bite my head off, darling. I hope I look as good as she does when I am her age.'

'If ever you get to her age,' he said.

'What do you mean by that?'

But the lift had reached the bottom level, the doors had opened and a party of four couples, wielding their quips, were mustering each other into the lift. Savanna and Helga pushed out past them, went out of the building and down into the plaza into the wind that swooped and climbed like storms of invisible birds. The fountain spun off water like silver sawdust from a saw and they had to walk wide of it to avoid being sprayed. They crossed the plaza, their tempers sharpened by the abrasive wind, and came out into Pitt Street. Savanna hailed a cab, it drew into the kerb and he opened the door.

'Aren't you coming with me?' Helga said.

'No,' he said, closing the door on her. 'From now on, you're on your own.'

2

Monday, December 2

Leslie Gibson looked at the cheque for ten thousand dollars, then added his crabbed signature to it. He didn't know within a hundred thousand dollars what he was worth these days, but it still was a painful exercise, a case of financial arthritis, for him to sign a cheque for more than fifty dollars. Jesus Christ, he thought, the things a man does when he's afraid!

'I think it's wonderful,' said Miss Kingsley, his secretary, and took the cheque. She handles the bloody thing more casually than I do, he thought. But then she didn't have to sign it. 'If the cancer appeal could find fifty men like you, they'd have their money in no time.'

'You think there are fifty men like me?' A wicked grin lay at the corner of his mouth like a venomous lizard; but she had worked too long for him to be trapped. He recognized her caution and allowed the grin to open up into a harmless smile. 'I don't think Sydney could stand fifty old buggers like me, Frances.'

She smiled back, not offended by his language. She was in her forties, a homely woman who was in her own way as tough as he was. She had had to be to survive twenty years with him. 'It would be an interesting thing to see, anyway. I'll have this cheque delivered by hand.'

'And get the receipt. We'll need it for the tax man. It's deductible. There are qualifications to my philanthropy, Frances.'

'It doesn't alter the thought, Mr Gibson. You may get a halo despite yourself.'

She went out, closing the door quickly behind her before he could reply. They conducted an undeclared war, each trying for the last word, and she usually won. He muttered to himself, looked at the stub in his cheque-book, then dropped the book in a drawer of his desk. He sat back in the high-backed leather chair that made him look smaller and more wizened than he actually was, and gazed about his office. It was a large room, panelled on three walls and with the fourth wall a curved floor-to-ceiling window that looked out towards the harbour and the Opera House. Two long shelves held rows of books: bound copies of business journals, books on mining, shipping, forestry, several volumes of *Punch* cartoons, biographies of other, bigger tycoons than himself, and every book he had been able to lay his hands on that told him something of Australia's history. Though his empire was now big by Australian standards, he no longer worked as hard as he once had; it had taken him some time to accept Glenda's demand that he must slow down, but over the past two years he had started to delegate authority. He still came to the office every day, but he did no more than two hours' work. The rest of the time he spent reading his favourite subject: history, and particularly Australian history. He had left school at twelve years of age, but his education had not stopped there and then. He belonged to a breed of men who were now dying out, the men who had filled in their lonely hours in the Outback devouring books, reading and re-reading, discovering worlds to which they had never belonged.

Half a dozen prints of early nineteenth-century Sydney were hung about the room and on one wall there was a Hans Heysen painting of an Outback shack that reminded him of his birthplace. On the opposite wall hung a Dobell painting of Edie Creek, in New Guinea, where Gibson Industries had all begun.

He stared at the Dobell painting and the slightly stylized scene became real as he saw again the men working their small gold mines in the New Guinea hills, felt the heat, tasted the dull stale food, experienced the racking shivers of malaria, watched other men die of scrub typhus. That had been before the Japs had come, when he had made enough money to start dreaming about a future. Then he remembered the retreat over the mountains, the small groups of men like himself, miners, planters, timber men, fighting the Jap advance patrols, and he remembered the three bullet wounds that had eventually resulted in his being invalided back to the mainland.

He had survived all that and now here he was in a luxurious office, protected by Miss Kingsley and his wealth, impregnable to every outside threat. Yet he was still afraid, scared to philanthropy by the thought of what could kill him from the inside: cancer.

Miss Kingsley buzzed on the office phone. 'Mr Savanna is here.'

'Bring him in.' He wondered what the hell Jack wanted. He had been on the point of going to bed last night when Savanna had rung and asked to see him this morning. Knowing Savanna, who rarely called him at all, let alone at ten o'clock on a Sunday night, he had not asked what he wanted; he had known at once that it must be something important, not to himself but to Savanna and possibly Josie. He hoped he was not going to be involved in some domestic crisis, a divorce or something, between the two of them. Other people's lives and problems were their own concern. He did not rise as Savanna came in but just waved him to the chair on the opposite side of the desk. 'What's on your mind, Jack?'

'You, Les.' Savanna had lain awake most of the night wondering about his approach to Gibson and had decided that the direct one was the best. It was the one Gibson would understand.

Gibson showed no surprise; he had at once closed up, suspicion providing its own armour. 'Yeah? Go on.'

Savanna looked towards the door to the outer office. 'Are we likely to be interrupted?'

'Only if I press the buzzer for her. I'll do that, Jack, if you waste my time.'

Savanna had not expected the interview to be easy, but now Gibson's rudeness seemed to put him more at ease. He sat back in his chair, gazed at the unfriendly old man for a long moment, then said, 'Les, you're going to be blackmailed.'

Gibson didn't even blink. 'Who by? You?'

'No. A German girl I know named Helga Brand.'

'One of your fancy pieces?' He saw the look on Savanna's face and he laughed, a sound that hinted of lung cancer. 'I know about 'em. Not their names, but you've had half a dozen over the past ten years. You haven't been doing the right thing by Josie for a long time. I got no time for fornicators, Jack.'

The old-fashioned term almost made Savanna laugh. 'Les, you're the last one should give me a lecture on morals. I know of at least two men who committed suicide because you broke them.'

'There was only one. The other bloke was gunna die anyway, he had cancer. He felt a twinge as he said the word; it was already at work on him, the very thought of it eating its way into him. 'He just got nasty, had a last shot at me before he blew his own brains out. The coroner took no notice of his note.'

'Well, even one suicide would prey on most men's conscience.'

'I think about him sometimes, but he doesn't worry me. It was business. He was weak, he just couldn't stand the idea of being broke. I could lose all this—' He waved a hand at his surrounding. 'Lose the lot. But I wouldn't blow my brains out. I might even start in all over again.'

'You probably would,' said Savanna grudgingly.

'Anyhow, I got my own set of morals. They don't allow for blokes who two-time their wives.'

Savanna shook his head in good-humoured exasperation. 'I don't know why I bothered to come. I've spent the whole week-end thinking about this, giving myself a headache, not

104

sleeping——' He shook his head again. 'I came here to give you a warning and I walk into a lecture on what I should do with my spare time.'

Gibson's hand was close to the buzzer on his desk. 'Jack, get to the point or get out.'

'All right,' said Savanna savagely. He sat up and leaned forward. 'This girl, Helga Brand, is going to ask you for a hundred thousand dollars.'

Savanna had to admire the old man's control; there wasn't a shadow of any reaction on the mottled, lined face.

'What for?'

'Les, your boats—or anyway one of them the one I was out on the other night—it's smuggling in drugs. The stuff is dropped from some overseas ship in waterproof packages and Bixby and his crew pick it up and bring it in. I don't even know if you're in on this——'

Gibson took his hand away from the buzzer. 'Thirty years ago I'd have kicked your balls off for that remark.'

Savanna hesitated, then nodded. 'Okay, I take it back. You have morals about drugs, too, have you?'

'Bloody strong ones. Go on. What about this girl? How did he get into it?'

Savanna made a weak gesture. 'That was my fault.' He told Gibson what had happened on the morning of his arrival back from the overnight trawler trip. 'To tell you the truth, I was a bit scared of Bixby. I think he could be a mean bastard without any trouble, a real stand-over merchant. When I told her about him and the drugs, she suggested I should blackmail you. I just thought she was joking. Then Friday night—well, then I got a whole new picture of her. Up till then I don't think I'd thought anything of her but a good lay who took some money on the side.'

For the first time Gibson showed some expression; his small beak of a nose twitched with distaste. 'I'm not interested in what you thought of her. Harlots aren't worth anyone's opinion.'

Savanna couldn't help it: 'You could change places with Father Wrigley, you know that? Jesus, Les, I didn't think you were such an old wowser——'

Gibson twisted his mouth sourly at the comparison with Wrigley, but didn't seem to mind being called a strait-laced prude. 'What's this girl planning to do?'

'I'm not quite sure what she's planning. She just said she was going to ask you for a hundred thousand dollars or she'd make trouble for you.' He paused, getting used to the new view of Helga; she had become another person since Friday night. 'I think she might, too. I thought I knew her pretty well, but now I find out she can be as calculating as——'

He paused again and Gibson said, 'As me? That what you mean? Then we oughta be a good match for each other, oughtn't we?' He stared at Savanna, his bright blue eyes as hard as pieces of glass, his thin lips tucked in till his mouth was only another line in his lined face. 'Why did you come and tell me all this, Jack? Wasn't she gunna split the money with you?'

'That was her original idea,' Savanna confessed frankly. 'But when I turned thumbs down on it, she said she'd bite you for the lot herself.'

Gibson's eyes were still hard and bright. 'Did it occur to you to put the bite on me yourself?'

Savanna wondered for a moment if Gibson would appreciate honesty. Then he decided against it: Gibson hadn't got where he was by being honest. 'It never entered my head. I've got my set of morals, too.'

Gibson grunted as if he found it impossible to believe that Savanna had any morals at all. But all he said was, 'Just as well. You'd have been sat back on your arse before you knew what hit you.'

Savanna complimented himself on his good sense in not having been honest. 'What are you going to do about Helga?'

'Where does she live?'

Savanna told him.

Gibson swung round in his chair, looked out the window. Savanna sat ignored, cut off from the old man by the high-backed chair. He wondered if he should get up and walk out of the office, then decided against it. Gibson wouldn't let him go like that, and he was not going to get half-way to the door to be called back like some cattle dog. Because he knew

106

he would come back if he were called, though he was not quite sure why. Where had the rebel gone that had once been himself?

'You didn't tell me, Jack——' Gibson was still staring out the window, the back of his chair still turned to Savanna. 'Why did you come and tell me all this?'

Savanna had been trying to find the answer to that all night. 'I don't quite know,' he confessed. He took out a cigarette, lit it as Gibson swung back in his chair. 'I don't think there's any love lost between you and me, is there?'

'If there is, I've never missed it. They'll ruin your health.' Gibson waved away the smoke of the cigarette as it drifted towards him. He coughed, a reminder of the sixty a day that he himself had once smoked. 'You didn't come to me to spite this girl, did you?'

'I don't think so. That might be part of it, but I'm not even sure of that. Do you remember the reason for every action, every major one, that you ever took?'

'I don't remember them, no. But I know there *was* always a reason. I didn't get here by accident.' He looked around the room without pride, just acceptance. 'There were accidents of luck, but I knew enough to take advantage of them.'

'Well, all I know is, I'm not here by accident. I'm——'

'You're what?' Gibson said as Savanna paused again.

'You're not going to believe this. I don't know that I believe it myself. But I might be here because of Josie.'

Gibson looked sceptical. 'You're right. I don't believe it.'

Savanna shrugged, but persevered with his explanation, if only to explain it to himself. 'Josie has a lot of respect for you. Some of what Glenda feels for you has rubbed off on her.' Gibson blinked, as if he had just been surprised. 'You don't believe that, either, do you?'

For the first time Gibson showed a weakness: 'I'd like to. But that doesn't explain why you're concerned about me.'

'Only indirectly, Les. I think I might be here because I wouldn't want Josie to be disappointed in you. If ever this came out into the open, it would knock Glenda for a loop. And that would hurt Josie. She's had her disappointments in me. I wouldn't want to see it piled on her.' He drew on his cigarette, blew out smoke, then shrugged again. 'It's not a very convincing reason for my being here. But it's part of it.'

'What's the other part?'

It's a catharsis, an urge to be delivered of all the worries that have plagued me now for five years. I've reached a stage where I've become one huge aching boil and if I can open it up, even to you, everything will come out. It won't work, of course, and the hope is stupid. And you wouldn't believe what I'd say, anyway, because you're too tight, too closed up against the world, ever to believe in the value of catharsis. But a man sometimes has to talk to someone, even an enemy.

But all he said was, 'Maybe it's just that I don't believe in blackmail.'

Gibson sat silent, sucking on his thin lips. He was not afraid of what this girl Helga would do to him and he certainly wouldn't give her any money. But he hated the thought that an outsider, an absolute stranger, could suddenly and without warning threaten his impregnability. He had arranged his empire against every emergency, against takeovers, economic depression, wars; he had believed till a few minutes ago that his only weakness was the vulnerability to disease of his own body. And now this girl, this *harlot*, was threatening him as if he were no stronger, no more unassailable, than this weak-kneed bastard of a brother-in-law sitting opposite him. She would have to be taught a lesson. And so would Bixby, the man who had opened the crack in the fort.

'Leave the girl to me. Just don't tell her you've been to see me.'

'Don't hurt her, Les. I mean physically.'

'I don't knock women around. Blokes like me, the ones who don't have much time for women other than our wives, we're usually the ones who treat 'em best. It's bastards like you, the playboys, who knock 'em around.'

'You're wrong there.' Savanna stood up. He was still not sure that he had done the right thing in coming to see Gibson, but he felt a curious relief, as if at last the boil was coming to a head of its own volition. 'I've never hit a woman in my life. But if you hurt Helga, I'll come back and belt the living daylights out of you. I'll be bastard enough to take advantage of your smallness and your age. You might be the only man left I *could* belt. And I'd do it, don't make any mistake about it.'

Gibson stared up at the tall man opposite, thinking: twenty-five or thirty years ago he could probably have taken on a football team and done the lot of them. The army didn't give him his medal because it liked the look of him; he must have done something courageous to get it. What happened to him? When did his particular cancer begin eating away at him?

'Do you love this girl, Jack?'

Savanna shook his head without hesitation: he loved Silver, but he wasn't going to mention her name to Gibson. 'Not at all. But I *liked* her. And that's been something. She's suddenly turned out to be a bitch, but I still wouldn't want her hurt. Just see that she's not, Les.'

Gibson continued to stare at Savanna. He's weak and he's buggered up his life, but maybe there's a spark of decency somewhere in him. 'All right, Jack. She won't be hurt. But she's gunna get the shit scared out of her.'

Savanna grinned. 'Unlike Father Wrigley, she doesn't like vulgarity. Watch your language in front of her, Les.'

Gibson had one of the moments of insight that had made him so successful in business. 'I thought you might have a slap at him sooner or later. It sticks in your craw, doesn't it, that I'm taking him to Europe with us?'

Savanna hesitated, then nodded. 'There are better things you could do with your money.'

'Like helping you out of the hole your business is in?'

'Yes,' said Savanna, wondering how Gibson knew the state of Olympus's finances.

It was Gibson's turn to grin. 'That would do me no good with Glenda. You should get on better with her, Jack. In the long run I only spend my money for her.'

Savanna was at the door. He turned and looked back at the wizened little man hunched like a baboon in the big leather chair. Then he smiled, a little sadly. 'It's a pity there's so much bastard in you, Les. There's a spark of decency in you that you've never really given a chance.'

Gibson smiled inwardly, his expression not changing at all.

That's two sparks: between us we might have started a bushfire of decency. 'I don't regret anything.'

'I don't believe that.' Savanna waved at the books on the shelves. 'What were you looking for there? A man doesn't read history unless he feels he's missed something. What was it, Les?'

'I wasn't looking for my character there, if that's what you mean.'

'What then? Are they all just there for show, trying to give yourself an air of breeding?' Savanna shook his head, smiling without malice. 'You'll never be a gentleman, Les, no matter how many books you read, no matter how much education you give yourself.'

'I know that,' the old man said flatly. 'I never wanted to be a gentleman. A long time ago, long before I had any money, I realized that *having* money didn't make you a gentleman. I'm talking about the old definition of the word. There are very few of them here in this country, but there's a bloody lot who like to *think* they're gentlemen. It's more than having money or education. It's breeding, I suppose, and it's got to go back a long way. There was an Englishman once said, "Gentilitie is naught but ancient riches." The more I read of history, the more I realize he was right on the knocker when he said that. My money is too new for me ever to be a gentleman.'

Savanna looked at him with new interest. 'Then the books——?'

'I've got a sense of history, Jack. You're not gunna believe this'—he smiled as he tossed Savanna's phrase back at him —'but I don't like to think everything started and is gunna end with me.'

Savanna said nothing for a moment, then he nodded. 'Don't hurt Helga,' he said, abruptly opened the door and went out.

Gibson hunched himself more in his chair and chewed on his lips. A spark of decency that each had recognized in the other: Jesus, he thought, whatever went wrong? And felt an unfamiliar taste in his mouth, one that he did not recognize, the salt of regret.

Then he coughed, felt the pain in his chest and shivered.

He sat up, reached for the phone. 'Get me Phil Bixby. He's one of the trawler captains.'

'Where do I find him, Mr Gibson?'

'Frances, if I bloody knew where to get him, I wouldn't be asking you.'

'Yes, Mr Gibson. Mind your ear, I'm going to hang up.'

He put the phone back on its cradle and grinned. He might have fallen in love with Frances Kingsley if he had not met Glenda first.

3

Bixby arrived within the hour. He came lumbering into the office, dressed in slacks, blue sports jacket and bright orange shirt. There was no awkwardness or embarrassment about him; he had already guessed why the Old Man had sent for him. He looked around for the Old Man's brother-in-law, but there was no sign of him. He went to sit down in the chair opposite Gibson, but his bottom didn't reach it.

'I didn't invite you to sit down,' Gibson snapped.

Bixby straightened up, his thick-featured face flushing. 'Okay, Mr Gibson. What can I do for you?'

Gibson never wasted time with his employees, especially ones he was about to sack. 'You can stop picking up drugs on my boats, that's the first thing. The second thing is, you're drawing your time, you and all your crew. The third thing is, you're gunna pay a visit to a girl named Helga Brand and warn her to keep her mouth shut. If she doesn't keep it shut, you're gunna have the demons down on you and you'll go up for seven to ten years. The judges are getting pretty severe on bastards who bring in drugs. And you've already done time once. Second time up they're always ready to give you the maximum.'

Bixby took a match out of his pocket and chewed on it. Then he looked at the chair beside him, looked back at Gibson, then sat down in the chair. He crossed one leg over the other, showing a length of bright orange sock to match the shirt, and sat back.

'If I ain't working for you any more, Grafter, then I ain't asking you whether I can sit down or not. If you brought me up here for a talk, then I'm gunna have it in comfort. I left school a long while ago, sport, and I'm too old for lectures. But first, let me get a few things straight. What's this about me running drugs?'

'You pick 'em up somewhere outside after they've been dropped and you bring 'em in with the ordinary fish catch.'

'Who told you that? That poofter brother-in-law of yours?' Bixby laughed, a rumble in his chest more like an indigestion sound. He undid his jacket and the orange shirt stretched tight across the muscles of his broad chest. Though he was a heavy beer drinker, twenty years of trawler fishing had kept him from running to fat. He was a violent man, taking pride in his ability to frighten others, a bully who had recognized there was no other way of asserting himself and making his mark in a world that preferred to ignore him. But he was not an unintelligent bully and he knew he was not going to frighten this little old sonofabitch behind the big leather-topped desk. 'You'd have a bit of trouble proving it, Grafter.'

'I don't have to prove anything,' said Gibson, not offended by the nickname; there had been a time when he had taken pride in that. It hurt Glenda to hear him called the name; but she wasn't going to be meeting this lout on the other side of the desk. 'You're not working for me any longer, so you won't be using my boat and it'll be none of my business. But that still leaves the girl. If she starts talking, you'll have the demons watching you. And they'll get you sooner or later.'

Bixby chewed on his match. 'You've become a sanctimonious old coot, haven't you? I can remember a time when I was doing some smuggling for *you*.'

'Not drugs. I was bringing in gold then, and gold never hurt anyone. Anyhow, that's all past now.'

'Yeah, you've made your pile, ain't you?' Bixby snapped off the match in his teeth, leant forward and dropped the two chewed pieces into the ashtray on the desk. 'What d'you want me to do with this piece?'

Gibson stared at the ashtray as if he might pick it up and hurl it at Bixby's head. Then he looked up and said, 'Tell her to keep her mouth shut. I don't care how you do it, but don't rough her up. If you scare her enough, she might take to the idea that she oughta go back to Europe. She's a Hun. I'll pay for her ticket.'

'Why would you do that, Grafter, if it ain't none of your business?'

But Gibson had all the answers ready: 'If you were picked up, they'd start investigating all my boats. That'd cost me money and it wouldn't make the rest of the crews too happy.'

'How much do I get as a'—Bixby grinned—'a golden handshake?'

Gibson picked up the ashtray, dropped the two pieces of match into the waste basket beside his chair, then put the ashtray back on the desk well away from Bixby. 'A month's pay.'

'That ain't much. I could tell 'em a few yarns about the gold we used to bring in.'

'That was nearly twenty years ago. As you say, you'd have a bit of trouble proving it. Consider yourself lucky I was able to warn you. If the girl had gone to the demons about you——'

'Why would she do that? If she's the piece who was with that feller Savanna, a blonde bit, she ain't the public-spirited sort. I seen her kind around too much—they ain't innarested in anyone 'cept themselves. Did she come and try and put the bite on you?'

'I've never seen or heard from her,' said Gibson, and felt that odd little thrill that always came when he was able to win a point merely by telling the truth. So much of his life in business had been taken up with double-dealing, prevarication and outright lies that the truth had become a luxury to be appreciated. That was something else he had learned from his reading of history: only the liar knew the full value of truth. 'She's your concern, not mine. If you can persuade her to go back to Germany or anywhere she wants to go, I'll pay her air fare, just to stop any interference with my boats. Economy class,' he added as an afterthought, not wanting to reward sin too extravagantly.

Bixby took out another match, chewed on it, then nodded.

'Okay, you win. But I dunno how you do it, Grafter, you got me beat.'

'Do what?'

'Stay outa gaol.'

Gibson permitted himself a confiding smile. 'I'm careful and I don't act like a damned fool. See the girl, then phone me up what she's gunna do. I'll give you the fare in cash when you're ready to buy the ticket for her. Just give me some warning, so I can have the money.'

'Don't you trust me?'

'Would you?' said Gibson.

CHAPTER SEVEN

I

Thursday, December 12

'WHO DO WE go to see first?' asked Clements. 'This bloke Savanna or old Grafter Gibson?'

'What have we got on Gibson so far? Just the photos of him and his wife. Nothing else.'

'Are you going to pass him up then?'

'We'll get around to him. But Savanna looks the better bet. Just the one photo of him and his missus. But that gabby woman next door to Helga's said she'd seen a handsome, grey-haired feller knocking on Helga's door. Or rather, she said he had a key.' Malone picked up the photo, turned it round towards Clements. 'He's grey-haired and I think you might say he was handsome.'

'I never know what handsome is, not the way some women see it. What else have we got on him? Personally, I'd rather try Gibson. I'd like to see how these millionaires live.'

'Russ, mate, you're too frivolous-minded. Is that all you want to do as a copper—go around interviewing millionaires in luxury homes?'

Clements thought about it, then nodded. 'Yeah, I think I'd settle for that.'

Malone shook his head. 'A snob cop. I never thought I'd live to see the day. It's these TV films, *Burke's Law* and that.'

Clements took out a handkerchief, blew his nose. 'Think I'm getting a summer cold or something.'

'It was that chilly atmosphere up at Helidon's last night. It might be even worse at Grafter Gibson's.' Then he turned round as Inspector Fulmer came into the room. 'We went to see Walter Helidon last night.'

'I know,' said Fulmer gravely, like a bishop who had just heard there had been heresy in his diocese. 'The Commissioner has just been on the phone to find out what it's all about. Seems Mr Helidon called him this morning, wanting to know couldn't you have gone to see him at his office instead of worrying his wife at home.'

'We tried his home because we thought he'd prefer the privacy there.'

'It seems you weren't too diplomatic——'

Malone didn't answer that. Instead he said, 'Are you on our side or not, Tom?'

'I'm not on Helidon's side, if that's what you mean. But from what he told the Commissioner, you could have been a little politer. I'm supposed to be ticking you off for your attitude towards *Mrs* Helidon.'

'I wasn't upset so much by her——' Then Malone shruggetd 'All right, tick me off.'

Clements sniffled in the background, wiped his nose again. 'We didn't get much co-operation up there, Tom.'

Fulmer said nothing, then at last nodded. 'All right, consider yourselves ticked off. Now, do you think Helidon had anything to do with the girl's murder?'

Malone, though his tongue sometimes got away from him, had learned the value of caution. A police sergeant, on four and a half thousand dollars a year, wasn't expected to be a judge. Fulmer had been known to jump on a junior constable who had once advanced an opinion that prostitution would never be wiped out so long as men had penises. Fulmer might think that life was either white or black, but Malone, for the time being, was prepared to stay in any grey corner he could find.

'We still have a way to go before I start naming suspects. We've got enough clues, God knows——' He gestured at the objects, now labelled, that lay on his desk. 'They've checked the blood on the sheets we found in the laundry basket—it doesn't match Helga's. They've found slivers of skin under one of her nails and a thread of blue material under another of them. We can't check on Helidon's blood group till we lay a charge against him. But he was wearing a blue suit last night and in all the photos of him he has on dark suits that could be blue. And when he took his glasses off last night there was just a faint mark, it could have been a scratch or even an old scar, on his eyebrow. I couldn't see properly, the room wasn't that well lit. We've still got several others to question. Any one of those could wear blue suits or jackets and could have a scratch on his face. I'd rather wait, Tom, before I start giving an opinion.'

'You're right,' said Fulmer. He picked up one of the chocolate boxes, still tied with a pink silk ribbon, from Malone's desk. 'Fancy, isn't it? What prompted you to bring these in? Lots of women eat chocolates.'

'I don't think women buy themselves fancy boxes, not girls who live alone.' He glanced at Clements, who was wiping his nose again. 'They usually buy them by the pound or half-pound, loose.'

'Well, you'd know more about that than I would. My wife's fancy runs to liquorice allsorts.' It would, thought Malone, and she'd follow them with a lemonade chaser. Fulmer picked up a label to which two tiny objects were affixed by scotch tape. 'What's this? Two chewed matches?'

'They were in an ashtray. The dead girl didn't look the sort who would chew matches.' Malone kept his voice dry, but behind him he heard Clements smother a sound that could have been either a sniffle or a snicker.

Fulmer glanced across at Clements, then looked back at Malone. 'All right. But don't get yourself confused by following up too many leads. Not if they're going to lead you away from where most of the evidence points.'

It's almost as if he *wants* Helidon to be the murderer, Malone thought. As if, by arresting a Cabinet Minister, he'd be proving his own integrity. Wowsers, with their interfering puritanical hatred of other people's pleasures, were bad enough. But a wowser cop could be dangerous.

He and Clements drove out to Double Bay, taking one of the chocolate boxes with them. Clements's eyes had now begun to run with his cold, so Malone drove. It was hot again today and the car radio told them that bushfires were raging on the city's outskirts; a firefighter or two might die before tonight and a dozen families lose their own homes. But that was someone else's misfortune: two cars went speeding past, surfboards strapped to the racks on their tops, heading for Bondi and escape from the heat. Malone's foot automatically trod down on the accelerator as the cars whizzed by him, but then almost at once he lifted it.

'Let 'em go,' he said to himself as much as to Clements. Then he looked at the unhappy Clements as the latter wiped his streaming eyes. 'Do you think anyone really cares whether we find out who killed Helga?'

'Well, *I* don't, right now,' said Clements.

'You want to knock off and go home?'

'Not yet. I'll see how I feel tonight.'

'You *do* care, you bastard. You'd hate it if I solved this thing on my own while you were home taking Aspros and hot lemon drinks.'

Clements blew his nose, then nodded. 'I guess so. Funny thing is, Helga was a whore and a possible blackmailer, but after last night at the Helidons' I'm a bit on her side.'

'You've just made me feel better,' said Malone.

'Why, were you getting a cold, too?'

'No, Just a dose of conscience.'

Clements sniffled. 'Don't pass it on to me. I got enough to worry me as it is.'

They found the candy store, a chi-chi shop that looked as if it, too, should have been decorated with a pink silk bow. They both went in, filling the tiny shop like a couple of bulls. The woman behind the glass display counter peered at them from a barricade of soft centres, nougat squares and a rainbow of ribbons. It was obvious that she expected either a hold-up or the shop to be wrecked: these were not the sort of men who bought expensive fancy chocolates for their girl friends.

Clements said, 'Do you have any menthol jubes?'

The woman blinked: he might have asked her for boiled lollies. 'In *here*?'

Malone laid down the box he had brought with him. 'Is this your only shop? You don't have another branch?'

The woman shook her head, still entrenched in her candy fort. 'The only one. Something is wrong?'

Malone showed her his badge, then produced the photos of Walter Helidon, Leslie Gibson and Mr and Mrs John

Savanna. He had had the photos copied and had snipped off the captions identifying the subjects; in an investigation you didn't have to take everyone into your confidence. 'Do you recognize any of those men? Did any of them ever buy chocolates here regularly?'

The woman almost collapsed with relief when she realized she was not going to be either held up or arrested; she grabbed the photos and peered at them as if Malone had just returned a long-lost family album to her. Then she put a long-nailed finger on the face of John Savanna. 'Yes. He comes in here regularly. At least once a week, sometimes twice. A very nice man, always buying for his wife. That is his wife? We should have more men like him.'

Malone noted the scold in her voice and determined to take some chocolates to Lisa. 'How long has he been coming here?'

'Oh, a long time. Maybe one year, maybe two.' She shrugged, more relaxed now. She looked at Malone with an appraising eye, half-coquette, half-saleswoman; she ignored Clements, a man who asked for menthol jubes. 'You should try our chocolates.' She picked one out of an open box on the shelf behind her, pushed it daintily in the direction of Malone's mouth, standing on her toes to do so. Malone, without thinking, opened his mouth and the woman popped the chocolate into it. 'Nice, eh? Your wife would like, yes?'

Out of the corner of his eye Malone saw Clements carefully studying the traffic in the street outside. He chewed on the chocolate, swallowed it and said, 'Sorry, my girl friend likes liquorice allsorts.'

That was even worse than menthol jubes. The woman sniffed silently, wondering why she had ever left Vienna for this barbaric outpost.

Malone said, 'When was this man last in here?'

'Not this week. Last week, maybe? Yes, I think so. Last week, at the beginning. But not since.'

Malone thanked her, debated whether he would buy a box of chocolates for Lisa, saw the prices on several boxes, changed his mind and left the shop, followed by Clements.

'It looked like feeding time at the zoo,' said Clements. 'Just as well the Bishop wasn't there to see that. Did you see her face when you said your girl friend liked liquorice allsorts? You stabbed her right in her plump tit then, mate. Well, where do we go from here? To Savanna's home or his office?'

Malone had checked on Savanna, learned that he ran a small studio called Olympus Film Productions. 'We'll take his office. He won't be at home at this hour, not unless he's apologizing to his missus for being such a two-timing bastard for the past year or two.'

Waterloo, where Olympus struggled like something from the early days of Hollywood, was only a few miles from Double Bay but a geological age away in social strata. Factories and warehouses occupied most of its area, turning it into a brick and corrugated-iron desert at the weekends; squat oases of terrace cottages stood with doors wide open inviting any breeze that might blow in from Botany Bay hidden to the south behind the wadis of alleys and treeless streets. The Falcon drew up opposite a terrace of cottages and the women-folk came to their doors, scrutinizing Malone and Clements with the frank, unhypocritical stares of natives who resented and suspected strangers. The women nodded to each other, recognizing coppers as plainly as if Malone and Clements had been in uniform, and anchored their hips and shoulders against door jambs, waiting for the action. Malone, feeling at home as much as if he were in Erskineville, got out of the car. Then he sniffed.

'Beer and meat pies. The national perfume.'

'I dunno that I'd like to be squashed in between them,' said Clements. 'You could go home every night smelling like the wharfies' annual picnic.'

But Savanna didn't smell like a waterside workers' picnic, even if his office smelled like the site for it. He wore some tangy perfume, either a hair dressing or an after-shave lotion that had remained on him perhaps longer than usual; whatever it was, it was plainly noticeable. Malone sat down opposite Savanna in the small office and looked at the producer carefully, thinking: this bloke wouldn't be out of place in his own commercials. Old Spice for the dark chin, Pantene Blue for the grey hair, the weekend farm somewhere up in Marlboro country; put a patch over one eye and he'd probably get a lifetime's free supply of shirts. But no hero of a TV commercial had ever looked as ill at ease as Savanna did, unless it was the feller with halitosis before he got the magic cure.

'Helga? I find it hard to believe—I mean, that she's dead. Like this. I thought she had gone back to Europe.' His hands were on the desk in front of him and he rubbed them together as if he were cold.

'Did you know her well?'

'Well, I *knew* her. She—she worked for me several times. She was a model, you know. I'm——' One hand left the other and strayed to the carved African head that doubled as a paper-weight. Malone noticed that he had big strong hands, with long supple fingers that picked up the heavy piece of stone as if it were no more than a piece of pumice. 'I'm sorry to hear of her death. Especially like—like this.'

'Was she a girl who would have made enemies?'

Savanna didn't answer at once, but stared at the carved head. Then he looked up. 'I don't know, to be honest. I suppose we all make enemies at some time in our lives. Most of us just never recognize them, that's all. She could have had enemies. I don't know what sort of life she led before she came out here from Germany.'

Malone told him what sort of life she had led in Hamburg. One eyebrow went up, but he showed no real surprise. 'She certainly disguised it pretty well. She always seemed to me a perfect lady—I just wish some of our other actresses and models knew how to behave as well.'

'How did she behave when you were alone with her, Mr Savanna?'

The long fingers tightened on the stone head and Malone prepared to duck. Even Clements sat up straight at the blunt-ness of the question. 'What's that supposed to mean, Sergeant?'

'Chocolates. You've been taking her chocolates once or twice a week for at least twelve months.'

Savanna put down the head, reached for a packet of cigarettes lying on the desk. He took out a cigarette and Malone waited to see how he would light it; but he reached into his pocket and took out a lighter instead of a box of matches. Malone watched him carefully, recognized the playing for time; but Savanna wasn't as good at the game as Helidon had been. The strong fingers, playing with the lighter, now looked suddenly as fragile as twigs.

'You chaps don't miss much, do you?'

'We try not to.' He had begun to notice other things about Savanna: the worn cuffs of the silk shirt, the cuff-links that did not match. Things looked as if they might not be going too well for the producer: the Pantene Blue being used a little more sparingly, the Marlboro being smoked a little closer to the cork tip: had Helga, too, started to prove a bit too expensive?

'I read about that girl being found down at the Opera House. I mean I glanced at it—I don't usually follow murder cases——' He glanced at them. 'Does that make me sound callous of other people's tragedies?'

'No,' said Malone, having already decided that Savanna, whatever his faults, was not callous. 'Most people are not interested in murder, unless it's a particularly juicy one.'

'If you'd described this one as a juicy one—I mean, you saw the tattoos on her behind? Well, if that had been mentioned, I'd have known at once it was Helga.'

'We're still a bit strait-laced,' said Malone. 'If we'd announced that to the papers and they had printed it, we'd have had questions in Parliament about bounds of decency and all that. The public mustn't be offended. Would you have come to us and identified Miss Brand if we had printed that description?'

Savanna puffed on his cigarette. 'That's a leading question, isn't it? Am I entitled to any warning—you know, anything I may say et cetera?'

'If you wish,' said Malone. 'I must warn you anything you may say et cetera.'

'Thank you,' said Savanna, and managed a smile. 'No, Sergeant, I probably wouldn't have come near you. I'm a married man and my wife doesn't know anything about Helga. It's not that I would be afraid of her if she found out —I'd just rather not—not hurt her.'

'You do admit you've been seeing Helga regularly?'

'Yes, I've been seeing her on a—non-professional basis, if you like to call it that.' To Malone's surprise, Savanna suddenly looked relieved at the confession; he actually sat up straighter, seemed to square his shoulders. 'That's why I'm, well, upset by what you've told me. About her being—murdered, I mean.'

'When did you last see her?'

'Last Friday week.'

'You're very sure of the day, aren't you?'

'I——' Savanna did not look the sort of man who would ever be embarrassed, but that was what his smile suggested. 'Those were my days—my visiting days, if you like. Tuesdays and Fridays.'

'You visited her last Monday week,' said Malone.

Savanna's hand strayed to the carved head again, but Clements leant across and moved it out of his reach. Savanna looked up in surprise, then gave a half-cough, half-laugh. 'Why did——? Were you expecting me to throw it at you?'

Clements glanced at Malone first, then said, 'You never know. We went to question an old lady a coupla weeks ago and she threw a knife at us. And she was only wanted for busting a neighbour's window, not for murder.'

Savanna asked very evenly, 'Am I wanted for murder?'

Clements glanced at Malone again. That's right, Russ, the latter thought, leave the hard ones to me. 'Nobody's wanted yet, Mr Savanna. Except the man who killed her.'

'Do you think I killed her?' The phone on his desk rang and he picked it up. 'Yes? No, Betty, I can't take any calls right now. Tell them I'll call them back.' He listened to the girl on the phone for a moment, then looked at Malone. 'This is an important one, a contract I've been trying to get for weeks.'

'How long will it take?'

'Ten, fifteen minutes perhaps.'

Malone looked around the shabby office, sighed, then looked back at Savanna. 'Sorry, Mr Savanna. Tell 'em you'll call back. Tell them you have another important client here, if you like.'

Savanna bit his lip, then he nodded, spoke to the girl and hung up the phone. 'I saw you looking around the office.

You're not very impressed, are you?' Malone hesitated, then shook his head. 'Six months ago I wouldn't have told anyone this. But now I don't care any more. I'm going bankrupt. That contract'—he nodded at the phone—'might have staved off the evil day.'

'I'm sorry. I didn't come here to make sure you'd go bankrupt. But you'll have to make up your mind what's more important. Getting a contract or telling the truth about you and Helga Brand.'

Savanna stubbed out his half-smoked cigarette. 'Put like that—all right, what do you want to know?'

'Did you visit her last Monday week?'

Savanna's eyes flickered for a moment, as if he were trying to get something into focus: Malone, the question, perhaps even a memory or an alibi. 'No. I told you, Tuesdays and Fridays were my days. God, that sounds bloody, doesn't it? Makes her sound like a stud mare. She wasn't that,' he said, and his voice softened a little. 'At least, I didn't think so.'

Malone let a few moments of silence pass; Clements smothered a sniffle. Malone had his own idea of what sort of girl Helga had been, but he knew that some men could love a whore with the blind adoration of someone loving a saint. Savanna might not have loved Helga, but it was obvious that he had felt a long way from hating her. If he had loved her, that would have given him a reason for killing her: to keep her from the other men who saw her on the other days of the week. 'What did you do that day? Where were you?'

Savanna seemed to be searching his memory. 'I—I was here at the office. I worked back.'

'Till what time?'

'I'm not sure. Six, six-thirty.'

Malone nodded to Clements. 'Get the secretary in here, Russ.'

Savanna sat silent as Clements ushered in the secretary. She was a small, neat brunette in a mini-skirt and a sleeveless blouse that exposed the start of the swell of her bosom. Clements blew his nose, peering at her over the mask of his handkerchief. Malone thought, I don't know how I could concentrate if they had birds like this working as secretaries at

Y Division. She was in her twenties, but gave the paradoxical impression of being a very experienced sixteen-year-old. But her experience did not include being questioned by detectives; her worried puzzlement only seemed to accentuate her young look. 'Mr Savanna can't remember what time he left the office last Monday week. Would you have any idea?'

The girl looked at Savanna, was even more worried and puzzled by the look of anguish on his face. 'I—I'm not sure. Is this something serious, Mr Savanna?'

Savanna nodded. 'I'm afraid it is, Betty. It doesn't matter. I've remembered what time I left here. You may go, Betty.'

'Just a moment,' said Malone. 'What time did Mr Savanna leave here, Betty?'

The girl glanced at Savanna again, then looked back at Malone. 'It was about three o'clock, I think. He—he was going around some of the advertising agencies.'

Malone thanked her and after another look at Savanna, a pleading one as if she were asking him to forgive her if she had said the wrong thing, the girl went out of the office. Malone waited till the door closed behind her, then said, 'You didn't go to any advertising agencies, did you?' Savanna shook his head. 'Where did you go?'

'I'm afraid that's something I'm not going to tell you.' There was no antagonism in Savanna's voice, nor even emphasis; Malone recognized the dispiritedness, the almost melancholy weariness creeping over the man. When they reached that stage it was hardest of all to get any information out of them; the threat of arrest meant nothing, as if it were almost some sort of escape. 'All I'll say is, I didn't see Helga. I went to her place, I'll admit that. I don't know what the time was, maybe half-past four or five. But she didn't answer the door and I left.'

'Did you have a key?'

Savanna half-shook his head, then changed his mind. 'Yes.' He took a key-ring out of his pocket, unhooked a key and dropped it on the desk. 'You may as well have it. I shan't need it again.'

'Why didn't you use it to enter the flat when you got no answer? Did you always wait for her to open the door?'

'No. But that was a Monday.' He ran his hand across his

cheek; despite his grey hair and his air of sophistication he looked young and embarrassed; principles did not sit well on him. 'It may sound stupid to you, but I just decided I'd be a gentleman, that I wouldn't butt in on her if there was someone else there.'

'It doesn't sound stupid. A couple of policemen have been known to be gentlemen. Constable Clements is one.'

Clements looked pleased and surprised by the compliment; he sniffed again and took out his handkerchief. Savanna bowed his head. 'Touché, Sergeant.'

'What sort of girl was Helga? I mean apart from her—profession?'

Savanna didn't reply at once: it was as if he had never really thought of Helga having a profession. 'Well, she was beautiful. But then you must have seen that? Or was she——'

Spare him the details, Malone thought. 'No, we could see she had looks.'

Savanna looked relieved. 'I'm glad she wasn't too—too knocked about. I don't think she was vain, not like some women, but she was careful of her appearance. She never looked—well, like a tramp. She was always neat and—tidy, I suppose. She was pretty houseproud, which sometimes didn't seem to go with—well, with what else she offered, if you know what I mean.' Suddenly he shook his head, like a man shaking water from his eyes. 'Christ, I hate talking about her like this! It's like dissecting a corpse.'

'That's what she is now,' said Malone, not unkindly. 'And we're trying to find out who made her one. You still won't tell us where you were from three o'clock, when you left here, till you went to Helga's flat?' Savanna shook his head. 'Would your wife be able to help us?'

Savanna sat up. 'Don't bring her into this, please.'

'Does your wife know about Helga?'

'No.'

'Those missing two hours—I don't like asking this, Mr Savanna, but is there another woman besides Helga?'

'What sort of character do you think I am?' His indignation was genuine; he was too weary for play-acting.

'I asked a question, Mr Savanna. I didn't put an opinion.'

'It amounted to the same thing.'

I've lost this little sparring match, Malone thought: I've let him work out his answer. 'Did you spend the time with another girl?'

'No,' said Savanna, but his emphasis was just a little too forced.

Malone switched to another tack. 'Do you know Walter Helidon?'

Savanna's brow creased. 'Helidon? You mean the Cabinet Minister? No, never met him. Why?'

'Helga was going into business with him. Some sort of boutique.'

'She never mentioned it to me.'

'Maybe she was keeping it as a surprise for you. Do you know Leslie Gibson?' That's another surprise for you. He saw Savanna's eyes widen for just a moment, the hand quiver as it came up to smooth down the already smooth grey hair.

'He's my brother-in-law. Don't tell me he knew her, too?'

2

'I never even heard of her,' said Gibson, harshly but unworriedly. 'And I don't appreciate you coming here to question me about her.'

'We tried to get you at your office, but your secretary said you wouldn't be in again today.' Malone's own voice was just as harsh; he did not like this sour old man who looked like an aged and vicious parrot, one with a bit of eaglehawk in him. He knew of Gibson's reputation for ruthlessness and this first meeting with the man only confirmed what Malone had expected. As with the Helidons there was going to be no sympathy for the dead Helga here. 'We have to do our work where and when we can, Mr. Gibson.'

Clements had been delighted when they had failed to contact Gibson at his office and had had to come out here to the penthouse flat on top of the tall block at the end of Point Piper. As they had ridden up in the smooth, silent, walnut-panelled lift he had said, 'I remember when he bought this unit. A hundred and eighty thousand dollars he's supposed to have paid for it. If I had that sorta money I don't think I'd care what people thought about me.'

'You mean as a cop? I think even the Commissioner might come over for a beer with you. You'd be the only cop living in this neck of the woods.'

Point Piper was an arm pushing out into the harbour east of the city proper. A recent survey, one of those so popular with that new breed of sociologists, the market research men, newspaper circulation managers and professional burglars, had placed the small peninsula at the very top of the residential status areas; the same survey had shown Malone's home suburb, Erskineville, down at the bottom. The area had accepted its rating with equanimity though with some ruffled surprise, as if it could not understand why it should have been included in any rating at all: it was rather like a London survey rating Buckingham Palace as a desirable residence. Expensive houses, some of them old and garnished with Victorian bad taste, and expensive home units, all of them new and not all of them in good taste, clung to the ridge that formed the spine of the Point. To the west was a splendid view of the city and the Harbour Bridge; to the east was a view across Rose Bay to Vaucluse, number two in the status areas; the residents need never be offended by a sight worse than a view of each other. At one time it had been as exclusive as one of the city's more select clubs, but over the past ten years many of its residents had decided that money had an exclusivity all its own and had sold their old homes to developers, who had knocked down the houses and replaced them with towering blocks of co-operatively-owned flats. In Malone's childhood and youth Australians had been reared to the idea that flats were only for renting; when the developers came to sell the flats they had built a new name had to be coined for them: home units. People who had been regular visitors to the Fair Rents Court when they had been renting flats, now rushed out to pay ransom prices for home units. The developers, dedicated to desecration, continuing the spoiling of the harbour foreshores that had been started by their ancestors a hundred years before, moved on and Point Piper became architecturally indistinguishable from any other better-class residential area of Sydney. Yet the Point still had its own aura, a suggestion in the air that still smelled of money, old money that still had value, pounds as distinct from the new dollars. It was Grafter Gibson's money that had allowed him to find his slot in the tall filing cabinet that was called Eureka Towers.

Eureka Towers was at the very end of the Point and the Gibson flat was at the very top of the block. Clements kept sneaking a look out through the wide windows at the city sky-line and the Bridge silhouetted against a salmon sky. Then he would glance covertly around at the luxurious room in which they sat.

'You're gunna give your eyeballs a hernia,' said Gibson. 'Get up and have a good look.'

Clements grinned, sniffled, stood up and began to move about the room. Gibson gazed at him as if to make sure that Clements was not going to put some of the ornaments in his pocket, then he looked back at Malone. 'You upset the wife when you came to the door and said you were police. We've never had a demon come to our door, not in all our married life.'

'You've been lucky then,' said Malone, and saw the old man stiffen. 'I mean, we often have to knock on doors to bring bad news. The uniformed police, I mean. News of an accident, a death, something like that. They never pick us to bring the good news. A lottery win, for instance.'

'Are you looking for sympathy?'

'Would we get it?' I'm not going to let this old bastard push me around.

Gibson grunted, recognizing this detective had an independence of his own. 'All right, what about this girl? Why come to me about her?'

Malone told him about finding the photos of him and Mrs Gibson in the manilla folder in Helga Brand's flat. 'We understand your brother-in-law, Mr Savanna, knew her.'

Gibson's face showed a momentary flicker of distaste. 'He might have. He gets around a bit. But I've never met any of his —interests. Certainly not this girl. I dunno her from a bar of soap.'

'Possibly you didn't *meet* her. But did she ever phone or write you?'

Gibson studied Malone, aware now that this man knew how to detect the split hairs in an answer. He did not lose his air of antagonism, but a gleam came into his eyes, as if he welcomed this opportunity of fencing with an opponent. 'Why would she do that?'

'We think she might have been in the blackmail game.'

Gibson blew out as if spitting something off his thin lips.

'You're an insulting bastard, Sergeant. Do you blokes ever pick each other up for insulting behaviour?'

'We don't have to,' said Malone. 'We get our monthly quota just picking up civilians.'

The gleam brightened in Gibson's eyes; with a little effort he might allow himself to enjoy this encounter. 'What makes you think this girl would have something on me so's she could put the bite on me?'

'I'm not suggesting she had anything. I'm just trying to find out why she had several photos of you and your wife in a file.'

'Were ours the only photos?'

'No.'

'Who else's?'

Malone shook his head. 'You really don't expect me to tell you that.'

Gibson sat still in his chair, his small body rigid, only his eyes moving as he looked at the two detectives. Clements was standing by the big window, his back to the view of the city now nailed against the sky by the copper rivets of its lights. Malone sat on a couch, a long silk-and-tweed upholstered affair that might have cost as much as half his year's salary. Even while he had been questioning Gibson he had been taking in the luxury of their surroundings. The Helidon home had had its suggestion of wealth, but this was unmistakably richer, though he was too unsophisticated in such matters to be able to explain the difference. Perhaps it was the panelling of the walls, or the thick Persian carpet, or the three paintings on the wall, any one of which could have been by an Old Master. Gibson lived in a penthouse, the symbol of ultra-modern living, yet he had surrounded himself with an interior that suggested a much older, more gracious time. Yet, and Malone could not explain the feeling to himself, there was the impression that, though this was Gibson's home, he was not at home here. His real home was somewhere else, back in the almost forgotten geography of his early life. Was there an Erskineville in his beginning, too?

At last Gibson said, 'And that's all you have? The photos? No mention of my name, nothing like that?'

'No.'

Gibson stood up. 'That's it, then. Come back when you've got something more. But not before.'

Malone rose, keeping his temper in check. 'We'll come back if we have to, Mr Gibson. Our apologies to Mrs Gibson if we upset her. But we don't solve murder cases if we worry about upsetting people. Helga Brand was probably upset when who-ever killed her wrapped his mitts round her throat.'

Gibson grunted, then looked at Clements, who was taking a farewell look around the room. 'See anything you like?'

'The lot,' said Clements candidly.

Malone had paused in front of one of the paintings. 'Who's that by?'

'Canaletto,' said Gibson, and for the first time showed some interest in Malone as a person instead of as a policeman. 'You know anything about painting?'

'Nothing. But I saw one like it in the National Gallery in London. One of the Grand Canal in Venice.'

'London, eh? That was a bit off your beat, wasn't it?'

'I went there for a holiday. As a change from ———.' He named one of the beach villages not far from Sydney where Al Capp would have found more inspiration than Canaletto.

Gibson let them out of the flat, closing the front door on them before they were in the lift. He walked back into the big living-room as his wife came out from the television den where she had retreated when the two policemen had arrived. She was dressed in a silk shirt and silk slacks that did nothing for her but hide her nakedness. Glenda Gibson was one of those unfortun-ate women who had begun too late in life to spend money on her clothes; any figure and any flair she might have had were lost in the years when finances and not fashion had dictated what she should wear; it had been only in the last ten years that she had begun to appreciate just how much her husband was worth. She went now to the most expensive French shop in Sydney, but the effect only suggested Racine recited in a broad Australian accent.

'What did they want, hon?'

'Nothing,' said Gibson off-handedly, moving towards his study.

'It wasn't nothing,' said Glenda. 'I was listening. They mentioned a girl who'd been murdered. And some photos of us. Les——?'

He stopped, came back and took her hand. 'Love, there's nothing to worry about. The girl must've been a crank or something. There wasn't just us, there were other people's pictures, too. But it doesn't concern us, take my word for it.'

She looked at him with the anxiety that only real love can generate. 'Les, don't get into any trouble. Not now. It's too late.'

He didn't ask her what she meant: he knew. At sixty-eight years of age, everything was too late. He leant forward and kissed her; her cheek felt like rice paper beneath his lips. 'All our trouble is behind us. Believe me, love. This is nothing.'

She said nothing, but she had noticed the trembling in the hand that held hers. She looked after him as he went on into the study. He's getting so small, she thought, so small and old. She prayed for him every night, but tonight she would pray longer and harder. She knew there was no one else in the world who would pray for him and that hurt her more than she would ever let him know. There was a bitter loneliness about loving a man whom no one else loved.

Twenty-two storeys below, Malone and Clements came out of the building and walked across to their car. Some people were arriving for a cocktail party in one of the flats. The women swept by the two policemen on a current of perfume and gay expectation; the men followed in their wake with lemming-like resignation. Clements glanced back at them.

'I think I might come back and see old Grafter, see if he could build my bank balance into a decent holding. Say half a million. Then I think I'd move in here. At heart I guess I must be a plutocrat. That's why I can't lose on the ponies or the dogs. Money just naturally gravitates to me.'

'Start thinking like that and it'll start going the other way. But you can have your little chat with Gibson when we come to see him the next time.'

'We're coming back?' There was no surprise in Clements's voice; he had been looking at the luxury that had surrounded them, but he had missed nothing of the reason for their being there. 'When?'

'I'm not sure yet. He may never have met Helga, but he knows something about her. Otherwise he wouldn't have asked if we had anything else on him other than the photos. Innocent men don't ask those sort of questions. They take their innocence for granted.'

'Well, if he was mixed up in her murder, then you were right. About the two men being in it. Old Grafter couldn't have got her from her flat down to the Opera House on his own. So who else do we look for?'

'The bloke who chewed those matches.'

They drove back to the city on the steel tide of traffic moving in for the night's entertainment. They climbed the hill to King's Cross, past the raw eczema of neon, past the girls coming out to begin their night's work. Malone looked out at them, wondering how many of them would finish up as Helga Brand had. The funny thing was, he had never met a pro who had felt sorry for herself. He wondered how Helga had felt on the last night of her life.

CHAPTER EIGHT

I

Monday, December 2

HELGA BRAND chose another chocolate from the box beside her, bit into it, then had a moment of doubt. She looked at herself in the mirror across the room, shrugged and ate the chocolate. She had put on a little weight over the past month, but it did not matter; there would be time to take it off before she got to München. And if German men were as they had been when she had left Hamburg six years ago, they wouldn't mind some plumpness in the right places on a girl. Though in those days she had been dealing with men lower down the social scale than those she was aiming at when she got to München.

She felt a thrill of anticipation and for a few moments was lost in contemplation of what her life would be like in the Bavarian capital. It would be fun to get back to a *real* city after the collection of suburbs that was Sydney. And the German men, especially the Bavarians, though they might be unsubtle, were at least lavish in their treatment of women who gave them what they wanted. Which was more than the *knauserig* Australians, the stingy ones, were.

She looked around the comfortable flat. She had always had a passion for neatness and taste and it showed in what she had chosen to surround herself with. The living-room was the sort of room where most men would be at ease; she had learned at an early age that the average business man preferred his eroticism in the bedroom. The pictures on the walls showed her nostalgia for her homeland; the biggest was a photograph of the Aussenalster, the lake glittering in an August sun and the yachts poised like birds about to take flight. The books on the nest of shelves in one corner were mostly popular novels, but there were also half a dozen picture books of Germany. There was nothing to remind her either of the Reeperbahn or the farm near Hanover: her mementoes were illusions as much as anything else, but she was practical enough to recognize them as such.

She continued to look around the room and allowed herself another illusion, the fantasy of what would surround her in Germany if she were, as she was here in Sydney, the mistress of both a Cabinet Minister and a film producer. It must be the puritan that still hung about in the corners of even the most libertine Australian, the reluctance to spend extravagantly on anything sinful. A whore's life could be profitable in Australia, but never that of a mistress.

She had never liked the whore's life on the Reeperbahn. She had not run away from the farm and gone to Hamburg to be a prostitute; but there had been no great moral battle when a travelling salesman at the hotel where she had worked as a chambermaid had offered her twenty marks after she had slept with him one night. She had been fifteen then but had looked eighteen; and she had found the experience neither frightening nor revolting. The journey to the brothel on the Reeperbahn had been both quick and gradual, almost a night-by-night progress. The next four years had bred a disgust for men and an early acceptance of the thought that she could never love a man; but she had known no other way of earning so much money: and having money, lots of it, was her main aim in life. She had fled to Australia when one of her regular customers had threatened to cut her up because she had been stealing money from him. She had found no trouble in getting work as a model when she had arrived in Sydney; the local photographers were always impressed with any girl who had had overseas experience. But their fees were not high and after a year or so she had started looking around for other sources of income. There had been several men before she had found Jack Savanna and Walter Helidon. She smiled now as she thought of them, the big-time spenders of pennies.

She took another chocolate, then picked up the large manilla folder with its file of newspaper clippings. She had started the collection almost six months ago when she had first thought of going back to Germany. There had been no definite thought in her mind of how to use the collection or even that she would; she had begun to put the pictures and clippings aside for a rainy day, in much the same way as her farmer father had taught her to bring home firewood, even in summer, against the possibility of an early winter. She had always been a practical girl, despite her extravagance, though never a calculating one: at least not till this past week. If she had been calculating at an earlier age she would have done better for herself than the brothel; and she would certainly never have listened to the suggestion of Gruen, the brothel owner, and had those embarrassing marks tattooed on her bottom. She would have those removed as soon as she got back to Germany. But not in München. In Essen or Dortmund, some city she would not be likely to visit again. She had left one identity behind her on the farm near Hanover, another in Hamburg, and she would leave Helga Brand in Sydney. An entirely new girl, Helga? (she must start dreaming up a new attractive surname), would arrive in München to begin a new, rich life. She turned over the collection of photos and clippings, her passport to the new life, and reached for a third chocolate.

Then she heard the key in the lock. She sat up at once, pushed the manilla folder under the heavy armchair in which she sat, and looked towards the small entrance hall as Walter Helidon came in and closed the front door behind him. The weather had been up and down in its temperature the past few days and today was another warm day. Walter was sweating and she felt repelled as she always did, though she had never let him know.

She got up, pulling down her skirt. Usually when Helidon arrived she was waiting for him in a negligée or a brief mini-skirt and blouse: he was a man who asked for the obvious in sexy attractiveness. But this afternoon she had dressed as for a business interview; after all she had invited him to come to talk business. She glanced at herself in the mirror, at the pale blue dress with the white collar and cuffs, and thought: I could be his secretary.

'Darling,' she said, and smiled.

'What's the smile for?'

'I was thinking I could be your secretary. But then she would not call you *darling*. Or would she?'

'I'm in no mood for jokes.' Helidon walked across to the sideboard against one wall and poured himself a stiff gin-and-tonic. He looked at her, but she shook her head. He took a sip of the drink, savoured it, nodded, then sat down in the chair she had just vacated. 'We're going to have a straight talk, Helga. No mucking around, understand?'

'Can politicians talk straight, darling?' She ran her fingers lightly over the top of his head as she passed him and sat down opposite him. 'I'm joking, Walter. I'll stop it. Talk straight. Did you bring the cheque?'

He took another sip of his drink, then wiped his face with the silk handkerchief he took from his pocket. He had not removed his jacket, as if he, too, saw this only as a business talk: he was going to avoid looking at home. 'No. Not the twenty thousand.'

'How much, then?' She felt a momentary stab of angry disappointment, but her face showed nothing.

'You shouldn't have gone to see my wife, Helga. I don't say I'd have given you the twenty thousand, that's a ridiculous amount, no man would be that foolish——'

'Not foolish,' she said. 'Generous. There are some generous men in the world.'

'Not in this city. Not like that,' he said, and there was almost a note of pride in his voice, as if Sydney men who kept mistresses were good businessmen who kept prices down.

'No,' she said, but he missed the irony in *her* voice.

'If you hadn't gone to see my wife,' he continued, 'I could have done something for you. For this boutique, I mean.' She had forgotten her original excuse for asking for the money and he stopped when he saw the blank look on her face. 'That was what you wanted it for, wasn't it?'

'Yes,' she said, putting the dream of München out of her mind for the time being. She might have to play her cards differently to get the money out of him and already she was beginning to shuffle the pack in her mind.

'I thought you'd have known better, Helga. I mean, than to

137

go and see my wife. Don't you know most wives won't pay to keep their husband's names out of the paper? Would I have been coming to see you these past two years if my wife was the sort who loved me enough to pay twenty thousand dollars to keep my name out of a scandal?'

Helga smiled. 'I think I *do* know women, darling. I went to see your wife because I thought she would pay to keep *her* name out of the newspapers. And I think she will, once she realizes I am in earnest.'

Helidon sipped his drink, composed his face into his Cabinet Minister's image, the one of decision. 'I've been thinking. It would be a good idea, a very good idea indeed, if you left Sydney and went back to Germany. Or anywhere you want to go.'

'Why do you think that would be a good idea?' She kept her voice expressionless, putting on no face at all.

He evaded her question: he was an old hand at such a practice. 'I'll give you your air fare to wherever you like to go. In fact I already have it here.' He took a cheque from his pocket. 'It's for a thousand dollars, made out to Helga Brand Proprietary Limited.' He smiled, trying to improve the atmosphere between them; but it was his politician's smile and she recognized it. 'That was a nice touch, a very nice touch indeed. My wife was quite impressed by it.'

'You mean she *liked* it?'

'Well, not exactly liked it, no. She thought it showed you were—business-like.'

'I think the word she would have used was calculating, Walter,' she said, and from the expression on his face she knew she had been close in her guess. 'A calculating bitch? I don't underestimate your wife. But you seem to be under-estimating me.' He looked puzzled. 'Thinking you could buy me off with a thousand dollars!'

'But that wasn't all of it,' he protested, hurt that she should think he was stingy; didn't he have the reputation at the Assembly of being the first always to pick up the tab for a lunch or drinks? 'I'll give you another'—he thought quickly: how much would be reasonable?—'two thousand dollars. Three thousand all told. You don't have to use the thousand dollars for air fare, if you don't want to go back there. You can go to Melbourne, Perth, anywhere you like. Just so long as you get out of Sydney. And you'll have something to get you started in your boutique wherever you want to open it. Go to Perth—they wouldn't know anything about *real* fashion'—he spoke with the Easterner's disregard of anything west of the Blue Mountains—'there's a lot of money there now——'

She leaned forward, hating him now for his meanness, for his bland assumption that she could be bought cheaply, for all the boredom she had felt with him over the time she had known him. He was a little man, a mediocrity who thought small, an *Australian*: suddenly she hated all Australians, the whole lucky country as they called themselves. She hungered to be back among her own people whose mentality she understood: 'It isn't going to be as easy as that for you, Mr Helidon!' Her voice became guttural, harsh: this was a different sort of passion from the one that made her speak German in bed. She suddenly swept into a torrent of her own language, hurling obscenities at him that he did not understand; she grabbed the cheque from him, ripped it into small pieces, threw it at him, the confetti of abuse. He sat back in his chair, brushing the pieces of cheque from him as if she had showered him with dirt, almost cowering before her fury; the foreign language confused him, made her more threatening because he did not understand her. Then she stood up, struggled to regain control of herself, spoke in English again: 'Get out! Don't come back till you bring me what I've asked for! And I want it by tomorrow night! Now get out!'

He was sweating profusely as he stood up; he took off his glasses as they began to mist up. He peered at her, trying to match her anger with his own; but all at once he was afraid, sensing a recklessness in her temper that might lead to disaster. Abruptly he made up his mind to give her all she asked for. 'All right, you'll get it!' He tried for some fury in his own voice, to show that she had not frightened him into giving way. 'I don't have another cheque on me. I'll be back tomorrow night——' He struggled for some sarcasm, anything to salvage something from her victory over him: 'That is, if you don't

mind me coming on a day that isn't mine? It'll be Tuesday—
I'm a Monday man——'

She smiled at once, moved closer to him but didn't make
the mistake of trying to kiss him: she was too shrewd to be
coy at a moment like this. She moved just close enough to
him to let him smell her perfume, revive the memories, if only
in his blood, of what he had once had, of what, in effect, he
was paying for.

'*Liebling*, I'm glad it's going to be this way. I didn't want
us to part bad friends—we've been *good* friends too long.
Tomorrow evening will be fine——' Jack Savanna would not
be back, not after their last meeting: her Tuesday and Friday
man was gone forever. He would be the one she would miss,
the only man to whom she had ever said *Ich liebe dich* and
almost meant it. 'I'll be here. Alone.'

Helidon had caught the smell of her perfume; he knew that
something he had enjoyed was now over and he felt a physical
twinge of regret. He stifled a sigh, nodded, put on his dark
glasses and went out of the flat. Helga closed the door, locked
it and walked to the window and looked out. A minute passed,
then Helidon appeared on the pavement below, walking with
that quick, suspicious walk that always amused her: he *looked*
like a man hurrying away from an hour or so with his mistress:
the dark glasses only added to the effect. Poor Walter, always
afraid of being found out. But he had been found out, she
guessed, years ago: by his wife, by herself, by his political
opponents: a man who had only one talent: ambition.

She turned away from the window, saw the torn-up cheque
scattered on the floor. Perhaps she had been hasty doing that;
at least it would have been a deposit on what he was going to
pay her. But in the event she had done the right thing; it had
proved to Walter that at least *she* wasn't thinking small; he
would be back tomorrow with the full twenty thousand.
Meanwhile, tomorrow morning she would go and see Mr
Leslie Gibson about the hundred thousand. That might be
more difficult, but he, too, had a wife who would probably
pay to keep her name out of the newspapers. A woman who
was a vice-president of the Daughters of Mary, who figured
three times in the manilla folder in photographs with the

Archbishop, who had had an audience with the Pope, wouldn't want her husband being exposed as connected, however remotely, with drug smuggling.

She went out to the kitchen, got a dustpan and small broom, came back, swept up the pieces of the cheque and dumped them in the waste-paper basket. She did it with all the neat efficiency of a *hausfrau*; her mother had trained her well, if for the wrong profession. Then she went into the bedroom, took off her dress and underwear, put on the green silk dressing-gown and went back into the living-room. She sat down, chose a chocolate from the box, then picked up the small leather-covered diary on the table beside the chair. She opened it and with a ballpoint pen made an entry: *Walter came this afternoon. Is coming back with the money.* She looked at it with satisfaction; then she glanced idly at the entries, some just one line, others more detailed, for other days. The entry for the previous Friday disturbed her: *Had argument with Jack.* She would call him before she left Sydney, say good-bye and hope that there would be no bitterness.

Sunk in a mood of sweet despondency, she jerked her head up in surprise when the doorbell rang. Stuffing the diary into the pocket of her dressing-gown, she got up and went to the door. She pulled back the lock, opened the door, expecting to find Helidon there.

Despite the dark glasses the woman wore, she recognized her at once. 'Why. Mrs Helidon! This *is* a surprise——'

2

Savanna pushed open the glass door to the entrance to Helga's block of flats and slowly began to climb the stairs. As with his visit to Gibson, he was not quite sure why he had come to see Helga; it certainly wasn't that he expected any sex with her. He was not even sure that she would let him into the flat; this was Monday, not his day for visiting her. Perhaps it was his day for saying good-bye: he had just said good-bye to Silver, forever and after twenty-two years of foolishly hoping . . .

'You know,' he had said as they had sat in the lounge of

the Wentworth looking out through the tall glass walls at the breeze rocking the umbrellas in the outdoor garden area, 'I've never really thought of us as being divorced. Separated, yes. But not divorced.'

'That's foolish, Jack. Or worse.' She was dressed in a cinnamon linen dress that set off the golden tan of her arms and the pale silver of her hair; other men in the room besides Savanna were looking at her, none of them guessing her true age. There was a youthfulness to her smile that excused the small wrinkles that appeared around her eyes when she did smile; and her bare arms, still firm, showed none of the dimples that so often gave away a woman's age. 'Separated couples don't have another spouse each—I love that word, spouse—and children. You have your daughter and I have my four kids. We're divorced, Jack, make no mistake about it.'

'I didn't mean it in that way, the legal way.' He sat back in his chair, cradling his drink in his big hands. He looked at her with careful tenderness, not wanting to offend her. 'I'm still in love with you, you know that.'

She did not deny that she might know it. She stirred her Tom Collins, the same sort of drink he had ordered for her when they had first met twenty-seven years ago. He had suggested it this time when the waiter had come to take their order and, smiling, she had agreed. She was not afraid of sentiment, so long as he did not try to take it too far. He would be taking it too far if he kept on with this line of talk: 'I think we'd better change the subject, Jack.'

A man sat at a nearby table morosely staring into his beer. A red-haired woman joined him, obviously having just come from the ladies' room, and he looked up and said, 'Geez, you were long enough! I thought you'd fell in.'

'Drop your voice,' said the woman, pulling dignity about her like a tattered shawl. 'This isn't the Leagues Club.'

Savanna and Silver looked at each other and smiled. They had not been married to each other long enough for their relationship ever to have reached the stage where they had become just the spare parts of each other's life. The break, when it had come, had been swift and sudden.

'Whatever happened to us?' He continued to look carefully

at her, as if trying to trace in her face all the years of her that he had missed. She's still beautiful, he thought. She must be forty-eight or nine, but she still leaves every other woman in this room for dead. Her figure was still good, perhaps a trifle fuller in the bosom and round the hips, but he didn't mind that. She had not entirely escaped the erosion of time, but you had to look hard, cruelly, to notice the faint thinning of the lips (like roses drying out, he thought; the Australian sun attacked so many women that way) and the tendons beginning to show through on the backs of her hands. She could still move him more than any woman he had ever met.

'We went into all that a long time ago,' she said, ignoring her own advice to change the subject. She was safe with him so long as they did not move out of the hotel lounge. She had been in her bedroom when he had called from the reception desk and she had been on the point of asking him to come up. Then something had warned her, not against him but against herself; and she had told him she would meet him in the lounge. 'Perhaps I didn't have enough patience in those days.'

He remembered his irresponsibility, his inability to settle down after the war. 'Do you have patience now?'

'You learn it living in the country. You have to, that's if you don't want to go off your head. We live by the seasons up there, Jack, not by the clock. And you come to respect them —the seasons, I mean.' That's the only thing you and Josie have in common, he thought. Josie's garden, her part-substitute for himself, had made Josie aware of the seasons. 'I wasn't brought up to bush life, but now I love it. Each time I come down to the city, I can't get back to the property soon enough.'

Her husband, Claude Carson, ran a sheep and stud cattle property about two hundred miles north-west of Sydney. Savanna had never met him but had seen photos of him in newspapers and farm magazines: a tall bony man, eyes squinting beneath the brim of his pork-pie hat, sun cancers showing like freckles on his lean cheeks: he was almost the archetype of the man on the land. 'It's none of my business— no, it *is* my business. Are you happy with Carson?'

143

'Why is it your business?' she said, knowing the danger she was exposing herself to by asking the question.

'Your happiness is my business.'

'Do you mean that, Jack?' she asked, thinking he sounded too glib. But he nodded and she felt ashamed for doubting his sincerity. 'Yes, I am happy with him. He's a good man and a wonderful father. The kids adore him.'

'Do you?'

'*That* is my business. Don't torture yourself, Jack. I'm happy with Claude and that's all you need to know.' She put down her glass and stood up. It was time to go; once again she felt the warning against herself. Oh Jack, she cried silently, why did I learn patience when it was too late? Her eyes misted and she turned away, leading him through the tables towards the lifts.

They passed the red-haired woman and her husband, coupled in argument, the only mutual passion they had left: 'All you ever do when we come out is drink!'

'That's the only bloody reason I come out!'

Silver walked a little quicker, her eyes clearing now. She and Jack might have finished up like that if they had gone on together. What love she still had for him only remained because she had cut herself off from him. When they reached the lifts she turned and held out her hand to him.

'Good-bye, Jack. I've had my last Tom Collins.'

He held her hand in his, saying nothing for the moment. He could not remember ever having felt so unutterably sad, not even when she had said good-bye to him twenty-two years ago. It seemed to him that here outside the lifts of the Wentworth, surrounded by strangers gay with drink and careless of tragedy, his life had just suddenly come to a dead end. Quietly, without any callousness, she had just removed all the seasons from his life.

'Good-bye,' he said. 'Be happy.'

Her mouth quivered. 'Thank you, Jack.' Then the lift arrived and she stepped quickly into it, not knowing whether it was going up or down and not caring. Just so long as she escaped before she surrendered.

Savanna gazed blankly at the closed doors of the lift. Then

144

he went back into the lounge and had another drink, pouring it down his throat like a man gulping at the quick merciful release of poison. It was then, despondent as a condemned man, that he decided to go out and say good-bye to Helga. He would go home to Josie tonight and, though she would not know it, he would be all hers, for what he was worth.

He drove out to Double Bay, parked his car and crossed the road to the store in the shopping plaza. The woman in the store, a buxom Viennese, smiled at him as soon as he came in the door.

'The usual, sir?' She took down the box of chocolates from the shelf behind her, began to wrap it. 'I envy your wife, you know? If I eat our chocolates, the weight I got to watch. One pound of chocolates, seven pounds of me, you know? She tied a fancy ribbon round the package. 'There, make it look attractive. What a pity all husbands are not like you, eh? We'd make a fortune in this store, you know?'

Savanna smiled. This woman, a romantic, would understand his mood of this afternoon. But he should have been buying the chocolates for Silver or (a pang of conscience) Josie. He paid for the box, thinking this would be his last extravagance as far as Helga was concerned, went out of the store and along the street to Helga's block of flats. He pushed open the glass door and slowly began to climb the stairs.

Helga's flat was on the third and top floor and he had just reached the second floor when the woman came running down the stairs. She passed him without seeming to see him, but in the instant of her passing him he saw the tears running down her cheeks behind the dark glasses and saw the broken string of pearls clutched in her hand. She went on down, her high heels clicking like small hammers on the marble stairs, then he heard the glass door open and shut and then there was silence. He paused, then shrugged and went on up to the third floor. There had been something vaguely familiar about the woman, but she wasn't someone he knew.

He automatically took his key-ring out of his pocket, selected the key to the flat, raised it to the lock, then stopped. This was not Tuesday or Friday, his days. He held the key an inch from the lock, then abruptly he dropped it and the key-ring back into his pocket. He had come to say good-bye and he would do it, if it were possible, without any friction between them. Decorously, like a youth calling on a girl for the first time, the box of chocolates tucked under one arm, he pressed the buzzer. He heard it buzz, sharply and insistently, and he waited. He thought he heard a movement in the flat, but Helga did not come to the door. He hesitated, then pressed the buzzer again. He waited half a minute, beginning to feel foolish, wondering why he had bothered to come without phoning her first. She was in there, all right, with someone else, some other mug she was setting up to be taken. Suddenly angry, he took the key out of his pocket again.

Then the door of the flat next door opened. A woman in a house smock, her hair in curlers, came out with a large cardboard carton full of screwed-up newspapers.

'Just moved in,' she said cheerily; she had the sort of face that instantly said she was a friend to the world. 'Still unpacking. You our neighbour?'

He slipped the key back into his pocket, hoping she hadn't seen it. 'No. Just a visitor. But my friend doesn't appear to be home.'

'Wouldn't know.' She went on downstairs, flinging words back at him over her shoulder; the curlers glinted like antennae on her head, she had messages for everyone. 'These are the old type of flats. Nice thick walls, you don't hear a thing. You should've seen what we were in before. Walls like tissue paper——' Her voice trailed away as she disappeared down the stairwell.

Savanna looked at the open door of the woman's flat, then at the closed door of Helga's. Then abruptly he swung round and went quickly downstairs and out into the street. No matter how thick the walls were, if he went into the flat and there was another chap there with Helga, everyone in Double Bay would hear what happened next. He would come back and say good-bye to her on *his* day, Tuesday, when his anger might be a little more under control.

He was half-way across the road when he saw Bixby. The trawler captain was walking away from him, but there was no mistaking him. Savanna stopped in mid-stride, was almost run down by a car whose driver yelled at him for being a bloody stupid dill, then he recovered and went on towards the car park. There was no reason why Bixby should not be in Double Bay; after all it was a harbour suburb and Bixby brought in his boat not far from here. But what was he doing in Helga's street? Had Grafter Gibson got the idea of using *him* to talk to Helga? Savanna halted beside his car, pondering if he should go back and warn Helga. Then he shook his head, like a man talking to himself. Let the Monday man, whoever he was, look after her.

He got into the car, dropped the box of chocolates on the seat beside him. He looked at them, then suddenly he smiled. He would give them to Josie. She would get them only by default, but even so he felt better for the thought. If today was the day for good-byes, it could also be the day for a new start. He might even ask Josie about the seasons.

Helga looked at her broken nail, then felt suddenly squeamish as she saw the sliver of skin and the blood under it. Still breathing heavily from exertion and anger, she stumbled into the bathroom and thrust her hand under a tap. She leant on the basin, her hand still under the tap as if she were trying to staunch a gush of her own blood instead of washing off the tiny streak of Norma Helidon's, and stared at herself in the mirror. There was a slight bruise on her cheek where the other woman had hit her and the collar of the green silk dressing-gown had been ripped. I could have killed her! she told her reflection; then all at once her anger went and she was afraid. Afraid of herself and the web she had created.

She had known from the start that the blackmail she had planned would not be easy. Men, even weak men, did not give away large sums of money without some sort of fight; especially self-made men like Walter Helidon and Leslie Gibson. She knew of the mercilessness that lay behind the acquisition of wealth: charity never paid dividends of riches.

She had expected to see the worst side of Walter Helidon's nature; but she had not expected the venomous opposition that Norma Helidon had shown. Walter's wife, the society matron, the queen of the charities, had come here this afternoon and shown all the alley-cat spirit of the girls Helga had once seen brawling on the Reeperbahn.

'Walter's been here, hasn't he, Miss Brand? I saw him down at the car park. No, we didn't speak to each other,' she had said as she had seen Helga's questioning look. 'He didn't see me. He looked as if he weren't seeing anything. I just hope he gets home safely,' she added, and for a moment her voice softened; it contrasted strangely with the harsh note that had been in her voice from the moment she had entered the flat. Then the harshness came back, as if she could not control it: 'I'm sure you wouldn't want him hurt. Or has he paid you the money?'

Helga leaned against the sideboard, drawing her gown tighter about her. Norma Helidon had sat down as soon as she had entered the flat, as if her legs had been able to carry her only this far and had then run out of strength; but she sat on the edge of the chair, her knees close together, her gloved hands clutching her handbag so tightly that the cream leather of it was dented. She had taken off the sunglasses she had been wearing and there was a pinched dark look to her eyes as if she were in pain.

'Why did you come, Mrs Helidon?'

Norma ignored the question. 'Has Walter paid you the money?'

Helga hesitated: how much would Walter confide in his wife? Then she shook her head, decided that from here on it would pay her to be nothing but honest and frank. After all she was selling them only the truth. 'Not yet. He is coming back tomorrow with it. He is being very reasonable.'

'He's being stupid,' Norma said flatly, a wifely opinion without malice. 'He has been stupid all along, getting mixed up with a girl like you.'

'Whose fault was that?' Helga couldn't keep the malice out of her own voice. Though she had never looked for a husband, had, with reservations, always enjoyed what her own life had brought her, there had always been part of her, the inheritance of Lutheran puritanism from her mother, that had envied the security of the woman who had a husband. 'You should have been a better wife to him.'

'I've always been a good wife to him.'

'You didn't give him what he wanted——'

'What you gave him, you mean?' She glared at Helga, voluptuous in the green silk, and became aware of her own body with the breasts that had begun to sag, the stomach that protruded when released from its expensive girdle, the buttocks with their dimpled porridge look. Oh God, she thought, they always have youth on their side. Why couldn't Walter have fallen for an older woman? But knew the question was foolish even as she asked it of herself. 'Giving him perverted sex——'

Helga smiled. All these wives were the same: any sex a man got outside his marriage bed had to be perverted. Walter had certainly had a fundamental approach to sex when she had first met him, an attitude that reduced the act to a simple athletic exercise: he seemed to look upon it as a test of his stamina and she had half-expected him to get out of bed and mark up his score on the wall, as if he were playing darts. She had had to teach him a lot, but what they had indulged in each Monday and Thursday had been nothing to the experiments she had been expected to perform, and had loathed, in her days in Hamburg. 'It wasn't perverted, Mrs Helidon, except to a perverted mind. A man is entitled to having it more than once or twice on a Sunday morning. Sex is more important than the *Sunday Telegraph*.'

Norma flushed, a mixture of anger and embarrassment. 'He really talked about me, didn't he? Oh my God, discussing me with a trollop like you——!' Her gloved hand went to the double strand of pearls she wore, as if words were stuck in her throat behind them.

Helga snapped, 'Only once—that was all he ever talked about you! We had other things to do—to talk about. I didn't give him just sex—I *listened* to him, gave him an audience. When did you last do that? What do you *want*, Mrs Helidon? To ask me to give him up?'

Norma Helidon nodded, her hand still at her throat.

'For nothing?' Helga shook her head angrily. 'I'm giving him up—but not for nothing! You—he and you—you have to pay for all the boredom I have had for two years——' She was suddenly finding reasons for her extortion: *she* had been acting the role of his wife while his real wife had been engrossed in her social activities: she became almost self-righteous, the blackmailer who had all at once found she was not so sinful. 'If it hadn't been for me, it would have been someone worse —at least I have been discreet—you owe me for that——'

'I can't let him pay you.' Norma's voice was hoarse now, a croak. 'It would be buying him back from you——'

Helga took a step forward, leant down till her face was close to the other woman's. 'That's for him to decide. He will not be paying for himself—he will be paying for you. And perhaps he will not think you are worth twenty thousand dollars——'

It was then that Norma hit her. The gloved hand came up in a sudden involuntary blow; Helga saw the look of hatred in Norma's eyes even before she felt the pain in her own cheek. She grabbed at the strands of pearls, cursing obscenely in German; then Norma clutched her by the collar of the dressing-gown and she heard the silk rip. In a moment they were wrestling, swaying together in the middle of the room to a slow rhythm like women without male partners at a tea dance. Norma's handbag and sunglasses had fallen on the floor; then the strands of pearls followed them, individual pearls slipping off the strings and scattering about the carpet like white dried peas. Helga continued to curse in German as she fought, but Norma struggled silently, the only sound coming out of her being an occasional great sob. An airliner went overhead as it headed down towards the airport south of the city; its jets coned into the one great scream that filled the room like the fury of the women who fought there. They did not move from the spot where they had first grappled; each of them stood with her feet firmly planted in the carpet. Then abruptly they broke apart, as if the horror of what they were doing had suddenly stepped between them like a referee. Norma dropped to her knees. She knelt there, her head hung on her breast, and now the sobs were coming out of her in awful tearing gasps. Helga staggered back, leaned against the door that led to the kitchen.

'Get out! Get out!'

Norma did not look at her. She lifted her head for just a moment and took a deep rasping breath; then she got down on her hands and knees, and, still sobbing, like some huge lumbering dog in pain, she began to crawl about the carpet. Helga, still recovering from the struggle, her gaze still blurred by her exertion, stared at the other woman in puzzled shock: had she gone out of her mind? Then she saw the gloved hands fumbling with the scattered pearls. Norma crawled around, still making the awful sounds deep in her throat, picking up every pearl she could find. Helga stared fascinated, unable to move even when Norma came crawling across the floor to pick up a pearl beside her foot.

Then slowly, the sobs subsiding, Norma got to her feet. She looked around for her handbag and sunglasses, picked them up and put on the glasses. Then without a word she stumbled to the front door, opened it and went out, one hand clutching the pearls to her breast as if she were trying to hold in her life's blood.

Helga straightened up, moved quickly to the door, closed it and locked it. She went back into the living-room, looked at her hands and then saw the blood and the sliver of skin under her nail.

She was in the bathroom when she heard the door buzzer ring. She turned off the tap and waited. It rang again, but she did not move. She did not want to have to face Norma Helidon again so soon. She had just witnessed the destruction of another woman and she was frightened and sickened by what she had done. And frightened and sickened by the thought that if they had continued to fight she would have killed Norma Helidon. When she had looked in the bathroom mirror she had looked deeper into herself than ever before and had seen the abyss of darkness there that she had never suspected.

She waited another five minutes, but there was not another buzzing from the front door. She dried her hands, went out

151

to the living-room, got her sewing basket and moved to a chair. She slipped out of her dressing-gown, fingering the torn collar, and was standing in the nude when the door buzzer rang again. She hesitated, then she slipped on the gown again. She did not want another scene with Norma Helidon, but it was obvious the woman was not going to go away. New neighbours had moved in next door and Helga was enough of a *hausfrau* to know that one way of avoiding involvement with neighbours was to give them nothing to gossip about. The best thing to do was to let Norma Helidon in and see what else she had to say.

She moved to the door, opened it, then stared in puzzlement at the man in the orange shirt who stood there. She had seen him before, but for the moment she could not remember where or when. Then recognition came, and with it shock; this was the man who, in an indirect way, had triggered off her decision to get home to Germany before Christmas. Suddenly afraid, she tried to slam the door.

But Bixby was already pushing it back against her, was grinning widely round the matchstick stuck between his teeth.

CHAPTER NINE

Friday, December 13

MALONE saw the calendar as soon as he opened his eyes in the morning. He knew what his mother would have done as soon as she had opened her eyes: an extra Hail Mary would have been said to ward off the Devil, and the saints would have been told to get off their tails and keep a sharp eye out today for sinners like herself. Well, I'd welcome the Devil this morning, he thought, if he brought along with him the feller who killed Helga Brand. There were times when, if the murder had not been too brutal or disgusting, he enjoyed the actual detective work. A lot of it might be dull routine stuff where you plodded from point to point, but at the end of each day there was a certain satisfaction: you had advanced from where you had started in the morning and you had done it from your own reasoning and, he admitted, sometimes your own guesswork. It was the putting together of a jigsaw puzzle, only in your case it was played for keeps and there were no prizes. No cop in his right mind ever considered a murderer a prize. But this Brand case was one he was *not* enjoying, one that filled him with a sense of unease. Yet he could not explain why. Maybe it was the Irish in him, the pessimism of the Celt who would never really enjoy Heaven when he made it because he would know by what narrow margin he had missed the alternative. The pessimism that made an intelligent, unsuperstitious man scowl at a date on a calendar.

The phone rang and he reached for it wearily: why couldn't Russ Clements wait till he got to the office? But it was Lisa and at once he smiled and sat up. 'Are you up, darling?' she asked.

There had been girls he had known to whom he could have given a crude answer to that one; but not to Lisa. They were uninhibited in their talk when in bed together, but she was a lady over the phone. Also, he was learning about himself as he learned about her.

'Darling, what's the matter? How long have you been awake? Are you ill or something?'

'I was just thinking, that's all. How long does it take to become a gentleman?'

'Longer than it takes to become a lady, I'm afraid. Gentlemen are born, ladies can be manufactured.'

'Where'd you get that little gem of cynicism—some PR release?' He thought about it for a moment, then said, 'Maybe you're right. But it cuts me out.'

'No, darling, it doesn't. You're a gentleman. You may not recognize yourself as one, but you are. Women look for different things from what a man looks for in a gentleman.'

'Such as?'

'What sort of conversation is this at this time of morning? I'm in my bra and pants, trying to get ready for the office.'

'Just the time to discuss with a man whether he's a gentleman or not. Go on.'

'Well——' Her voice was disjointed for a moment, as if she might be struggling into a dress. 'Well, a man judges a gentleman by the way he reacts to society as a whole. A woman judges him by the way he reacts to her. Or anyway this woman does.'

What a wonderful girl! She knew just how to make a man get up and face Friday, the 13th. 'I love you, Dutchy.'

'I wondered.' Another pause, heavy with breathing.

'What are you doing? You got another gentleman there with you?'

'I'm trying to do up my zip. You didn't call me last night.'

'I didn't get in till ten-thirty. We worked back——' He had left the office at eight o'clock, but, too tired to come home and cook something for himself, had gone out for a meal with Russ Clements at the Leagues Club. They had stayed on there drinking, neither of them getting anywhere near drunk but just enjoying the relaxation and isolation from what had occupied them since early that morning. It had been eleven-thirty, not ten-thirty, when he had finally got home. Much too

154

late to ring a girl with excuses why you had not called her earlier, especially a girl who could smell beer on your breath even over the phone. No beery gentleman would call a girl at that hour. 'What's the matter? Our date's on tonight, isn't it?'

'Unless you're going to be working back again.' Sounds just like a wife, he thought. Mrs. Scobie Scold Malone. Then she said, 'Scobie, Mrs Helidon called me last night about nine o'clock.'

He swung his legs out of bed, sat up straight. 'Go on.'

'She wants me to prepare a release that she is resigning from the committee of the Blue and Red Ball.'

He sagged with disappointment, then began to laugh. 'Is that all? Christ——'

'Don't swear at me, Scobie. No gentleman does that.' She managed to chide him without sounding priggish.

'Sorry. But honestly—why tell *me*? I couldn't care less what she resigns from. You know what I think of charity committees, *those* sort, the ones who never get their hands dirty.'

'Darling.' She had forgiven him for swearing at her; her voice was gently patient, like that of a kindergarten teacher leading a child into the mysteries of human nature. 'When Mrs Helidon resigns from the presidency of the Blue and Red Ball, she is resigning from the human race. Kings have abdicated thrones with less space than this will get in tonight's newspapers.'

He stood up, idly scratching the itches that had built up during the warm night. He always slept naked and now, trying to sort out what Lisa had just told him, his brain still half-asleep, he pulled up the blind to let the morning sun stream in.

A girl standing at a window in a house across the street looked at him, looked again, then waved appreciatively. He pulled the blind down again: he was in no mood to start the day right for strange girls.

'Darling, are you still there?'

'Yeah. Lisa—look, I appreciate you calling me. But do me a favour—don't become a detective.'

There was silence at the other end of the phone and he

knew he had offended her. Then, stiffly, as if she had also just zipped up her voice: 'All right, Scobie.'

'No, don't hang up! Darling, I know you're trying to help me. And you have. What Mrs Helidon is doing, well, it means she's got *something* on her mind. But I think it's best we start off on the right foot. We don't want a married life where we *both* have headaches, I mean about police business. I've thought about it and I don't think I should have talked to you the other night about it. This case, I mean.'

'Is it giving you a headache?'

'I think it's going to.'

'Then I want to share them. I don't want to be the sort of wife who is only wrapped up in her own affairs. I think those wives are *dull*——'

He was about to say, *We're not married yet.* But something told him that would not be a politic thing to say to a girl; he knew enough about women to know that they never took a statement for just what it was worth; not when they were in the mood that Lisa was in this morning. They could embroider it with more meaning than a school of philosophers; everything you might say was taken down and used as evidence against you. He sighed. 'All right, we'll share the headaches. But *please*—no detective work. I won't be a PR character and don't you try to be a policeman. Okay?'

Lisa was a sensible girl: 'Darling, I had no intention of doing any police work. For one thing, I don't like violence —that is one thing we must *never* talk about. Promise?'

You don't know me, he thought. What ever gave you the idea I liked violence or even talking about it? 'Promise.'

'But when I pick up things like *this*— Don't you think it's *interesting*? I've never met anyone so socially ambitious as Mrs Helidon. And then all of a sudden, just overnight, she decides she is going to retire. Why would she do that unless something serious, really serious, had happened to her or her husband?'

'You're starting to sound like a policewoman,' he said gently. 'No, you're right. But leave me to worry about it.'

She sighed. 'All right, darling. I'll try not to be a busy-body. But it has me intrigued why——'

'Stay away from it,' he warned. 'Now I'd better shower and get dressed. I'm standing here naked in front of the window and there are seven girls across the street making inviting signs——'

'Pull down the blind!'

He grinned. 'I think you're jealous. See you tonight.'

He hung up, showered, dressed, then pulled up the blind. The girl across the street, tired of waiting, had gone from her window. He collected the morning paper from outside his door and read it while he ate his breakfast of toast and coffee. There was nothing in the paper about the Opera House murder; Helga Brand had been worth only a day's run in the news; she would not make the papers again until her murderer was arrested. State Parliament had risen for the Christmas recess; Walter Helidon was not reported as having said anything in the Assembly. He looked at the latest cricket scores, but it was force of habit, a nostalgic reaction: ten years ago he had played for the State and there was still the occasional regret that he had not tried harder, had not persevered to see if he could play for Australia. It was all behind him now, the muscles would never again have the strength they had had in those days, and he would never know how good he might have been.

He scanned the other pages, but the rest of the news was forgotten as soon as he read it, a sure sign that he was worried. He had always done his best to have a detached attitude towards a case, but he had never entirely succeeded. Sooner or later he became emotionally involved and his judgement would suffer. So far there had been no emotional involvement in the Brand case, but he could feel the detachment crumbling away like a wall of sand. Against the grain of his cooler judgement, he found he was *wanting* the murderer to be Walter Helidon.

Last night before he had left the office he had sat down and dredged his memory, bringing up things forgotten in the silt of all that had happened since. He remembered the facts that had emerged in the case of land exploitation in which Walter Helidon had been involved; the Fraud Squad had been called in not to collect evidence against Helidon, but against a man named Bax, his brother-in-law. In the final outcome there had not been strong enough evidence to warrant laying a charge against Bax, but Malone had learned enough to realize that Helidon was less than lilywhite, that Bax, though the principal offender, had not been the originator of the suspicious land deal. Malone and the other members of the Fraud Squad working on the case had shrugged and moved on, accepting cynically that Helidon was only one in a long line of politicians in New South Wales who had used their position for their own ends. There had been major rogues such as Crick and Willis at the turn of the century, but Helidon had been only a minor one and the memory of him had soon been lost as Malone, over the years, had gone on to cases involving larger villainies.

But now he remembered that he had taken a dislike to Helidon because of the man's egoism. Egoism, he had read in a psychiatrist's report on another case, was the theory that self-interest was the basis of morality. He had been arrogant in his answers to the questions put by Malone and his senior colleague on the fraud case; and the same arrogance, though more controlled, had been there in the interview on Wednesday evening. A man's arrogance and egoism were not enough to indict him, but they did not help a policeman to have an objective and dispassionate attitude towards him. Especially one like Malone who, despite his efforts to the contrary, could always become so emotionally involved. I'm a poor cop, he thought. The best cop was the one who thought like a criminal, who might even have been a criminal but for some hiccup of fate. The worst one was the cop who too often put himself in the mind of the victim.

Malone washed his breakfast crockery, made his bed and rearranged some of the dust on the more conspicuous furniture. His mother came in every Friday to do the flat properly, so tonight it would look spick and span for another week. As he was leaving he stood at the door of the flat and looked around at what was—no, not *home*. He had never called it home; it was always *the flat* or *my place*. Home was still the terraced house in Erskineville, even if he would never go back to it. But this flat was, for what it was worth, *him*: he had put his mark on it in a more subtle way than those people who hung their name on a plate at their gates. The Qantas travel posters of London and Rome, his dream of another life: the framed photograph of himself in action as a fast bowler, the relic of the past; the photo of Lisa standing against a cloudless sky, the dream of the future: all of it evidence against him. And the two rows of books, paperbacks and second-hand hardbacks, on the cheap do-it-yourself bookshelves: some best-selling novels, half a dozen detective novels by Simenon and Ross MacDonald, a history of crime and detection, a book on the psychology of the criminal mind, three or four travel books: the mental range of the accused. The rest of the flat had been there when he had rented it, a grab-bag of furniture that made it identical with a hundred other flats within a mile of it. Malone looked at it, compared it with the luxury in which Helidon and Gibson lived, and thought with a feeling of self-disgust: Maybe that's it. You resent what the other fellers have got with their bending of the rules. You've become what you always swore you'd never be: a dissatisfied cop. It hurt to think that the feeling had only begun since he had asked Lisa to marry him.

He went quickly out of the flat, slamming the door behind him. He found a parking ticket on his car, put it in his pocket and swore at a parking policeman, one of the Brown Bombers in their khaki uniforms, who could be so conscientious at eight-thirty in the morning. He got into his car, already warm with the morning heat, and drove into Surry Hills, the inner section of the city where the Criminal Investigation Branch had its headquarters. He found a parking spot, hoped there wasn't another conscientious Brown Bomber in the area, went into the CIB and upstairs to the Fingerprint Department.

CIB headquarters had once been a hat factory. A government short of money and imagination had bought it and converted it; in another ten years it would be obsolete and, Malone was sure, another government would look around for something else that could be converted. That seemed to be the official approach to so much in Australia: improvisation. As he rode up in the lift he remembered what he had seen of Scotland Yard when he had been in London and thought of the shots you saw of Los Angeles police headquarters in television films. Some cops didn't know when they were well off. Then he thought: Quit it, Malone. Next thing you'll be leading the university students in a riot against the Establishment.

He got out of the lift and walked down the passage between the partitions that marked the various departments. Voices murmured behind the closed doors: they could have been muted echoes. He wondered what bewildered ghosts wandered through here in the shank-end of the night. Hatters' formers, hardeners and stumpers, smelling of steam, they would wonder at the new tradesmen who occupied their old work-places, the fingerprint, forgery and ballistics experts who could reconstruct a crime with the same skill as some of the ghosts might once have re-blocked a hat. As he came to the door of the Fingerprint Section he remembered when a man had been picked up who had had no fingerprints. Mystified, they had held him for further questioning, the old euphemism for what-the-hell-goes-on-here, and on the third day prints had reappeared on his fingers. Then they had learned that the man was a hat stumper, worked all week with his hands in near-boiling water or under steam, and by the end of each week his fingers were smooth of prints. If he had worked in this particular factory, his ghost must be bursting his ghostly gut laughing.

The Fingerprint Section was the best in the country and one of the three or four best in the world. Malone, with the frank admiration of the unscientifically-minded man for those who had mastered the science of their craft, always enjoyed visiting the section. And the men who worked there always enjoyed having him: trapped among their filing cabinets, their eyes myopically focused to the fingerprint sheets in front of them, they often felt their contribution to crime solution was overlooked and they always appreciated the opportunity to illustrate that a policeman was nothing without the aid of forensic science.

'None of the prints we collected are in our records,' said Hawkins, the man who brought the file to Malone. He was one of the civilian members of the section, an elderly grey man in a grey dustcoat whose face was as lined as the prints he put down in front of Malone. 'But that isn't to say we can't help you. Take this one, for instance. We found them on the telephone, the key, and on pieces of that broken glass. Standard type of print. Nine over one, U over U, MMO over MM, eight over sixteen. But no scars, no wearing down of the whorls or loops. They belong to a man who probably hasn't done a tap of manual work in all his life, certainly not for the last twenty years or so. He'd be a professional man. Or maybe a con man.'

'Could be either,' said Malone, and found himself thinking again of Helidon. 'Those were the only male prints you found?'

'We went back again yesterday when you asked us, went over the place with a cloud of powder. Nothing, Scobie, other than the three we had already picked up. Miss Brand must have been a good housekeeper, one of those sort that goes over everything every day with a duster. The wife is the same. I'm always telling her they'll never find a fingerprint in our house.'

'What about the cup and saucer on the draining board in the kitchen?'

'They'd been washed and wiped. Nothing on them. There were some biscuit crumbs on the draining board, but no prints on the biscuit tin. That had been wiped clean, too.'

Malone raised an eyebrow. 'She wouldn't have been *that* house-proud, dusting off her biscuit tin. If she'd done that, she'd have got rid of the crumbs, for sure.'

Hawkins puckered his face into a net of wrinkles. 'I'm only telling you what we found and what we didn't find. There were no prints at all in the kitchen, not even hers.' He tapped the file on the counter between them. 'That's the lot, Scobie. The man's, Helga's and the ones we found on the side table, those of another woman. If anybody else was in the flat that night, he left no prints.'

'Somebody else was there,' said Malone, remembering the chewed matchsticks. 'And if he went around wiping off his prints, he wasn't an amateur.'

He thanked Hawkins, went downstairs and found he had

collected another parking ticket. He looked around, but the Brown Bomber had disappeared; they were the world's best guerilla force bar none. He drove down to Bridge Street, parked his car where he knew he would not get a ticket, right outside the Police Commissioner's office, then walked down to Y Division and gave the parking tickets to Smiler Sparks.

'Look after those for me, Smiler.'

Sergeant Sparks came as close as he would ever get to a grin. 'They put one on the Superintendent's wife's car yesterday. He reckons the next Brown Bomber he sees, he's gunna run him in for loitering.'

Russ Clements was in the detectives' room arranging some more Christmas cards that had arrived in the morning mail. He blew his nose as Malone walked in, sniffed and wiped his eyes. 'I was looking at one of these cards a while ago, tears running out of my eyes and The Bishop came in and said he was glad to see I was sentimental. Here's one from Charlie Duggan. They finally got him in New Zealand, he says, and he's doing seven years.'

Charlie Duggan had been a whimsically cynical con man who had been the bane of the Fraud Squad when Malone had worked on it. All of them had admired Charlie's ingenious schemes and had had almost an affection for him each time they had picked him up; Malone could remember the gettogethers in the Squad room when detectives and con man had sat around and, with shaking of heads, discussed the gullibility of John Q. Public. The Squad had never been able to nail Charlie for more than a six months' sentence and then only once. They were convinced that what Charlie had said was true: 'Even the judges and juries admire me, fellers. We're all con men, even you fellers, but only some of us make a career of it. We've all got a streak of larceny in us. And so long as a con man doesn't rob an old lady of her savings, most of you say good luck to us. Everybody would love to live on his wits—if he had any.'

If only all crims were like Charlie, Malone thought. But they weren't: Charlie had been an exception. 'Blow your nose again. We're going out to see Mrs Helidon.'

'You gunna ask the Minister's permission first?'

'You heard what The Bishop said the other day. Treat it as a routine case. We don't usually ask a husband's permission to question his missus.'

Clements struggled into his jacket. 'If this thing gets out of hand, I just hope The Bishop is there to back us up.'

'He'll be there. Someone as self-righteous as he is wouldn't miss the opportunity.'

<h2>2</h2>

Pymble dozed under its green blanket of trees and shrubs beneath the brass sky. Over to the east smoke boiled up like a dark storm: the bushfires were eating at the city's perimeter; but here, so far, no one was worried. Cicadas whirred and somewhere at the far end of the road a lawnmower buzzed like a gentle snoring. The solid brick homes behind the approaches of their large gardens looked as impregnable as castles; swimming pools sparkled like modern moats. But Malone knew from experience that no home was impregnable. The people who lived in them were their own white ants.

Norma Helidon herself opened the door to them. 'I think you might have phoned, Sergeant——'

'I'm sorry, Mrs Helidon. The police can't afford to make appointments.'

'No. No, I suppose not.' She led them through the living-room and out into a loggia that faced on to a large swimming pool. Beyond it was a garden where flowering shrubs blazed like frozen fires in the morning glare. A white poodle gambolled among the shrubs like a lamb that had been shorn by a drunken shearer: ruffles of white hair stuck out at odd parts of its skinny frame. It looked at the two strangers, uttered a bark that wouldn't have been out of place in a lamb, and went on with its game.

Here beneath the vine-covered loggia it was cool and green. They sat down on some white iron outdoor furniture and Norma Helidon said, 'Coffee?'

'I think it might help.'

'To make the atmosphere easier?' She was dressed in a blue

silk housecoat and her make-up was as complete as if she were on her way to one of her many committee meetings: she looked as cool and elegant as a fashion model. But no amount of make-up could ever hide the pain in the eyes; only dark glasses could do that. She took a pair of them from the pocket of her housecoat, put them on, then poured three cups of coffee from the percolator that stood on the glass-topped, iron-legged table beside which she sat. 'Do you always try to do that for your victims, Sergeant?'

Her hand was shaking as she handed Malone his cup, but he pretended not to notice it. 'We don't call them victims any longer. Our public relations office advised against it. How are your public relations, Mrs Helidon? I'm told Miss Pretorious is very good.'

The cup rattled in its saucer as she handed Clements his coffee. 'Are we going to sit here all morning and swap insults?'

'I apologize,' Malone said, and suddenly felt sorry for the woman. He suspected that beneath the veneer there was another woman altogether, one who might have had a warmth and affection for other people instead of just a use for them. 'I didn't come here to do that——'

'But I rub you up the wrong way? All right, Sergeant, I apologize, too. Now why did you come?'

He took a small envelope out of his pocket, rolled two pearls into his palm. 'Are those yours, Mrs Helidon?'

Her hand went instinctively to her bare throat, then dropped back in her lap. 'I—I don't think so. What makes you think they might belong to me?'

'We found them in Helga Brand's flat. And four or five crushed ones. No, wait a minute,' he said as he saw her face stiffen beneath the dark glasses. 'I told you, I didn't come here to insult you. It doesn't matter what you think of Helga, to me and Constable Clements she was a girl who was murdered. Once someone is murdered they become respectable, at least as far as being entitled to having their murderer convicted.'

'I didn't murder her, Sergeant.'

'I'm not saying you did. But one way of finding out who

did kill her is by eliminating everybody else who might have. Now I've been making some inquiries about you——'

'Where?' Her voice was sharp. 'From Miss Pretorious?'

Malone wondered if he kept his face blank; out of the corner of his eye he saw Clements pause with his cup halfway to his mouth. 'I don't go to public relations people for my information.'

'I don't think the police public relations would like that recommendation,' said Norma Helidon tartly.

He smiled, conceding her the point, trying to break down the chill that still lay between them. 'I got my information from other sources. A newspaperwoman, if you must know. She told me about your trademark, Mrs Helidon. The pearls you're never seen without.'

She was silent a moment, then she nodded, making her own concession. 'That's right. I suppose they are what you call my trademark, though it isn't an expression I'd have used myself. But I don't wear them when I'm alone around the house.'

'You weren't wearing them the other night,' said Clements; he sniffed and took out his handkerchief. 'When Miss Pretorious was here. Wouldn't you wear them then?'

'I probably was wearing them,' she said evenly. 'You just didn't notice them. But then men rarely do notice such things. Women wear jewellery for other women, didn't you know that?'

Malone looked at Clements, who blew his nose, then shook his head emphatically. 'You weren't wearing them, Mrs Helidon.'

'If Constable Clements says you weren't wearing them,' said Malone, 'then I'm afraid you weren't. I'll admit I didn't notice, but then I never notice what anyone is wearing. Including what I'm wearing myself, according to my—girl friend. But Constable Clements could have been a fashion spy.'

'You had on a blue silk dress, a little bit darker than that housecoat you're wearing. You had a gold bracelet on one wrist and that watch you're wearing on the other——'

'All right,' Norma Helidon broke in; lipstick discoloured her teeth as she bit her lip. 'Perhaps I wasn't wearing the pearls. But I have them. They are inside in our safe. I have three sets and all of them are intact.'

'May we see them?'

The swish of the housecoat as she rose was like the sound of a scythe. 'My husband isn't going to like this when he hears of it.'

'I'm sure he won't,' said Malone as he and Clements followed her into the house. The poodle barked after them and Clements, holding back, turned and blew his nose at it. 'I understand he's already complained to the Commissioner.'

'And what did the Commissioner say?'

'I don't know. He never confides in us. But he didn't say to forget the case.'

She was four or five steps ahead of him as she led him through the living-room. He sidestepped a wide lounge and as he did so he almost fell over a small side table. He looked down and saw the rack of pipes. His mind offered no thought or suggestion; his hand went down of its own accord, his little finger went into the bowl of a pipe, he lifted the pipe from the rack and dropped it into his pocket. *We've all got a streak of larceny in us . . .*

'I'm glad to see you keep your valuables in a safe. You'd be surprised the number of women who leave their jewellery lying around like bits of clothing.'

Norma Helidon had led them into a bedroom big enough to have contained the whole of Malone's flat and had space to spare. The room was dominated by a huge four-postered bed canopied in blue silk; blue silk seemed to be another of her trademarks.

Clements, the lover of luxury, raised his eyebrows. Norma Helidon saw his expression reflected in the big mirror that made up one wall.

'You notice décor, too, Constable?'

'Only in an unofficial way,' said Clements, and Malone thought: the boy is learning. He's not going to let her squash him. 'We don't have much in the way of décor back at the office.'

Norma Helidon moved to the mirror, pressed one end of it

and a section of it opened out. Behind it was a small wall safe. 'I believe the usual thing is to hide safes behind pictures. I hope you won't give away our secret.' She took out a large leather box, offered it to Malone. 'All in a lump like that, it looks terribly vulgar. I try not to wear it all at once.'

Malone smiled. The woman had guts, whatever faults she had. He looked in the box. He had no idea of the worth of the jewellery it contained, but he guessed it would run into thousands of dollars. To a man who had given his girl a fifty-dollar engagement ring and still felt the pain of the extravagance, this was an Arabian Nights' treasure chest. The box was divided into compartments and in one of them were three pearl necklaces, all of them complete as far as he could judge. He nodded, but picked up one of the necklaces.

'I apologize again.' Then he held one of the loose pearls in his hand against the necklace. 'This one would match, though, wouldn't it?'

Norma Helidon took off her dark glasses, peered at the pearl. 'Yes, I think it would. But it isn't as difficult to match pearls today as it used to be. These are cultured pearls—mine and those loose ones you have. I think you'll probably find that those two pearls belonged to Miss Brand. A girl like her would be sure to get gifts like that.' The sneer in her voice was as rough-edged as a file.

'I guess so,' said Malone, and held back from asking if her husband might have given gifts like that to Helga. Then he said casually, 'You never met her, did you? I mean, at her flat?'

'No.' Norma Helidon turned round, put the box back in the safe. She closed the wall mirror, looked at herself in it, put on her dark glasses and turned back to face Malone and Clements. Like her husband she had learned how to mark time while her mind slipped into gear: the effort was not lost on Malone. 'No, I never met Miss Brand other than at charity functions. And then only once or twice.'

Malone and Clements left five minutes later. At the front door Malone said, 'Is it your maid's day off, Mrs Helidon?'

'No, I'm afraid she's left us.' Now that they were leaving, Norma Helidon seemed more relaxed; the edge had gone from

167

her voice. She took off her dark glasses, blinked in the glare from the red gravelled drive, but did not replace the glasses. 'It's terribly difficult to keep girls. She was the fourth we've had in two years. You bring them out here, she was Italian, and they're no sooner here than they start thinking like Australian girls, that there is something wrong with being a servant.' She smiled, but there was no dagger in it this time: 'Or do you think like that, too?'

'I am a servant,' said Malone, grinning in reply. 'A public servant. What was your maid's name?'

Her smile froze on her face. 'Why?'

'Just as a matter of interest,' he said, trying not to make too much of it.

She hesitated, then said, 'Rosa Calvorsi.'

'Does she have any relatives out here, do you know?'

'None that I know of. She came to us through one of those service bureaus.'

'Well, we hope you're not without a girl too long. This is a pretty big place to run on your own. Good-bye, Mrs Helidon.'

'Will you be back?' Her voice tightened a little.

Malone shrugged, smiled again. 'Who knows? But don't expect us to phone if we do come back. It's against the rules.'

'Don't you ever go against the rules?'

'Only when they get in the way.'

As they walked out to their car parked in the street Clements said, 'Why'd you pinch the pipe? You thinking of taking it up?'

'How else are we going to get Helidon's fingerprints?'

'Clev-er. You should be a detective. Did you notice her make-up was a bit thick on her throat? When she put her hand up to her throat that time, she wiped a bit of it off. There was a small nick there. It could have been made by someone's fingernail when they snatched her pearls off.'

'Clev-er. You could be a detective, too.'

As they drove away Malone looked back. Norma Helidon still stood in the doorway of her house. The sun struck slant-wise across the veranda and the pale silk glittered like a gas flame in its brightness. As they went farther down the road it seemed to him that that was all he could see, the blue flame: Norma Helidon herself had been consumed by it.

I wonder if I've had the wrong idea, he thought. I wonder if she killed Helga and Helidon is only trying to protect her?

CHAPTER TEN

I

Monday, December 2

BIXBY took his hands from round Helga's throat and let her
drop to the floor. Her dressing-gown fell open and she lay
there like an invitation that mocked him. He knew by the
look of her that she was dead; nonetheless he felt for her pulse
and put his ear to her breast. There was nothing: he had
killed her, all right.

He sat back on his haunches, staring at the nude body
with none of the lust that had gripped him when he had first
come into the flat. Outside in the street a car horn hooted twice
and a girl's voice shouted that she was coming. Somewhere
below a kid walked out of the flats with a transistor turned full
up: Tom Jones was pining for the green green grass of home.
The refrigerator started up in the kitchen, bottles in it rattling
together, and he jerked nervously. Then he got slowly to his
feet, his legs feeling as stiff as tree stumps, and automatically
he took a match from his pocket and began to chew on it. He
backed into a chair and collapsed into it. Jesus, what a mess!

He had had no thought of physically harming her when he
had come to the flat. When he had first pushed his way in the
front door and seen the lush body outlined beneath the green
silk, he had had ideas for a moment or two; but then he had
put them out of his head, figuring that would only lead to a
fight. And he hadn't come here to fight, at least not for a
bit of *that*.

He had no principles against hitting a woman; some of
them deserved no better. He had been married twice and both
wives had left him because of his ill-treatment of them; but
he had never felt that he had been in the wrong, had always
been convinced that they had asked for the beltings he had
given them. But he had not come here to belt this dame, only

to hint that she might get done over if she didn't take his advice and get out of Sydney. He had thought that no more would be necessary. He had never warned off a woman before, but he had played the game with several men and they had taken the hint and quietly disappeared.

It had been different with this piece. 'If Mr Gibson sent you, you go back and tell him I'm not frightened of him! I'll come to see him tomorrow and I want the money!'

He had smiled at her because just then he did not believe her opposition would amount to more than a few hot words. 'Old Grafter dunno anything about this. I just run a little something on the side and I'm telling you—it's none of your business!' His voice grated, but he was not really angry yet; it was all part of the act of frightening her. 'All you gotta do is get outa Sydney. Go back to Europe—anywhere you like—but blow! I'll give you the fare.'

'Everyone's trying to put me on a plane!' He wrinkled his brow at that; had old Grafter himself been on the blower to her? 'Well, it's not going to work! Now get out!'

She went to push past him, to open the front door. It was then that he hit her, not a heavy blow by his standards. But she staggered back, the red mark of his hand on her cheek. She glared at him, her mouth open; then abruptly she whirled and picked up the glass Helidon had left on the side table. Bixby ducked, but he was not quite quick enough; the glass bounced off his shoulder and crashed into fragments against the wall behind him. He moved in on her as she rushed at him with her fingers clawed. They met like lovers in the middle of the room, but there was no love in their embrace: her fingers clutched at his face, he took hold of her throat. She tried to scream, but he pressed tighter.

'Shut up, you bitch!'

He had never had to deal with a woman who fought as she did. She scratched his face, tore at his eyes, tried to twist her head to bite the hands at her throat; she kicked him in the shins, the knee and the crotch; and every blow she made wrote her death warrant. He could feel the fury taking hold of him, the mixture of anger and sexual excitement; he drew her body in under him as he tightened his grip on her throat. He bent her back beneath him, cursing obscenely as she struggled like a woman in a storm of passion and he could feel the sex rising in him as to the moment of climax. Then suddenly she went limp beneath him and at the same instant his blurred gaze cleared. He took his hands from round her throat and let her drop to the floor.

Now he sat in the chair and stared at her. The gown was wide open and her nude body sprawled on the carpet like that of a woman exhausted and sated by sex. But he had never felt less like having a woman; he even shuddered, as if he found the thought of her as a woman repulsive. Jesus, what a mess! All because he hadn't been able to control his bloody temper. What the hell was he going to do?

He should have waited till another day, maybe tomorrow, before coming to lean on her. He had arrived in Double Bay an hour or so ago and had come to the flats, been halfway up the stairs when he had seen the bloke in the dark suit and dark glasses letting himself into Helga's flat. He had gone outside again, crossed the road and sat on one of the seats in the small park opposite. After a while he had seen the man come out, still wearing his dark glasses, and hurry off down the street. He had waited a while, then he had crossed to the flats and was just about to go in when a woman, also wearing dark glasses, had pushed in the front door ahead of him. She had looked at the names on the mailboxes just inside the door, put her finger on the one marked Helga Brand, then gone up the stairs. Bixby had seen all this from just outside the glass front door; at once he had turned round, re-crossed the road and sat in the park again. Later he had seen the grey-haired joker, Savanna, arrive, go into the flats and a moment later the woman in the dark glasses come rushing out. Christ, it had been busy. Helga looked like she had more visitors than the bloody Prime Minister. He had waited a while; then, not wanting to be recognized by Savanna when the latter came out of the flats, he had got up and decided to go down to the pub for a beer. He had just begun walking down the street when out of the corner of his eye he had seen Savanna coming out of the flats. He had kept walking, not quickening his pace, hoping the grey-haired poofter wouldn't have seen him.

Maybe all those visitors, Savanna, the bloke in the dark glasses, the woman, had also been leaning on Helga. *Everyone's trying to put me on a plane,* she had said. If they all had been leaning on her, putting the arm on her, no wonder she hadn't been in any mood to listen to him when he'd arrived.

He reached into his pocket, took out another match and began to chew on it, dropping the first match on the carpet beside his chair. That old sonofabitch Gibson would kick up a stink about this. He hated to admit it, but he was afraid of Grafter; the old bastard had too much money, too much power. The stand-over stuff, the bashing with a bottle or a piece of iron pipe or a bicycle chain, that was okay with the small-time mugs around Paddington and the Cross; but it was no argument at all against a man who could buy all the protection he wanted, could probably buy even some of the demons if he needed them. They were going to be a problem, too: the demons. He hated the police with a passion that bordered on insanity; twice he had tried to kill a cop and only his poor marksmanship with a pistol had let him down. Each time the police had not known who was shooting at them and so he was still free to kill one of them when the time and his aim was right. But now he had killed, not a demon but a dame, and he was surprised at how he felt. Empty and let-down, the way he felt after he had got out of bed from doing some troll he had taken home for the night. Post-coital blues he had once heard a bloke call it, though he hadn't really understood what the joker had meant: it had been a university student who had come on to the trawler as a temporary while one of the crew had been sick. He had lasted two nights, talking all the bloody time about sex as if it was something he was studying for a degree for up at the university: some of the bloody intellectual ones gave more time to the crotch than they did to the brain. Finally Bixby had thrown him off the boat, disgusted with the little creep. Still, whether the jerk had been right or not, that was how he felt now: the post-coital blues. Only there hadn't been any coitus or whatever they called it. Just murder.

He stood up, throwing away the chewed match, and looked out the window. It would be dark in another hour; better to wait till then. He went to the front door, locked it and came back into the living room. They'd made a bloody shambles of the place, wrestling the way they had. He wondered if the people next door had heard the commotion; if they had, they must have decided not to interfere. He went into the bathroom, bathed the scratches on his cheek and around his left eye, cursed, spat thick saliva into the bowl, and went out to the kitchen. He did not turn on the light, but moved about in the dusk of the small room. He put on the kettle and made himself a cup of coffee. He found some biscuits in a tin in a cupboard and he stood there in the slowly darkening room, sipping coffee and eating a chocolate biscuit, while he decided what to do.

He would have to get her body out of here, get rid of her somewhere. If she was found here, there was no guarantee that Gibson, if the heat got too hot for himself, wouldn't put the finger on him. Maybe not put the demons on him, but hire someone else to get rid of him. Bixby knew that there were always starters in Sydney these days for an elimination job, young mugs who would do it for five hundred bucks and didn't even want to know who had hired them. He wouldn't put it past old Grafter paying for such a job if things got nasty.

No, the best thing would be to get rid of the troll, dump her somewhere she'd never be found; then go and tell Grafter that she'd taken the hint and already gone back to Europe. He'd collect the air fare from Gibson, six or seven hundred bucks, pocket it and write the whole thing off as a neat night's work. But where the hell was he going to dump her so she'd never be found? No use tossing her into the harbour; even if she was weighted there was no guarantee she'd stay down on the bottom. Anything could release her: sharks, even skin-divers; there were so many skin-divers around these days the bottom of the bloody harbour must look like Pitt Street at peak hour. Someone or something could free her and there'd she be, floating up to the top and coming back to haunt him. He remembered the Shark Arm case, he'd been just a kid then, when a couple of mugs had done in a bloke, got rid of him in the water, and bugger me, a couple of weeks later some fishermen catch a shark out at Coogee, put it into some local baths and the bugger spews up the dead bloke's arm, complete with tattoos that identified him. No, the harbour wasn't the shot.

He finished his coffee, put down his cup and saucer and turned to go out of the kitchen. Then he saw the newspaper lying on the shelf beneath the cupboards. The room was quite dark now but for a streak of light that came through the window; he looked out and saw the tall block of flats next door and the bright light that lit up an outside flight of service stairs. The streak of light fell right across the newspaper and he saw the headline: *Minister Would Welcome Ideas*. Then two words jumped out of the story below: *Opera House!* Of course! That was it! He trembled with excitement as the idea took hold of him. Just the place!

He had worked at the Opera House as a labourer for three months about four or five years ago. He had just come out from doing eighteen months for breaking into a factory out at Botany and stealing car radios, and for a while he had found it difficult to get back on the trawlers. He remembered he had been working down below in the Opera House and some gabby engineer, a bloke named Gershwin or Kernel or something, had told them the rooms down there were to be boarded up and never used: they were just part of the foundations. One of those rooms would be just the shot! Dump her in there and she'd never be found, not until they pulled the abortion of a place down and built something else as stupid and useless.

He went back into the living-room and over to the window that faced down on to the street. The kerbs had been lined with parked cars when he had come into the flats, but they must have belonged to people who worked at stores in the neighbourhood; there were plenty of parking spaces now, including a couple right in front of the flats. He went into the bedroom, found a handbag on the dressing-table, searched through it and found a key-ring with two keys on it. He went to the front door, quietly opened it and tried one of the keys in the lock: it fitted. Then he stepped out on to the darkened landing, closed the door silently behind him and went down the stairs.

He was on the second floor landing when he was flooded

with light as a globe immediately above his head came on. He blinked in the sudden brightness after having been in the dark for almost an hour, bumped against a wall; he opened his eyes, already starting to feel the sweat breaking on him, and looked quickly around for whoever had switched on the light. But there was no one there; and when he peered over the stair-rail he could see no one on the first floor landing or the ground floor entrance hall. He gulped in a deep sigh of relief. The light must have been on a time switch.

He went out of the flats, walked two blocks, collected his car, a grey Valiant, and brought it back and parked it in front of the flats. He sat in the car for a minute or two wondering if it was worthwhile going back upstairs for the dame's body. What if some busybody in the flats caught him bringing her downstairs? They'd yell bloody blue murder and have the demons, the fire brigade and probably the bloody army there before he could shut them up. But against that, if he left the body up there in the flat it would be no time before he'd have Grafter Gibson on his neck. And there was the six or seven hundred bucks he'd collect for the air fare the girl was supposed to have used: that wasn't to be sneezed at. He'd need some sort of worker's compensation to tide him over till he could find another boat. The Maltese, the drug pedlar, wasn't going to like it when he told him he'd lost his boat and they would not be able to pick up any more drug packages till he'd got a new one.

He got out of the car, leaving it unlocked, went into the building and quickly up the stairs. He was sweating by the time he reached the landing outside Helga's flat: not from exertion but from fear that someone would have their front door open, would see him and remember him if and when the demons came poking around here. He fumbled with the key as he put it in the lock, but then the door was open and he slipped quietly into the flat, closing the door behind him. In the darkness he stumbled over a chair, bumping the bruised knee where Helga had kicked him; he gasped with pain, then cursed the bitch for what she had done. He crossed to the window, drew the curtains, then fumbled his way to the light switch.

He looked about the room, wondering if he ought to do something about cleaning up the mess. But the sooner he got out of here, the better. Eventually someone was going to come here looking for the dame and they would probably get on to the coppers; but people disappeared every day in the week in a city as big as Sydney and most of them never got their names in the paper. Old Grafter might learn she had disappeared and he might wonder if she really had got on a plane for Europe; but if she never came back, and she wouldn't for sure, then he wouldn't worry any more about it. Get out of here as quick as possible, that was the shot, and get rid of the body.

He went right round the flat, wiping his fingerprints off everything he might have touched. He went out to the kitchen, washed his cup and saucer, dried them and put them on the draining board. He wiped the coffee jar and the biscuit tin and the door of the cupboard from which he had taken them. He went back into the living-room, switched off the light, then wiped the switch. He pulled open the curtains again, getting enough light from the street lights outside to see what he was doing, then he bent over Helga.

He pulled the silk dressing-gown about her and tied up the cord. Even dead she looked a bit of all right; she'd have made a good tread, he'd have bet on that. He lifted her up to sling her over his shoulder, then felt something in the pocket of her dressing-gown. He fumbled in the pocket and brought out the small leather-covered book. A diary: it might be worth hanging on to. He slipped it into his own pocket, then lifted her body on to his shoulder. She was not easy to hold: the silk kept slipping on her body and she felt ready to slide out of it. He grasped her tightly, feeling a certain stiffness already creeping into her. Maybe he had waited too long; he didn't know how long it took for rigor mortis to set in. He'd better hurry.

He opened the front door a few inches, using his handkerchief to keep his prints off the doorknob; then he stepped out quickly, closing the door behind him. He went down the stairs, feeling his arm slipping on the silk of the gown but not wanting to stop to take another grip of her; he was in a cold sweat and he had the crazy feeling that his legs were going to give way beneath him. He heard a door open on the top landing, but by then he was on the bottom flight of stairs. He tried to move more quickly, stumbled, lost his grip on the body and it slid off his shoulder. He made a frantic grab, got a grip on the dressing-gown and swung Helga round. She seemed to stand up in front of him for a moment, her wide-open, blood-streaked eyes only inches from his own; he jerked his head back, stumbled again and almost fell over. Then he grabbed her, swung her up into his arms, reached the lobby and went out through the front door as he heard the clack of a woman's heels coming down the stairs.

A car was backing into a space at the kerb two cars in front of him. He hurried across the pavement, jerked open the door of the Valiant, dumped the body into the rear seat, slammed the door and ran round to get behind the wheel. He fumbled with the ignition, pressed the starter and cursed frantically when the engine didn't fire. Out of the corner of his eye he saw a man and a woman, the woman talking a blue streak, come down into the lobby of the flats and move towards the glass front door. He pressed the starter again, heard the engine cough, then start up. A moment later he was drawing out from the kerb just as the man and woman came out of the flats.

He drove back towards the city, turned down a side road that led to Rushcutters Bay. He knew where he would be able to find a small boat without any trouble. From now it was all going to be plain sailing.

2

'You shouldn't have gone there,' said Walter Helidon. 'That was just plain stupid. What did you think you'd achieve?'

'I don't know.' Norma, slumped in her chair, stared at the pearls lying in her lap. 'I thought she might listen to reason. Sometimes women can talk to each other——' She looked up. '*You* talked to her, I gather. About me.'

He poured himself a drink his third since Norma had come

in less than an hour ago. 'God Almighty, does Rosa have to have her television up that loud?' From the back of the house, from the small rear wing where the maid had her room, came blurred shouts; if one listened carefully it was possible to detect that the shouts had something to do with dog food: a dog barked and was answered by the poodle somewhere else in the house. 'Are Italians deaf?'

'Some Australians are. I just said something to you. You talked to that girl about me.'

He took his drink and stood in front of the marble fireplace. No fire had ever been lit in it; Norma had not wanted the marble discoloured by smoke. Everything in the room still looked as if it had just come from the interior decorator's showroom; varnished with the protective coating of mere possession, the room was designed for show and not for use. We call it the living-room, Helidon thought, and how much of our living has it seen?

'I shouldn't have done that,' he admitted. 'But we're not going to get anywhere—*us*, I mean, you and me—if we stay together and you go on throwing her up at me——'

'You threw me up at her.' Then she sighed and gathered up the pearls in her hands. 'No, you're right. Don't expect me to forgive you for what you've done. But you're right—we must forget her. I'll try if you will.'

'That will be easy——'

'Will it?' She had more capacity for self-torture than he had, she was a woman; but she realized what she was doing to herself and she stopped: 'No, I shan't ask you that. If you stop seeing her——'

'I have to see her again,' he said. 'Just once. To give her the money. Unless you want to give it to her?' Then he saw the look on her face and he added hastily, 'No, that was stupid. I'm sorry, very sorry indeed. I didn't mean anything.'

'Can't you post it to her?'

He shook his head. 'She could say she never received it. We're going to pay her once and once only.'

'Not *we*,' she said. 'You're paying her the money.'

'It's for both of us.'

'It might be. But I don't want to think that I ever paid a penny to her. I hate her, Wally, and whether we talk about her or not, nothing is ever going to change that.' She opened her hands and looked down at them and the pearls that lay in her palms. She saw the picture of herself crawling around the carpet looking for the pearls and she shuddered. Oh God, how could I have degraded myself so much? Suddenly she opened her hands flat and let the pearls fall to the floor. She stood up and went out of the living-room. A moment later he heard her shut the door of their bedroom.

Helidon made a move to follow her, then stopped. Better to leave her to herself; he wouldn't know what to say, anyway, if he did go into the bedroom after her. It was coming home to him now that he had never really made a success of the politics of their marriage; he knew how to canvass for votes, but he had never realized that it was sometimes necessary to canvass for love and understanding. Ambition had always been his disease and he had infected Norma with it. For the last ten years that had been all they had had in common. It had left him without words, or even the gestures, that would be needed if he went into the bedroom.

He jumped as he heard a shot. But it came from the back of the house: someone had been shot between the commercials. He made a step to go and tell Rosa to tone down the volume of her set, then decided against it: while she was out there, wrapped up in whatever was going on on the screen, she wouldn't care what was going on in here. He and Norma had not had their money long enough for him to feel completely at ease with their servants; an egalitarian society never drew a clear enough line between servants and their employers. Should you fight with your wife with a maid in the house?

He turned back and went into the small study off the living-room. He sat down at the leather-topped antique desk and wrote out a cheque for twenty thousand dollars payable to Helga Brand Proprietary Limited. He stared at it: the price of stupidity. He had read somewhere that no man in public life was entitled to a private life and he had scoffed at the idea; but now he was beginning to realize that the man who had expounded the principle had not been such a fool. He wondered how much Helga would have asked for if he had been just a private individual.

He got up, went through to their bedroom and knocked on the door. There was no answer and for a moment he felt a sick panic: had Norma done something foolish like trying to commit suicide? He turned the knob, pushing against the door expecting it to be locked; but it opened at once and he almost fell into the room, only saving himself by holding on to the door. Norma lay on her back on the bed staring at the ceiling.

'I'm going out,' he said, and his voice trembled with relief at finding she was all right. 'I'll take the cheque to her, get it over and done with. I'll be back in an hour.' She made no answer, didn't even look at him. He hesitated, fumbling for the words he knew he didn't have. 'I mean it, darl. Only an hour. I won't stay there. Just give her the cheque and come straight back. Will you be all right?'

She still did not look at him, but she said, 'When you come back, I don't want to hear a word of what's happened. We never mention her again.'

'No,' he said. 'We're finished with her.'

He went out to the car. He drove carefully into the city, over the Harbour Bridge and out through the neon-lit congestion of King's Cross. American servicemen on leave from Vietnam wandered the pavements of the Cross; they were all dressed in civilian slacks and shirts, but there was no mistaking them. They were just boys and they all had a look of innocence about them; it was strange, but Helidon had noticed that all of them seemed to look like country boys. It was as if the months of war in Vietnam had stripped them of any sophistication they might have had. They wandered the pavements looking for girls, and Helidon, passing them in the Mercedes, hoped they found none like Helga. But even as he wished better for the young Americans, there was the lingering regret, only half-confessed, that it was all over with Helga.

He drove out to Double Bay, parked the car in Helga's street, feeling secure now in the darkness, and crossed to the block of flats. He took his dark glasses out of his pocket, then dropped them back again. He would look more conspicuous wearing dark glasses at night than if he were without them. He went into the building and ran quickly up the stairs. By the time he was outside Helga's door he was puffing; he'd do better from now on to spend his Monday and Thursday evenings at some gymnasium. He would do just that; he glowed with the self-righteousness of the newly reformed. He let himself into the flat with his key, closing the door behind him. He switched on the light, then stopped, staring through into the living-room.

Norma had told him she and Helga had fought, but they couldn't have caused *this* much destruction. The room looked as if a battle, not just a struggle between two women, had been fought in it. A glass lay shattered on the floor; he could see the mark where it had been hurled against the wall. All the chairs but the heavy lounge chair had been overturned; the coffee table lay on its side, two of its legs snapped off. A chocolate box was upturned on the floor, its contents scattered about and crushed into dark stains on the yellow carpet. One of the heavy drapes that curtained off the small dining recess had been pulled down and lay like a bundled body behind the heavy lounge chair. He felt sick, shutting his eyes against the picture that suddenly sprang into his mind of Norma and Helga fighting, rolling and tumbling about this room like two savages and causing this chaos.

Then he opened his eyes and called, 'Helga?'

He waited, then moved towards the bedroom. But it was empty; so were all the other rooms. He came back into the living-room, frightened now. Where had Helga gone? Had she decided not to wait for the money, was already on her way to see one of the publishers of the political scandal sheets?

He picked up the phone, dialled his home number. He waited for what seemed a long time; he began to wonder if Norma was going to answer the phone and once again he got the sick feeling of panic. Then the ringing stopped and she said, 'Hullo?'

'Darl, it's me. She's not here.' He looked around the room again as if expecting Helga to appear from some corner he had overlooked. 'Darl, the place is a wreck. You must have had a terrible donnybrook with her.'

There was silence for a moment, then she said, 'I can't remember doing any damage——'

'You must have. You probably didn't notice. The coffee table has a couple of legs broken, you tore down a curtain. And there's a broken glass—— Did she throw a *glass* at you?'

'Nothing like that. I tell you, as far as I can remember we didn't damage the place at all——' She broke off, then her voice faltered as she came on the line again: 'Darling, come home. Quickly!'

He looked around the room again, feeling even more afraid. He would not come here again, but he did not look around trying to store memories. It would be best if he could forget everything that had happened in this flat. 'I'll be right home, darl.'

He was at the door when he paused, wondering if there was anything in the flat that belonged to him. He went back into the living-room, then through into the bedroom and bathroom: he could find nothing that could be identified with him, that she could produce as any sort of evidence that he had been a regular visitor here. He took his key out of his pocket and dropped it on the small table beside the front door. He looked at it for a moment, felt the temptation of it. Then he turned his back on it; he had told Norma he was finished with Helga and he meant it. He would call Helga tomorrow, meet her somewhere else and give her the cheque. Besides he would not come back here again. Someone else but Norma and himself had been here this evening and only God knew what had happened after Norma had left.

He went out of the flat, closing the door after him. He was half-way down the stairs when he heard the man and the woman, the woman talking continuously without seeming to draw breath, coming up the stairs. There was no way of avoiding them. He missed his step, recovered, and went on down. He nodded to the couple as he passed them, then he had reached the lobby. He opened the glass door and as he went out he heard the woman, her voice magnified in the stair-well, say, 'His face looked sorta familiar——'

He was out in the street, half-way to his car, when he remembered the cheque he had given Helga this afternoon, the one she had torn up.

But it was too late now to go back and search for the pieces. His key was inside the flat.

CHAPTER ELEVEN

I

Friday, December 13

'MAKING PROGRESS?' asked Kerslake, mouth working; he had a week's questions bottled up. 'See you've learned the name of the girl. Read nothing else, though. Not getting far?'

'It takes time,' said Malone. 'The Opera House wasn't built in a day.'

Kerslake jerked his head under the jab, acknowledged it. 'True, true. Well, if we can help——'

Malone and Clements had driven back from Pymble and Norma Helidon to headquarters. Malone had given the pipe he had taken from Helidon's rack to Clements and asked him to take it up to Fingerprints at the CIB. Then he had lapsed into silence and Clements, miserable with his cold, had concentrated on his driving. He had automatically slid behind the wheel when they had come out of the Helidon house and now he was wishing he had given the wheel to Malone. But he recognized that Malone had something on his mind, something that was worrying the Irishman more than his own cold was worrying himself.

'What's eating you, Scobie?' he said at last.

Malone hedged. 'If you had to put all that money of yours on the murderer right now, where would you lay it?'

'You mean out of Helidon, Gibson and Savanna?'

'There are two other starters—Mrs Helidon and the bloke who chewed those matches.'

Clements pulled up at a red light, glanced out at two long-haired youths in a souped-up Holden. The passenger grinned insolently across at him, while the driver kept revving the engine; then all at once recognition dawned in the eye of the passenger and he spoke out of the side of his mouth to the driver. The latter took his foot off the accelerator and the two of them slouched down in their seats, gentlemen of leisure out for a breath of fresh air. The light turned green and Clements took off; in his mirror he saw the Holden ambling away from the light at no more than twenty miles an hour, holding up traffic in the lane behind it.

'Forget them.' Malone had noticed Clements's reaction to the two youths; Clements at twenty-six was well on his way to being an arch-conservative. 'They were doing nothing.'

'It's the long hair. I'd like to run 'em all in just on suspicion.'

'Of what?'

Clements had not yet reached the fossilized stage of conservatism: he could still laugh at himself. 'Anything. But——' He stopped, smiling, and said, 'You're letting your own suspicions get away a bit, aren't you?'

'How's that?' said Malone, at once on the defensive.

'I think you've already decided one or both of the Helidons killed Helga.' Malone said nothing and Clements took the car up the approach to the Harbour Bridge and through the toll gates before he went on: 'I'll admit I'm a bit with you. I can't see any connection Gibson would have had with her. And Savanna—well, I guess he could have done her in. He could have had reason to—if she was blackmailing him, going to tell his wife or something. Still——' He shook his head. 'I think it was one of the Helidons. Or both. But we're supposed to be objective. And it still doesn't account for the bloke who chewed those matches. He could have been another one of her customers, you know. Her Saturday or Sunday bloke.'

Malone shook his head. 'Not unless he came on the wrong day. She was done in some time on the Monday. She'd have cleaned up the remains of any Sunday visitor. The living-room was a shambles, but you heard what Savanna told us—she was house-proud. The rest of the flat looked it. The kitchen, the bedroom, the bathroom—they were like exhibition rooms. She wouldn't have left any dirty ashtrays overnight from Saturday or Sunday. The other feller was there on Monday all right. But we don't know who he was or what motive he had—unless he'd just been called in to help get rid of her body. We know Helidon had a motive—if she was blackmailing him, as I think she was. Mrs Helidon had a motive, too. She wouldn't be the first wife who'd killed her husband's girl friend.'

'Yeah, I'd lay money she'd been to Helga's flat. She was too nervous all the time we were looking at those pearls. And they matched, all right. She could have had them down to the jeweller's any day last week and had them re-strung in a hurry.'

'That maid would know. Try and trace her. Try the Italian social clubs. These migrants usually go to their own community clubs when they first come out here. Someone at one of them might know her.'

Clements sniffled and made a face. 'I was thinking of going home to bed.'

'Go home afterwards. Go round the clubs first, sample some of that Chianti and garlic. It's supposed to be good for colds.'

Clements took the car down the Cahill expressway, flying across the glass face of the city. 'What are you gunna do?'

'I think I'll go and see my Old Man. Ask him to help me do a bit of detective work.'

'He won't like that.'

Con Malone didn't. When Malone left Kerslake and went down into the basement of the Opera House, having borrowed a helmet and a torch, Con was with him, grumbling and muttering like an old soldier who for the tenth day running had drawn latrine duty. 'Dunno why you can't do your own dirty work.'

'I'm trying to show you that not all police work is dirty,' said Malone, grinning in the gloom at his father. 'Now, can you string me up some lights in here?'

'What are you looking for?'

'A chewed matchstick.' He took a match from the box in his pocket, chewed one end, then showed it to his father. 'Like that.'

Con Malone looked around the chamber, at the debris of timber and old newspapers, milk bottles, beer bottles and one wine bottle, lengths of rope and sheets of corrugated iron, and the single iron bed-head that leaned against one wall like the bars for a window that had never been constructed in this dungeon. 'You want your bloody head read! Find a match *here*?'

But he went away to get the lights and Malone sat down on a length of timber, the torch at his feet, and waited. He slipped the chewed match back into his pocket. The room was as silent as a tomb; what sounds could be heard from outside had the ghostly effect of echoes, calls from another world. What a place to finish up, he thought; and once again felt the sympathy for Helga Brand. I'm in the wrong game. If I expected gentle deaths for everyone, I should have gone into a seminary, as Mum wanted me to. But even as he had the thought, he knew there was no guarantee that the deaths in a seminary were any less violent than Helga's had been. The priest might die with no marks on his throat, but no one knew the haemorrhage of despair there might have been in the man's heart. For all he knew of Helga, deep inside her she might have welcomed her own death.

I wonder if Helidon could give me the answer to that one if I asked him? But here I go again: why do I keep choosing him as the murderer? It was okay to arrest vagrants and loiterers on suspicion; maybe not strictly legal, but it came under the heading of prevention of crime and that was a good enough reason. I told Mrs Helidon this morning: you go against the rules when they get in the way. But you couldn't afford to go against the rules when it came to arresting a man for murder. There was no death sentence in New South Wales, but if Helidon were arrested his life would be finished as surely as if the rope had been strung round his neck. The case against Helidon had to be watertight, had to be based on evidence that would be even more convincing to Malone himself than to a jury. When he laid the charge against Helidon there must be no doubt in his own mind about the facts. Suspicion, prejudice if you like, must be entirely eliminated. Whatever Helidon had got away with seven or eight years ago in the land deal case had no bearing on this case. Charlie Duggan, the cynical con man, had once said, 'Looked at from my side of the fence, justice is nothing more than civilized revenge.' Well, he must see he did not prove Charlie had been right.

Con Malone came back with a long lead to which were connected two high-wattage globes. The room abruptly took shape: hard, cold, uninviting, lacking any mystery. 'What are the police rates for casuals?' Con Malone wanted to know.

'You're doing this as a public duty, didn't you know?'

'Am I?' Con made a rude remark about that; but he made no attempt to walk out. 'Well, we better start over where the body was, then work back in a line towards the door. Right?'

Malone looked admiringly at his father. 'Didn't I tell you? I got all my detective talent from you.'

'I had more bloody pride than to join the police force, but your Uncle Seamus, he killed a copper in The Troubles back home in the Ould Country, you know that? They put up a statue to him, my word they did.'

'Who?' Malone grinned. 'The copper or Uncle Seamus?'

'Bloody funny.'

They spent half an hour searching the chamber, but they found no chewed matches. At last Con Malone straightened up. 'We're wasting our time, Scobie. Nobody's been in here who chewed matches. Or if he was, he was too busy to be chewing 'em. You think he might be the bloke who done her in?'

'I don't know,' said Malone, still riding tight on his own suspicions. 'But if he didn't kill her, he'll be able to tell us who did.'

'I don't think I'd snitch on a mate,' said Con Malone. 'Not even for murder.'

'Not even if they murdered Mum or me?'

'That'd be different, but!' Con looked shocked, as if he had never thought that anyone close to him could be murdered.

'It always is,' said Malone a trifle sadly.

He took one more look around the chamber, then Con Malone took down the lights and they made their way up through the maze of passages, out of the cool, damp gloom, and came out on to one of the outdoor podiums above the wide expanse of steps. They stood there in the threatening heat; Malone took some time to adjust to the assault on his senses. In front of them the city, all glass and concrete, glittered like a broken escarpment of pure quartz: people worked behind those glass cliffs, the buildings were *alive*, but you would never know it: the sun blazed on them, the windows reflected a blinding uninhabited infinity. Behind him he could hear the sound of hammering, magnified a thousand times by the giant horn of the roof shell: it pounded against his eardrum. He shut his eyes, wishing he had brought some sunglasses with him. When he opened them and looked down the long broad flight of steps he saw a party of Japanese coming up, little men in dark business suits whose helmets looked like white bowlers. At their head, dressed in the same farcical uniform, was Walter Helidon.

'Well, Sergeant Malone!'

Helidon paused at the top of the steps and Malone waited for him to doff his helmet; but Helidon knew when political politeness could descend into ridicule. He excused himself from the group; the Japanese moved on under the guidance of one of Helidon's officials. Malone looked after them as they moved on up another flight of steps, their cameras clicking like the hammers of empty guns; the Japanese must be the world's most indefatigable photographers, Japan itself would soon be buried in a snowdrift of pictures of other parts of the world. Con Malone also looked after them. Then he spat, an old-timer who had no time for old-time enemies. He stepped to the end of the podium, stood looking out at the skyline of the city as if viewing it for the first time. But it wasn't the Japanese who had driven him there. It was bad enough to be seen in the company of his son, the policeman, but to be seen in the company of both a policeman and a politician from the other party was more than his life was worth; there were certain lengths to which an old Labour radical could never go; even to have spoken to the Japanese would have been more forgivable. Malone and Helidon were left alone on the top of the steps.

'A trade delegation,' said Helidon, nodding after the Japanese. 'They weren't very impressed when I told them we had been working on the Opera House for ten years. Seems it took them only fifteen years to re-build the whole of Hiroshima.' He took out a handkerchief, took off his glasses, wiped the sweat from his face, then replaced the glasses.

Malone recognized the ritual: he waited for the remark that had to follow: 'My wife called me. You've been up to see her.'

'Yes,' Malone said cautiously; again he felt his dislike of the self-assured politician coming to the surface. 'I hope we didn't upset her too much?'

'What do you think?' Helidon snapped. 'My wife isn't used to being questioned by the police. Neither am I, for that matter.'

'As I remember it, Mr Helidon, you told me that once before.'

'Have you got some sort of grudge against me, Malone?' Helidon looked at him warily.

'No,' Malone lied; or thought he lied.

'You left my wife with the distinct impression that you did not believe what she had told you.'

Malone tried to look surprised; somewhere up in the roof-shell a workman laughed, the sound a giant giggle of mirth. 'I don't know how she got that idea. The questions were only routine.'

'Don't treat my wife as a suspect, Sergeant. I'm warning you. If you bother her again, I'll have a word with the Commissioner. You have no grounds at all for questioning her the way you did.'

Malone felt himself get hot, far hotter than the sun had made him. Keep cool for Christ's sake, Malone! Don't knock the Cabinet Minister arse-over-charlie down the steps, not in front of the Japanese: this isn't the Diet. The group had turned to look back at the city: Malone and Helidon were centre stage, right in the line of their gaze. 'I'm acting on instructions, sir. I was told to treat this as a routine murder case and that's what I'm doing. The only way to solve any case is by asking questions.'

'You have no questions you have to ask my wife. Come to me with them if you have any. Though I can't imagine what else we'd have to tell you.'

Malone hesitated, then put his hand in his pocket, took out the chewed matchstick and held it in the palm of his hand. He did not know why he had not thrown the match away down in the basement chamber; but he had learned to profit from his unexplained actions and he never queried them. He had the Celt's respect for mysterious influences, the visions hidden but felt.

'Do you know a man who does that? Chews matches?'

Helidon looked down at the tiny frayed stick. He stared at it while his hand went to his pocket, took out his handkerchief again. He did not take off his glasses this time, but wiped his face and ran his handkerchief round inside his collar. Then he said, 'No, no one. No one at all.'

'You're sure?'

'Very sure, indeed. Was that one of the questions you asked my wife?'

'No.' Then Malone looked towards the group of Japanese as they began to move into the main building. 'I shan't keep you, Mr Helidon. I think your friends from Hiroshima are getting a little impatient. You're probably losing face.'

He spun round and walked along the broad podium to where his father stood. Con Malone turned, his face squeezed into a wrinkled gourd by the glare of the sun, and nodded at Helidon as the politician disappeared into the dark shadow of one of the giant shells.

'Didn't know you knew him. Seen him on TV the other night. A smarmy bastard like all his sort. He's got nothing to do with this case, has he?'

'No,' said Malone, and could still see the look of utter fear that had been in Helidon's eyes when he had looked down at the chewed match.

'His mob gets away with murder,' said Con Malone. 'But even he wouldn't go in for the real stuff. He'd be too gutless, they're all gutless today. He'd be the sort'd pay someone else to do it.'

Malone looked sharply at his father, then forced a grin. 'You're starting to sound like a real cop.'

Con spat disgustedly at a passing seagull. 'I pity that poor girl of yours. She dunno what she's marrying.'

You're right, Malone thought. And wondered what questions had been in Norma Helidon's mind when she had married Walter Helidon.

When Malone got back to Y Division headquarters, Inspector Fulmer was in the detectives' room.

'How's it coming, Scobie?'

Malone put down the sandwiches and bottle of milk he had brought in with him for his lunch. 'Not easy. I've just been talking to Helidon again.' He summarized his conversation with Helidon. 'He knows who killed her. Or if he doesn't know for sure, he's got a bloody good idea. I thought he was going to have a heart attack when I showed him this.' He took the chewed matchstick out of his pocket. 'But I think you'll have to start backing me up, Tom. I don't think the Commissioner is the sort who'd let himself be pressured by any politician. But I just don't want to be sent for and have to lay all my cards on the table at once. The truth is, I don't have all the cards right now.'

'You won't be sent for.' Fulmer was walking up and down, rubbing his hands together; Malone had never seen him so animated. 'I'll see to that. You might as well know——' He stopped, smiling like a bishop who had just been canonized before they had buried him. 'I'm the new Divisional Superintendent. It's going to be announced officially on Monday. Harry Chester is retiring—bad heart. I'll see you're not worried, Scobie. Go ahead on the case just the way you were.'

Malone congratulated him. 'Who's coming in as Div. Inspector?'

'It hasn't been decided yet. Pity it couldn't be you. But your day will come.'

'There are at least ten fellers ahead of me. I'll be fifty before I make Inspector. That's the worst of the Public Service. You always have to wait till the bloke ahead of you dies or retires before you get promotion. I could be the greatest cop in the country and I could still not make Inspector before I was forty-five at the least.'

Fulmer nodded sympathetically. 'I never thought I'd make Super so soon. I thought another five years at least.'

Malone grinned. 'You could make Commissioner yet.'

Light gleamed for a moment in Fulmer's dark eyes; then he shook his head. 'That will never happen. John Leeds still has six years to go before he retires as Commissioner and there are four other men who could make it ahead of me. In six years' time I'll be within two years of retiring. They'd never consider me.' Promotion to the top was a mathematical calculation: Fulmer's sums and his dreams did not add up to a common total. His guard let down by his elation at his unexpected promotion, he did not seem to realize how much he was confiding in a junior officer. The gap between sergeant and inspector was not much: it allowed for confidences and even argument; but on Monday he would be a superintendent, another species altogether. He looked at the Christmas cards on the mantelpiece. 'Could not have come at a more appropriate time. A wonderful Christmas present for my wife.'

I wonder if he'll promote her, Malone thought. He had met Fulmer's wife at several police functions: a small dowdy woman who stood as much in awe of her husband as a cadet policeman would. 'Well, anyway, it'll be nice to know you're standing between me and the Commissioner.'

'You'll have nothing to worry about. If Helidon can contribute anything more, you go at him. We don't have to be respecters of position in a murder case. It would be nice if you could wrap it up before Christmas.' He nodded at the matchstick. 'Find that fellow and perhaps that will be it.'

He left and Malone sat down to his lunch. He put his feet up on his desk, picked up an early edition of the afternoon paper. Other detectives drifted in, all of them looking worn out by the heat. Nobody discussed the cases they were on; each man respected the troubles of another. Malone read the newspaper, marvelling at the amount of trouble there was in the world outside his own bailiwick: the war in Vietnam, the guerilla fighting in the Middle East, the war in Biafra, an earthquake in Turkey, floods in Italy, Australia in trouble in the cricket Test against the West Indies. Only the advertisements seemed to have the right happy note: spend your money and enjoy a bankrupt Christmas. Malone drank his milk, wondering why it tasted a little sour.

Then his phone rang: it was Lisa. 'It's in the papers.'

'What is?'

'Mrs Helidon's abdication. Didn't you see it? It is headlines in the women's section.'

He flipped over the pages of the newspaper to the women's section, an area of print normally as esoteric to him as the pages of *Cybernetics Weekly*. The story of Norma Helidon took up half a page and was illustrated with a photo of her in evening dress: evidently she had not given any interviews this morning. But the writer of the story had not been lost for words: the Virgin Mary, Malone mused, had retired from the scene with less fuss.

'I called her,' Lisa said in his ear. 'She told me she will not be wanting our services any longer. She said her health was not good and she was thinking of going abroad. But that wasn't for publication. Don't you think that's interesting?'

'You're playing detective again.'

'All right. I'm sorry. But I thought you would like to know.' The coolness was in her voice for a moment, but then it went when she said, 'Am I seeing you tonight?'

'A beer, a sausage roll and thou beside me—what more could a man want?'

'A little culture,' she said, and hung up in his ear.

It was three o'clock before Clements returned. He came in, his jacket over his arm, his shirt stuck to his back and chest with sweat, his eyes streaming. He flopped down in his chair, blew his nose, wiped his eyes and slubbered like an exhausted horse.

'Donna ask me whata sorta day itsa been!' He threw back his head and laughed, an hysterical sound. 'I've just spent five bloody hours talking broken English and pidgin Italian. If there's one thing I've learned, it's that I'm no linguist!'

Malone grinned, held up a paper bag. 'Had your lunch? There's one sandwich left.'

'I've been doing nothing else but eat and drink ever since I left you. I'm chockablock with pizza and capuccino. They didn't want to know me at first in the clubs, but once I convinced them I wasn't looking for Rosa to pinch her, were they hospitable and talkative!'

'Why did it take you five hours then?'

'The first six clubs, there was someone at every one of 'em who thought he knew her. Then everyone'd get into the act.' He shook his head, still laughing. 'They've all asked me back on their Guest Night. I think I'll go, too. Some of these Italian birds aren't bad. Especially Rosa. When she's out of that maid's uniform she's a bit of all right.'

Malone said patiently, 'Where did you find her?'

Clements grinned. 'Sorry, mate. Well, I got on to her at the seventh club, one out in Paddington. They gave me her address—she's moved in with an aunt and uncle out that way.' He stopped smiling, blew his nose again. 'She didn't leave the Helidons. Mrs Helidon sacked her. Gave her two months' pay and told her to get lost.'

'Rosa say if she gave any reason for the sacking?'

'None, except that she and Helidon had been upset by the death of an old friend and were thinking of going abroad.' He put his big hand down on Malone's desk as if he were laying a card there. 'Helga had been to their house. Rosa remembered her—she was there the week before she was murdered, Rosa couldn't remember the night. But when Helga was leaving, Rosa heard her say something about seeing Helidon on the Monday. She couldn't remember exactly what it was, her English isn't that good, but she remembered it. Evidently she came to the front of the house, was about to go into the living-room to ask the Helidons if they wanted something to eat, when she saw the two of them looking as if they were just about to start a fight. Helidon was holding his cheek as if his missus had clocked him one. Rosa beat it back to the kitchen.'

'What else did you find out?'

'I asked her about the pearls. I was right—Mrs Helidon *had* had them in to a jeweller's last week. Rosa saw them on the dressing-table one morning—she thought it was the Tuesday but she couldn't be sure—the string was broken and they were lying loose. She asked Mrs Helidon about them, but Mrs Helidon gave her the brush-off, said there'd been a bit of an accident and not to worry about them. That day Mrs H. took them into town to have them re-strung.' He stood up. 'I'll be back. I've got a gallon of capuccino I've got to get rid of.'

When he came back Malone said, 'I think we'll go out and see Savanna. Then if we've got time, we'll make another call on Grafter Gibson.'

Clements looked surprised. 'Why those two? Why not go out and see the Helidons again?'

Malone still lay back in his chair, his feet still up on his desk. But he could feel the tension within himself, the coming to a decision that worried him because he had anticipated it long before he had had good grounds for it.

'Who do you think killed Helga?'

Clements had been about to fix his tie which he had loosened. He stopped with his hand to his collar. 'You asking me to lay it on the line? Getting ready to charge someone?'

Malone didn't reply at once, then he nodded. 'Yes.'

Clements fixed his tie, patted it down against his still-damp chest. Then he said, 'Either Helidon or his missus. The bloke who chewed those matches was probably in on it, but whether he did the actual job or was just there to help get rid of the body, I'd lay money the Helidons were the ones who thought up the idea.'

'That's the way I see it, too,' said Malone, and felt as if a weight had been lifted from him. He stood up, put on his jacket. 'Okay, let's go and see Savanna.'

'Why him? And then Gibson?'

'Because I want to be a hundred per cent sure. I want those two absolutely in the clear before we go to the Bishop and tell him we want a warrant for Helidon.'

Clements blew his nose, wiped his eyes. 'I guess you're right. But this time next week I think I'm gunna have more wrong with me thana cold in the head.'

3

Savanna was not at Olympus. Malone and Clements swam up to his office on a heavy current of meat pie and beer smells: the bakery and the brewery seemed to be doubling production for the Christmas demand. The secretary, her crisp appearance wilted at the edges by the heat, looked up distractedly as they entered the tiny outer office. 'No, Mr Savanna *isn't* here! Suddenly everything's happening and he's taken the day off.' The phone rang and she snapped into it for a minute or two, then slammed it back in its cradle. Then for the first time she seemed to remember who they were and some of the temper went out of her face, to be replaced by a grey look of concern. 'Mr Savanna isn't in any trouble, is he? I mean, you're not from the, you know, Fraud Squad or whatever it is?'

'He hasn't been cooking the books, has he?' Malone said.

She found the energy to shake her head vigorously. 'I do the books. We're in the red—my word, are we in the red!— but there's nothing crooked in them. He's not in trouble, is he?' she repeated plaintively.

'No,' said Malone. 'In fact, he's helping us. What's his home address?'

The girl gave it to them, but not till she had looked at them suspiciously again. For all her impatience with her boss for taking the day off, it was obvious that she had a deep loyalty to him. Outside in the steaming heat again Clements said, 'That girl would never give evidence against Savanna.'

'I wonder if his wife will? I wonder if he's told her yet about Helga?'

Savanna was in his garden when Malone and Clements drove out to Rose Bay. He wore a pair of shorts and no shirt and though he was tanned there was the beginning of sunburn on his bony shoulders, as if he might have spent all day out here in the garden.

'It's not a good day for planting,' he said, gesturing at the border plants lying on the piece of wet sacking, 'but they'd be dead if I left them much longer. My wife usually does all this. I'm not much of a gardener——' He stopped, brushed the dirt from his hands and looked at the two detectives. 'What am I talking so much for? You're not interested in me as a gardener, are you?'

'Maybe some other time.' Malone looked around the garden. If Mrs Savanna took care of all this on her own, then she did not have much else to occupy her time. The house, a Spanish villa with Australian overtones, the stone koalas at the foot of the steps and the iron lacework along the veranda, was set back from the street about forty feet; the whole of the front area, with the exception of the driveway, was taken up by a thickly planted garden of hibiscus, camellia, magnolias and multi-coloured semi-tropical shrubs. There did not seem to be another square inch of soil in which anything else could be planted; it was as if Mrs Savanna had gone on planting and planting because there was nothing else she could find to do; she would not be the first wife he had met who had empty hours to fill. He looked back at Savanna. 'Does your wife know about Helga Brand?'

Savanna bit his lip, then nodded. 'I told her this morning. That was why I took the day off. She—she didn't take it too well.'

'Do women ever take that sort of thing well?'

Savanna shrugged. In his ragged shorts and thonged sandals, his long hair unkempt and hanging about his ears, he looked no lady-killer. 'I debated whether I'd tell her. I didn't want to hurt her. You see——' His mouth twitched as if he were in pain; but he was only trying to smile. 'I don't like hurting people, especially women. That's why I couldn't have killed Helga.'

'Why did you tell your wife, then?'

Savanna shrugged again, a nervous gesture as much as an answer. 'I don't know. I wanted to be honest with her, I suppose that was part of it. And to be honest with you'—he managed the smile this time—'I knew you'd be back some time to see her or me. And I didn't want her to find out about Helga from you.'

Malone looked at Clements, read the expression in the younger man's face, knew Clements felt the same way as he did: they were both beginning to like Savanna. 'Could we go inside, Mr Savanna? I can see a couple of curtains moving in your neighbours' windows. I don't know why, Constable Clements and I don't think we look any different from anyone else, but people always seem to recognize policemen from a mile away. We don't want to spoil your reputation.'

'It will be spoiled sooner or later,' said Savanna with only mildly bitter resignation. 'Unless you can keep me out of the murder trial.'

'You sound pretty sure we're going to bring someone to trial.'

'Don't you always?'

'Most of the time, but not always. Some cases we never wrap up. Others we solve, but don't have enough evidence to bring them to court. There are two men walking around Sydney now, we know they committed murder and they know we know, but we'll never get them up before a judge.'

'Well, I hope you get this fellow,' said Savanna; and Malone was puzzled why the grey-haired man suddenly looked afraid. But he said nothing as he and Clements followed Savanna up the steps into the house. Clements almost fell over one of the stone koalas and Savanna's mouth twitched again in another unsuccessful attempt at a smile. 'They were here when we bought the house, Somehow I've never had the heart to get rid of them. It seemed un-Australian.'

'You don't seem to have the heart for a lot of things, Mr Savanna.' Malone's voice was gentle, not unkind, and Savanna was sensitive enough to catch the exact tone of it.

'Too true, Sergeant.' He held open a screen door, ushered them ahead of him. 'But nobody chooses his own heart, does he? Not even the transplant patient. This is my wife.'

Malone recognized the look on Josephine Savanna's face. He had seen it before on the faces of women who had built a life on the sand of delusion, who had substituted self-deception for happiness; when everything collapsed they had nothing else to fall back on, no foundations on which they could build again. Her eyes and mouth looked bruised, as if she had been physically hit by her husband; if she had had any dignity to begin with, it had been stripped from her like a tattered gown. She nodded dumbly at Malone and Clements, her eyes wincing a little more when she understood that they were police.

Savanna led them into a living-room where good and bad taste fought a battle in which neither was the winner: a delicate Swedish vase looked ready to crack under the half a dozen plastic flowers it held, a boy in a small Arthur Boyd painting raised the gun that he couldn't fire at the ceramic ducks flying up the opposite wall. Malone, giving Savanna the credit for the good taste, wondered how much time he spent here, if he had at some time given up and Josephine Savanna had surrounded herself with her own comforts.

Savanna went out to the kitchen to get some beers out of the refrigerator and Malone and Clements were left uncomfortably alone with Mrs Savanna. The three of them sat in silence for almost a minute, then Josephine Savanna said, 'You haven't come to—to make trouble for my husband, have you?'

Malone wanted to tell her that it was not the police's job to make trouble, that ordinary citizens did well enough at that on their own. 'No, Mrs Savanna, your husband is in the clear as far as we're concerned.'

'He's been a good husband——' She gestured around her, as if providing a home was evidence enough that a man was a good husband. 'And a good father, too.'

For the first time Malone saw the photographs on the bookshelves. One could have been of Josephine Savanna some years ago, but it was hard to tell: she looked too effortlessly happy: expressions, Malone realized, could date as much as hair styles. In the other photo a pretty girl in a mortarboard and gown smiled with all the confidence of someone whose worst fears were over: she had graduated and everything from now on would be easy. 'She's very attractive.'

'She's in England, she's doing a post-graduate course at Cambridge.' She looked up at Savanna as he returned with three beers and a lemonade on a fancy wickerwork tray. She took the lemonade as he handed it to her, but didn't look at it. 'I was telling them about Margaret. You've given her everything she ever wanted.'

'Not just me. You, too.' He gave Malone and Clements their beers, sat down and sipped his own. 'We're trying to decide what to do. Whether to write and tell her everything or—Jesus Christ!'

He suddenly broke off, put his hand over his eyes. His other hand shook and some beer splashed out of his glass and dropped on his bare knee. The breakdown was so sudden that Malone's hand jerked in surprise; the beer splashed in his own glass. In the heavy silence that followed sounds spilled in from outside the house like a gritty wind: next door a child whined that Larry had hit it, a transistor radio in a garden had Aretha Franklin telling that she took what she wanted. Malone and Clements sat in stiff embarrassment; they were accustomed to scenes like this, but they were never comfortable in them. Josephine Savanna stared at her husband for a moment, but she didn't rise and cross to him as Malone had expected. Instead, she looked back at the two detectives, took a sip from her lemonade, put the glass down on a small table beside her, then folded her hands in her lap. The change in her was remarkable. It was as if having witnessed the total collapse of her husband it was now time to start re-building, herself and him. There was no malice or even satisfaction in her attitude. It was the decision of someone who still had faith in self-deception: all you had to do was close your eyes against the bad, believe only in the good. There would be no more other women in her husband's life, he had learned his lesson, he would love only her from now on, would be the good husband and father in the image she had created.

Malone coughed. 'I think we'd better get on with it, Mr Savanna. Maybe I'm being a bit more candid than I should be, but we don't think you had anything to do with Helga Brand's murder. But we still haven't accounted for that two hours of yours on the afternoon of her death. Where were you?'

Josephine Savanna had been gazing at Malone, relief blossoming in her face like a pale blush as she heard him say that Savanna had had nothing to do with the murder; but now abruptly her head swung back towards her husband on Malone's last words. The hands tightened in her lap, the fingers became entwined bones. The expression on her face was as eloquent as if she had cried out: Oh God, there's not another one!

Savanna took his hand away from his eyes; there was a shine in the corners of them, but he had not succumbed to weeping. Malone was glad of that: he did not like to see all the iron taken out of a man. Savanna stared at the detectives, but didn't cast even a side glance at his wife. At last he said, 'I can't prove I was anywhere. I just drove—drove out to Bondi. I sat on the promenade there for, I don't know, an hour, an hour and a half, I couldn't say. I—I was going to tell Helga it was finished between us.'

Josephine Savanna's hands relaxed: the relief came back into her face. But Malone knew Savanna was lying, even if now was not the time to accuse him of it: there were certain things, whatever they might be, that Savanna was not going to admit in front of his wife. 'Why were you calling it off? Was she trying to blackmail you?'

Savanna laughed, a dry hacking sound. 'How can you blackmail a bankrupt? She knew how broke I am——'

'You never told me.' His wife's voice was flat, devoid of surprise or accusation.

Savanna looked at her now, as if some sort of danger had passed. 'I didn't want you to worry——' The concern for her in his face was genuine: he's not lying this time, Malone thought. 'One of us was enough.'

'Do we have any money at all?' Then she bit her lip, looked at Malone and Clements. 'I'm sorry. That's something my husband and I can discuss later.'

Malone asked a few more questions, but only as a matter of form. The interview was over, but for the one important question; and he did not want to ask that in front of Josephine Savanna. He nodded to Clements, who gulped down the last of his beer, and the two of them stood up.

Malone looked at the photo of their daughter. 'I wouldn't tell her just yet. Just in case we never need to call you to court——'

Husband and wife looked at each other, then Savanna nodded. 'Thanks, Sergeant.'

The two detectives said good-bye to Josephine Savanna, who acknowledged their farewell almost off-handedly; she had something more important on her mind, she was going to build a new life with her husband, starting from rock-bottom scratch. Savanna followed Malone and Clements down to the front gate.

'You're still not going to tell us where you were that afternoon?' Malone said.

Savanna made a pretence of exasperation. 'I've told you!'

Malone shrugged. 'You're not trying to protect someone else—another woman?'

'You asked me that question once before,' Savanna said evenly. 'No.'

There is another woman, Malone thought; but she really didn't matter any more. He didn't press the point, but put his hand into his pocket, took out the chewed matchstick he had shown to Helidon.

'Do you know anyone who does that—chews matches?'

There was only a momentary hesitation on Savanna's part; but, Malone had to admit, it could have been the hesitation of puzzlement. 'I don't know. I suppose I do. But I couldn't name them off-hand. A lot of men do it, don't they?'

'Not that many,' said Malone. 'Good-bye, Mr Savanna. When you decide to tell us where you spent that couple of hours that Monday, give us a ring. In the meantime we can always get you here?'

Savanna looked back at the house; his wife stood behind the screen-door like a ghostly image. 'Where else would I go?'

4

'Where do we go from here?' Clements asked as they got back into the Falcon. 'Gibson's office or his home?'

Malone looked at his watch. 'If you were an elderly millionaire, where would you be at four-thirty on a Friday afternoon—in your office or at home?'

'If I was a millionaire, elderly or otherwise, I'd *never* be in my office.'

'Righto, just follow your natural parasitical inclinations.'

'That's a good one,' said Clements, blowing his nose for the tenth time in the past half hour. 'You've started to sound educated since you became engaged to your Dutch bird.' He headed the car towards Point Piper. 'What d'you reckon about Savanna?'

Malone stared ahead of him at the tidal wave of traffic sweeping out of the city towards them. The day was still hot and the traffic had a molten look to it: if you touched any of the passing cars you would be charred at once. 'I don't think he had anything to do with Helga's murder.'

'What about those two hours?'

'I don't know about them,' Malone confessed. 'Maybe he did go out to Bondi, sat out there for all that time.'

'I don't believe that.' Clements waited for a break in the traffic so that he could turn right. He waited a minute or two, then he edged his way across the stream; there was a multiplying screech of tyres that stretched back a hundred yards towards the city and the drivers of the leading cars in the three lanes blared their horns at him. Clements took the car up the road that led to the block where Gibson lived. 'He was somewhere else but Bondi for those two hours. You think he might have been with another dame?'

'I've been thinking that.'

'Why didn't you ask him, then?'

'I don't know. I think I just felt sorry for his wife. She'll get over his affair with Helga—some women have that much resilience. And she'd be one of them. But I don't know that she could take it if he was running a second one on the side. I'll bet it wasn't a woman who first suggested polygamy.'

As they drew up before Eureka Towers, Clements said, 'You've been at this game longer than I have. Do you always reckon it's worthwhile becoming concerned about the women?'

Malone didn't reply at once. How could you not become concerned with pain? Then he said, 'I could be wrong. But yes—I can't help being concerned about them.'

'The ones like Helga, too?'

'You heard what Smiler said the other day—I waste my time on sixteen-year-old whores.' He got out of the car, waited for Clements to come round and join him. There was the beginning of a breeze from the south; it banked up against the tall block above them, then spilled round the edges as a small wind. 'I just don't know, Russ. One of the older blokes once told me—never become involved. He's right, I know that. What I haven't learned yet is how you turn yourself off from involvement.'

Clements shook his head in the same morose way as when he had won at the races for the third time running. 'I hope we don't have to pick on Grafter Gibson's missus. She's too old to take a beating.'

'I looked up Grafter in *Who's Who*. They've been married for thirty-five years. No kids. Anyone who could stand him for that long on her own could stand up to anything. Still——' He pressed the button for the lift. 'Let's take her gently if she's there.'

A part-aboriginal maid, night-dark eyes staring at them suspiciously, let them into the Gibson penthouse. Glenda Gibson, in a black velvet pants-suit, just falling short of elegance by twenty years and twenty pounds, greeted them with equal suspicion.

'My husband's not home, Sergeant.' She had just come from the hairdresser's and her hair had a stiff, unnatural look, as if it could be taken off and set aside on a shelf. It did not sit well on the warm, sincere face beneath it. 'But if you'd like to wait——?'

She offered them a drink and after some hesitation Malone asked for a bitter lemon for himself and Clements. He had a feeling that Gibson would not like it if he came in and found two policemen sitting back in his living-room quaffing beers; the offence would be only venial if the drinks were bitter lemons.

The two detectives sat there in the huge air-conditioned living-room watching the late sun turn the harbour into a verdigris-streaked shield on which black ships stood like heraldic charges. The maid flitted around the edges of the room, a dark wraith whose eyes never left the two policemen: she was concerned for her mistress. A tall grandfather clock struck five and Glenda Gibson looked at it with approval, as if time were a household pet to be rewarded for good behaviour.

'My husband will be home in a quarter of an hour. He's never late. Yet he never carries a watch.' There was no mistaking the pride in her voice; her husband was her king, president and prime minister. But she was troubled by the intruders at the gates: 'I just don't understand why you have to see him. We live a very simple life,' she said, unconscious of the luxury amidst which they sat. Her whole life was Les and whatever he wanted; all the rest was just background. She put down her glass, the sherry in it barely touched. She stared at them, her face crumbling a little under the blue-grey siege-cap of her hair. 'He's an old man, you know.'

'We know, Mrs Gibson,' said Malone gently. 'We haven't come to arrest him or anything like that.' He looked around the room, changed the subject: 'You must be very happy here.'

Mrs Gibson stared at him a moment longer, then seemed reassured. She glanced about her, then shook her head. 'I don't like the height. I think I must have verti-whatever-it's-called. I never go near the windows. I always look at the view from here, the middle of the room. You're never too old to make mistakes,' she said, and looked around the room again. 'We made one buying this place. But it's too late now to move again.'

'It should be no trouble,' said Clements, trapped by her frankness into an undiplomatic frankness of his own. 'I mean, you have the money——'

'It's not the money, young man. It's the time it takes for a place to become your home. That's a bad cold you have. Would you like some aspirin or something?'

Gibson came in the front door as the clock struck the quarter-hour. Glenda Gibson beamed at Malone and Clements as if her husband had just arrived walking on water; then she rose, crossed to him and kissed him fondly and without embarrassment on the cheek. There was nothing remarkable in that, Malone thought. What was remarkable was that Gibson, a man Malone would never have suspected of any public demonstration of affection or emotion, returned the kiss as if he and his wife were alone in the room. He still wore his hat and after he had kissed his wife he turned away, hung the hat carefully on a hat-rack and only then looked at Malone and Clements.

'You should have come to see me at my office,' he said

raspingly. Then he nodded to his wife. 'Excuse us, Glenda. They won't be staying long.'

'No, I'm staying, Les. They said it's nothing serious, so I want to stay and hear what it is. If it *is* serious——' She fluttered one hand, 'I'll still stay.'

Gibson did not argue with her. He walked to the drink cabinet built into one of the panelled walls, poured himself a whisky-and-soda, and without looking at the two detectives said, 'If it's about that girl, what's her name, you're wasting your time.'

'Maybe,' said Malone. 'But I'm afraid we're the ones who have to decide that, Mr Gibson.'

'What girl?' Glenda Gibson turned to her husband. 'The one they talked about last time?'

Gibson said nothing for a moment, looking at Malone; but Malone let him answer. 'She was the girl they found down in the Opera House.'

'The Opera House one!' Her voice jumped ridiculously, almost a little girl's squeak of surprise. 'What the devil——?'

Malone let Gibson continue with the answers: 'It's nothing, love. Like I told you, there were some pictures of us, newspaper pictures, in her flat. She'd been collecting them or something.'

'But why?'

Gibson let Malone answer that one. Malone took his time. They had nothing at all on Gibson; but they had to be sure he had nothing on *them*. Gibson had money and was at the top of the heap, and it was part of the cynical nature of Sydney that it always believed that any man who had achieved both money and position could not have done so without some pull in influential quarters. Malone was not as cynical as the worst of Sydney's voters, but neither was he foolhardy.

'We think the girl was building up a list of people to'—he glanced at Gibson—'to swindle.'

There was just a momentary gleam of appreciation in Gibson's eye: this copper wasn't such a mug. 'It happens all the time, Glenda. It had to happen to us sooner or later. But she's dead now, so there's nothing for us to worry about.'

'Who killed her? Someone else she was trying to swindle?'

'We don't know,' said Malone. 'We're trying to find out if someone who knew your husband gave her your name. We've been to see Mr Savanna,' he said to Gibson.

'Jack?' Glenda Gibson's head jerked round to her husband again; she could have been watching a tennis match that only occasionally came alive for her. 'Did he know her? I wouldn't put it past him—I wonder if Josie knows?'

Gibson looked into his glass. 'If she didn't know, it's time she found out. She's been living in a fool's bloody paradise too long.'

Mrs Gibson jerked her head back at Malone and he said quietly, 'She knows, Mrs Gibson. She took it all right.'

Clements nodded. 'I wouldn't worry about her.'

'I always worry about her——'

Gibson moved across, sat down beside his wife, put a hand on her arm. 'That's the trouble, Glenda. Josie doesn't really want anyone to worry about her. She enjoys her little bit of bloody misery.' He turned back to Malone and Clements. 'You've probably recognized that my brother-in-law is several sorts of bastard. But he's attractive to women——'

Glenda shook her head vehemently. 'I can't see a thing in him!'

Gibson smiled and pressed her arm. 'Josie wouldn't agree with you, love. She'd rather settle for one night a week of Jack than have bugger-all of him. Sergeant, if he gave my name to this girl, was he in on the swindle?'

'Only you would know that,' said Malone. 'I was only guessing that she was thinking up some swindle. It could have been something else.'

'What?' said Glenda Gibson.

Gibson realized he had opened the subject too far by his vindictive swipe at Savanna. 'It could be—er—anything. Girls like her get up to all sorts of tricks. But I'd had nothing to do with her,' he snapped at Malone. 'Nothing. She was a complete stranger to me. I'd never seen her or spoken to her or had a letter from her. A complete stranger, take my bloody word for it!'

It was Glenda's turn to be comforting. 'Don't get worked

up, hon. I don't think they're accusing you of anything. Are you, Sergeant?'

'No,' said Malone, and knew the interview was going to get nowhere by being prolonged. The attrition of questions would never wear down Gibson; the old man was solid rock. Malone stood up, took the chewed match from his pocket and held it out. 'Do you know anyone who does that, Mr Gibson?'

Gibson's eyes narrowed just a fraction, but he shook his head at once. 'No. What's that got to do with what we're talking about?'

'Nothing,' said Malone; then looked at Glenda Gibson. 'What's the matter, Mrs Gibson? Do you know someone who does that?'

'I don't suppose it means anything——' She glanced at her husband, then stopped, shook her head. 'No, I was mistaken. Lots of men do that.'

'Not too many,' said Malone, keeping his voice even. 'And if needs be, I'll try to track down every one of them in Sydney. Go on, Mrs Gibson. You were going to say something——No, please, Mr Gibson! Don't interfere. Or has your wife jogged your memory?'

'I don't know,' Gibson grunted. 'I don't know what she was gunna say.'

'That man who came up here the other night,' said Glenda. 'Clixby or Dixby or something. One of your trawler captains. He chewed a match.'

Malone said nothing, sat down again, waited for Gibson. At last the old man nodded, took a sip of his whisky, nodded again. 'I'm getting old. I don't notice people's habits any more. Feller named Bixby. He used to be one of my trawler captains.'

'Used to be?'

'I'd sacked him. Found out he was only declaring two-thirds of his fish catch each time he came in. Him and his crew were flogging the other third to some wholesaler they'd teamed up with.'

'Why did he come to see you here, Mr Gibson? Was there some argument? I mean, did he resent being sacked?'

'He didn't love me for it, if that's what you mean. But there was no argument, was there, Glenda? You didn't hear us having words, did you?'

'I was only in here for a minute,' Glenda Gibson told Malone, anxious to repair what she now recognized as an indiscretion. Les had said nothing to her, but she knew his silences as well as she knew his words and gestures. 'But then I was moving around the flat all the rest of the time, I mean I didn't leave here. I didn't hear one raised word—no argument, nothing like that——'

'Why did Bixby come to see you, Mr Gibson?'

Gibson finished the whisky in his glass. The old bastard's mind is still sharp, Malone thought. He only needs a second or two to come up with a story: 'He'd been with me, off and on, a long time. Twenty years or more. I just wanted to know why he wanted to take me down.'

'Why not at your office?'

'He rang me and said he'd rather see me at home, said he couldn't wait till the next day, he was going away or something. I didn't expect any trouble from him. I didn't get any.'

'Did he tell you why he took you down?'

Gibson grinned. 'Same old story. He said I had too much for one man, I wouldn't miss the bit him and his crew were taking off me.'

'People are like that,' said Glenda, her hand on Gibson's arm again. 'As if Les had never worked for what he's got.'

'What *we've* got, love,' said Gibson, and even to Malone's sceptical ear the old man did not sound sickly sentimental. This ruthless old crook and his feather-brained wife have got something my mum and dad have never achieved: understanding. And he felt suddenly sad for Con and Brigid Malone with their tongue-tied love for each other. Protect Lisa and me from that, O Lord. Give us pain, give us despair, but never forget to give us understanding.

Clements said, 'I think I know Bixby. He hasn't always been with you, has he, Mr Gibson? You said off and on. When he was off, was he in gaol?'

Gibson shrugged, looked at Clements for the first time. 'He could've been. I don't keep track all the time of all the people

I employ. I suppose there's a couple thousand of 'em, maybe more, spread throughout the firms I own. They come and go and, I suppose so, they come again. That's what Bixby did. What he did while he was gone, I wouldn't know and wouldn't wanna know.'

Clements saw Malone's inquiring look. 'Bixby's not a common name. If he's the bloke I'm thinking of, he did time out at the Bay. I can't remember what for, but he had some sorta record. We could look it up.'

'When did you see him last, Mr Gibson?' Malone asked.

Gibson looked at his wife. 'Last Friday,' she said. 'I remember because we were going to that Christmas charity party at the golf club. '

'You haven't seen him since?'

Gibson shook his head. 'I don't want to see him again. He's finished, far as I'm concerned.'

Malone stood up. 'Well, that's it, I think. We shouldn't be worrying you again, Mr Gibson. Nor you, Mrs Gibson.' He liked the old woman and he was pleased when she returned his smile. Any woman who could find the amount of happiness she had with an old bastard like Gibson was no ordinary woman. 'We'll get Bixby's home address from your wages office and give him a call. He may be able to help us.'

'But how?' asked Glenda.

But Gibson pressed her arm. 'It's none of our business, Glenda. Let the police look after it. It's none of our business.'

Malone and Clements said good-bye, drove back to the city through the cool southerly buster that had sprung up. Trees that had been stunned by the heat of the day came alive again, danced like corroboree blacks beyond the street lamps. Malone was driving, and Clements, slumped down in his seat with his handkerchief wiping his eyes, suddenly sneezed.

'I'm gunna get bloody pneumonia out of this.'

'What are you doing tonight?'

'I was gunna go to the trots. But I dunno, maybe bed would be the best place. Why?'

'What did you remember about this bloke Bixby?'

Clements sneezed again, wiped his nose. 'More than I let

on back there. I wonder if he was running some game with Helga? If he was in on the blackmail bit? I've run into him a coupla times. He's a stand-over merchant, he got booked several times for beating up other blokes. He might've been the one put Helga up to the idea of blackmail.'

'Could be. If he'd been with Grafter for twenty years, even off and on, he could have found out something about the old bastard. Well, we'll find out when we find him.'

'If he's gone away, as Grafter said he did, that might not be easy.'

'Has anything been easy on this since we started?'

When they got back to their office there was a message to ring Hawkins at the CIB.

'Scobie? About time—where've you been? Friday night's my night up at the Leagues club with the wife——'

'Sorry,' said Malone, losing some of his respect for the Fingerprint Section; crime for them evidently wasn't a twenty-four-hour job as it was for some people. 'What's the news?'

'Well, we checked those prints on the pipe you sent up. They match the prints on the phone, the key and the pieces of that broken glass. It's the same feller, all right. Any idea who he is?'

'No,' Malone lied. 'But we're getting close.'

He hung up and told Clements the report on the finger-prints.

'You want to save some money tonight?'

'How?'

'Don't go to the trots. Go out and check on Bixby. It might take a bit of running around, you'll have to dig up the wages clerk at the trawler firm—*someone* should be there, a trawling outfit wouldn't close down at night—' Then he shook his head. 'No, it can wait till tomorrow. Forget it.'

'Tomorrow's Saturday. I'll still have to dig up someone to get that address. I'm as impatient as you, mate, to get this thing cleared up. I'm like you now—I think Helidon is the guy we want. But we want to be sure. And like you said, the only way we're gunna do that is by elimination. It could be that there's only Bixby to be eliminated. Let's get him out

of the way as soon as we can. Just one thing——' He blew his
nose, wiped his streaming eyes. 'While I'm tearing around
tonight, what are you gunna be doing?'

'Thinking,' said Malone. 'And taking Lisa to dinner.'

'One of these days,' said Clements, 'I'm gunna be the senior
bloke in a team. And I'm gunna run the junior joker right off
his bloody feet.'

'I said exactly the same thing myself ten years ago,' said
Malone. 'What are you hanging around for? Start running.'

CHAPTER TWELVE

I

Friday, December 6

BIXBY pressed the bell of the Gibson flat, heard the deep tone of the chimes behind the heavy oak door, nodded appreciatively and waited. The old bugger knew how to spend his money, all right; anyone living in this block didn't have to worry about whether he had butter or margarine on his bread. Bixby wasn't surprised when a maid opened the door, though he couldn't remember ever having met one before. Some forgotten instinct prompted him to take off his straw hat.

'I'd like to see Mr Gibson.' He saw the girl's refusal in her face even before she spoke. 'Tell him it's important. I won't keep him long. The name's Phil Bixby.'

The girl looked him up and down, nodded, then closed the door in his face. He felt his temper rise, flushing his face, and his hand crushed the brim of his hat. The bitch, her with a touch of the tarbrush in her, putting on an act with him! Then he stiffened, striving hard to control himself. Hold it, Phil. That's how you done in the other piece.

The door opened again and the maid said, 'Mr Gibson will see you.'

Bixby followed her across a small entrance hall and into a living-room larger than anything he had ever seen before. He trod on carpet that felt as if it had six inches of rubber beneath it; when he looked around he took in nothing he could remember, but he knew he was in the middle of more luxury than he had expected. Possessions meant nothing to him, it would have taxed him to remember what he had in his own flat; yet he could sense the value of them, knew they were the labels of how much most people were worth. Old Grafter, or his missus, had thrown the money around like confetti furnishing this joint.

Gibson stood in front of the big window that looked out to the harbour. He waved the maid away, waited till she had gone, then said, 'Nobody invited you here. So don't plan on staying long. What d'you want?'

Bixby took a match from his pocket, began to chew on it. 'I won't keep you, Grafter. I just come for the air fare for that girl. I had a talk with her. She's gone back to Germany.'

'Already?' Then Gibson turned as his wife, looking like a stout bon-bon in candy yellow, came into the room. 'This is my wife. Mr Bixby. He used to work for me on one of the trawlers.'

Bixby took the match out of his mouth, nodded. 'Pleased to meetcha, Mrs Gibson. Just a little business with your old— with the boss. Won't take a minute.'

Glenda Gibson acknowledged his greeting, then looked at her husband. 'Don't be long, Les. We're late for the party already——'

She went out, leaving behind her a whiff of expensive perfume that was lost on the two men.

Bixby glanced around the room. 'Nice place you got here, Les. Must've set you back a packet.'

'How much did the fare cost?'

'Let's say a round seven hundred dollars. I hadda do a bit of running around, get her on her way and things like that, you know what I mean?'

'When did she leave?'

'Day before yesterday.'

'You took your time coming for the money.'

'Look, I done the job, didn't I? It wasn't easy, you know, she's like all them Huns, pretty bloody stubborn. They don't give up easy. But in the end she saw reason. I got her on the plane and she oughta be in Germany by now. I've had other things to do, you know, that's why I ain't been for the money before. But I'm here now, Grafter. Seven hundred bucks, cash on the knocker.'

'It won't be cash.' Gibson stared at him for a moment, then he moved towards the door into his study. 'It'll be a cheque.'

'Make it to cash, then. I want the dough first thing in the morning. I might be going away.'

'The banks aren't open Saturdays. You'll have to wait till Monday. Something worrying you, Bixby? What made you forget that?'

Bixby chewed a little harder on the match. 'I dunno. I guess it's because I ain't been working this week. You lose track of the days. Okay, it'll have to be Monday, but make it cash.'

Gibson went into the study and Bixby, restless now, moved around the living-room, finishing up at the big window that looked west towards the city and the Opera House. From here he could see almost the whole of the last part of his journey last Monday night. Like he'd told Grafter, it hadn't been easy.

After he had checked that he could pick up a boat without any trouble in Rushcutters Bay, he had driven down to the Domain and along the road that led to the point. The Domain, like most parks, was deserted at night but for lovers in their cars. He had known that a man on his own in a car would be suspected as a Peeping Tom, it was a great place for creeps like that, and he had stayed only long enough to refresh his memory on how far he would have to go by water to get to the Opera House. He had parked above the path that led down to Fleet Steps. That's where he'd have to take the dame's body aboard the boat; that meant he'd have about three-quarters of a mile's rowing, if he kept to the shoreline, before he got round to where he could slip in under the Opera House pilings. Well, that wouldn't be so hard. But first he had to get the bloody boat around to Fleet Steps and that wasn't going to be so easy. He'd have at least two miles' rowing because he'd have to keep well clear of the naval depot at Garden Island otherwise he'd have the Navy demons butting in, wanting to know what he was doing around there at night. Going out into deep water to skirt Garden Island might mean he'd run into a Water Police patrol boat and those bastards wouldn't just wave to him and pass on; but that was something he'd have to risk. If he was going to get rid of the dame's carcass so that no one would ever find her, then the Opera House was the only shot and he would have to take all the risks it meant getting there. Now, standing in

Gibson's living-room, he knew he could have taken her up the bush somewhere, up to one of the thickly timbered valleys in the Blue Mountains, and buried her there; he could even have taken her up to the outskirts of the city, left her in the scrub somewhere right in the path of the bushfires that were raging: she'd have been no more than a blackened skeleton in no time. But somehow those ideas had never occurred to him that night. He was a stranger to anything ten miles inland from the heart of the city; he had been a water man all his life and physically and mentally he stayed by the water. He guessed it was some sort of animal instinct.

It would have been a bloody sight easier burying her up in the bush. He had driven out to Alexandria, stopped in a street where there were only factories dark and silent for the night, transferred the body from the back of the car to the boot, then driven back to Rushcutters Bay. He'd gone looking for a small boat, found one and quietly sculled it away through the school of yachts moored in the small bay. That had been easy. The long row out round Garden Island and back inshore below the Domain had been the tough bit. He had sweated all the way, not from the rowing but because he had been dead scared the Water demons would appear. But finally he had made it, moored the boat beneath the steps, climbed up to the road, walked back through the Domain and caught a cab down outside the Woolloomooloo wharves. A girl there, doing no good with the merchant sailors, had tried to pick him up; she was probably still wondering why he had so savagely knocked her back, probably thought he was a queer or something. By the time the cab had dropped him back at his car at Rushcutters Bay it was almost midnight. He waited there another hour, chewing matches, sitting in the dark and beginning to wonder what he was going to do for cash now he was out of a job. He might have to go back to the game, doing over factories for whatever he could get out of them. A new game had started up over the past few months, bank hold-ups, but that didn't appeal to him. You had to carry a gun for that and if ever the demons landed you and you had a gun on you, they saw you copped the lot when they got you into court. The bank jobs might give you cash in a hurry, but sooner or later you got caught. Whereas a good factory man, if he was careful, could go on forever.

At one o'clock he drove back to the Domain. Most of the lovers had had enough for the night; those blokes who hadn't made it had given up and gone home and those that had had probably run out of steam. Two or three cars still remained, but anyone who was still at it at this hour wouldn't be looking up to see what was going on outside their own bedroom in the back seat. He got the body out of the boot, but she was harder to carry now than when he had brought her out of the flat. She wasn't completely cold yet, but she'd started to go stiff; he noticed when he lifted her head that her lower jaw was completely locked. He lifted her on to his shoulder, cursing the silk dressing-gown; he wondered for a moment if he ought to throw it away, then decided against it. He wasn't squeamish, but he didn't fancy the idea of handling her naked. He knew there were creeps who did women when they were dead, but he knew he'd never come at that. Maybe he was being bloody stupid, a real wowser, but dead women should have something on them. It was what his first wife, the silly bitch, would have called *decent*.

It was another hour before he'd got her hidden down in the basement of the Opera House. There had been a few moments when he could have done with some help, when it had taken all his strength to handle her up from the boat. He'd been stopped by no one, but once he'd had to hold the boat steady in under the pilings when a security guard came to a spot right above him and flashed his torch around. It had not been easy, just like he'd told Grafter, but now she was buried there in the Opera House, in her own private tomb, the biggest bloody mausoleum in the world, and like as not she'd stay there forever. There had been nothing in the papers so far about her being missing and it looked like no one was going to care. For all the world and Grafter Gibson knew, she'd gone back to Germany.

Gibson came out of the study with the cheque. 'That finishes it. We shouldn't hear another word out of her. Unless——' He drew back the cheque as Bixby reached for it. 'You didn't rough her up at all?'

Bixby was all innocence. 'Why would I wanna do that? I told you, I hadda argue with her, but what woman don't argue? I admit I told her something *might* happen to her, but soon's I said that, she got the point right away. You won't have to worry about her again, Grafter. She's gone and gone for good.'

Gibson handed over the cheque. 'All right. Now you go and you be gone for good, too. If ever I hear you're hanging around any of my boats, I'll have the police down on you before you know what hit you.'

Bixby was going to make some threatening retort, but he abruptly thought better of it. The old bastard didn't know it, but he held the whip handle; if ever he found out the girl had been killed, Old Grafter wouldn't think twice about cracking that whip. 'I told you, I'm going away. I'll be gone by Tuesday.'

'Where are you thinking of going?'

Bixby grinned, put on the straw hat, ran his hand round the brim. 'That depends, you know what I mean? I got some other business to attend to. If that pays off, I might even take a trip overseas.'

He was at the door now, but he paused and looked back and around the living-room. 'You got a real nice set-up here, Grafter. Just shows how far you can go when you're smart, don't it?'

'Yes,' said Gibson. 'Just keep it in mind.'

2

'I'm working for the Aboriginals this Christmas,' said the young girl, clanking her gold bracelet, the lucky charm of the Darling Point tribe. 'It's my conscience, darling. And I want to learn to throw a boomerang.'

'A queer jockey?' said the Wahroonga matron. 'But how do the poor horses like that?'

'Cost me seven thousand dollars,' said the grazier down from the country. 'The wife thinks money is vulgar—until she wants some.'

'It's just my bloody luck to be right-hand man to a left-handed boss,' said the young executive.

Walter Helidon moved among the shrapnel of the cocktail chatter. The Christmas charity party was being held at the Royal South Shore golf club and in those rare moments when he looked back to his beginnings he marvelled that he was a member of the club. As a boy he had caddied here, but that had been over thirty years ago; the members he had caddied for were either dead or too old now to remember the tow-headed boy named Wally. In those days the club had had as many restrictions as any royal household; it revelled in its Royal title as if it had been made part of the King's own domain.

Applicants for membership were scanned as if they were to be honoured with a barony; the blackball was holed in one more frequently than the golf ball. Overnight-rich men were barred, as were professional turf men such as trainers and jockeys, foreigners who were not diplomats, and Jews: there had been several cases of apoplexy when a Jew had been named as Governor-General of the country and the club had had to entertain a Yid as the Royal representative. Restrictions had eased somewhat since those days, but election to membership was still difficult. Walter Helidon had been elected because someone on the committee had suggested that the club never knew when a member who was a Cabinet Minister might not be an asset. Helidon had been delighted to accept the nomination and was now doing his best to reduce his handicap from 25 to 24. As a youth, playing in a caddies' competition, he had gone round the course in six over par, but he never boasted of that now and was only glad that his name had never figured among the prizewinners of the competition.

'Hullo, Wally.' Les Gibson sat in a window seat looking out over the course. He was clutching a glass in one bony claw and looked like a man interested in neither Christmas nor charity.

'Hullo, Les. You look like Scrooge. How did they get you to a thing like this?' Gibson was one man who would never be elected to membership and Helidon could only suppose he was here at the invitation of one of the charity women who was after a sizeable donation.

'At the point of a gun,' said Gibson. 'How's the eye? Last time I saw you a voter had just clocked you.'

Helidon managed a smile, humouring the old bastard. He had not forgotten the insults Gibson had handed him at their last meeting, but in the political game you could only harbour grudges against opponents from other parties, never against an uncommitted voter. You never knew when you might need him. 'With all your money, Les, what do you vote?'

'Communist. They're the only ones who can afford to be honest—they'll never get into power in this country, not with the millions of reactionaries we call the easy-going, democratic Aussie.' He looked around the big room at the easy-going democratic reactionaries who remained oblivious of his contempt of them. 'The voters are the same, Wally, Hypocrites, every bloody one of 'em, all voting out of their pockets. The only honest voters today are the radical kids, the demonstrators.'

'They'd be pleased to have you as one of their backers. Why don't you give them a million or two?'

'I wouldn't back 'em. I'd shoot the bloody lot of them. If ever they did get into power, I'd be one of the first for the chopping block. I admire 'em, Wally, but I'm not bloody stupid. I admire tigers, too, but I wouldn't want one as a pet.'

Helidon felt in a benevolent mood. After all, Christmas was the time to be charitable, even to old crooks like Grafter Gibson. And he had heard no more from Helga, so maybe she, too, had been touched by the Christmas spirit, and had decided to call it quits and leave him alone. He suddenly felt in the mood to enjoy the party and he said, 'I think I envy you, Les, in a way. You've got enough money and you're old enough to have all your worries behind you. You can say and do exactly what you like.'

Not quite, Wally, thought Gibson. But all he said was, 'The time to be honest is when you're young, not when you're old. The truth doesn't improve with age.'

'I still envy you.'

'You could be the same as me if you wanted to give up politics. But if you did that, Wally, you'd die of anonymity. You wouldn't be the first, but I think it'd be a terrible bloody death in your case.'

Helidon's benevolent mood disappeared as quickly as the smile from his face.

'Have you ever had a kind word to say to anyone, Les? Or vice versa?'

'Yes,' said Gibson, his mottled face screwed into a smile that could have been malicious or affectionate, depending upon who saw it. 'Here she comes now.'

Glenda Gibson, rustling like old leaves in her yellow silk, came up to them. 'Mr Helidon, I've just been talking to your wife. She's so pleased and so must you be!'

'Why?' Helidon was puzzled. Norma, still suffering from the reaction to her fight with Helga last Monday, had been in no humour for the party and had only come because she was chairwoman of the charity committee.

'What was in the papers this morning—that's she's been made president of the Blue and Red Ball.'

'That's headline news?' Gibson asked dryly. 'When's the inauguration? You gunna wear a top hat, Wally?'

Helidon kept his temper. 'Don't be too critical, Les. We may have over two and a half million people, but we're still a small town. And the women do some good.'

'You'll be saying the same for you politicians next.'

'Now that's enough of that, Les,' said Glenda. 'No matter what the size of a place is, little town or big city, there always has to be someone at the top.'

'Christ Almighty,' said Gibson, grinning lovingly at her, 'you're starting to sound as if you wished you'd be in the running.'

Glenda looked at Helidon. 'Could you imagine me as a society queen, Mr Helidon, with *him* as my consort or whatever they call it?'

Helidon's smile did not have to be forced this time. 'An impossible picture, indeed, Mrs Gibson.'

He moved away and Gibson looked after him. 'When he

was born I bet they squeezed him out of his mother like shaving cream out of a tube. He's so bloody smooth.'

'Maybe he *has* to be, in his position. You shouldn't be so critical, Les. He can't afford to be as frank as you are.'

'He'd never offend anyone, not even his missus, for fear she mightn't vote for him. He spends his whole time pussy-footing around, never wanting to get out of step. He's a dull bastard and there's no getting away from it—if he just swore or got drunk, I'd think a bit more of him. Not much, but a bit. Have you had enough, hon? Let's go home.'

'In a while. The Archbishop would like to meet you.'

'The Cardinal? I've met him.'

'No, the Anglican Archbishop.'

'Jesus, Glenda, isn't one set of God-botherers enough for you?'

'Now don't be like that, Les. You know what Father Wrigley says—we should all try to be ecumen-whatever-it-is.'

'If being ecumenical means being matey with Father Wrigley, I'd rather be a bigot.'

'I think I'd rather have him visit us than that Mr Clixby or whatever-his-name was who came this evening. You do have some rough-looking men working for you.'

'He's not working for me any more,' said Gibson, regretting the seven hundred dollars it had cost him but thinking how easily the girl had been got rid of. 'You won't be seeing him again, hon. Now where's the bloody Archbishop?'

Walter Helidon, on the other side of the room, was just starting to feel the effects of his third martini. He looked about him, thinking: this is the cream of the city, and mock cream though I may be, they're mixing me in with them. He lifted another martini from a passing tray and toasted himself. He might never go any higher than this, but this was good enough. Helga had been wrong: you didn't get this far if you were no more than a schoolboy. Merry Christmas, Walter.

'You look pleased with yourself.' Norma Helidon, throat encircled by the repaired string of pearls, paused beside him. She flashed her smile at a gabble of young girls as they swooped by like predators on their way to take down the older men for as much as they could get in the name of charity; in the background their escorts waited with the smug satisfaction of young men who knew that what they would offer the young girls later in the night would be more welcome than a charity donation. 'I wish I had your self-delusion.'

'I told you before we left——' He smiled at a woman, recognizing her as one who worked for him in his electorate; he and Norma stood side by side like a firing squad shooting smiles instead of bullets. 'If Helga was going to get in touch with us again, she'd have done it by now.'

'Have you tried to get in touch with her?'

'Yes,' he admitted after a moment's hesitation. 'I rang her twice to try to tell her she could have the money. There was no answer. Personally, I think she's had second thoughts about what she was up to, has got scared and done a bunk. After all——' He switched on another smile, this time at a couple whose respective ancestors had come out with the First Fleet: his as convicts, hers as army officers: both heritages were now respectable, though, in the new national spirit, his was the more to be envied. Convicts, so long as they were four generations removed, were now considered the best of stock. 'We're both a little more important than she thought. She may have got scared of our position.'

Norma, with some of the candour she had almost forgotten, changed her smile to a wry one. 'You're kidding. No girl like her was ever a respecter of position—even if we had any. A new Premier, and you could be out of the Cabinet tomorrow. As for me——' The smile widened again in recognition of another passing couple, this time Louise County and her husband, a small thin man with the resigned look of one who had chosen to surrender in the battle of the sexes. Louise was said to have defeated him on their honeymoon twenty years ago and he had been walking wounded ever since. 'Being chairwoman of a committee composed of a dozen women like Louise isn't *position*. It's just civilized masochism.'

'What's got into you? What's happened to the social snob I was married to?'

'Listen to who's talking. I lost my snobbery on the living-room floor of your girl friend, along with my best string of pearls. I had to get down on my hands and knees to find out I'd also lost my pride.' She turned to him, the smile frozen on her face like a grimace of pain. 'Let's go home, Wally. I'm feeling terrible.'

They went out through the slowly swirling crowd that, its preoccupation with itself thickened now by drink and gossip, would not miss them. As they got into the car Norma slumped back in her seat, took off her pearls and put them in her handbag, and sighed quaveringly as if she were on the verge of tears. Helidon sat quietly beside her, something telling him that this was a crisis moment in their marriage, even more critical than when she had found out about Helga. Their life together from now on started here.

'Would you give up politics if I asked you to?' She did not look at him directly; there was more apprehension in her voice than threat. 'Not right away, but as soon as you could.'

He said warily, 'You're asking a lot.'

'I know. But I'm trying to save our marriage.'

'We're all right, darl——'

She was massaging her throat, as if she had just removed a rope from it instead of the string of pearls. 'We don't have a marriage, Wally. Even Miss Brand told me that.'

'I thought we weren't going to mention her again?'

'I'm not throwing her up at you. I'm trying to be dispassionate about her——' She stopped, as if she found being dispassionate was not an easy emotion. 'But she told the truth. We don't have a marriage. We have a—a social arrangement.'

'There are plenty worse marriages than ours.'

'A man's answer.' She turned round to him, gaining more confidence. 'Wally, I *mean* it. Our marriage isn't going to last the way it's going. Oh, we might stay together for convenience's sake. There are a lot of our friends who have marriages like that. But——' She faltered, then went on: 'I want something more than that to look forward to. I think I've just discovered I was happier as the dull woman I was ten years ago. At least then we were in love.'

'I love you now,' he said and meant it.

'You probably do. And I love you. I really do, darling.

226

But——' She regarded him thoughtfully. 'How long will it last if we go on living separate lives? That's what we're doing, you know. We sleep in the same room, but not in the same bed——'

'Whose fault was that?'

She waited a moment before she admitted, 'Yes, it was my idea. And I'm sorry now.'

'We can buy a double bed tomorrow.'

'All right, we'll do that. But that's not going to be the solution. We have to start living together *all* day. Even when we're apart. Does that make sense to you?'

He nodded slowly, still unsure of her. She was asking him to give up all he had worked for over the past ten years, the life that for him was the only life worth living. He loved politics, got almost a sensual as well as an intellectual pleasure out of them. He had reconciled himself to the recognition that he would never be Premier, the ultimate satisfaction (he had no interest at all in Federal politics and never even thought of being Prime Minister); he had achieved a complacency of mind that, with parallel smugness, he knew very few men managed. He had at least another fifteen years, probably more, of public life to be enjoyed: neither the voters nor the Party would ever ask him to do what Norma was asking. He would agree with her for the time being, but he would try to change her mind in the weeks ahead. They could still have the life she wanted if she gave up her charity committees.

'What would we do?'

'We could go abroad. Travel—take our time——'

'It makes very good sense, indeed.'

She smiled, relaxing. She leaned across and kissed him on the cheek. 'We'll be happy, darling, I promise you. But while we're making a new start——'

'Yes?'

'Give up saying *indeed*. I'm not one of your voters, darling.'

He smiled, loving her now as much as when their marriage had begun. 'I'll watch it. Let's go home and vote for each other in bed.'

An hour and a half later she got out of bed and reached

for her dressing-gown. 'Don't put it on,' he said. 'You used to walk around naked when we first got married.'

The shadow of Helga passed between them, but they looked at each other frankly as if neither of them had seen it. He wants me to act like his whore did, Norma thought. What was the perfect wife supposed to be: a servant in the kitchen, a lady in the drawing-room and a whore in the bedroom? But she said nothing of that, only looked at herself in the big wall-mirror. 'I looked better in those days.'

'You look all right now,' he said, shutting out the image of Helga, being doggedly faithful and loving. 'You look—*womanly*.'

She came back, leaned across to him as he sat up in bed and kissed him. 'Was it really good?'

'We haven't lost the knack. All we needed was to forget everything but ourselves. I'm just glad Rosa has gone.'

'I forgot everything, everything but what we were doing. But if you asked me to remember——' She smiled, kissed him again. 'We don't need to remember it. It'll happen again. Often.'

Then the phone rang. He picked it up automatically: it could be the Premier, his own secretary, a voter, anyone: even Helga. It was a voice he had never heard before, a rough voice full of gravelly menace: 'Mr Helidon? I think you and me might get together.'

'Who's this?'

'My name don't matter right now. But I got a diary here that's got *your* name in it, you know what I mean? It was given to me by a girl named Helga, an old friend of yours. You remember her?'

He looked at his wife. He had been about to pull her back into the bed with him when the phone had rung; but now all the sex ran out of him. He put his hand over the phone. 'Don't get cold. Put your gown on.'

Puzzled, she said, 'Who is it?' Then her face flushed. 'It's not *her*, is it?'

He shook his head. 'Some man.' He took his hand away from the mouthpiece. 'I'm not interested in what you have. You can tell Miss Brand to——'

'To go to hell?' The voice chuckled. 'She's gone back to Germany, sport. She ain't innarested in you any more.'

'Then why did she leave you her diary?' Helidon saw his wife's head jerk up.

'She owed me a favour I done her. But don't let's get into any long natter over the blower. You have a boat, Mr Helidon, it's moored off the Yacht Club. Wuddia say I meet you on her tomorra morning, say ten o'clock? And don't bring anyone with you.' The voice hardened. 'You couldn't prove anything right now against me. But I got a lot here might worry you. See you at ten.'

The phone went dead in Helidon's ear. Slowly he put the instrument back on the bed table, stared at his wife sitting naked and middle-aged on the bed beside him. 'More blackmail,' he said, and wanted to weep. 'It's not over at all. A long way from over, indeed.'

3

Saturday, December 7

Bixby saw the blue Mercedes come down the narrow street and swing into the parking lot of the Yacht Club. He walked across as Walter Helidon, in dark glasses, blazer and linen slacks, impeccably dressed even as a victim, got out of the car.

'G'day, Mr Helidon. Right on time.'

Helidon looked at the big, rough-looking character in the red checked shirt, blue trousers and fancy-banded straw hat. A racecourse urger, he thought: what would Helga have been doing with a man like this? 'What's your name? That's the first thing I want to know before we start talking.'

'I don't think you need to know that——'

'That's where you're wrong.' The dark glasses hid the anxiety he felt; this man looked capable of physical violence and Helidon had always been afraid of violence. But he was in control of his voice and he did his best to get into control of the situation. 'If this thing goes as far as you seem to think it's going to——'

'How's that?'

'Blackmail. That's what you're after, isn't it? I'm not going to pay out money to someone whose name I don't know.'

'You've decided to come good with the cash, then?'

'I didn't say that——' Helidon's voice rose a little.

'Don't get excited, sport. Let's go out to your boat. We wanna keep this calm, you know what I mean? That's the shot, eh?'

The club house and moorings were as busy as a cormorants' nest site. Weekend sailors were preparing their boats; some yachts were already nosing out towards the broader waters of the harbour. No one took any notice of Helidon and the tough-looking man with him as the two of them went out in one of the club's runabouts; everyone, even a Cabinet Minister, lost rank here at the weekend and became no more than someone indulging his favourite sport. The man in the red shirt, if he was noticed at all, was taken for a tradesman going to do some work on Helidon's yacht. Helidon was known as a soft-hands sailor; he had never been known to scrub a deck or wind a rope.

'Nice craft you got here.' Bixby clambered aboard the yacht. She was an ocean cruiser-racer based upon a successful Sydney yacht, *Freya*: a 39-foot craft with an 11-foot beam that Helidon had bought with the vague idea of entering her in the annual Sydney-Hobart race, but so far he had taken her no more than ten miles out to sea and had been sick most of the time. But a gale would have made him no sicker than he was now on this smooth backwater of the harbour. 'Must've set you back a fair packet.'

'We didn't come out here to talk about the price of my boat.' Helidon took off his blazer and sat down. The sun, criss-crossed by gulls, blazed down and he was wishing he had brought a hat with him; if this talk went on too long he was going to get badly burnt from the glare off the water. He should have cut the talk short back at the parking lot, got into his car and driven off. He had already lost a tactical point by coming out here; it conceded that he was willing to listen to this man's proposition. He tried for some authority: 'Get to the point, But first, what's your name?'

Bixby hesitated, then gave his name. He had never pulled

a job like this before and he wondered if other jokers who went in for blackmail kept their names out of it. But if he played his cards carefully this bloke Helidon would have nothing on him. 'Helga told me you'd already paid her some cash.'

Helidon remembered the cheque for a thousand dollars which Helga had torn up and thrown in his face. His bank had not called him this week to query him on the deposit of a pieced-together cheque. And if Helga had already gone back to Germany, as this chap had said last night on the phone, then it was pretty obvious she was not going to try to cash the cheque. 'You're wrong there. I paid her nothing.'

Bixby sensed the assurance in the other man's voice. For just a moment he lost his own confidence; then he remembered the diary in his hip pocket. The entries were straight enough: a bloke couldn't misunderstand them. 'I told you, sport, Helga left me her diary.'

'Why did she do that? How well did you know her?'

'Ah, we were old friends, sorta.'

'Were you the pimp who ran her?' Helidon realized his mistake at once.

'Oh, you admit you knew what game she was in? No, I wasn't her ponce. Like I said, I was just a friend. Not even one of her customers. But you were, weren't you? Pretty regular, too. Every Monday and Thursday.' Bixby had been looking carefully at Helidon in his dark glasses and now he remembered the man he had seen going into Helga's flat last Monday afternoon. 'Did you say good-bye to her last Monday?'

Helidon said nothing, wondering how much this man knew. He could not see Bixby as a friend of Helga's, she had been so fastidious and highly critical of certain types of Australian men; but then he had read that whores often sought as friends men entirely different from their clients, and maybe Helga's kink had run to having someone like this lout. He was as big and crude as a bull and maybe that was what she had wanted. He felt a sudden angry embarrassment, as if he had proved sexually inadequate. Knowing his own fastidiousness and, yes, his lack of stamina, it could have been part of her bitchy revenge that she should have exposed him to a man like this. But why had she so suddenly decided to leave for Europe?

Bixby grinned. 'Never mind what you said to her. I seen you going into her flat last Monday. I was gunna call on her m'self, but when I seen you I went away and give you your time. What did you say to her? She made up her mind pretty quick to go back to Germany.'

A yacht slid by, its auxiliary engine ticking over, its crew freeing the sails for quick raising as soon as they were out far enough to catch what breeze there was on the water. The skipper of the yacht waved to Helidon. 'Don't look so glum, Walter! There'll be a nor'-easter this afternoon—plenty of good sailing!'

Helidon forced a smile and waved back. He rubbed the top of his scalp, feeling the sun biting in through his thinning hair, and looked back at Bixby. 'I didn't say anything to her, nothing that would have caused her to hare off to Europe the way she appears to have done. Are you sure *you* didn't say something to her?'

Bixby spread his hands. 'Why me? Her and I got on very well. We were always doing favours for each other.' He took a match from his shirt pocket, began to chew on it. 'No, all she said was that you were coming back with some cash for her.' He had memorized everything in the diary that had anything to do with Helidon, beginning with the name, address and phone number among the list of other names, addresses and phone numbers at the beginning of the small book. His mind was not subtle, but like the minds of many habitual liars he could turn fiction into fact in his own imagination. Her diary had said: *Walter came this afternoon. Is coming back with the money.* That was as good as talking to her, wasn't it? He kept her alive in his mind till she would have told him all about Helidon that he would want to know. 'Did you go back and see her?'

'Yes, but— When did she tell you all this?'

'She rung me Monday evening, after you'd been there the first time.' He had caught Helidon's slip; the bastard had given himself away. He'd just have to watch he didn't do the same thing himself; watch out for the old tongue. 'I picked her up, took her out for a drink. She said then she was gunna go back to Germany. Then she gimme the diary, said I oughta get in touch with you. I rung her the next morning when I'd read the diary, but she'd gone. Did you give her the money she asked for?'

'I did,' Helidon said abruptly, taking a chance that Helga had not confided too much in this brute. 'It was probably what she used to go back to Europe.'

'How much was it?'

Then she hadn't told him. 'That's between me and her, I think.'

Bixby chewed on his match, then dropped it between his feet. 'Yeah, I guess so. What we're really talking about is what's between you and me. I think it'd be worth a fair bit to you to keep your name outa the papers, wouldn't it?'

'One question,' said Helidon. 'Did you and Helga have a fight about anything?'

Bixby managed a look of surprise. 'Me? Fight with her? Why?'

'Nothing.' Then who had wrecked Helga's flat? That is, if this chap was telling the truth; and Helidon could not be sure whether he was or wasn't. He had always prided himself on being able to read other men: the salesman who sells himself, as he had been doing all his life, has to know his market. But upset and frightened as he had been this past week, his perception had lost its edge: suspicion was a cracked prism through which to view anything, let alone the truth.

Bixby watched him for a moment, then looked about the yacht. 'How much you say this set you back?'

Helidon had recovered. 'I didn't.'

Bixby grinned, feeling more confident every minute. 'No, you didn't. Well, I got a fair idea of boat prices. About fifty thousand dollars, I reckon. This your main pleasure, sport? I mean, besides girls?' He grinned again as he saw Helidon flush. 'I'll let you off light. How about ten thousand? You pay up and I'll let you have Helga's diary and you won't hear another word from her or me.'

'Did she tell you to speak for her, too?'

Ah, you ain't going to catch me that way, sport. But watch the tongue, Phil, watch the tongue. 'No, she didn't, come to think of it. But you think she's gunna bother to come all the way back from Germany to bite you for a few more bucks? Not Helga, sport.'

Helidon took out his handkerchief, spread it over his burning scalp. He sat there like some placid red-faced old woman, only the dark glasses, like empty sockets, suggesting the death's head beneath the smooth plump skin. 'How do I know I can trust you?'

'You don't,' said Bixby, grinning cheerfully now. 'But you're a politician, you know nobody trusts anybody these days. You just gotta take the chances. If I give you the diary, what else will I have on you, see what I mean?'

Helidon thought quickly. He had never written Helga even a note, never put his name to any present he had given her, always paid her in cash each week. The only time he had ever signed his name—'I gave her a cheque for a thousand dollars. She tore it up. Where's that?'

'I wouldn't know about that.'

There had been just a moment's pause before Bixby had answered: Helidon couldn't be sure whether he was telling the truth or not. 'What would you know about the other man who visited her on Monday? Didn't she mention him, too?'

Bixby felt his nerve-ends beginning to tighten. 'What bloke was that?'

'The one who wrecked her flat. Didn't she mention him?'

'No, sport. If anyone wrecked her flat, it must of been after she left it.'

'But it was wrecked on Monday night!' Then Helidon realized his second mistake.

'Look, Helidon, let's quit buggerizing about.' Bixby decided the only thing to do was ride right over this bastard and get out of here quick; the last thing he wanted to do was end up discussing last Monday night. 'Helga didn't mention anyone else but you. If someone else was there in her place and done it over, maybe it was another one of her customers working dirty water off his chest when he found out she wasn't there. Some blokes are like that—they get very shirty

234

when they don't get their bit right when they're expecting it.' He had been like that himself on one or two occasions; but he'd done over the trolls themselves rather than their flats. 'Let's get that ten thousand, I'll give you the diary and we'll call it quits.'

'I can't get it for you this morning. You'll have to wait till Monday, till the banks are open.'

Bixby ground his teeth, as if he still had a match between them. Jesus. Monday was going to be a bloody busy day for him at the bank: cashing old Grafter's cheque, cashing—no, wait a minute. 'I don't want a cheque, sport. I want it in cash.'

'You'll get it by cheque or nothing. As you said, why should I trust you? If I turned up with the cash I wouldn't put it past you to knock me over the head and make off with the money *and* the diary. And then you'd be back for more. It'll be a cheque, made out to cash if you like, but that's as far as I'll go.'

'You know, Helidon, you ain't in a position to lay down the law about anything. I could finish you off, you know that?'

'I could finish you off, too, have you thought of that? I could call your bluff and turn up with the police on Monday. How would you like that?'

They sat there in the bright blue glare hurling threats at each other; but they were like two duellists, each of whom was not sure how many bullets were in the other's gun. Bixby resorted to the weapon he knew best: 'You do that, sport, and some time, sooner or later, you'll get your head kicked in.'

Helidon recognized the real menace in Bixby's voice. Suddenly he was afraid; sweat broke on him and streamed down his face. He took the handkerchief from his head and wiped his face with it; and as he did so he knew he had lost what little advantage he had, for the moment, gained over this thug. 'All right. No police. It will still have to be made out to cash, though. I've got several appointments Monday. Come to my office at four-thirty.'

Bixby shook his head. 'Nothing doing. You might have the place bugged, try to get some evidence on me. You're talking

235

about trusting me. Why should I wanna trust you? Christ, you been two-timing your missus, what's to stop you pulling a fast one on me? I give you the diary, you gimme the cheque and when I go to cash it, you've rung the bank and stopped payment. Ah no, sport. Cash it's gunna be and no argument. I'll meet you in the middle of the Harbour Bridge footway. That way nobody can see what we're passing to each other. And I can see whether you got any demons with you. I tell you, Helidon, if you bring 'em and they lay a hand on me, I'll blow the lot about you and Helga. I'll go to the cooler, but Christ, you'll be on the front page of every paper in the country. So no tricks, sport. Ten thousand in cash and no tricks. Remember. I'll phone you Monday what time we'll meet.'

'But how do I get there? You can't stop a car on the Bridge—'

'You'll have to walk. It'll do you good.' Bixby stood up, looked at the sweating, abject figure slumped in the cockpit of the boat. 'I dunno what Helga saw in you, sport. You must've paid her well.'

CHAPTER THIRTEEN

I

Saturday, December 14

MALONE looked at Lisa as she lay sleeping beside him, marvelling at the flawless bloom of her cheeks, at the length of the lashes on her closed eyes, at the fullness of the slightly parted lips that seemed even fuller this morning from last night's bruising kisses. How does a man deserve such luck? he thought. He slid out of bed, went out to the kitchen and drank a glass of orange juice. He knew he was going to be kissing Lisa again in a few minutes and he knew what a man's breath, especially a beer drinker's, could smell like first thing in the morning. He was always amused at the scenes in movies where lovers woke in the morning and instantly devoured each other as if they had a mouthful of Sen-Sens. But maybe there was no bad breath in Hollywood, not even first thing in the morning.

He took a glass of juice back into the bedroom and gently woke Lisa. She rolled over on her back, throwing the sheet off the upper half of her, and looked up at him. For a moment she did not seem to know where she was; then she smiled slowly, as if remembering something from a dream from which she had not yet entirely wakened.

'A naked man in my bedroom. What would my mother say?'

'It's Saturday.'

'Oh, that's different, then.' She sat up, took the glass from him, sipped the juice. 'Saturday is the morning for naked men around here.'

They had gone to bed often since her return to Sydney, but last night was the first time he had stayed all night with her. There had been no spoken reason why he had not stayed before; it had been as if they had each decided that they

237

would not make a habit of living together before they were married. Buried deep in Malone there was still an old-fashioned morality: long ago the nuns and brothers had taught him that marriage was a sacrament, not just a legal arrangement, and the ideal, though tarnished over the years, was still there. He did not want to *slide* into marriage, to stand before a priest or a registry clerk and have legal approval placed on something that he and Lisa had been doing for maybe months. He had sufficient candour to acknowledge that he was really only splitting hairs, that whether he went to bed with Lisa for two hours or ten, they had already started their marriage. But old habits, old teachings, clung like grass burrs: principle had to be honoured, even if it were now only plastic.

Last night it had been Lisa who had suggested he should stay. 'Don't go, darling.'

'You want *more*?'

'No, Yes. No.'

'That's a clear-cut answer. Or is that what they call double-Dutch?'

'Darling, of course I want it again. But that's not the reason I said stay. You're worried, aren't you?'

He didn't answer at once, then he said, 'Does it show that much? Even while I'm making love to you?'

'No, it didn't show *then*. But at dinner—and even now. You have something else but me on your mind. You won't sleep if you go home, will you?'

'I don't know that I'll sleep much if I stay here.' He grinned; then his face sobered. 'You're right. Just as well a man doesn't need his mind to make love, otherwise I'd have been impotent tonight.'

'I'll debate that bit about needing your mind to make love some other time——' She lifted herself on to her elbow, leaned over him. 'Darling, what's troubling you? Is it this case?'

He nodded. 'When you were working in London, how much do you reckon the diplomats let prejudice colour their judgement?'

Even in bed she was intelligent, which was more than he

238

had met in any of his other girls. 'Darling, are you trying to compare justice with diplomacy?'

'I suppose so. No comparison, eh?'

'None at all. Someone once said that justice is truth in action.' Charlie Duggan wasn't the one who had said it. But Malone didn't mention him: maybe Lisa would not understand Charlie. 'Diplomacy is only compromise in action.'

'You know, you're the first naked philosopher I've ever met. Do you always think better with your clothes off? Maybe you should get together with that Beatle and his wife, the ones with the bare bum wisdom.'

She bent her head, kissed him, then bit his lip. He flinched and slapped her shoulder, but she said, 'Be serious.'

'I am. I'm trying to laugh so I won't feel my headache. But it doesn't work.'

'I know. My mother told me that, when the Nazis were in Holland during the war. She said they used to joke among themselves, laugh at the Germans' pomposity and stupidity. But the Germans were always still there in the morning.'

'You don't like the Germans, do you?'

'No.'

'That's prejudice talking. There are some good Germans.'

'Was your Helga Brand a good German?'

'I don't know that she was a good anything, except maybe a good whore. But it's not her I'm prejudiced about. I'm very objective when it comes to murder victims. I'm supposed to be objective about the murderer, too. But that's the hard part in this case.'

'You know who the murderer is?'

'I think so.' He was silent for a moment, his hand idly stroking the smoothness of her back. 'On the evidence I've got I could lay a warrant against him tomorrow. But——'

She waited for him to go on; then she said, 'Who is it? Walter Helidon or his wife?'

His hand stopped flat against her back, his fingers pressing into her. '*His wife?*'

'It's not her, then?'

'Why should it be?'

239

'I didn't say it *should* be. But it could be, couldn't it? She had enough reason to kill Helga Brand.'

'Would you kill a girl who was trying to blackmail me? One who'd been my mistress?'

'That's not a fair question. How does one know what one would do in a particular circumstance? I like to think I'm a law-abiding, moral person. But I've sometimes wondered why the Dutch didn't kill more Germans, especially since they hated them so much.'

'There's a moral difference about killing in wartime. At least, there's supposed to be. But maybe your Dutch friends didn't kill the Germans because they had to live with them.'

'That's just what my father said. He said if they'd killed a German, there'd have still been ten others there in the morning.' She kissed the end of his nose. 'My parents are going to like you, you know.'

'Don't tell 'em where we had this discussion. Do you really think Mrs Helidon might have killed Helga?'

'You don't, that's obvious. You've already made up your mind, haven't you? About who killed her, I mean. Mr Helidon?'

He nodded slowly.

'What's your worry then, darling?'

He shrugged. 'Asking me to put it into words, I don't know that I can. It's just—well, I think I'd judged him before I'd really built up a case against him. I knew his background. He's a man without much in the way of principles—or he was when I last met him. He got away with something he shouldn't have, and I guess that rankled with me—I mean when I remembered it. I haven't been thinking about it for seven or eight years.'

'What was it?'

'No, I'm not telling you that. He got away with it, so it's closed now. But I'm trying to tell myself that he *has* to be the murderer and whether I or anyone else worked on it, the answer would still come out the same. But I'm afraid if I have to get up in court and give evidence, they're bound to notice the prejudice in my answers. I won't be able to help him. I *want* him to be the murderer. And I'm not sure that it isn't just because I didn't nail him last time.'

She moved closer to him, lying on him, and took his head in her hands. 'Darling, if he's the murderer, then you or anyone else's prejudices don't matter a damn. The jury will decide, not you. You shouldn't let yourself become involved like this.'

'I had that told to me before.'

'Just become involved with me. *There*. Don't go home tonight.'

And now it was morning and the problem, like the Germans in Holland, had not gone away during the night. 'Did you sleep well, darling?'

'Like a log.' Which was true; but only from exhaustion, not from peace of mind. 'But I've got to go to work now. I'll get myself some breakfast.'

'I'll get it for you while you shower. What would you like?'

'After last night, a piece of steak and some eggs. The eggs nice and runny.'

She made a face. 'First thing in the morning?'

'Anything is good first thing in the morning. Especially this.'

'No, darling. Aah . . .' Then later she said, 'Do you still want your steak and eggs?'

'A double helping now. What do Dutchmen eat after making love first thing in the morning?'

'You're always asking me those sort of tricky questions. Let me up.'

'Get your bosom out of my hand.' Then he stopped smiling and kissed her gently on the bruised lips. 'I love you, Lisa. Prejudiced about you, in fact.'

'Don't ever change, darling. And always be with me in the mornings.'

2

Clements, looking as miserable as a wet fowl, was arranging the latest batch of Christmas cards on the mantelpiece when

Malone arrived in the office. 'Here's one from Milly Morrow. Remember she used to work out of the pubs along the Quay? Never made more than three quid a night in her life, I reckon. She was a poor picker. Says she's retired now and working as a cook on a sheep station up near Coonamble.' He grimaced as he looked at the cheap fancy card, an old whore's pathetic nostalgia for a sad past: the only friends she had left from it were policemen. 'Dunno I'd like that, her being a cook. She'd had the clap more times than I've had a cold.' He blew his nose. 'You think we oughta write her boss and warn him?'

'Let him find out himself. She can give him the clap for Christmas. How's your cold?'

'Bloody awful,' said Clements, eyes streaming. 'I'm going home pretty soon.'

'How did you get on last night with Bixby?'

Clements wiped his eyes, peered closer at Malone. 'What happened to your lip? You have a fight with Lisa?'

'Don't you know a love bite when you see one?'

'Who gives a copper love bites? You're just unique, mate. Well, anyway, about Bixby.' He spread his hands. 'Bugger-all. I dug up his address, he has a flat out at Bondi, went out there, nobody home. The neighbours said they hadn't seen him since last Tuesday or Wednesday, they couldn't remember which.'

He sat down on the edge of a desk, looked soberly at Malone. 'Does that change the outlook?'

Malone had sat down at his desk, was slowly flipping through the file on the Brand case. 'I don't know.' He looked up, asking Clements to make up his mind for him. 'What do you reckon?'

Clements had a direct attitude that may not have helped the cause of justice but did not give him headaches. 'Look, Scobie, we've got nothing on Bixby at all. Nothing at all. The chewed matches don't prove anything—it could have been any one of a dozen other guys. We don't even have a connection between him and Helga.'

'There's a thin one. Gibson's photo was in Helga's file and Bixby worked for Gibson.'

'I don't think I'd want to look into that one. That opens up another ant-hill. We could go on for bloody ever that way. If you're gunna trace every bloke who ever had anything to do with her, what about all of them she must've had back in Hamburg? Any one of those could have turned up here in Sydney. If she was on the game back there for five or six years, she could have been underneath half the German merchant navy at some time or other. We don't know why she left Germany. What if she'd run out on some ponce and he finally caught up with her out here?' He shook his head. 'Let's settle for what we've got, Scobie. They're not asking us to be the jury. All we have to do is put enough evidence for a case to be made out against Helidon. We've got more than enough.'

Then Inspector, soon-to-be-Superintendent, Fulmer came in. He had, if anything, become more pontifical. 'It's time, gentlemen, that we let justice take its course. Mr Helidon should be given his chance to answer our suspicions, don't you think?'

Christ help us if he should ever get to be Commissioner, Malone thought. He'd be issuing papal bulls instead of warrants.

'Russ and I were just discussing that.' He saw Fulmer look at him expectantly and he wondered: is he waiting for me to call him *sir* now? No, I'll wait till Monday before I start that. But he sat up straighter in his chair. Fulmer was his backstop on this case and he might need the new Superintendent if things got sticky. 'I think it's time for a warrant.'

Fulmer nodded. 'All right. But I'll have to see the Commissioner first. He's come in this morning, for some reason or other. There's something going on up there at his office.'

'Do you think it might have something to do with Helidon?' Clements asked. 'Would the Premier have got word of what we're up to?'

'Possibly.' Fulmer's long jaw came up. 'But it's not going to make a darned bit of difference. We'll get that warrant.'

Then, as if the Commissioner had been listening to him,

the phone rang in Fulmer's office. He went into the small room, came out a minute later. 'I'm wanted up there right away.'

'Is it about Helidon?'

'I couldn't say. But it will be about him before I leave there. Wait here till I come back.'

He should have said *Till I return*. And there should be a roll of drums as he's going out now; or better still, a heavenly choir. Fulmer went out, *strode* out, and Malone sat back and put his feet up on his desk.

'Well, that's it,' he said to Clements, and heard the relief in his own voice as if he were listening to a stranger. 'It's out of our hands now.'

Clements shrugged and blew his nose; he was too miserable and not involved enough to feel relief. 'It's been more interesting than most jobs. At least we got to see how the other half lives.'

'You're a reactionary snob, mate.'

'You've said that before. If you're trying to insult me, you're on the wrong track.'

'I think you'd like to have had your name on one of Mrs Helidon's invitation lists. I could just see you at the Blue and Red Ball.'

'Somehow I don't think Mrs Helidon's lists are gunna be worth two cents from now on.' He blew his nose again. 'I think I'll hang around till Tom comes back. If we're gunna serve that warrant this afternoon, I think I'd like to be there, cold or no cold.'

Malone, to fill in the time till Fulmer returned, got up and moved across to the ancient typewriter and began to type out a new, more precise report on the Helga Brand case. As the facts came up on the paper under the pressure of his fingers, he felt his relief increasing: the evidence against Helidon was irrefutable, would stand up to even the most objective searching. Prejudice didn't enter into it: Helidon was the murderer.

Then the phone rang. 'Sergeant Malone? This is the Commissioner's secretary. Inspector Fulmer asked me to give you a message. He said not to wait, that nothing more was going

to develop on the case you and he were discussing. He said
he would see you first thing Monday morning.'

'Can I speak to him?'

'I'm afraid not. He's still with the Commissioner.'

Malone hung up, looked across at Clements, who had sat
up in his chair. 'We can go home. There's something going
on up at the Commissioner's office and they don't want us
to know about it. We stop work till Monday morning.'

'Do we keep a tail on Helidon? I mean, say he decides to
to a bunk. Bixby's gone into smoke somewhere. What if
Helidon decides to follow him?'

'We're going to do what we're told, mate. You go home
and enjoy your cold in bed and I'll take Lisa out to the beach.
I'll see you Monday morning.'

Clements looked as if he needed further convincing; then
he sneezed, blew his nose and gave up. 'Righto. But if Helidon
disappears over the weekend, you can get someone else to
help you find him. I think I'll spread this cold into a month's
sick leave.'

Wiping his eyes, he went home. Malone turned back to the
typewriter, finished off the last page of his report. As he
pulled the sheet out of the typewriter two other detectives,
Kildare and Welch, both of them perspiring freely, came into
the office. They had the look of men who had been expecting
a free weekend and had suddenly discovered they were going
to be working overtime.

'What a bloody scorcher!' Kildare gasped, dragging off his
jacket. 'I was gunna go out to Bondi this afternoon, spend
all the time in the water. You finished with the typewriter,
Scobie?'

'All yours.' Malone shook his new sheets together, found a
new manilla folder for them; he couldn't remember ever
having been as neat and careful about a report. 'You got to
work?'

'The Water boys have just fished a feller out of the harbour.
Had his skull bashed in.'

'Well, he's your pigeon,' said Malone, closing the manilla
folder and laying it on his desk. He felt suddenly glad now of
the opportunity to spend the weekend with Lisa. Helidon

could wait. 'I'll have that swim at Bondi for you, while you're tearing around in the heat trying to find out who he is.'

'Oh, we know that already,' said Kildare, sitting down at the typewriter. 'The Water boys recognized him. He was a trawler captain named Phil Bixby.'

CHAPTER FOURTEEN

I

Thursday, December 12

'THEY'VE JUST BEEN HERE,' said Savanna. 'They're probably on their way to see you now.'

'Did you know she had a picture of me and Glenda in that file of hers?'

'Les, I didn't know a thing about any file. Not till the police mentioned it. She evidently had other pictures in it, too——'

'Who of?' Gibson's voice crackled over the wire: the sharp old mind was already at work.

'I—I don't know. They didn't say.' A newly-found caution took a slippery hold on Savanna; if he could avoid it, he was not going to be involved in any further conspiracy. If Walter Helidon's photograph had been in Helga's file, if he had been her man from some other day in the week, that was Helidon's business and he didn't want to know. This whole disaster had started because he had been burdened by a knowledge he hadn't sought. 'Christ, Les, why did you have to let this happen?'

'Pull your head in, Jack,' Gibson said evenly; he could have been discussing a minor business deal that had gone wrong. 'I had nothing to do with this. And neither did you,' he added as a grudging concession; Savanna remarked the reluctance in the rough old voice. 'We'll go and see our friend, see what went wrong. You better pick me up—we don't wanna be too conspicuous.' Rolls-Royces have their disadvantages then, Savanna thought, dredging some dry humour up out of the wreck of himself: they are not the best car in the world for someone trying to make discreet inquiries about a possible murderer. 'I'll phone you when the demons have left here. Stay there at your office. Don't go home. We don't want Josie in on this.'

247

Leave me something to decide for myself, Les. Let me be the one to protect Josie; I don't need you to tell me how to look after my wife. But he said nothing because he knew the old man was right: he hadn't looked after his wife. 'I'll wait, Les.'

An hour and a half later he picked Gibson up at the entrance to Eureka Towers. The old man came out of the front doors as soon as the Jaguar pulled into the forecourt, opened the car door and slid in with the agility of a man half his age. 'Righto, don't let's waste any time. Bixby lives out at Bondi. I've rung him, but there's no answer. We'll call on him.'

'Bixby? For Christ's sake—you didn't get *him* to warn off Helga?'

'It was the best idea at the time. He was the one gunna get into trouble, not you or me, for bringing in the drugs.'

'Yes. But him——' Savanna shook his head. 'He's a thug. I don't think he'd give a second thought about belting a woman. And that's what he's done.'

'We don't know he even laid a hand on her. That's what we're gunna find out.'

'And if he did——?'

'Then we just make sure we're not connected with it. Leave it to me, Jack.'

Savanna, despite his sick depression, could not help but marvel at the change in Gibson. *The old bastard has shed twenty years. Is this what makes a man a success in business, the ability to thrive on a crisis? No wonder you never made it, Jack: a crisis always sat you back on your bum, like a good hard tackle in football. Or maybe it was just that there had been too many of them. A crisis a day never kept the bailiffs away. Quit the sick jokes, Jack. You are right in the middle of the sickest joke of all.*

'How do you feel about the girl being dead?' It was hard to tell whether Gibson's question was a kindly one or just a matter-of-fact attempt to put everything into perspective.

'Sick.'

Gibson looked appraisingly at the younger man, who at this moment, with his grey hair and his sallow face, looked the older. 'You had more time for her than you admit, didn't you?'

'Les, you don't have to love a girl to be upset because she's been murdered. There's such a thing as charity.' He found enough courage to shoot a weak barb: 'As distinct from philanthropy.'

'You and I had better give up sparring with each other,' said Gibson, unoffended: he knew why he gave his money away. 'We've gotta stick together on this.' He smiled, a spasm on his thin lips. 'I never thought the bloody day'd come when I'd have you as a partner.'

'I'm no happier about it than you are. How did you get on with the police?'

'All right, I think. That Malone, the sergeant, he's no idiot. He mentioned, too, that there were other pictures in that file. I wonder who else she was trying to put the bite on?'

Savanna made a pretence of concentrating on his driving. If Walter Helidon *was* involved with Helga, it was no concern of his and Gibson's. But he knew he was deluding himself, shutting the door on something he did not want to know about. *He* had been involved with Helga, had half-loved her if the truth had to be faced, and if there was any decency left in him he could not say it was no concern of his who had killed her. And Walter Helidon might have killed her. . . . His hands shook on the wheel and the Jaguar momentarily slipped sideways.

'Christ, you drive like this all the time?' Gibson sounded only irritated, not scared. 'You better pull yourself together, Jack. When we see Bixby——'

'I'm not going to see him.' Savanna slid the car into the kerb, switched off the engine. This street in Bondi had the bare, treeless look of so many streets in Sydney's seaside suburbs: sunbaked arroyos whose walls were the red-brick flats that lined either side of the roads. We're developing our own pueblo dwellers, Savanna thought; and looked out at the particular pueblo in which lived Bixby, the probable murderer. He turned in his seat, faced Gibson directly. 'You go in and see him on your own, Les. I'm not shirking any of my responsibility for this whole mess, except for this bit. I told you I didn't want Helga hurt.'

Gibson returned the stare. 'What are you planning on doing? Doing a bunk, hiding out till it all blows over?'

'I'm not entirely gutless. Despite what you may think,' he added as he saw the smear of contempt in Gibson's eyes. 'I'll be around to answer the police any time they want to see me. But I'm having nothing to do with Bixby.'

'You scared he might take to you?'

'I don't know. But if it came to a donnybrook, I wouldn't lie down and take it. I've been sitting in my office ever since the police left, thinking about the last twenty-odd years. And, yes, thinking about the next twenty, or however many I've got left. I decided I'd got about as far down as I could go. Or anyway, as far as I wanted to go.' He paused and looked out through the windscreen at the deserted street. The pueblo dwellers were inside at their evening meal; their empty cars lined the kerb like barricades. The street ran down to the promenade and from the beach beyond there came the faint thunder, like the rumble of a distant war, of a rolling surf. A distant war, he thought: Christ, when was I ever out of a war? We all carry our small wars with us, like original sin. I wonder what Father Wrigley would make of that one, coming from a full-time atheist? 'I once won a medal——'

He paused again, as if embarrassed to bring up his war experiences. But Gibson said nothing, showed no expression. It was no encouragement for Savanna to go on; but at least Gibson had not moved to get out of the car. He might never talk to Gibson again and he wanted to put the old man straight on a few things.

'They gave it to me for being brave, they said. That wasn't what the citation said, but that was what they meant. I wasn't brave, or if I was, it was a reflex action. I went in and killed four Japs in a machine-gun post—it was them or me and the six chaps with me. Now I think it's cowardice to lie down and let someone kill you, but I don't think it's bravery to stand up and try and stop the other feller from chopping off your head. But don't ask me to define the difference. Perhaps it's no more than taking a gamble on which way you die. I remember we were pinned down in the mud for half an hour by those Japs before I decided I'd had enough. Well, I'm like that now, Les. I've had enough. I haven't a single bloody idea what I'm going to do, but I'm not lying down any more. And if I went in there——' He nodded at the block of flats where Bixby lived. 'If I went in there and Bixby started to throw his weight around, who knows, I might try for another medal. And that might bring the police back to us quicker than we want them.'

Gibson continued to gaze steadily at Savanna, his face showing nothing of what was going on in the sharp old brain. Jesus, what a waste, he thought. This bloke might have been something; but somewhere along the line they took the marrow out of his backbone. But who? Or what? But he said nothing, asked nothing; just looked hard at the stranger named Jack Savanna. Then he nodded abruptly, got out of the car and went into the flats.

He was back in less than five minutes. 'Not there.'

'Do we wait?'

'No, we'll go home. We'll wait for him to come to us. If he did do in the girl and the demons get on to him, he'll come to me, put the bite on me for money to get out of the country.'

'Will you give it to him?'

'No. I gave him some money—it was supposed to have been for the girl's air fare back to Germany. I checked with my bank this afternoon—he cashed the cheque first thing Monday morning. That's all I'll give him. If I gave him any more, that would be aiding and abetting a felony, or something just as bad. If they caught him, they'd be on to me and I might get anything from three to five years. I've stayed out of gaol so far. I'm not gunna spoil the record this late in the piece.'

'What will you do then?'

'If he killed the girl, I'll turn him over to the police.'

'But you sent him to see her——!'

'Not to kill her. That was never on the ticket. I told him to scare her on to a plane out of the country—I didn't tell him to do her in. When that happened, if he was the one who did kill her, then he was on his own.'

'We'll still be dragged into it.'

'I've survived worse things.' Then it was his turn to stare

out through the windscreen. 'I just hope it won't tear the guts out of Glenda, that's all. She's always telling me it's too late now for us to have any more trouble.'

Savanna said, 'You can put the blame on me. Tell her you were trying to get me out of trouble.'

Gibson glanced sideways at him. 'How would Josie take that?'

'I don't know. But whatever it does to her, it'll be the last hurt I'll ever give her. There's Margaret, you see. I think I've already lost her. I'm not sure, but I think so. She never writes to me, only to her mother. You can sometimes get over losing your wife——' Sometimes, but not always: not the wife you would love till the day you died. But Silver was not Margaret's mother; and he knew now, had finally accepted it, that Silver was gone forever. From now on there had to be only Josie. 'You don't get over losing a daughter. Or a son, I guess. I'm standing up on my hind legs again—for Margaret, I suppose, as much as anything. If ever she comes back to Sydney and sees that her mother and I are trying to make a go of it, that I'm only half the bastard I used to be—well——' He turned his hands over on the wheel in a gesture of supplication to a God in whom he didn't believe; but there was some fate, *something*, in which you finally had to place your faith. 'You never know. In time she may regret losing me as much as I've regretted losing her.'

The two men sat there in a silence that had nothing to do with the quietness of the street outside the car. They were like explorers who had come across each other in an alien country: their discovery of each other was made suspicious by the surface familiarity. Each knew he had found more in the other than he had been looking for and they were embarrassed by it: one did not look for bonuses in a relationship that had been closer to enmity than friendship. A car came slowly down the street, the two youths and two girls in it peering out at the names of the flats: Ideal Haven, Beauview Hall— 'There it is!' The car jerked to a halt and the four young people fell out and ran into Paradise (the rest of the name, Court or Hall, had fallen off the front of the flats: even Paradise was jerry-built). A dog chased a cat across the road, suddenly lost interest in the pursuit, came back, raised a leg against the front wheel of the Jaguar, then trotted on down the street. A man and a woman came out of the flats where Bixby lived and went down towards the beach, carrying a low-voiced argument between them like something of which they were ashamed. A television set suddenly blared somewhere— 'Thirteen people died today in bushfires'—and at once the street seemed to come alive. The evening meal was over: time for television, for argument, for going out. People came out, got into cars, roared off down the street, racing to God knew what destinations. Children came out to escape the heat of their homes, ran around in the only slightly less stuffy heat of the evening. It's another country, thought Gibson; not snobbishly but only because he was suddenly lonely for Glenda.

'Let's go home, Jack.'

They rode home without any talk between them; yet each man felt that at last there was some communication between them. Neither of them might ever admit it and the tenuous contact might die for want of further understanding; but each man rode back to Point Piper nursing his own small discovery of the other. Explorers of wider continents than a single man had returned home with less.

Just before he got out of the car Gibson said, 'Can you have lunch with me tomorrow?'

Savanna hid his surprise: Gibson had never before invited him even to have a drink. 'What time?'

'One o'clock. The Union Club.' Gibson had achieved membership of the citadel of the Establishment during the war years when, as a wounded hero and a pioneer from New Guinea, he had been admitted because the club committee had thought it would be unpatriotic not to do so. By the time they had realized the true side of him, his vulgarity, his don't-give-a-damn-for-anyone and his financial skulduggery, he was too rich and powerful to be disbarred without causing a scandal. But if his connection with the murder of Helga Brand ever came out into the open, he would certainly be asked to resign. He wouldn't miss the club, since he had no friends there, had no friends anywhere; but he might as well get as much out of his membership subscription while it lasted. 'You ever been there?'

'My father used to belong to it.'

Gibson raised an eyebrow, then grinned. 'Your point, Jack. He probably belonged there more than I do. Good night. Don't lose any sleep over Bixby.'

I shan't sleep, Savanna thought: that's asking too much. But it won't be Bixby who'll keep me awake. There are too many other figures in my nightmares. Including myself.

2

Friday, December 13

Walter Helidon saw the calendar as soon as he opened his eyes in the morning. It was a small day-by-day calendar in a silver-plated frame, a Christmas present from Norma; the frame also held a small notepad and a silver pencil. He raised his head from the pillow and saw his nervous scrawl on the pad: *Bixby will call office at 4.30.*

Norma came into the bedroom carrying a breakfast tray. She was in her dressing-gown and had done her hair, but he noticed she wore no make-up. Normally she put on powder and lipstick as soon as she got up in the morning; in one of their more acrimonious moments he had once told her that a woman's unmade-up face at breakfast was less appetizing than cold soggy toast. But this morning it did not trouble him and he was just glad she was *there*.

'I've had mine. Did you want something more than toast and coffee?'

He shook his head, took the glass of apple juice she handed him and gulped it down like a man dying of thirst. He drank the juice every morning, not really liking it, because he had read in the Medical pages of *Time* that it acted as an anti-coagulant against the previous day's intake of cholesterol. He had never bothered to check with a doctor if the claim was true; like most men who hated strenuous exercise he was prepared to accept any easy way to health. This morning he would have gulped down hemlock with the same thirst. He had woken from the worst night he had ever spent, lost in nightmare country, to a day that, if superstition meant anything, promised no better.

'You haven't eaten a proper meal for two days. You can't go on like this, darling.'

'I'd just get the heaves if I tried anything solid.' He spread his toast with honey straight from the comb, another health food: he couldn't remember what *it* was supposed to do. 'It's no use, darl. I won't be able to eat a good meal till all this is over.'

'When will that be?' She sounded resigned, as if she knew his answer would be:

'God knows.'

'Do you think Bixby was the one who killed—her?' She couldn't bring herself to say *Helga*: it sounded too familiar, as if she had accepted the girl as part of her own and Walter's life.

'I don't know,' he said despairingly .'He could have. He probably did. But what do we do? Ring up the police and put them on to him?'

'Why not?'

But there was no hope in her voice and he recognized it. 'Darl, all we can do is pray he'll be satisfied with the money he wants this afternoon.'

'I haven't prayed in years. I've forgotten how to.'

'Well, *hope*, then. I don't know how to pray, either. Unless they're the same thing.'

'Do you think he might not call this afternoon? I mean, he didn't call you on Monday when he was supposed to——'

'He'll call, all right.' He put down the toast and honey after taking one mouthful.

He had waited all day Monday for Bixby to call; then all day Tuesday and still no call. He had begun to believe that Bixby had lost his nerve and decided not to go through with the blackmail threat; but, just in case, he had brought home the ten thousand dollars and put them in the safe behind the big wall mirror. There had still been no call from Bixby by the time he had left the Assembly on Wednesday and by then he had been convinced he had nothing more to fear from the man.

He had come home Wednesday evening with an almost jaunty relief; he had even been looking forward to taking Norma to the police widows' charity dinner, the sort of function he normally abhorred. They could decently escape from it at ten o'clock, then go on to the Silver Spade, where he had had his secretary book a table. Tony Bennett was singing there and he was Norma's favourite; he would request Tony to sing *C'est Si Bon*, which was her favourite song. It would be like old times, the sort of times middle-aged married couples so rarely recaptured.

Then he had reached home and the two detectives, Malone and Clements, had been there.

When they had gone he had sunk into the leather chair. Norma came back into the room, sat down in the red empress chair, looked down at her hands clasped in her lap and said without looking up, 'Did you know she was dead?'

'How would I have known? God, darl, do you think I could have kept that from you?'

'You kept it from me about you and her being——' She shook her head. Then she looked up. 'Wally——?'

'What?'

'Nothing.'

'No, not nothing,' he said more harshly than he had intended; he could feel himself trembling, coming apart inside. 'What were you going to ask me?'

'No, you couldn't have——' Her hands writhed in her lap like snakes' heads battling each other to death.

'You were going to ask me if *I* had killed her. Jesus Christ, darl, do you think I'm capable of murder?' He dropped his pipe into the ashtray beside him. His hand clawed at the arm of the chair, his nails scraping against the leather. He stared across at his wife sitting in the chair where Helga, *his mistress*, had sat only—how long ago was it? It could have been only last night or it could have been a year ago; the image of her came and went in his mind like a tide, sometimes so close he could feel and smell her, other times so distant as to be no more than a ghost. And as he gazed now at his wife

256

she, too, seemed to retreat, became a ghost. He leaned forward, reached out a hand to her: she came back, became real again.

'Darl, I *couldn't* have killed her! No matter what she was going to do to us—I couldn't have killed her!'

Norma got up from her chair, crossed to him, took his head in her arms and pressed his face against her bosom. He leaned forward into her, putting his arms round her waist, and began to weep. She, too, began to cry. They were locked together like that in an agony of despair when they heard the footsteps of the maid on the tiles of the entrance hall.

'Signora? Oh, *scusi*——'

'No, it's all right, Rosa.' Norma moved away from her husband, wiped her eyes with a handkerchief. 'Mr Helidon and I—we just heard of the death of an—an old friend.'

'Oh, signora, I am so sorry——' The maid had lost her embarrassment at once; she had the Italian affinity for grief, understood the emotional release of tears. 'You will not be going out, then?'

'Yes.' Helidon's voice was again unintentionally harsh. He stood up and felt his legs ready to collapse beneath him; he held on to the back of his chair like an old man. 'We'll be going, Rosa. We *have* to——' The last sentence was addressed to Norma. Her face was blank for a moment, then she understood and nodded.

'Lay out my things, Rosa. Mr Helidon and I will go to the dinner.'

The maid uttered more condolences on the death of their old friend, then went through into the bedroom. As she did so the phone rang in the study. Helidon walked stiff-legged through into the smaller room and picked up the phone. Norma followed him to the doorway, stood there waiting as if she expected every phone call from now on to concern both of them, to be important to them.

This one was: 'Helidon? It's your mate here. Sorry I ain't been on to you before. I hadda go outa town Monday unexpectedly.'

'What sent you?' The rasp in Helidon's voice was intentional this time; he felt the gathering of an unexpected strength. He motioned to Norma to come into the study and close the door. 'You read about Helga's murder?'

There was just a moment's silence on the line: 'Don't start talking like that, sport. How would I know about that? It ain't even in the papers tonight. It's just come over on the news. That's the first I heard of it.'

'It was in the papers on Monday, when they found her down at the Opera House.' The clipping of her death had been lying on his desk for two days and he had not known it was Helga. Again there was the feeling of sadness, of something lost forever. Then he saw Norma looking at him with pain and fear in her eyes, and he tasted his treachery like bile.

'I read that bit, but I never connected it with Helga. It didn't mention her name, like. Not till tonight's news on the radio and TV.' There was another short silence, then Bixby said, 'I was coming to see you tonight. Got as far as your front gate. Then I seen you had visitors.'

'Where are you now?'

'It don't matter. I'm not gunna come and see you now, not tonight, anyway. Did you get the money on Monday?'

'Yes.' Helidon's legs were still weak; he sat down at the desk. But there was nothing wrong with his voice now: 'You don't sound very upset about—about Helga's murder. Not for an old friend.'

'I ain't laughing about it, sport, you know what I mean? I ain't the weepy sort, but I'm gunna miss her.' Again there was the silence. Then: 'I'd just like five minutes alone with the bastard who done her in. Wouldn't you?'

Helidon looked at his wife standing with her back pressed against the door: aged, afraid and all he had left in the world.

'No,' he said. 'Now what do you want? Are you still thinking of blackmail?'

'What's to change my mind?'

'Well—*this*. What's happened to Helga.'

Something that could have been a chuckle or a bad connection came over the wire. 'I don't think she'd want me to back out now. Someone will have to buy a headstone for her. You wouldn't want her buried in a pauper's grave, would you?'

'You bastard,' said Helidon, and almost wept again. Norma crossed from the door and put her hand on his shoulder; he could feel the clutch of her fingers through his jacket. He looked up at her and shook his head; but, thankfully, he saw she misunderstood the reason for the pain in his face.

'I'll call you tomorrow, Helidon. At your office, some time after lunch. If you've got the money, hang on to it, don't take it back to the bank. It'll be safe enough till I come for it. Hooroo, sport. It's a shame about Helga, but I wouldn't lose too much sleep about it. You still got your missus.'

The phone went dead and Helidon put it slowly back on the desk. When he let go of it, his fingers remained clamped in a claw; he had not realized he had been gripping the instrument so tightly. There was a knock at the door and he jerked his head up in shock. But it was only the maid, not Bixby.

'Signora? Shall I make some tea? You and the signore, it would help you——' The maid's voice was full of sympathy: death, even that of someone she did not know, had made her one of the family.

'Thank you, Rosa. We'll be out in a moment.' Norma looked down at Helidon still sitting cramped and stiff at his desk. 'What did he want, Wally?'

'I don't know. I mean, if he wants *more*. We haven't lost him, darl—he's still with us.' Then he looked up. 'She'll have to go. We can't have her around—not now. We'll have to be on our own till this is over.'

'But I can't get rid of her like that. I can't run a place like this on my own——' But she saw the agony in his face and then she nodded. 'All right, I'll tell her in the morning. Do you still want to go to this dinner?'

'No. But we'd better.' He stood up, easing his body out of the chair. 'Outside—I mean out of the house—we've got to go on as if things were normal. If we suddenly cancelled tonight, those two detectives would hear about it and they'd be back in the morning to find out why.'

The next morning, Thursday, the police came back anyway. That afternoon Bixby rang him at his office. 'I see you had some visitors again. The bulls. They seem pretty interested in you, ain't they?'

'How did you know? Have you been watching my house?'

'Well, let's say I was driving by, eh?' Bixby's humour died somewhere down the line; it came through to Helidon as a threat. 'Then they went over to the Opera House to see you, too, didn't they? Looks like they got you tabbed for something, sport. I don't think we better meet today. I'll give you a call tonight at home.'

The rest of the day had been a blur to Helidon, one in which he was vaguely aware of being rude and irritable with his secretary, offhanded with a fellow Minister and then, at the last minute, cancelling a meeting with his Department chief. He went home early, sitting cramped in the corner of the back seat of the official car and looking over his shoulder every time the car pulled up at a traffic light.

'You expecting someone to be following us, Mr Helidon?' the driver asked.

'What? No.'

'I thought maybe Mrs Helidon. I mean, she had your car. You know, doing a bit of Christmas shopping and that.' The driver was a small sharp-featured man with a tireless tongue and an equally tireless curiosity. Helidon had tolerated him in the past because such men were invaluable as sources as to what was going on in government circles; White Papers and official memoranda never told half of what one could find out from an inquisitive, talkative official driver. The trick was to see that you never gave him anything he could pass on about you. 'I was a bit surprised when you sent for me this morning. I mean, Thursday you usually drive yourself. You want me Mondays and Thursdays from now on?'

He had forgotten this was Thursday, Helga's day. 'Yes, I think so, Wilf. It's getting to be too much, battling the traffic every day.' He looked over his shoulder again, but in the charge of traffic behind them there was no sign of anyone who looked like Bixby. Or the two detectives, Malone and Clements. He turned back, saw the itchy eye of the driver in the rear-vision mirror. 'I'm just looking at it, the traffic, I mean. Wondering why a man chooses to live in the city.'

'Not thinking of retiring, are you, sir?' The sharp little face was as alert as that of a hunting dog.

Norma had brought that up again this morning. 'No, Wilf,' he said, and somehow managed a smile. 'This is my life.'

When he let himself into the house Norma was sitting out on the loggia staring at the smoke-clouded sky to the north. 'Twenty homes have been burnt up there at Terrey Hills. I was listening on the radio. The people lost everything they had.'

'Yes,' he said, only half-hearing what she had said. He sat down, picked up the small bell on the glass-topped table and rang it. 'I had no lunch. Rosa can get me a sandwich and a cup of tea.'

Norma stood up. 'I'll get it. Rosa left this morning. You asked me to——' Even the dark glasses did not hide the ravaging of the last twenty-four hours. I've made an old woman of her, he thought; and put his hand up to take hers. 'There's only some corned silverside. I didn't feel up to going shopping today.'

'Forget it. I'm not really hungry. Indeed, I'm——' Then he stopped. 'Sorry.'

'What for?'

'Indeed.'

'That's the least of my worries now.' But she smiled and kissed the top of his head. 'There are other people worse off than us, I suppose. Those people up there.' She nodded towards the north and the threatening clouds of smoke.

'Yes,' he said, and felt ashamed that he had no real sympathy left to bestow on other people.

They stayed home that night and at ten o'clock, worn out waiting for Bixby to call, Helidon went to bed. At ten-thirty the phone rang at last. 'I think we better get together tomorra, sport, I'm gunna need a bit more money.'

'How much?'

'Wuddia say to twenty thousand?'

Helidon closed his eyes: irony brought its own pain. Norma, lying beside him, reached for his free hand and held it tightly. 'That's too much——'

'I don't think so. Look, Helidon, things don't look too bright for you. The bulls are on to you, all right I'd lay even money you're their number one suspect. Now if I just rung 'em up and said I could send 'em Helga's diary——'

'What's in the diary? You haven't told me a thing yet.'

'And I'm not gunna. That's what you're buying, a pig in a poke. All I'll tell you is, you're gunna get your money's worth. Twenty thousand dollars, in cash. I'll ring you at your office again tomorra, say four-thirty, and tell you where we can meet. Have a good night's sleep, sport.'

Helidon held the phone against his ear for a moment, deaf even to the dial tone. Norma spoke to him, but he didn't hear her. Then he felt her nails digging into him and he came out of the wide-eyed coma that had gripped him. He put the phone down, scrawled a note on his bedside pad that Bixby would call him at four-thirty; then he slid down in the bed, gathered Norma in his arms and held her to him. They lay there in the expensive shelter of their bed like two people in an air raid who knew that the bomb to hit their house was already on its way.

And now it was Friday the thirteenth, the day for disasters. He put aside the breakfast tray and got stiffly out of bed. It was years since he had been vigorously athletic, but over the past week it seemed to him that he had become old and infirm. He stood up on legs that felt awkward and painful in the knees; Norma took hold of him as a nurse might take hold of a patient getting out of bed for the first time in weeks. They looked at each other in the wall mirror and Norma struck a spark of wry humour. 'Mr and Mrs Dorian Gray.'

'Don't,' he said.

The official car called for him an hour later and he drove into the city in silence: Wilf, the driver, talked all the way but Helidon heard nothing of what he said. His office was in the State Government block, a beautiful dark grey tower that the citizens, with the local talent for belittling anything that embarrassed them with its pretensions, had dubbed the Black Stump.

When he got out of the car the driver noticed the two brief cases for the first time, the full one and the empty one.

262

'Expecting a heavy weekend, sir?' When Helidon looked blank, he nodded at the briefcases. 'Paper work. You gunna be taking stuff home?'

'That's all government is these days, paper work. Isn't that what they say, Wilf?' But the ten thousand dollars in one of the briefcases dragged him down more than all the paperwork of all his years in parliament.

He rode up in the lift to one of the upper floors, silently nodded good morning to his secretary, went straight through into his office and immediately decided he had done the wrong thing in leaving the house at all. He was too sick and abstracted to be able to go through today's programme; Cultural Development, never an urgent matter in this State, would not suffer for another day's delay. He called in his secretary, told her to cancel all appointments for the day, assured her there was no more wrong with him than an upset stomach; then he took the empty briefcase, went down to his bank, drew out ten thousand dollars and did his best to remain oblivious of the teller's inquiring eye. But he could read the question in the teller's mind: why would a Cabinet Minister, for the second time in a week, want ten thousand dollars in *cash*? Other people drew amounts as large as that, but they were usually cranks of some sort or bookmakers. Why would a Minister want twenty thousand in cash? And Helidon was sure he could read the second question in the man's mind: was it to pay off blackmail?

He went back to his office, the notes feeling like a ton of lead in his briefcase, and spent the rest of the day, for want of something to fill in the time, trying to catch up on Departmental paperwork. His secretary kept popping in and out to ask how he was; at lunch time she brought him some dry biscuits, a glass of milk and a stomach sedative. At four-thirty she called on the inter-office phone.

'There's a gentleman on the phone, Mr Helidon. He sounds like a man who called the other day. Do you want to be troubled by him?'

'Put him on, Paula. I know who it is. It's a private matter.' He knew he could trust her if he told her that; she would not listen in on the conversation.

There was a click, then Bixby said, 'G'day, been a scorcher, hasn't it? You got the extra necessary?'

'I have it. Now what?' It was an effort to keep his voice cool and calm.

'Well, I don't think we wanna be too conspicuous, you know what I mean? So how about we meet on your boat again? Make it eight o'clock, it'll be dark by then. Don't bother to wait for me—I'll be out on the boat. And remember, sport. No one else but you and me, okay?'

When Bixby hung up, Helidon called Norma. 'I'm meeting him on the boat at eight o'clock. I should be home by nine.'

'Darling, do you think you should? I don't trust him. What if——?'

'If what?' But he knew what she meant and his tone softened. 'Darl, he won't try anything—*drastic*.' It was an inadequate word for murder. 'I'll tell him that you know where I am. All he wants is the money. I'll give him that and get the—the diary in exchange. And then——'

'And then?' But she didn't want an answer. Before he could reply she said, 'Wally, don't bring the diary home. I don't want to see it. Burn it or tear it up. Anything.'

'You won't see it, darl,' he promised, determined to protect her from now on from any further pain or worry.

'Will you come home first?'

He hesitated. There were over three hours to fill in before he had to meet Bixby. But if he went home he knew what a wrench it would be to leave there again when the time came: unsafe though it had been to the invasion of Helga and Bixby, it was still the only haven he knew, the only place where there was any comfort. 'No, I'll stay here till it's time. But come in and pick me up at the club. Wait for me in the car park.'

'I'll be there at eight. You shouldn't be with him too long. And darling—*be careful*.'

God, he thought as he hung up, whatever made our love go cold for as long as it did?

At five-thirty his secretary came in, smartly dressed, freshly painted: Friday night was her night on the town with the girls. Helidon had remarked this local phenomenon before and now, to allay her concern for him, he tried for a light note: 'Hunting night again, Paula?'

'We don't *hunt*, Mr Helidon. It's just a girls' night out.'

In night clubs and restaurants he had seen the groups of women all determinedly enjoying themselves without the company of men; but the occasional girl's head would turn as a good-looking man went by and a wistful look would come over her face, as if she knew that what she was enjoying with the other women was only second best. On a sudden impulse he took out his wallet and extracted five ten-dollar notes. 'I don't know how many there are of you, but let the dinner be on me.'

'But, Mr Helidon——' She was surprised and uncertain. A girls' night out should not be paid for by a man: it was a surrender of their independence.

'Call it a Christmas present,' he said, still unsure why he had made the gesture, but aware of the twenty thousand dollars in the two briefcases standing by his chair. A bunch of lonely women were entitled to some donation, if a black-mailer was worth twenty thousand. I wonder what she would say if I put the briefcases on the desk, opened them and told her to take as much as she wanted?

Reluctantly she took the fifty dollars. 'Thank you, Mr Helidon. We'll drink a toast to you. Shall I call your driver?'

'No, I'm—I'm going out with Mrs Helidon. Enjoy your-selves.'

'Oh, we always do,' she said, but she was a little too emphatic; behind her thirty-five-years-old, not unpretty face there was a hint of the effort it took to enjoy what was less than she dreamed of. 'Have a nice weekend, Mr Helidon.'

He sat on in the office in the deepening dusk, not getting up to turn on the lights when the furniture of the room finally became indistinguishable. He had turned his chair round and sat facing out towards the harbour. A half a mile away and below him he could see the floodlit shells of the Opera House; he had been staring at it for a full five minutes before he realized what it was; then he abruptly swung his chair round and looked back into the darkness of the room. When at last he switched on a desk lamp to look at his watch he had made up his mind not to come back to this office in the New Year. He would resign from politics and take a long trip overseas with Norma, start a new life and begin to enjoy more fully the money he had made.

He reached for a sheet of notepaper, took the gold pen out of his pocket, wrote *Dear Mr Premier*. One part of his mind noted how steady was his hand: the act of resignation was not so difficult after all. He put all he wanted to say on one sheet; he had never been noted for short speeches or memoranda, but this one could not have been shorter and still made its point. He folded the sheet with his customary neatness, making sure the corners matched, put it in an envelope and sealed it. He put on his jacket and hat, picked up the two briefcases, went down in the lift and handed the envelope to the night duty porter.

'See that gets to the Premier tonight. At his home, if necessary.'

'She'll be right, Mr Helidon. Good night. Have a nice weekend.'

He caught a cab over to the Yacht Club, asking the driver to pull up at the entrance to the car park. He walked down through the car park to the boat attendant's office on the jetty below the club house. The attendant, a man in his early thirties but already scarred and bleached by sun and salt into the effigy of a much older man, was in his office.

'Never get away before nine or ten on a Friday night. You want me to run you out to your boat, Mr Helidon?'

'No, I'll be right, Jack, if I can just borrow one of the runabouts.'

'Any one you want. You look loaded down there.'

'Paperwork, Jack. I'm going outside the Heads tomorrow and dump it all at sea.' He felt far better than he had all day, almost a little light-headed. Now that he had made his decision to resign, the twenty thousand was more than blackmail money: it was the price of a new life, one he was surprised to find he was looking forward to.

As he drew in beside the yacht the dark bulk of Bixby rose up out of the cockpit. He hesitated, then handed up the two briefcases. Bixby took them, put them down, then reached

266

out a hand to help him aboard. When Helidon took hold of the hand he felt the strength in the rough calloused fingers and all at once his new-found relief went out of him. This hand in his could be the hand that had strangled Helga.

He almost fell into the cockpit, sat down at once, feeling his legs weakening again. Bixby sat down opposite him, a dim burly shape against the lights of the distant club house and those on one or two yachts whose owners were on board their craft. There was the rattle of matches in a box, then Bixby's hand went up to his mouth.

'The money in the briefcases?'

Helidon had to clear his throat before he could reply. 'It's there.'

'That's the ticket. It don't amount to much, does it? I never seen twenty thousand in cash before. Somehow you'd think it'd amount to a pile Jack Rice couldn't jump over.'

Helidon wondered who Jack Rice was; then remembered it was a famous hurdle horse with a prodigious leap. It was a cliché to say of something that Jack Rice couldn't jump over it; and the cliché suddenly reduced the bizarre moment to a sordid little business deal. Helidon straightened up, knowing now he could handle the next few minutes. 'Do you want to count the money?'

'Nah, I don't think so.' Bixby took the briefcases, opened them, lifted out the bundles of notes one by one, fingered a few notes as if to satisfy himself that it was money, then dropped the bundles into the large suitcase he produced from the darkness at his feet. 'If you've weighed in short, I can always come back.'

'I don't want to see you again after tonight.' Helidon would never know what made him make the next remark: perhaps it was regret for the lost Helga, perhaps it was the curiosity that might become too much of a burden as time went on: 'Do you know who killed Helga?'

Bixby was bent over, lost in the shadows of the cockpit. He snapped shut the lock of the suitcase, a sound like the clicking back of the hammer of a gun, then slowly straightened up. 'Why would I know that, sport?'

Helidon leaned back, felt something jabbing him in the

base of the spine, put a hand behind him and removed it. 'Why didn't you turn up on Monday?' His voice seemed no longer to belong to him; he was drugged now by the passion to *know*. 'You must have known something—nobody else recognized Helga from the description in Monday night's paper. Did *you* kill her?'

'I'd keep your voice down.' Bixby's hand went to his mouth, took out the chewed match, dropped it. 'Sound carries over water. You oughta know that.'

Helidon struggled to lower his voice, but he was on the verge of hysteria now. Everything had been there in his subconscious, hazy as a partially developed film, deliberately submerged by fear and the primitive urge for self-protection. But now he was unable to stop himself: 'You bastard! It must have been you! Oh Christ, gimme the diary and go!'

Bixby stood up, moved towards Helidon. The latter swayed aside, already feeling the death blow before it was delivered; but Bixby was only lifting the suitcase up on to the gunwale. Helidon twisted his head round, for the first time saw how Bixby had got out here to the yacht: a small rowboat lay in the larger boat's shadow, bouncing gently on the ebbing tide.

Bixby rested the suitcase on the gunwale and looked at Helidon.

'I think I'll hang on to the diary just a bit longer, sport. You got some ideas in that head of yours that you better have a second think about.'

He leant over the side to drop the suitcase down into the rowboat. Helidon leant farther away from him, felt the something sticking into his hip this time. His hand felt for it, felt the cold iron head of a wrench. He looked up, saw the big dark shape still bent over the side of the boat. He had a vague feeling of disembodiment, like a man coming awake in a place he did not recognize. His hand came up with the wrench clutched in it; it was the action of a man brushing away a nightmare. He saw the shape of the wrench go past his face, but there was nothing he could do to stop it; Bixby's head, as he straightened up, came right into the arc of the swing. The heavy iron met the bone of the skull with a crunch that would echo in Helidon's ears forever. Bixby made a soft sound, half grunt, half hiss, then he fell over the side into the rowboat.

Helidon dropped the wrench into the rowboat. Then he leaned over the side of the yacht and was violently ill.

CHAPTER FIFTEEN

I

Saturday, December 14

MALONE drove up Pacific Highway through the sparse Saturday lunchtime traffic. He had waited in the office for Fulmer's return, then at last called the Commissioner's office: no, they were still in conference and the secretary had no idea when it would end. Malone, impatient, frustrated and worried, had finally left a message with Kildare and Welch. 'Tell Tom Fulmer I've gone up to see our friend at Pymble.'

'I thought you said you were going out to Bondi?' Kildare looked up from his two-fingered report on Bixby's death.

'Who's your friend at Pymble?' Welch asked.

Be cautious, Malone. You're still some way from nailing your first Cabinet Minister. 'You'll read about it in the papers.'

He escaped from the cool dark room into the hot brilliance of the day, and now as he approached Helidon's street in Pymble he hoped he had done the right thing in coming up here alone and on his own initiative. But he had to know if Helidon was still around. He had nothing with which to connect Helidon with Bixby's murder; but Bixby almost certainly had had something to do with Helga's murder. And Helidon might be the only man who knew what that connection had been.

He got out of the car and went up to the front door of the house. Even before he rang the bell he knew there was nobody home. Experience over the years had taught him to feel when a house was empty; it was a sixth sense that had saved him a lot of time and trouble. But he rang the bell anyway, twice; then he went round the side of the house to the back garden. The swimming pool winked invitingly. That's what I should do, he thought: strip off and spend the afternoon in the water waiting for Helidon to come home. Except that Helidon might never come home.

There was a splash from a pool next door. He pushed between some hibiscus, looked over the fence into the neighbouring garden. Two children splashed in the pool, heaving and diving like ungainly dolphins. A fat man, oozing out of his trunks like brown blancmange, sat under an umbrella listening to a race broadcast on a transistor radio.

'Excuse me,' said Malone; but the man could hear nothing but the Donald Duck voice of the race caller. Malone waited resignedly. You did not interrupt anthems or prayers: why interrupt a race broadcast, which was something of both? The race finished and he tried again: 'Excuse me, do you know if Mr and Mrs Helidon are away?'

'They were there this morning.' The fat man sounded sour; he must have backed a loser. 'They could be down at their boat.'

'Where's that?'

The fat man told him, then turned up his radio, getting the starters and riders for the next race. Malone left him to his tribal ceremonies, went out to the car and drove back to the harbour. He felt a mixture of relief and trepidation when the attendant at the club house told him that Mr and Mrs Helidon were out on their boat. The attendant took him out and as they approached the yacht he could see the Helidons sitting unmoving in the cockpit of the yacht. Neither of them rose as the runabout came alongside and the attendant, puzzled, looked up at them.

'You want your visitor to come aboard, Mr Helidon?'

'If he wishes,' said Helidon tonelessly. 'Welcome aboard, Mr Malone.'

He has his wits about him enough to call me *Mister*, not *Sergeant*. Malone clambered up on to the yacht, dropped his jacket on a seat and sat down opposite Mrs Helidon. Helidon himself was in the chair behind the wheel. Both of them were in cotton shirts, slacks and canvas shoes; and both of them wore blue terry-towelling hats against the fierce beat of the sun. Beside them Malone felt stiff, conservative and overdressed. He took off his tie in an attempt at informality and equality. After all, this was a long way from a formal police call. Now that he had been reassured that Helidon was still here in Sydney, had not done a bunk, his misgivings about leaving Headquarters returned.

'What is it this time?' Helidon said wearily.

'It's about a man named Bixby.'

Neither of the Helidons turned a face towards the other, but Malone was sure that behind the dark glasses they both wore there was a quick exchange of glances. 'I don't know anyone named Bixby.'

'He was a trawler captain, worked out of the harbour here.' Malone watched Mrs Helidon closely as he said, 'He had a habit of chewing matches.'

But there was no reaction at all from Norma Helidon. All she said was, 'What has this Mr—Bixby?—got to do with my husband?'

'Probably nothing at all.' Malone squinted against the glare off the water, wishing he had brought his dark glasses with him from the car. I'm at a disadvantage here; my Irish face, in this glare, is going to be as readable as one of those large-type books for the nearly blind. The only thing to do was to attack: 'But we think Helga Brand knew Bixby. And I—we think he was in her flat on the day she was murdered.'

Helidon's hand was on the wheel. The knuckles whitened, but he managed to show no other reaction. He looked at this policeman, wondering how much he knew. He had had no sleep at all last night and a fierce ache had tightened across his brows from temple to temple. Malone was leaning back against the gunwale where Bixby had fallen over into the rowboat. Thank God there had been no blood to wash off the yacht; Bixby had bled out his life into the rowboat. And that was somewhere out in the harbour now, God knew how many fathoms down.

'I still don't see what that has to do with me.'

All right, you asked for it, Malone thought. 'We think you were there that day, too, Mr Helidon. We found your finger-prints on several things in the flat. The phone, a piece of a broken glass, a key——'

Helidon's hand tightened still harder on the wheel; his

knuckles looked as if they might burst right through the skin. But he said nothing, because his tongue had suddenly become swollen in his mouth; and Norma snapped, 'That's ridiculous! How would you know they were my husband's fingerprints?'

Even behind his dark glasses Helidon's grateful glance towards his wife was evident. 'Yes, how would you know they were my prints?'

'I borrowed one of your pipes.' Malone reached for his jacket, took the pipe out of a pocket and held it out to Helidon.

But Helidon could not put out a hand to take it. God, could they find fingerprints on a boat and wrench after they had been in the water for some time? After he had recovered from his violent vomiting he had laboriously got down into the rowboat and lifted the suitcase back on to the yacht. He had climbed back, put the money back into the briefcases, then dropped the suitcase down into the rowboat again. He had looked down at the crumpled heap, that he could not bring himself to believe was a dead man, in the bottom of the rowboat. What would happen if he just pushed the rowboat off, let it go with the ebbing tide? But he knew that would be leaving too much to chance. Shivering with fear and revulsion at what he had done, he determined not to leave any more to chance.

He had gone down into the cabin of the yacht, found a spike and a wooden mallet. Then he had got down into the rowboat, tied the runabout on behind it, picked up the oars and stroked the rowboat out and away from the yacht. He did not know how long he rowed, nor where his strength came from; when he finally pulled in the oars he was exhausted. He sat slumped, a pain pulling his chest together: Christ, what if he should have a heart attack, if someone in the morning should find the two of them dead here in the same boat? He had raised himself then and got to work. He had taken Bixby's legs, pulling them beneath the seat so that the body was firmly wedged there. There was a painter on the front of the rowboat and he had taken that and roped one of Bixby's arms to the seat. Then he had got into the runabout, leaned over precariously and driven the spike into the bottom of the rowboat. He had almost fallen back into the rowboat as he

273

had tried to wrench the spike free again, but at last it had come out in his hand and he heard the gurgle of water coming into the bottom of the rowboat. He had sat there in the runabout, shoulders hunched, head bent, and waited till the rowboat had sunk from sight. Then he had started up the motor of the runabout and cruised quietly back to the yacht. He would never know how Bixby's body had got free of the sunken rowboat and been found by the police.

'Isn't there some law against taking a man's possessions out of his house without his consent, Sergeant?'

'Yes, I think there is,' said Malone. 'But as I told Mrs Helidon, we sometimes have to break the rules when they get in the way.'

'Do you think my husband killed Miss Brand?'

'We're not supposed to answer leading questions like that, Mrs Helidon.'

'Is it against the rules?'

Malone studied her carefully, searching for the crack in her; then he nodded. 'I'll ask you a question. Do *you* think your husband killed Miss Brand?'

He ducked as Helidon's fist swung past his ear. He fell off the seat, landing painfully on one knee, crouched waiting for Helidon to come out at him from behind the wheel. But Helidon made no further move; he had made his gesture in defence of his wife. He dropped his hands and sank back in his chair. His wife moved closer to him, put her hand in his. The two of them, blank-eyed with dark glass, faced the detective as he still crouched in the well of the boat.

Malone slowly stood up, picked up his jacket. 'I'm sorry about that, Mrs Helidon. I didn't mean it as a nasty remark. I'm just trying to do my job, find out who killed Helga Brand. I think you had better come into Headquarters with me, Mr Helidon.'

'Do you have a warrant?' There was no further fight in Helidon: he seemed to ask the question more as a matter of form, as if he were demanding some sort of protocol due him as a Minister. He had lost and he knew that it was only a matter of time before they charged him with the murder of Bixby.

When he had come ashore last night Norma had been waiting for him in the Mercedes in the car park. He had staggered up to the car, opened the door, thrown in the briefcases and fallen in on the seat beside Norma. She had put her arms round him and asked gently, 'Is it all over?'

'No, no.' He had shaken his head against her bosom and told her what had happened.

She had said nothing for a long time, just sat holding him to her. Then at last she had said, 'It's a terrible thing, Wally, what you've done. But it might be the end. It might all be over for us now.'

But she had been wrong.

'That will depend on the answers you give to our questions,' said Malone. 'But I'll warn you—I think we have enough evidence against you to ask for a warrant.'

'Thank you,' said Helidon automatically, as if Malone had granted him some concession. 'May my wife come with us?'

'I'm coming, darling,' Norma Helidon said before Malone could reply. She stood up, moved to the stern of the yacht, took hold of a rope and pulled in a small dinghy. 'After you, Sergeant.'

Malone went to clamber over the side, then suddenly stopped. He bent down, ran his finger along a groove beneath the seat on which he had been sitting. When he straightened up he was holding a broken and chewed match.

'Who did you kill, Mr Helidon? Helga or Bixby? Or both of them?'

2

The Premier sat behind his desk with the Attorney-General just beside him. The Police Commissioner was to Malone's right and just in front of him; Fulmer, the junior man in the room other than Malone, sat on a leather couch against one wall. Malone himself sat on a stiff-backed chair in the centre of the room and by now, twenty minutes after entering the Premier's office, felt that he, and not Helidon, was on trial. When he had arrived back at Y Division with the Helidons,

Fulmer had still been up at the Commissioner's office. He had called there and had been put on to Fulmer.

'We've just come out,' said Fulmer. Then: 'The Helidons? You have them down there? I think you've been a bit hasty.'

'I've only brought him in for questioning. You said to treat it as a routine case.' I won't call him *sir* till Monday.

'You should have waited to see me. Hold it a minute.' But it was five minutes or more before Fulmer came back on the line. 'The Commissioner has just been on to the Premier and the Attorney-General. Bring Mr Helidon up to the Premier's office in half an hour.'

'Tom, I don't want to front the Premier yet. I haven't put all my questions to Helidon——'

'You should have thought of that, Sergeant. Half an hour.'

Now Malone shifted uncomfortably on his chair, made a move to cross his legs, then decided against it. I'll bet even the Opposition Leader gets something more comfortable than this when he comes here. Out of the corner of his eye he saw John Leeds, the Commissioner, watching him closely; but it was impossible to tell whether Leeds was sympathetic or critical of him. There was some comfort that Fulmer was in the room to back him up, but so far Fulmer had said nothing at all.

'Well, you have a good case against Mr Helidon, Sergeant.' The Attorney-General was a small, bald-headed man who had the reputation of knowing the law backwards but had difficulty in remembering even his wife's name. 'But what do you think —do you think Mr Helidon killed this girl—this——' he looked at the file in front of him '—this Helga Brand?'

'Well—well, all the evidence points that way,' Malone said; then he felt abruptly angry and said more forcibly, 'You've just implied as much yourself, sir.'

The Attorney-General glanced at the Premier and the Commissioner, then looked back at Malone. 'Yes, yes. But with this new development with this man' —again he referred to the file— 'this Bixby—what do you think now?'

'Is it for me to decide, sir?'

'No.' Leeds had said very little since they had sat down, but his nod to Malone had been a friendly one when the latter had entered the room. Now he sat forward as if he had decided he was Malone's advocate. 'I'm sorry, Mr Croydon, but I never ask my men to make those sort of decisions. He would not have been asked to make it if we had been dealing with someone else but Mr Helidon. He'd have gone to his superior officer, in this case Superintendent Fulmer, and Tom would have made the decision as to whether a warrant was justified. But even he would not be deciding whether the man charged was a murderer. All he would be doing would be deciding whether there was a case for the man to answer.'

'I'm sure Joe knows the law, John.' The Premier smiled at both the Attorney-General and the Commissioner: he had been carrying oil for troubled waters so long that he was known to political journalists as Tanker Smith. He was a sharp-featured man with a lock of hair that always hung down over one brow, giving him a boyish air; but he had been in politics for thirty years and no boy could have survived the in-fighting he had been embroiled in during that time. He turned the smile on Malone. 'You do seem to have a certain doubt, Sergeant——?'

Is that the word for what I'm going through? Malone wondered. From the moment he had picked up the chewed match on Helidon's yacht there had been the horns of a dilemma gouging at him such as he had never experienced before. He had repeated his question to Helidon, but then he realized he was going to get no more information out of the Minister: Helidon was like a man who had just suffered a severe stroke. Malone and Norma Helidon had had to help him down into the dinghy. Malone had started up the out-board motor and the three of them had ridden in in silence through the empty moorings to the club house jetty. Norma Helidon, taking her husband's arm, had begun to lead him towards the blue Mercedes in the car park.

Malone had shaken his head. 'We'll go in my car.'

'Don't you trust us to follow you?'

'Put away the knives, Mrs Helidon. We're a long way past the insult stage.'

He opened the rear door of the Falcon, gestured for them to

get in. Then he got in behind the wheel, gasping a little as the hot vinyl of the seat burnt him through his trousers. He reached out to turn on the ignition, then stopped and turned round.

'If you're not going to answer those direct questions, I'll put it another way. Let's suppose you *didn't* kill Helga, but someone else, Bixby, had as much evidence as we've got that you did. Let's suppose he tried to blackmail you and you killed *him*. How close would I come with that guess?'

Norma Helidon looked at her husband, but he seemed still in a state of dumb shock. She pressed his arm, then turned back to Malone. 'Which murder are you investigating? Miss Brand's or this man Bixby's?'

I'm not fighting him any longer: he's given up. I'm fighting her and she is going to break every rule in the book. Because she's not a lawyer defending a client: she's a wife fighting to save her husband. I'm not up against justice: I'm up against love. 'I think they're connected, Mrs Helidon. I don't think I'll have much trouble putting them both in the same file.'

'Have you considered the possibility that Mr Bixby might have killed Miss Brand?'

You don't trap me that way. 'I've considered a lot of possibilities. They don't change the fact that the evidence is strongest against your husband.'

'You implied my husband might have killed Mr Bixby. What's your evidence for that?'

None, except a chewed match found on your yacht. But he was not falling into that trap, either. 'I only have to charge him with one murder, Mrs Helidon.' He looked at Helidon, who lay back in the seat as remote from and unheeding of the conversation as if he were alone. All at once his dislike for and antagonism towards the man went. *God damn it, Malone, don't get involved again.* Brusquely he said, 'One is enough.'

But now, here in the Premier's office, he wondered: which one? The murder of Helga Brand, on which there was almost certainly enough evidence to convict Helidon, but which he might not have committed; or the murder of Phil Bixby, on which there was practically no evidence, but which Malone was sure now Helidon had committed? *You do seem to have a certain doubt*, the Premier had said.

Malone looked at Fulmer for support, but the Bishop was playing Pilate: he sat quietly on the couch, his washed hands in his lap. Christ, what's happened to him? Malone thought. Treat it as another routine case, he had said; and now that it was no longer routine he just didn't want to know. What the hell had gone on in the Commissioner's office this morning?

'Yes, sir,' Malone said at last. 'I do have a doubt. I think Mr Helidon killed Bixby. I'm not so sure now that he killed Helga Brand.'

'Who do you think could have killed her?'

'It could have been Bixby,' Malone said slowly, and began to sense that all the hard slogging that he and Clements had put in over the past week had been for nothing.

Croydon rustled the file in front of him. 'So we could be taking Mr Helidon into court for a crime he didn't commit?'

Again Malone looked at Fulmer; but the latter was gazing steadily at the Premier and the Attorney-General. You bastard: you helped me climb way out here on the end of this limb. He turned back to Smith and Croydon, shifting in his chair so that his back was half-turned to Fulmer. He saw the flicker in the Commissioner's eyes, but he ignored it. I'm on my own here, so bugger them all.

'That's right, sir,' he said to Croydon. 'Unless we charge him with the murder of Bixby.'

'On which you have no evidence, at least none that would stand up in court?'

'None.'

Croydon closed the file, but he wasn't finished yet. 'Are you sure you just don't want a conviction of some sort, Sergeant? As a reward for all your undoubted hard work?'

Malone went momentarily blind with fury. He clutched at the chair beneath him, clung to it till his vision cleared. Then he looked directly at John Leeds. 'Am I on trial here, sir?'

For a moment he thought he had gone too far. He saw the flush on the Commissioner's face; then he realized Leeds's anger sprang from the same cause as his own. 'No, Sergeant, you're not! Mr Premier——'

'I understand, John,' said Smith, hands throwing out oil on either side of him. 'I'm sure Joe didn't mean it the way it sounded. I think we'd better have a private session on this, Sergeant——' He gave Malone a friendly nod. 'Would you mind waiting outside?'

Malone, his anger only slowly subsiding, got up and went out of the room. In the outer office Helidon and his wife, sitting uncomfortably on chairs like a two-person delegation waiting on the Premier, looked up as he closed the door behind him.

'Do they want to see me now?' Helidon, back in a political ambience, seemed to have recovered.

'Not yet.'

Malone went over to the window, stood looking out into the almost empty street. A derelict, seemingly oblivious of the heat, wrapped in a torn black overcoat against a perpetual winter of isolation, shuffled down the other side of the road, stopping to punch the parking meters as if he expected them to spill out a jackpot. A young couple, secure in the company of each other, laughed at him and went on up the street, too selfishly in love to spend even pity. Malone heard a movement and turned to find Helidon standing beside him.

'Why do you think he hates those meters so much?'

'Hates them? I thought he was just hoping for a windfall, even a five cents one.'

Helidon's eyebrows went up behind the dark glasses he still wore. 'You think a man that far gone still has some hope left?'

Malone looked after the shambling bundle slowly making its way down the street. 'I once sat and held the hand of a man who was trapped under his tractor. He'd had everything crushed out of him, but he still took an hour to die. The last word he said was, Tomorrow——'

Helidon took off the glasses, pinched the inner corners of his eyes. 'Maybe——' He went back and stood in front of his wife. 'I'll ask them to hurry it up, darl. They can't keep us in suspense like this.'

'We may as well get used to it,' said Norma Helidon. 'This may be only the beginning.'

Then the door opened and Fulmer looked out. 'Could you come in, Mr Helidon? And Mrs Helidon, too, if she wishes.'

Helidon took a comb from his pocket, ran it through his hair, tucked his shirt neatly into his slacks. He composed his face, disciplining it into the old urbane look. Norma Helidon took off her dark glasses, borrowed her husband's comb, ran it through her hair, checked her lipstick in the mirror on the wall. Then they took each other's hand and followed Fulmer into the Premier's office.

The door closed behind them and Malone was left in the outer office, feeling as alone and derelict as the overcoated wreck going down the street, still punching the meters and hoping for a five-cent miracle.

3

It was another half hour before the door to the Premier's room opened. The Commissioner came out first and his head jerked at Malone.

'Come with me, Sergeant.'

He strode on out of the office with his rolling seaman's walk and Malone, after a quick glance at the others still in the Premier's room, followed him. Leeds didn't look back; he seemed intent on getting out of a building that threatened to asphyxiate him. He went down the outside steps into the even more stifling heat of the street, turned the corner and went at the same fast rolling gait down towards Police Head-quarters and his own office. Malone galloped to catch up, then fell into step beside him. Leeds stared straight ahead of him, saying nothing, and Malone, wise in the atmosphere of superiors, kept his own mouth shut.

They went up to the Commissioner's office and as soon as he thumped down in his chair behind his desk Leeds let fly. 'Bugger and blast them!' Then he suddenly seemed to realize he had a junior officer with him; he looked up at Malone and glared. 'You didn't hear a word I said, Sergeant!'

'Not a word, sir.'

Leeds reached for the decanter of water on his desk, poured

himself a glass. 'Sit down, Scobie.' He was in control of himself now; his big reddish face lost some of its hue. He forced himself into the low gear that was his usual pace, became the relaxed, unflappable figure that was the public and police force image of him. 'There's going to be no charge.'

Malone was glad of the chair beneath him. 'On neither count?'

'Neither. The A-G put a very good case for forgetting the whole thing—both murders. The gist of his argument was the truth of justice.' Leeds succeeded admirably in keeping any tone of comment out of his voice. 'Should a man stand trial for a murder he didn't commit because we couldn't put him in the dock for a murder we know he *did* commit.'

'Give me time, sir, and I think I could dig up enough evidence on the Bixby murder.' But Malone's heart was not in it and he knew his voice gave him away.

'I think you've had enough of it, Scobie. Anyhow, it has been decided for us by the Premier and the A-G. No charges. It probably has nothing to do with their decision, but next year, you know, is election year.' This time he allowed himself a sardonic note; but only for a moment. 'Did you know Helidon had sent in his resignation to the Premier last night?'

'He didn't mention it.'

'Well, they've decided to accept it. It will be announced this evening for tomorrow's papers. He'll be retiring from politics altogether—on health grounds. Then he and his wife are going to take a long trip overseas.'

'May I have a drink of water?'

'Are you feeling faint?'

Malone grinned. 'Has a junior officer ever passed out on your carpet before, sir?'

Leeds smiled, stood up, crossed to a cupboard. He opened it, revealing a small refrigerator. He took out two cans of beer, came back, poured them into two glasses. 'As of now, we're both off duty. Here's to your health, Scobie.'

'Yours, too, sir.' Malone took a long swallow of the beer, then said, 'So this is going to be another one like the High Commissioner job in London? I'm to forget all about it?'

'You're to forget everything that happened up at the Premier's office. Superintendent Fulmer will take charge of the file and it'll go into the Classified section over there.' He nodded to a steel filing cabinet in one corner. 'You will do your best to accept the old philosophy of punters and policemen. You win a few, you lose a few.' He raised his glass. 'Here's to politics.'

Malone didn't drink to that. 'Do you mind if I ask, sir—did Superintendent Fulmer put forward any argument that the charge be pressed?'

'Tom Fulmer said nothing. I think he saw the way things were going, regardless of what we said.'

'But I thought——' But Malone did not go on: whatever he had thought of Fulmer's principles, something had happened to them up there in the Premier's office. He stood up. 'Well, I don't suppose it'll be the last one we'll lose, sir.'

'It'll be the last one I'll lose this way,' said Leeds. 'There is going to be another announcement in the papers tomorrow, Scobie. I'm retiring. No, not over this——' He waved a big hand as he saw Malone stiffen. 'Though it would be nice to think I had enough ethics to do so. But the Premier also got my resignation last night. I have only a few years of active service left in me. I'm going to Cyprus to run the United Nations force there. Canberra has asked for me to go. I'm Australia's contribution to law and order.' His ironic smile was hidden in his beer. 'It will be interesting to see how much politics I run into over there.'

'Who's to be the new Commissioner?'

'That still has to be decided. Several of the older Superintendents won't be starters—age, health, things like that. There will be a new look about the Force—younger men at the top.' He looked up at Malone. 'It's quite likely that Superintendent Fulmer will be Commissioner one day.'

And then Malone understood Fulmer's silence, understood that even the most rigid of men could be bent by the flame of ambition. Christ, he thought, what a dirty day. Tanker Smith was likely to be in power for the next ten years and when it came time to appoint the Police Commissioner after next he would not look twice at a Superintendent who had once tried

283

to press charges against one of his Ministers at the beginning of an election year.

'You may even be Commissioner yourself one day, Scobie.'

Malone smiled wryly. 'I'll have to outlive the present Premier.'

'Yes,' said Leeds. 'But don't expect to outlive politics.'

CHAPTER SIXTEEN

I

Tuesday, April 1

'YOU NEVER DID find out who murdered that girl,' said Brigid Malone. 'That one from the Opera House.'

'Anyhow, I'm glad I wasn't dragged into it,' said Con Malone. 'I still got me good name up at the pub. Can I have a bit more of that plonk?'

Malone poured his father another glass of claret. 'That's a bottle of the best French stuff. Lisa's father sent it up from Melbourne.'

'I thought it tasted different,' said Con Malone, giving nothing away.

'Like I said,' said Brigid Malone, 'if she'd been someone, you'd've found out who done her in. Don't you think so, Lisa?'

Lisa didn't look at Malone. 'They don't solve *all* the murders.'

'I still think——' Brigid Malone was unconvinced. 'More trifle?'

'How's your job, Lisa?' said Con Malone, sipping his wine. The sausages and onions had tasted better with the glass of French red-eye with it; but he wouldn't dare tell the Old Lady that. 'You busy?'

'I'm helping promote a new Society queen. That's the fourth since Norma Helidon went abroad——'

'I always liked her,' said Brigid Malone, an habitué of the Society pages; she knew nothing of what went on overseas, but she was conversant with the births, deaths and marriages of a world that was just as remote from her. 'She had a look of style about her——'

Malone sat back in his chair, letting the conversation swirl lazily about him. It had been an easy day today at Y Division. Come to think of it, things had been pretty easy since Christmas, since the Opera House murder. There had been an epidemic of bank hold-ups, but only one in Y Division; and Kildare and Welch had been landed with that one. They had never been told why they were to forget the Bixby murder and, because they were easy-going men, they had not persisted with their curiosity. They knew that someone had talked to someone somewhere, and they had been prepared to let it go at that.

An easy time for almost four months, Malone thought; but still the sour taste remained. He took another sip of wine.

The resignation of Helidon from politics had got less space in the newspapers than the abdication of his wife from Society. By the time Malone and Lisa had left for Melbourne to spend Christmas with her parents, the Helidons, as news, were as dead as last year's fashions. In late January Lisa had brought to Malone's notice a small item on the social pages of the *Sun*. '*Among today's departures by Qantas for London were Mr and Mrs Walter Helidon. They said they had no definite plans when they would return.*'

'Does that finally close the case?' Lisa had asked.

'It was closed the minute I walked out of the Premier's office that Saturday afternoon.'

'Don't sound so bitter, darling. Mother and Father liked you so much at Christmas because they thought you were so even-tempered.'

'Your mother told me I'd need to be even-tempered to live with you.'

'Do you want to get up and go home?'

'I am up——'

'Wait a moment till I get rid of this newspaper. We don't want Dorothy Dix between us at a time like this.'

It had been difficult to get rid of the bitterness; and Russ Clements had felt the same way. Driving out to the airport one day last month to pick up a man whom Scotland Yard, through Interpol, had asked to be questioned, Clements had said, 'I still think we should've tried to nail Helidon for the Bixby job.'

'You can try it in your spare time,' said Malone. 'It'll keep you from winning too much on the dogs and horses.'

'I haven't had a winner in three weeks,' said Clements happily. 'But seriously, Scobie, we shouldn't have let him get off scot-free.'

'He didn't get off scot-free,' said Malone; but he said it reluctantly. 'He had to give up the only life he cared about.'

'You're too bloody charitable,' said Clements.

I'm not, thought Malone. I'm just a bit older than you and I've had hammered into me some of the pragmatism of politics. It doesn't make me any happier and it certainly hasn't made me more charitable.

As they pushed through the crowd in the airport terminal a hand clutched Malone's arm. 'Going abroad, Sergeant?'

'Hullo, Mr Savanna. No, they don't give the police free passes on the airlines. You on your way?'

Savanna shook his head. He looked different from the man Malone had known in that week last December: the blue Pantene made the grey hair glisten like that of a younger man, he wore a new expensive suit, he seemed to have lost weight. But there was something else: he seemed taller, his eyes had a lively humour to them, he exuded a quiet confidence that just had not been there in the old Savanna.

'No, I'm out here to see the boss off.' He nodded across to where Gibson, mouth turned down, stood with his wife, Josie Savanna and a short fat priest who, beaming like an altar boy who had just been told he would no longer have to serve early Mass, was supervising the checking of their luggage.

Malone then remembered seeing a small paragraph that had said Gibson Industries had taken over Olympus Films. 'What's he like to work for?'

'He'll be better to work for while he's abroad. But don't quote me.' Then Savanna's smile died and he said tentatively, 'You never came back to us—about Helga.'

'No,' said Malone. 'I don't think we'll ever solve that one. We closed the file on it when we found Phil Bixby.'

Savanna's expression did not change: he might never have heard of Bixby. 'Well, maybe it's best that way. At least it didn't get into the papers what Helga had been. Back in Germany, I mean.'

'Yes. I just wonder if she cares now. So long, Mr Savanna.

Give my regards to Mr and Mrs Gibson. Oh, and to your wife. She looks well.'

'She's never been better. Goodbye, Sergeant.'

And that was it. As John Leeds, now in Cyprus, had said, *You win a few, you lose a few.* But if you had any principles, you never lost your sense of taste. You knew what would always taste sour every time you thought of it.

He took another sip of wine and looked across at Lisa, who would always taste good.